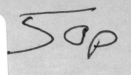

Francesca and Guy had never liked each other, not even as children, living in the splendour of their parents' opulent Park Avenue apartment. As they grew up, their animosity increased with each passing year, so that at the end they had not even spoken. Guy had caused them all to suffer – Francesca, Diana, Kathryn, and perhaps most of all Sarah. She was the only one who had loved him without reservation, but was that not perhaps a mother's privilege? Sarah had certainly paid heavily for her devotion – but then Guy had made everyone pay . . .

Also by Una-Mary Parker

Riches

Scandals

Una-Mary Parker

HEADLINE

Published by arrangement with NAL Penguin Inc,
New York, New York, USA.

First published in Great Britain in 1988
by HEADLINE BOOK PUBLISHING PLC

First published in paperback in 1988
by HEADLINE BOOK PUBLISHING PLC
Reprinted 1989

ISBN 0 7472 3109 5

Typeset in 10/12½ pt Mallard
by Colset Private Limited, Singapore

Printed and bound in Great Britain by
Collins, Glasgow

HEADLINE BOOK PUBLISHING PLC
Headline House
79 Great Titchfield Street
London W1P 7FN

This is for Sophie, Jessica,
Lucy, Amelia and Archie with all my love

ACKNOWLEDGEMENTS

I would like to thank these friends for their answers to my questions in the course of research, and for their support and encouragement, for which I am most grateful: Nigel Milne of Nigel Milne Ltd, S Kendall-Smith and S C Marriott of Paton and Co Ltd, John Rossant, Joanna Drinkwater and of course Susan Zeckendorf and Maureen Baron.

'It is public scandal that constitutes offence, and to sin in secret is not to sin at all.'

Molière 1622–1673

Prologue
1972

The woman's voice rose to a painfully shrill note that ricocheted round the courtroom, shocking the assembled company.

'No, no! Oh God, she didn't do it! I tell you, she didn't do it!'

Stunned, Diana Andrews realised it was her own voice, straining and choked, tearing at her throat, as she jumped to her feet in the crowded courtroom. London's Central Criminal Court, the Old Bailey, was packed for the last day of a sensational case that had titillated England for weeks.

There were urgent whispers of 'Hush ...!' and Diana looked round wildly. Her son, Miles, was gripping her arm on one side, and on the other Francesca Andrews, her sister-in-law, was squeezing her hand in sympathy.

But it wasn't their child standing there being accused of murder. No one could understand the anguish she felt as she watched Kathryn, a slim figure, her long dark hair falling smoothly down her back, her heart-shaped face bleached white, standing in the dock.

Diana tried to get a grip on herself but the tears were blinding her eyes and only one thought filled her mind. Guy. Guy Andrews, who had been her husband for over twenty long dreadful years. He had brought unhappiness and destruction to everyone around him and now he seemed to be reaching out from the grave, touching them all, and what he had been and what he had done was about to ruin Kathryn's life.

Diana's once exquisite face was ravaged, her thin shoulders hunched. No one would believe, seeing her now, that when she'd been a young girl she'd been regarded as a great beauty. Guy had done this to her, and although he was dead, he was going to reduce Kathryn's life to an empty tortured shell as well. A sob escaped Diana's lips.

The judge's impassive face remained folded in deep tired lines under his grey wig and his cold eyes stared straight ahead, but the learned barristers for the defence shuffled their papers uncomfortably and the jury sat rigid, shocked and embarrassed by her outburst. People in the public gallery were staring morbidly at Diana too, thankful it wasn't their daughter standing there, alone and condemned.

The final scene in the long drawn out case of the Crown v Kathryn Andrews had reached its climax. The eighteen-year-old girl stood accused of murdering her father and now the jury had brought in their verdict. Kathryn was standing motionless, uncomprehending, as if the shock had suddenly made her deaf.

The judge droned on, passing sentence in a flat dry voice, but his words weren't registering on either Kathryn or Diana. All they could remember was the jury's verdict, minutes before.

'Do you find the defendant guilty or not guilty of the murder of Guy Andrews?' the clerk of the court had demanded of them.

The foreman of the jury rose to his feet and looked the judge straight in the eye. He did not falter in his reply.

'Guilty, M'Lud.'

A great sigh, like the soft swish of a wave, rose and fell round the room and that was when Diana jumped to her feet, crying out, unable to control her feelings.

The journalists in the gallery scratched frantically in their pads. This was sensational! This would be front page banner headlines!

Kathryn Andrews, eighteen-year-old daughter of Lady Diana Andrews, found guilty of murdering her father, Guy Andrews, the eminent and popular Member of Parliament, whose vast fortune came from his family's giant corporation, Kalinsky Jewellery Inc.

Diana strained forward, trying to catch Kathryn's eye, desperate to convey to her, across the hot and crowded courtroom, her feelings of love and support, her deep wish to comfort. Most important of all, her unwavering belief in Kathryn's innocence.

Kathryn was staring into space, gazing at some far distant horizon, lost to the world, lost to her mother. Her large dark eyes, heavily fringed with black lashes, looked blank. Her small, full mouth hung slack, drooping at the corners like a small child's.

That face had become familiar to millions of people over the past few months, emblazoned on the front page of all the tabloids and on the television news programmes. The media had even shown snapshots of her as a laughing little girl, sitting on a pony, with her handsome father, her aristocratic mother, and her brother, Miles, grouped around her.

Like her mother before her, she'd been known as the girl who had everything: beauty; wealth; position.

Now the state was sentencing her to life imprisonment. At just the same age Diana had unwittingly imposed a sort of life sentence upon herself. And Guy had been the cause of it all.

Diana began to tremble, a quivering that started in her stomach and spread through her like an ague, as she clung to Miles' arm to prevent herself from falling. She blamed herself for so much that had happened. Her weaknesses and mistakes – Guy's weaknesses and sins – together they had forged a marriage that had been built on pride and greed, half-truths and deep fears.

At the beginning, when she'd been Kathryn's age, all she had wanted was to be loved. Nothing more. Had that been so selfish? Had she in some way turned Guy into the person he had become? The thought had always haunted her, somewhere at the back of her mind. It was too late now. The past was done. And Kathryn was having to pay the price.

Diana turned to her sister-in-law but Francesca was staring ahead, lost in her own memories of Guy.

Francesca shuddered as she looked round the

crowded courtroom. Guy was dead, but the trouble he had caused would stay with them for ever. Francesca and Guy had never liked each other, not even as children, living in the splendour of their parents' opulent Park Avenue apartment. As they grew up, their animosity increased with each passing year, so that at the end they had not even spoken. Guy had caused them all to suffer – Francesca, Diana, Kathryn, and perhaps most of all Sarah. She was the only one who had loved him without reservation, but was that not perhaps a mother's privilege? Sarah had certainly paid heavily for her devotion – but then Guy had made everyone pay.

Book One
1948

Chapter One

Francesca's face was filled with astonishment. 'You want to do *what*?' she asked Guy.

'I'm planning to live in England permanently and get married. What the hell's so strange about that?' Guy lounged back on the leather sofa in the library of their Park Avenue apartment, a long lean figure in an immaculately cut suit, his handsome olive-skinned face set in petulant lines of annoyance.

Francesca rose from the table in the window where she'd been studying for her MBA and went to stand by her brother. Her dark auburn hair tumbled around the regular features of her face and her brown eyes were wide with surprise.

'What's Mom going to say?'

Guy gave her a warning look. 'Don't go making trouble, Francesca. Let me handle Mom in my way.'

'Which is to get her wound up, like you always do.'

'Crap!' he expostulated. 'I never wind her up. Anyway, it's her fault. She and Dad sent me to England to be educated in the first place and now I like it there. I hate New York. I hate this apartment. Most of all I hate the thought of working for

3

Mom in the company. I intend to leave before she finally has me in her clutches.'

Francesca sank onto the sofa beside him. She was four years younger than her brother but at moments like this she felt ten years older. Guy, at twenty-four, was still juvenile in so many ways, and yet dangerously manipulative. Sarah, their mother, had indulged him ever since he'd been born, and he rewarded her with his endless demands and threats unless he got what he wanted.

'But what about the company? Don't you want to be any part of it?' asked Francesca.

Kalinsky Jewellery, Inc. Showrooms and offices on Fifth Avenue. Branches in Dallas, Los Angeles, Paris and Monte Carlo. Annual turnover: millions of dollars. Number of employees: several hundred. Advertising budget: over six figures. A great dark vulture of a company that Guy felt had over-shadowed his existence all his life and threatened to suck at his life's blood one day, until there would be nothing left of him but a heap of gleaming white bones.

'I don't want to have anything to do with it. I've no interest in the jewellery business and I never have had. All I'm interested in are the profits, and thanks to grandfather leaving me twenty-five per cent of the stock I do well enough.'

'Providing, of course, that Mom gives you an allowance,' Francesca cut in swiftly. 'And buys you all the clothes and cars you want, and pays for you to go on expensive trips.'

Guy sat bolt upright and ran a hand over his

dark, glossy hair. 'You seem to forget grandfather also left you twenty-five per cent,' he cried. 'And Mom is always buying you things, so don't accuse me of sponging off her. The trouble is you're jealous of me, Francesca. You hate it because I'm her favourite.'

Francesca gave a loud groan of irritation. They'd been having this silly argument since they'd been children and it was Guy's regular weapon when he was on the defensive.

'For the last time, Guy, I am not jealous of you. What makes me mad is that you have a wonderful future, all planned for you, as the eventual President of Kalinsky's and you don't even want it!'

'And you do,' he jeered. 'That's the bottom line, isn't it? You fancy yourself as a business whizz kid, swanning around the boardroom of Kalinsky's, running the whole show. What a joke! You'll get married and have babies like all your friends and that will be the end of that. Mom will never let you join the company. She told me herself.'

Francesca clenched her fists and decided she would not rise to Guy's bait. It was typical of him to try and undermine her confidence and this time she would not let him succeed.

'So who is this girl you're planning to marry?' she asked calmly.

Guy leaned forward, an eager expression on his face. 'She's a sweet little thing, just eighteen and incredibly naive. Her name is Lady Diana Stanton, and she's the daughter of the late Earl of Sutton. I met her at a tennis party in the spring, and she is just what I need to consolidate my position in

5

English society. Her family know everyone and I'm certain she'll have me.'

'That's disgusting!' exploded Francesca. 'What are you going to do with a wife, in the first place, and how can you possibly marry someone because they'd be useful to your ambitions?'

'Don't be so bloody stuffy, Francesca. Women marry for position, why shouldn't men?' Angrily, Guy reached for his slim gold cigarette case and took out one of the handmade du Maurier cigarettes he'd bought on his last trip to London.

Without answering, Francesca rose and went slowly back to her work. *God help the girl*, she thought grimly. *I wonder if she has any idea what Guy is really like?* Then she was struck by another thought. If Guy really intended to make his life in England, then surely that must leave an opening for her to realise her lifelong dream . . .

It had all begun when Francesca was six years old and had wanted to go to work every morning like her mother, though she wasn't entirely sure what Mom actually did. There was something so grown-up and independent about getting all smartly dressed, climbing into a waiting chauffeur-driven limo, with a briefcase full of important papers, and being whisked off to huge, opulent offices on Fifth Avenue. She concluded her mother must be a Very Important Lady.

Each morning, Sarah Andrews arrived at the elegant bronze and glass showrooms of Kalinsky's, and walking under the pale blue and gold window canopy, decorated with the company logo, a capital K in gilt, she entered the showrooms to greet her staff; her first duty of the day which she maintained kept them on their toes. Her eyes would move swiftly round the ornate showcases, lined with pale-blue moiré silk and filled with jewels that glittered and dazzled, to the pale-blue and gilt chairs, the pedestals of exotic flowers, the brightly lit chandeliers and the spotless pale-blue carpet. Having satisfied herself that everything was in order she then left the showrooms and, entering the building by another door, took the lift to the tenth floor. Here she had magnificent suites of offices for herself and the directors, and an imposing boardroom. Sometimes she stopped off at the ninth floor first, where the secretaries worked alongside those in the marketing, financial and advertising departments. Sarah's policy was to make her presence felt. Not a day went by without her checking out each employee.

On the occasions Francesca was taken to Sarah's office by her nanny, she was wide-eyed and envious of her mother's vast Louis XV desk covered with a line of 'phones that rang constantly. Her mother always seemed to be giving orders or making decisions to an unending stream of people, who called her 'Mrs Andrews' and treated her with great respect. The only clue Francesca had as to what her mother did was a plaque on the door that read 'President'. Perhaps it was like being President of the United States. Everyone was very nice to her when she visited her mother, talking to her in sweet coaxing voices as if she were a puppy.

'My! Aren't we getting a big girl, Francesca. That's a pretty dress you're wearing!'

Francesca would smile politely. She wanted to be where her mother was, in charge, behind a big desk, telling everyone what to do. There was one day in particular which stuck in her mind forever; a wet Friday afternoon, when she was due to go to her ballet class.

'I want to stay here, Mom,' she pleaded earnestly. 'I hate ballet, can't I stay and watch?'

'No, darling. Now run along.' Sarah Andrews smiled distractedly, her tired face creased in fine lines. 'Enjoy your class and I'll see you tonight.'

'I don't want to go to ballet.' Francesca planted her feet firmly, in their little red shoes, on the deep chocolate-brown carpet and glared at Sarah. 'I want to stay here,' she repeated.

'I'm afraid you can't. Momma's very busy. Anyway, you'd soon get bored, sweetheart. This is no place for a little girl.'

'You allow Guy to stay when he comes here!'

A flicker of annoyance crossed Sarah's face and she threw down her gold fountain pen irritably. 'Boys are different, Francesca. Anyway, Guy's older than you. He's ten now and one day he'll take over from me, so it's good for him to get an idea of what it's like here, but little girls don't want to bother their heads about such things. Now off you go, and have a nice time at ballet.'

The injustice of it bit into Francesca's heart, and her large brown eyes suddenly filled with tears. The patronising way her mother had dismissed her hurt deeply, making her feel a useless little fool, while Guy was being built up into something special just because he was a boy.

As she practised her *développés* and *frappés* she decided she was as capable of sitting behind a big desk as Guy. After all, her mother was a woman and *she* ran Kalinsky's!

Years later, Sarah was to remember that particular scene. Francesca's sparkling eyes as she watched what was going on in the office and her dejection when she was dragged away made Sarah realise the girl was going to be difficult. It was from that moment on that Francesca had shown a determination to find out as much about Kalinsky Jewellery, Inc. as she could. She drove her mother to distraction with her questions, refusing to be fobbed off by 'Oh, well, we've just had a busy day.'

By the time she was ten she wanted to know everything there was to know about running a jewellery company. Her endless questions varied from which stone was which, to the meaning of carats and where stones came from. She wanted to know how they were cut, polished and set. She asked who designed the fabulous necklaces and brooches she saw in the Kalinsky catalogue. More than that, she wanted to know how much everybody got paid in the company, from the top craftsmen to the assistants who sold the jewellery, and what the profit margins were.

Meanwhile she worked hard at school, determined to get good grades, and in doing so she frequently outstripped Guy although he was four years older. She shone at maths and geography;

her compositions were bright and original and her grasp of general knowledge put her at the top of the class. And all the while her interest in every facet of Kalinsky's grew.

Finally, when the questions became too much, Sarah told her to mind her own business. Kalinsky's had nothing to do with her. She should just think of herself as a very lucky little girl because the company allowed them to live in a beautiful apartment in Mayfair House, at 610 Park Avenue, with lots of servants, good food, lovely clothes and a nursery full of toys.

Francesca remained unconvinced. Her mother was a remote enigmatic figure, and there were times when she longed to get close to her, but it was always her brother Guy who came first. Everything had always been for Guy, since the day her mother had inherited Kalinsky's.

Sarah Andrews had been the only child of Howard J. Wayne, founder of Kalinsky Jewellery, Inc., which he had named in memory of his beautiful and fascinating White Russian mother. Sarah had inherited the quickly expanding company in her late twenties, when her father had suddenly died of polio. Over the years that followed she'd worked hard, learning the business and keeping it going so that one day she could hand over to Guy a healthy, vibrant corporation. They had been difficult years too. Her British husband, Doctor Robert Andrews, had persistently tried to persuade her to sell, get out, settle in England. He hated America and longed for the cool peace of the Yorkshire moors, where he had practised medicine. But

Sarah would not hear of it. With tenacity she learned how to run Kalinsky's under the tutelage of Henry Langham, who had been with the company since the beginning and was now a member of the board. Together they fought every threatened take-over bid, every prospect of a menacing merger, any boardroom chicanery. And Sarah was doing it all for Guy. One day he would take over from her and become President.

Francesca and Guy's father, Robert, had been a shadowy figure throughout their childhood. He had spent more and more time in his beloved England when they'd been small, and although he was both loving and kind, when she saw him Francesca was only aware of a look of deep sadness in his Anglo-Saxon blue eyes and the resigned droop of his shoulders. It was obvious that her parents had very little in common, and she was intrigued as to why they had been attracted to each other in the first place.

Sarah had always been wealthy, dominant and strong, and from old photographs she looked very pretty, with an abundance of chestnut hair and a vibrant smile that lit up her small-featured face. She had been educated by governesses, taken on trips around the world by her adoring father, shopping in Paris for her clothes by the time she was seventeen and making her début into New York society at the age of eighteen. Hers had always been the privileged world of the very rich, where money could get you anything you wanted, and that included people.

Robert, on the other hand, was the son of a

middle-class English couple, who had to work and save so he could go to medical school. Holidays, when they could afford one, were a week's stay in a cheap bed-and-breakfast, with yellowing lace curtains on the window and a strict landlady. At twenty-five, Robert passed his finals and worked as a doctor at St Bartholomew's Hospital in London until he had saved enough to buy his own practice in Yorkshire.

His parents, living now in genteel poverty, were therefore dismayed and shocked when he fell in love with the dynamic Sarah Wayne, whom he met when he was attending a patient in one of the minor stately homes in the area. Sarah was a house-guest, and to her host's surprise she asked if she could extend her visit. Within three months she and Robert were married and she had whisked him off to New York, where she assured him he could earn a lot more money if he specialised. He did. Five years later he was a highly respected ear, nose and throat specialist and he hated every minute of it. He longed to get back to his roots, his own people, and a quiet peaceful way of life, and as the years passed his trips to England became more and more frequent. Francesca overheard his arguing with her mother when she was eleven, and her heart was wrung with sympathy for him.

'One of the troubles, Sarah, is that nothing is mine!' he was saying. 'The house is yours. Our friends are all your friends. Even the children belong to you more than they do to me.'

'You're being ridiculous,' Sarah had snapped back. 'It's all ours! How could I help inheriting

Kalinsky's and all that goes with it? It's your problem if you've got a complex about having a rich wife, not mine.'

'You could sell the company and live the normal life of a wife and mother. What sort of home life do we have? None. You leave for the office early in the morning, and you come home when it suits you. We either entertain every night or we go out. At the weekend, we fly down to your place in Palm Beach. It's not only bad for our marriage, it's bad for the children.'

Francesca could hear Sarah groaning loudly, in a theatrical way. 'Here we go again,' she said wearily. 'All the old arguments. You must understand, Robert, once and for all, that I *cannot* sell Kalinsky's. My father entrusted it to me when he died, and now it is my duty to look after it until Guy is old enough to take over. I shall never understand why you hate it here in New York.'

Then there had been a short silence and Francesca had strained to hear what was being said. Her father was murmuring something in a low voice, and then she heard Sarah again, sounding odiously cruel.

'You can bloody well go back to England for all I care! You're nothing but a failure, a provincial small town failure, and God knows why I married you in the first place.'

The next day he had left for England, to return to the little village in Yorkshire that had been his real home. Six months later he was dead, from cancer.

Sarah, with Francesca and Guy, flew to England, where they saw him lowered in a plain oak casket into the rich, fertile soil of his beloved country. Francesca had wept bitterly. Sarah and Guy had not.

A part of Francesca was never to forgive Sarah for causing her father so much unhappiness.

'Guy, why are you going back to England again, so soon?' Sarah Andrews tried to keep the disappointment out of her voice. Guy had only been home for a couple of weeks and she'd really hoped that this time he'd come back for good.

'I've got masses of things to do over there. The London season is just starting up and I've got invitations to parties, balls, race meetings, everything that's going on. All my friends are in England you know, not here.' Guy looked at her accusingly and drummed his fingers on her desk. He'd arrived at her office at noon, hoping to catch her when she wasn't too busy, because he had a favour to ask. 'Mom, London's getting very expensive these days and I have to return hospitality. I need some more money.'

'Isn't your allowance enough?'

'Oh well, if you don't want to give me any more . . .' Guy shrugged and let the words drift away. It had exactly the effect he knew it would.

'No, that's all right, I'll write you a cheque now.' Sarah reached for her crocodile handbag and drew out her personal chequebook. 'How long are you going to be away?'

Guy's eyes narrowed as he tried to see how much she was making out the cheque for. 'Not long,' he said smoothly. 'The Mackenzies have invited me up to Scotland for the shooting in August, they have a castle in Perthshire, but I'll be back long before the fall.'

'I hope you will, honey.' She fiddled with the clasp of her diamond and gold bracelet nervously. 'I'm really going to need you here to start your training. We're always frantically busy during the run-up for Christmas and it would be wonderful to have you working alongside me.' Then she handed him the cheque with an indulgent smile and he scrutinised it quickly before putting it in his pocket.

'Don't worry, Mom, I'll be back and raring to go! Could you do something for me? Keep Francesca off my back. She's really got it in for me these days.' He rose as he spoke, and sauntered nonchalantly towards the door.

Sarah frowned. 'What has she been saying?' she asked sharply.

'You know Francesca. Always trying to make mischief.' Guy shrugged again, and Sarah thought she detected a tinge of sadness in his expression.

'Don't worry, darling. I'll see to Francesca,' she assured him. 'Thank goodness she's found herself a young man, quite a clever writer I believe, so that should keep her occupied. Now, you just have a good time in England, sweetheart, and get back as soon as you can.'

'Thanks, Mom.'

As he flew out of New York the next day his thoughts turned to Diana Stanton. They had met in inauspicious circumstances, and yet that meeting had sown such fertile seeds in his mind that he couldn't wait to return. Settling back in his first class seat, he recalled that day in the country.

Guy drove a hard volley shot over the tennis net and brought his score up to 6-2, 6-4, as his opponent, Richard Montgomery, chased madly after a ball that kept eluding his racquet.

'Shit!' swore Richard under his breath. The match was being observed from the grassy embankment that rose along one side of the tennis court by some of the girls who had been invited over for the day, and they could hear every word the players said.

'Your serve,' called Guy, trying to sound cool and keep the triumph out of his voice. He returned Richard's serve to perfection, but Richard swiped the ball with a low back-hander and it shot into the air and dropped into a far corner of the court.

'Out,' shouted Guy, unnecessarily.

Fifteen minutes later the two players strolled off towards the house, Guy glowing with victory and looking as immaculate as he had two hours before, Richard, flushed and sweaty, shambling behind. Tea was, fortunately, just about to be served, saving him from further humiliation. One by one the girls scrambled down the slope, joined by some young men who had been playing croquet, as they all made their way to the terrace.

'Come along,' crooned Richard's mother, Mrs Montgomery. 'Tea's ready. Come and help yourselves.' She waved plump fingers towards a table laden with small sandwiches and cakes while she poured lapsang souchong from a large silver teapot.

'Milk? Lemon? A little sugar?' she fussed happily.

She did so enjoy it when Richard invited his friends over.

The handsome group, casually elegant in well-tailored white sports clothes, converged like a flock of chattering swans, perching on wooden garden seats bleached to ashy grey from being left out through many English winters. Some of the guests sat on the stone balustrade while others lounged on the steps that led down from the rockery.

From the terrace, a daisy-flecked lawn sloped gently to distant flower beds filled with old fashioned peonies, lilies and clumps of lavender. To one side an ancient wooden pergola supported a tangled mass of pink roses, and the evening sun laced long shadows across the charming, lively tableau.

Amid the chink of fine bone china and animated talk, Guy lowered himself onto a wide stone step, his tea in one hand and a slice of ginger cake in the other. He was an elegant figure in his tennis whites. Tall, well over six feet. Lean, with long legs and narrow hips. Strikingly handsome, with very dark hair and eyes, and an olive skin. He looked younger than his twenty-four years. Through narrowed eyes, he now watched the people round him and listened to their conversation. It was heavily overladen with private nuances and interjections that he still didn't fully understand. They seemed to talk a language of their own and there was an unspoken understanding between them which made him feel isolated. A certain expression in their eyes, a secret sort of smile, a tilt of the head, and suddenly they were communicating with each other in a way that made him feel paranoid. Was it him they were laughing at? Or his dark green Bentley parked in the drive beside their battered little Austins and Morrises? Did they think his American accent funny, or his private wealth ostentatious? Whatever it was, and no matter how often they invited him to parties, they kept themselves apart, this nonchalant clan who guarded their exclusivity so jealously and who ganged up together with exquisite politeness to keep others out.

Ever since he could remember he'd been cultivating a sense of belonging but, half-American, half-British, he'd ended up in a sort of no man's land in spite of his money, in spite of his British education, in spite of the contacts he'd made. He wanted to emulate these aristocratic young men who ignored the trappings of their nobility because they could afford to take it for granted. The kind of men who wore shabby tweeds, patched with leather, their father's old evening clothes, their grandfather's hunting boots, who jokingly admitted they were broke and that they'd soon be hocking the family tiara to pay for a new roof, and who were so self-confident and self-assured they drove dilapidated old cars. Why couldn't they show respect or even liking for him? He was very rich, good-looking, a good sportsman, well-educated and excellent company. He returned their hospitality with lavishness. He sent their mothers bouquets of flowers if they invited him to dinner. And all the time they treated him with the sort of politeness they'd use when talking to an acquaintance.

He looked around him again at the cosy groups of twos and fours, offering each other lifts home after tea, deciding where they'd go for dinner. A cold feeling of isolation swept over him. How could he ever belong?

It was at that moment that a pretty girl with long blonde hair, a gentle face and a sweet smile, came and sat down beside him. She was wearing a pale pink linen dress and in her hands was a plate of chocolate biscuits.

'Hullo!' Her manner was friendly. 'I'm Diana Stanton. Would you like a choccy biccy?'

It had hit Guy like a spear of light. The answer, no matter how ludicrous and mad! It would require him to make enormous personal sacrifices but he was suddenly sure he could do it. And with an innocent little thing like this, he might even manage to have his cake and eat it. The answer was, of course, obvious. He must marry into one of these great families.

Chapter Two

Lady Diana Stanton slipped off her long pale-blue satin cape with its white fox collar and, with a shy smile, handed it to the cloakroom attendant, who tossed it over her arm and gave Diana a ticket.

'I say,' cut in a girl who was standing beside her, 'are you going to the Montagus' ball tomorrow night? I hear they've invited six hundred people – imagine!' She smoothed her long white kid gloves and turned to look at her reflection in the cloakroom's only mirror.

Diana joined her, a slim figure in a white organza ballgown, her long blonde hair held back from her face by small crescents of white flowers. A pink-and-white English rose complexion added to her great beauty and her pale-blue eyes were sparkling.

'Yes, I'm going,' she replied. 'Isn't it going to be fun? I hear there's going to be a rumba band too!' She laughed merrily, and the girl in pink sighed. Oh, to be like Diana Stanton! If she hadn't been so nice she'd have hated her! There was no doubt about it, Diana was the Debutante of the Year. Her photograph, by Cecil Beaton, had appeared in *Vogue*, *Tatler* and *Queen* magazines and she'd been depicted as a fantasy figure, drifting through the rose gardens of Stanton Court, her ancestral home, in flowing white muslin, her hands full of flowers.

More girls were crowding into the cloakroom now, hovering like butterflies in their gauzy finery, and the attendant was getting more disgruntled by the minute as she became swamped by dozens of evening wraps. The shrill babble of young female voices pierced the air as they jostled in front of the mirror.

'Has anyone got a spare hairpin?'

'I do hope David will dance with me tonight. He is coming, isn't he?'

'Oh dear, my lace fan is broken. Mummy will be furious.'

To Diana, who had spent all seventeen years of her life in the peace of Oxfordshire, the excited hysteria sounded like a flock of frightened birds.

'Shall we go?' She turned to the girl in pink, who was pinching her cheeks to make them appear rosy.

'Heavenly,' breathed the girl. Everything was heavenly with her. The music, the food, the flowers. Especially the young men. Leading the way, Diana entered the great marble hall of Londonderry House, where tonight's ball was being held. Beneath the glittering chandeliers her mother, the Dowager Countess of Sutton, waited for her, talking to some of the other chaperones.

'I'm longing for the day we can go to parties on our own,' whispered the girl in pink. 'The most heavenly young man wanted to take me home from

22

the Storridges' dance last night, but of course I had to refuse. Maddening!' she reflected.

Diana smiled again and gave a little nod but she didn't really agree. It was fun having her mother come to these parties and she wished her brothers could be here too, but Charlie was married now and busy running the home farm at Stanton Court, so he hardly ever came to London. And as for John, he was still up at Oxford and said he hated dancing anyway.

'Are you ready, darling?' Mary Sutton smiled warmly at her daughter, and privately marvelled at her beauty.

'Yes, Mummy.'

'Let's go then.' She turned to go up the magnificent red-carpeted staircase with Diana by her side.

At that moment, fluttering and jostling and giggling, the other girls came bursting out of the cloakroom to be scooped up by their mothers or grandmothers, forbidding looks demanding them to show some poise.

The Marchioness of Londonderry stood waiting to receive her guests at the top of the stairs, a regal figure in a huge diamond tiara and diamond chains that hung to her waist.

A footman was announcing each guest.

'Lady Sutton and Lady Diana Stanton,' boomed the sonorous voice. There was a perceptible hush and heads turned as Diana and her mother shook hands with the Marchioness.

'My dear, that gel is just too exquisite.' murmured an elderly chaperone to her companion as they sat on the little gilt chairs that lined the walls of the long, gallery-shaped ballroom.

'You mean Diana Stanton? Oh yes, she'll certainly make a brilliant marriage.'

'Of course, Mary Sutton has brought her up most beautifully,' interjected a third. 'Such good manners. And none of the dreadful modern fad for wearing a lot of make-up.'

Like rusty old jackdaws bedecked with glittering jewellery, the old ladies put their heads together, smoothing the fingers of their black-gloved claws.

'Mary only lets her meet the right people, of course.' The first one spoke again. 'I've always said it's so dreadfully important for gels to meet only the right people. It never works if they marry a man with the wrong background.'

The others nodded sagely.

'I remember my mother saying the same thing to me when I was a gel.' She waved the plumes of her black feathered fan. 'You must marry a man from the same background, she said, and that means he must also be Protestant and Tory.'

'Quite!' chorused the others.

At that moment they were joined by Mary Sutton whom they welcomed with much rustling and fluttering of fans. She was such a charming woman and they had felt so sorry for her when her husband, George, the dashing fifth Earl of Sutton, had been killed at the beginning of the war. She'd been left to cope with death duties, a large estate to run, and three children to think about. Diana had only been nine at the time. Charles, who succeeded to his father's title, was twenty and in the army, and

John, who'd been twelve, had just gone to Eton. Everyone marvelled at Mary's bravery and here she was, three years after the war had ended, bringing out her daughter and planning a ball for her. They eyed her with admiration.

'Well,' Mary Sutton accepted a glass of champagne from a liveried footman, 'Are we going to spend the evening sitting here or are we going to try to have a good time?'

Diana, still standing by the entrance to the ballroom, was already surrounded by a group of laughing young men, fresh faced and elegant in their white ties and tails. One of them stood out in particular, his dark head towering above the rest, his intense eyes never leaving Diana's face. She gazed back at him, her blue eyes filled with admiration and longing, hoping he would ask her to dance before any of the others did. Beside him these young men seemed like overgrown boys, fresh-skinned, shallow and very immature. Boys like her brother John who, for all the flattering attention they paid her, did not match up to her ideal of a romantic man. Guy was different. He was older, more sophisticated, and from the moment she'd seen him sitting on the Montgomerys' terrace he'd reminded her of Laurence Olivier as Heathcliffe in the film of *Wuthering Heights*. He had the same dark brooding eyes which suggested an inner loneliness, and the tall muscular body of an athlete, slim and lithe and elegant in expensively cut clothes. His olive skin and sensuous mouth gave him a slightly debauched look beside these innocent English boys, and Diana felt an inner trembling of anticipation as he stepped forward from the group.

'Would you like to dance, Diana?' he asked softly.

Her heart gave a great lurch and for a moment she felt breathless.

'I'd ... I'd love to,' she stammered, and a moment later she was floating away in his arms as a wave of music came spinning across the slippery floor, enveloping her, lifting her in its lilting rhythm, as she gazed up into his face.

Oblivious of everyone else that night, Diana floated on a cloud of happiness, glad that Guy seemed to want to dance with only her, thrilled when he suggested they go out onto the balcony that overlooked Hyde Park, where the trees rustled in the softness of the summer's night, and where he told her she looked beautiful.

'Do I?' she said, with a little laughing catch in her voice.

'You outshine everyone here tonight,' he replied, smiling.

But when at last the ball ended and Diana stepped into the waiting car with her mother, to return to the house they had rented for the summer in the heart of Mayfair, Mary's words brought her happiness crashing down.

'It was very rude of you to spend the whole evening with that young man,' she said, almost crossly. 'Everyone wanted to dance with you and one or two were quite upset when you refused.'

'But I wanted to dance with Guy!' said Diana,

her cheeks flushing. 'The others are just boys, and so silly. Guy has been everywhere, he's so much more grown-up than the others. Don't be angry, Mummy, I had the most wonderful time tonight. It's the best ball I've been to.'

Mary Sutton's lips tightened. While her daughter had been enjoying herself, she'd been deeply disturbed by what she'd heard about Guy from the other mothers. It wasn't just that he was a heavy drinker that worried her. She'd been told for a fact that he frequented sleazy clubs, splashing his money around whilst keeping company with prostitutes. He seemed to have no real friends and those that he did have sponged off him to excess. In fact his reputation couldn't be worse.

'I'd rather you didn't see him again, Diana,' she said grimly, thinking of all the nice eligible young men who adored her daughter.

'But we've asked him to my dance,' protested Diana. 'Don't you remember? We put him on the list after I met him at the Montgomerys'. I don't know what you've got against him.'

'His reputation leaves a lot to be desired. You'll get a bad name for yourself if people couple you with him.'

'Oh, Mummy, that's absurd. Times have changed, it's not like it was in your day. I've never heard that he has a bad reputation. Obviously he's had a few girlfriends, but then he is twenty-four.'

'It wasn't girlfriends I was referring to,' said Mary dryly. 'He goes with ... prostitutes,' she added, almost embarrassed. 'You can't be seen with a man like that.'

'Well, I don't believe a word of it,' said Diana defensively. 'Wait until you get to know him, Mummy. He's a marvellous person.'

In the darkness of the car, Mary and Diana sat in hostile silence for the rest of the journey.

'We seem to have many more boys coming than girls,' cried Diana, giving the guest list a final doubtful glance.

'That's as it should be,' her mother replied firmly. 'We don't want any wallflowers at our ball! Do you know, when I went into the cloakroom at the Maxwells' dance the other night, six girls – six, my dear – were sitting around chatting because no one had asked them to dance all evening! The poor things just couldn't bear the humiliation of sitting out in the ballroom with everyone noticing. The shortage of young men was a disgrace!'

'How awful for them,' said Diana, trying to imagine what it would be like to be a wallflower. 'I think I'd have gone home.'

'They didn't dare! Their mothers would have been furious! That would really have been admitting failure. Now, let me see that list again, darling.'

Mary Sutton, still in her velvet robe, although her white curly hair had already been dressed round her emerald and diamond tiara, sat on the edge of her four-poster bed and scrutinized the list of four hundred and fifty guests. One name stood out as if it had been written in large block capitals – Guy Andrews. Mary now bitterly regretted that the invitation had been sent before she had been warned about him. And of course, of all the acceptances that had arrived, his had been among the first. Mary glanced at her daughter with a worried expression, knowing that much of her euphoria sprang from the thought of Guy's presence tonight. Diana was looking out of the bedroom window now, her face alight with excitement.

'Doesn't everything look wonderful?' she exclaimed. 'I'm so glad we're having the ball here, instead of in London.'

Stanton Court, listed as one of the most beautiful stately homes in southern England, had been the home of the Sutton family for over three hundred years. Diana had been born here and she loved the old grey stone house and vast gardens that stretched in spectacular vistas as far as the eye could see. Today, though, everything seemed to have come particularly alive. Since dawn a small army of gardeners had been mowing lawns, clipping hedges and weeding the rose beds. Then the electricians had arrived to floodlight the grounds. All day the activity had gone on, as vans crunched up the drive to deposit trestle tables for the bar and hundreds of little gilt chairs which they placed in drunken stacks on the terrace. Diana liked the little red velvet cushions that went with them.

'Where d'you want this lot, miss?' a delivery man asked her, unloading more cushions.

Eagerly Diana grabbed an armful. The velvet was so soft and squidgy. 'I'll show you.' She led the way to the ballroom, so excited that happiness bubbled up in her chest, breaking into an explosive little laugh from time to time. Life was wonderful! It could even be described as 'heavenly'.

'Would you like a cup of tea?' Impulsively she turned to the red-faced, sweating man, sorry for him because he would not be at the ball tonight.

'Thanks, miss. There's four of us.' He mopped his face.

'I'll go and see about it straight away!' And she was gone, skimming along the corridors beneath the formal portraits of her ancestors, sorry for everyone who wasn't as happy and lucky as she was.

Now, as she had her hair done in her bedroom, the sounds from downstairs were more muted but no less thrilling. Hurrying footsteps, muffled commands, the chink of silver and crystal, a diplomatic merging of their own staff and the hired catering staff. At last it was time to put on her new ballgown. Minna, the elderly nanny who had looked after Diana and her brothers since they had been babies, was there to hook her up and tie her sash just as she had done when Diana had been a child.

'Is it all right, Nanny?'

Minna nodded indulgently. Her lovely little Lady Diana looked a proper picture! Her gossamer white lace dress had a huge crinoline skirt and ruching round her bare shoulders. Her tiny waist was encased in a wide blue satin sash. 'Like them portraits in the gallery!' Minna added, thinking of the painting by Romney of Diana's great-great-grandmother. Diana spun round in front of the mirror to get the full effect, and touched the cascade of white ribbons the hairdresser had fixed to keep her hair off her face.

'Will I do?' she asked anxiously.

'You'll do fine, my lovey,' Minna patted her arm. 'You'll be the belle of the ball. Now, mind you have a good time, and don't go drinking no champagne!'

'I promise, Nanny.' Eyes sparkling, cheeks flushed with happiness, Diana leaned forward and kissed Minna's withered cheek.

Downstairs everything was ready. Great banks of white flowers swelled to the ceiling, twining round the pillars in the hall, sprouting out of the corners of the rooms. Diana stopped to smell them, longing to gather great armfuls and press them to her breast. They smelt so – heavenly. Charles and his wife, Sophie, were already in the candlelit drawing-room with Mary Sutton, having a glass of champagne before the guests arrived. John, it was reported, was still struggling with the studs in his stiff shirtfront. Outside the gardeners had been detailed to light the flaming torches that lined the drive from the great wrought-iron gates half a mile away right up to the entrance of the house. The dance orchestra was tuning up; the waiters were plunging bottles of champagne into buckets of ice.

'I can hear a car!' cried John, rushing into the room.

Charles went to the French windows that over-looked the drive. 'There are lots of cars arriving!' he exclaimed.

Diana shot them all a look that was both excited and nervous. 'Is it beginning?' she gasped.

Obeying her mother's strict instructions, Diana danced with all the young men who clustered around her that evening, but all the while she was conscious of Guy, standing by the bar, his intense eyes never leaving her face as he watched her talking and laughing animatedly.

At last she could bear it no more and sped over to him, her smile slightly anxious.

'Are you having a good time?' she inquired. 'You don't seem to be dancing much.'

'I was waiting until you had done your duty as a good little hostess should.'

Rebuffed by the irony in his voice she stepped back and looked into his face. His features were composed, but his eyes glittered with annoyance.

'Oh! Well . . .' she said lamely.

Suddenly he smiled, a warm tender smile that made her heart melt.

'Don't worry, Diana. I understand. It's just that I thought it unnecessary of your mother to point out, when I arrived, that I mustn't monopolize you.'

Diana's face flamed. 'Oh, how frightful! I am sorry; Mummy should never have done that.'

Guy's smile deepened. 'Shall we make up for lost time?' he asked, slipping his hand round her waist. At his touch a strange excitement burned inside her. She looked up into his eyes and found them warm and gentle now.

'Yes,' she said softly.

When they danced he held her close, his cheek

almost brushing her hair, his hand holding hers tightly. Dazed and in the grip of a desire to have him hold her closer, Diana leaned against him, feeling the flatness of his stomach and the strength of his thighs against hers.

'How about going into the garden?' he murmured as if reading her thoughts. Diana ignored the warning bells that rang in her head and the thought of the lecture she would no doubt receive from her mother in the morning. She caught Charlie's eyes frowning at her as she and Guy slipped through the French windows and out onto the terrace, but she didn't care. All she wanted was to be with Guy, who was still holding her hand and leading her down to the garden, where the air was heavy with the maddening sweetness of the scent of roses, and the song of the nightingale could be heard coming from the distant forest.

'You have a beautiful place here,' said Guy, looking back at the great house whose windows blazed with a dozen chandeliers.

'You must come down one weekend,' suggested Diana recklessly. 'I could show you round properly then.'

'I'd like that very much.' He slipped his arm round her and gave her a little hug. 'Have you always lived here?'

'It's been in the family for over three hundred years. I was born here.' Diana looked at his profile, silhouetted against the moonlight, and thought how handsome he looked. More like Heathcliffe than ever; the outsider, looking into the rich man's home. Not that Guy didn't have money, she told herself. In fact, his family in America were probably much richer than the Suttons. Nevertheless, something strongly maternal in her wished to make Guy feel wanted and happy. It was obvious that he was misunderstood, lonely even. She squeezed his hand tightly.

'I'm so glad you were able to come to the party tonight,' she said.

Guy turned and looked down on her, and for a moment she hoped he was going to kiss her, but instead he flashed her a smile and left her feeling disappointed. There was something about that smile she didn't like, but it was gone in a moment, and with it her reservations.

Then Guy spoke. 'I feel honoured to have been asked. Who could wish for more than to be a guest of the "Deb-of-the-Year"?'

For Diana, the rest of the night passed like a happy dream as she danced and drank champagne with Guy, ignoring the looks of disapproval from her mother. The revelries continued until the dazzling floodlighting paled to nothing against the rosy mistiness of a rising dawn. Only then did Diana creep into bed, not to sleep, but to think about Guy, and long for the moment when she could see him again.

Chapter Three

Francesca snuggled closer to Marc as they lay together on the sofa.

'Go on,' she prompted, lifting her head to look at him so her heavy fall of chestnut hair swung about her shoulders. 'What comes next?' She looked at his profile and saw his brows were drawn together in deep perplexity, his lower lip stuck out in fierce concentration. 'Well?'

'Christ, I don't know!' Furiously Marc threw the typed sheets over the back of the sofa so that they landed on the floor with an explosive thud. Then he put his hands behind his head and looked up at the ceiling, a look of disgust on his face. 'I just can't write this fucking book – it isn't working.'

'Don't worry about it, honey.' She laid her arm across his muscular chest in a protective gesture. 'You've probably got writer's block. Lots of people get it. Why not take a break, relax a bit? Then tomorrow you can start afresh.'

Impatiently, he sat upright and, pushing past her, clambered off the sofa. 'You don't understand, Francesca, it's not as simple as that. I'm not tired! I just can't write! And my publishers are waiting for this book. God, it should have been delivered to them last week and here I am, stuck in the middle of the damn thing, not knowing what the hell to do next.'

Francesca glanced up at him and felt her heart melting as she looked at this man she loved so much. In that moment she'd have sold her soul to help him.

Marc Raven, at twenty-five, was the most magnetic man she had ever met. It certainly wasn't because of his looks, she laughingly reminded herself. At five foot eight and powerfully built, he already had a rugged, almost craggy, face, untidy dark hair that grew like a lion's mane and a crooked smile she found immensely attractive. His dark eyes, darker than hers, were the only gentle thing about him, except when he was angry, as he was now. Then they glittered dartingly under heavy dark brows drawn together in an almost straight line. His hands were deeply tanned, strong and well shaped, and very expressive. Francesca thought him almost beautiful in an unconventional way. There was an animal grace and virility that was deeply sexual, and his presence, as soon as he entered a room, was charismatic. From the first moment she'd met him at dinner at a friend's house, eight months before, she'd been totally hypnotised and fascinated. He was her first great love, and at twenty-one she knew she would never find anyone so wonderful again.

When Marc had been twenty-two he'd written his first novel, *Unholy Spectre*. It received sensational acclaim, broke sales records and made him a small fortune into the bargain. The film rights had been snapped up and the critics hailed him as the next Ernest Hemingway. Publishers wanted his next book at a phenomenal advance and it looked as if he'd got it made. Except that he could no longer write. At least not as well as he wanted to, in no way as well as *Unholy Spectre*. Despair and lack of confidence were now sapping his mind as he struggled desperately to finish his second book.

While Francesca studied for her MBA at Columbia Business School, Marc shut himself away in his smart new apartment on 76th and Madison, pounding furiously at his typewriter, and with equal fury filling up the wastepaper basket with crumpled white wads of paper containing one or two hesitant sentences. This second book meant more to him than the first for it would consolidate his position as a writer, but right now he was wondering if he could make it.

Her summer holiday was only a week away and Francesca wanted to spend as much time with Marc as she could, but his present mood forbade her to suggest any plans at the moment. She watched him now as he prowled round his masculine living-room with its big leather sofas, cluttered desk, book-lined walls and brass lamps shaded with green glass. He was pointedly ignoring the scattered manuscript as it lay on the floor, and by the hunched look of his muscular shoulders she knew she could expect another explosion. She didn't have long to wait.

'I really am desperate!' he suddenly roared. 'Everyone will think I'm a one-book writer! God, maybe I am!' He flopped down onto the sofa again, crushing her feet.

'Ouch!' Francesca let out a little yelp of pain.

'Oh, I'm sorry, sweetheart.' He shifted his position and rubbed her feet. 'I'm sorry to be inflicting all this on you.' A sad hint of his crooked smile crossed his face.

Francesca smiled back, a warm smile that lit up her velvety brown eyes and exposed her pretty, even teeth. 'Perhaps if you could remember how you wrote the first one, you could do it again,' she suggested tentatively. She didn't know a thing about writing but in the time she'd been with Marc she'd discovered he could be very touchy on the subject. 'I mean, you weren't living here for a start. Perhaps it's too big, too comfortable. Weren't you sharing rooms in the Village with a bunch of writers and artists? Hardly seeing anyone else, not having much money? Maybe now . . .'

She knew she had gone too far. She could feel the tension building up in him again, a pent-up frustration that showed in the grimness of his jawline and the tightening of his normally full mouth. Abruptly he rose again and, going round behind the sofa, picked up the manuscript and laid it on his desk.

'Is that it, Marc?' There was a note of fear in her voice. 'Is it me? Am I distracting you from your work?'

He looked at her long and silently, as if his thoughts were miles away, not with her at all, trying to search for an answer.

'No, honey, it's got nothing to do with you. Nothing at all,' he said at last, and he sounded weary.

But if it wasn't her, what could it be? Francesca curled up tighter on the sofa as if she were cold. Was it his parents, still running a bakery in Queens, refusing his help of money, refusing to acknowledge his success, cutting him out of their lives? They were deeply disappointed because he'd left the bakery at nineteen, saying he wanted better things out of life. He'd changed his name from Ravenska to Raven, which hurt them deeply, got himself a half share of a room in Greenwich Village and worked nights in a restaurant so that he could spend his days writing. While his parents toiled in their shop, his father getting up at three in the morning to bake the bread, Marc shared his food and his dreams with his new friends hoping for the big break. He was one of the lucky few, but his parents hadn't spoken to him since. Guilt, that's his problem, reflected Francesca. He doesn't feel he deserved his success.

'I ought to be going home in a minute,' she said in a small voice, as she got up from the sofa and smoothed the pleats of her red skirt.

'Please stay the night, darling.' He had his back to her so she couldn't see his face, but his voice sounded urgent.

'Oh, honey! You know I want to but Mom would go crazy! She still treats me like a kid. I think she still thinks I'm a virgin.'

'I know.' His voice was low.

'But I don't have to go right away – that is if you'd like me to stay for a bit?'

'Yeah!' Marc turned to face her and his eyes

were gentle and probing. He spoke softly. 'I'd like you to stay forever, sweetheart. God, I don't know what I'd do without you.' Then more intensely, 'Oh, I love you so much, Francesca.'

A second later she was in his arms, the flame between them that never went out igniting again, filling her with longing for this powerful tortured man whose arms held her tightly now and whose kisses stayed on her lips long after they had parted.

With infinite gentleness, he removed her cashmere sweater and then lingeringly traced the outline of her jaw with the tips of his fingers, while he kissed her mouth with great tenderness. Soon his hands were exploring down her back, round her hips and up to her breasts. Then he bent down and took one of her hardened nipples in his mouth, while his hand stroked between her legs, feeling her wetness as she pressed herself to him. Wave after wave of desire swept over her making her feel like a soft malleable sea anemone, opening and flowering towards him, longing to be taken, wanting his seed to fill her so she could drown in him.

Her hands were exploring him now, helping remove his clothes, feeling his rising hardness, knowing his longing was as great as hers, knowing too that he would prolong this tantalising ecstasy for as long as he could. Then they were lying on the soft depth of the leather sofa and he was parting her legs and entering her with powerful strokes, his eyes looking unwaveringly into hers until, with a final thrust, his mouth came crashing down on

hers as climax after climax left them shuddering
helplessly.

It was autumn and London lay bathed in mellow
dusty sunshine. The young social butterflies had
come up from the country for a final fling before
next year's debutantes emerged to command the
scene, and Guy was ensconcing himself in his new
penthouse flat in Arlington House, overlooking
Green Park. He did not intend to have a dull
winter.

By mid-October he was inviting Diana out
several times a week, and she was accepting with
alacrity.

'It's so wonderful, Guy,' she told him as they
dined at the Savoy Grill one evening. 'Mummy says
I can stay up in town from Monday to Friday in
future, as long as I go home at the weekends.'

She didn't add that her mother's scheme was
designed to enable her to meet lots of other young
men, in the hope she'd soon get bored with Guy.

Guy smiled indulgently at her enthusiasm.
'Where are you staying? Your family don't have a
place in town, do they?' 'A place in town' – he'd
learned that was how the aristocracy referred to
an apartment in London. They also had 'a place in
the country.' Never a cottage or a house or a
mansion.

'I'm staying in Cheyne Walk with Lady Benson.
She's an old friend of Mummy's. They came out
together.' Diana sipped her champagne, something Guy had given her a taste for, and smiled
broadly at him. 'I'm enjoying being in London much

more than I did during the summer. Everything seems sort of, well, different.'

Guy's dark eyes bore into her blue ones and she felt herself blushing. 'Of course things are different, Diana!' he said in a teasing voice. 'Before, you went around with a bunch of silly girls! You're having fun now because you're with me!'

Diana dropped her gaze, a deep thrill turning over her stomach. What he said was true. So terribly true! Guy made her feel grown-up and sophisticated. He took her to places like the Berkeley Hotel, where they danced to the music of Ian Stewart, or dinner at Le Caprice, which was always full of show-business personalities. Then there was the ballet and opera, race meetings at Sandown Park, film premières and charity balls. He'd even taken her to a nightclub in Leicester Square called The 400, where it was so dark you couldn't see the people at the next table. She had found that very exciting.

As if reading her thoughts, Guy leaned forward, laid his hand on her arm briefly and said, 'I've got tickets for *Kiss Me Kate* for Thursday evening. Would you like to come? We could dine afterwards at the Café de Paris and then maybe end up at the Orchid Room?'

Diana eyed him with adoration. Was there ever a kinder, more generous man? He seemed to be making a great effort to make her happy and he had so much money too! After a lifetime of living among priceless antiques and treasures, but never having enough spare money to go on a shopping spree, Diana had suddenly begun to appreciate money and what it could buy.

'Oh! I'm dying to see *Kiss Me Kate*! That would be wonderful, Guy.'

'Great.'

The moment of near intimacy was gone and he was being his usual breezy self again, but Diana was content. He'd taken her out every other evening for the past month and had spent two weekends at Stanton Court with her and her family. Surely that meant he must want to marry her, even though he had never attempted to be intimate with her?

The Orchid Room was as dark as The 400 but not, Diana suspected, as clean. Waiters were serving drinks at little tables with the instinct of bats in a dark cave, and couples, welded together, were edging their way round the tiny dance floor.

Would Guy dance with her like that? Was that why he had brought her here? Diana's heart lurched as a wave of longing, mixed with apprehension, swept through her. He'd never held her close, in fact no one had.

'Champagne?' Guy was flourishing the wine list gaily. 'It's so dark in here I can't read a damned thing – how about some Dom Pérignon?'

She nodded, suddenly reassured by his normal jolly manner. 'You're coming down to Stanton Court at the weekend, aren't you?' she asked eagerly. 'Charlie and Sophie are giving a dinner party on Saturday night, and on Sunday we've got some people coming over to play tennis.'

'Yes, I'll be there. What shall I bring?'

'Bring?' she looked puzzled. 'Well, your tennis

things I suppose, and a dinner jacket . . .'

'No, I meant in the way of presents. Something for your mother and Sophie, and how about that brandy Charles likes so much?'

'Oh, Guy! You don't have to give us presents every time you come to stay!' she protested. In fact she'd much rather he didn't. Guy and his lavish presents were something of an embarrassment to the Sutton family and left them with the uneasy feeling that he was trying to buy their favour. The sort of presents they usually received from their friends were pots of home-made strawberry jam, or a honeycomb from a proudly owned hive.

'Guy,' she began tentatively, 'my family don't have much money you know, not money they can actually spend, it's all tied up in trusts and things, and maybe, well,' she felt herself getting flustered, 'if you keep giving them such wonderful presents, they . . . well, it embarrasses them! They're not in a position to reciprocate and . . .'

'Oh Diana! You are sweet!' Guy was beaming at her. 'I understand all that, and why should they give me presents, anyway? They're so hospitable to me, the least I can do is take down a few trifles with me! Maybe some caviar for dinner on Saturday would be nice? And some Russian vodka to go with it?'

Diana bit her lip, wishing she'd kept quiet. Oh well, if her family didn't like it, it was just too bad. Whatever happened she mustn't risk upsetting Guy by saying anything more.

'So shall we go down on Friday in time for tea?' she asked.

'Great. Why don't I pick you up in the morning and then we could have a leisurely lunch somewhere along the way?'

She gave a sigh of pleasure. Life had become sheer heaven since she'd met him.

An hour later, Guy drove her back to Cheyne Walk, helped her out of the car and walked her up the lamplit path to the front door.

'It's been a fabulous evening,' he said with sincerity as she turned to say goodnight. 'Thank you for coming.'

For a magical second she felt his arms loosely around her, his lips just brushing hers, and then he was gone.

With trembling legs and her insides melting with desire, Diana climbed the stairs to her bedroom and stood there, gazing mistily into space. Guy was more than Heathcliffe, he was the hero of every romantic novel she had ever read, and every Hollywood film she had ever seen.

She couldn't wait for him to ask her to marry him.

Charles and Sophie Sutton looked at each other with worried expressions.

'So there it is!' Charles spread his large hands in a gesture of helplessness and slumped onto the chintz covered sofa. 'There's not a damned thing we can do, either. Diana's quite determined.' He tugged at the knees of his baggy cavalry twill trousers and slouched deeper. A worried frown puckered his pink weatherbeaten face, suddenly making him look older than his thirty years.

'Mother has handled the whole thing very badly,' he continued. 'She should have put her foot down at the very beginning, instead of letting Diana invite him here.'

'I think she thought that Diana would be keener on him than ever if she wasn't allowed to see him,' said Sophie reasonably.

'Humph! Well, it hasn't worked, has it? I've been doing some checking up; he was at university with some chaps I know, and I also have some friends in London who have met him. Sophie, he's rotten through and through. He sponges off his mother, he is a drunkard, and the company he keeps is the lowest of the low. His reputation stinks and the only women he's ever seen with, apart from Diana, are tarts! I mean, the whole thing is disastrous!'

'And she's in love with him,' said Sophie dryly.

They were sitting in the library of Stanton Court having tea, and had just heard from Mary Sutton that Diana was hoping to marry Guy. They were expecting her later that afternoon and as she had said Guy would not be with her this weekend, they were planning how to persuade her, once and for all, to stop seeing him.

Charles sipped his tea and looked thoughtfully at his wife. Thank God for Sophie, with her no-nonsense practical mind, her warm smile and her energy. Especially now. She was someone who could talk to Diana, woman to woman, make her see she was making a terrible mistake. Sophie's background and upbringing had been much more sturdy and vigorous than Diana's. The daughter of a general in the British army, she'd travelled the world with her parents and, at the age of twenty-two, had landed a responsible job in the Foreign Office.

Charles had met her at the local Hunt Ball and had been struck by her merry blue eyes and naturally curling brown hair. She was no beauty, but her personality was warm and reassuring.

Three months later they were married.

'I wish your mother had insisted she train for a job,' observed Sophie. 'Diana's living in a bygone age, you know. Other girls share a flat in town nowadays, and work at something. She seems to think you come out, have a glorious season and then marry the first eligible fellow who comes along.'

'I'm afraid that's Ma's fault. Because it was like that in her day she doesn't see why it shouldn't work for Diana too.'

'Well, somehow we're going to have to make her understand that if she married Guy it could ruin her life. If he's as bad as you say, he'll be running off with other women all the time and leading her a hell of a dance. He does drink a lot when he comes here but I've never actually seen him drunk, have you?'

Charles made a slight grimace. 'He's careful when he's here but only last week I heard, from the Montagus, you know, that he'd been so drunk in some restaurant that he was sick all over the place and had to be taken home.'

Sophie looked at him, appalled. 'Surely Diana knows all this? Hasn't anyone told her?'

47

'Don't they always say it's the wife who is the last to know anything?' he replied grimly. 'Well, this weekend I'm going to tell her, even if she gets upset. I'm going to spell it out!'

'Why does he want to marry her?' Sophie asked suddenly. 'Apart from the title, she's got nothing! Her little allowance barely covers the cost of her clothes.'

'Our name, though, could open all the doors he wants opened. The man's a terrible social climber, Sophie. It was the first thing I noticed about him when he came that first weekend. He'll use Diana to climb the ladder and when he's got what he wants he'll ditch her.'

'How can he be a social climber if he goes about with such awful types, prostitutes and people?'

'Maybe they are the only ones who are impressed by him, apart from Diana.'

Restlessly, Charles heaved himself off the sofa and wandered over to the French windows that led to the garden. The velvety lawns lay bathed in late mellow afternoon sunshine under a sky that was blue and clear. Beyond, the herbaceous border glowed with brightly coloured flowers and beyond that the oak trees were alive with crowing blackbirds. The beauty of the day jarred on him.

They had been such a happy family once but now that seemed like such a long time ago. Now Diana wanted to marry Guy Andrews and if she did, nothing would ever be the same again.

'Is that her car?' Charles spun around as they heard the swish and crunch of gravel on the drive.

'Yes,' said Sophie, taking a deep breath. 'I think it is.'

Dinner that night was a strained affair. Earlier in the evening Charles had told Diana, bluntly and almost brutally, what he knew about Guy. She had listened quietly at first, but then she had suddenly jumped to her feet, her face flaming with anger.

'You've got it all wrong, Charlie!' she cried. 'You've been listening to terrible gossip! Why are you paying any attention to people who are probably jealous of Guy, with his wealth and good looks, instead of using your own judgement? Has he ever been drunk in this house? Has he ever behaved badly? And I've never heard about him going to these clubs you mention or being seen around with dreadful women! I've never heard he's got a bad reputation!'

'You must remember you move in a very different circle, Diana.' Charles stood up also, and went and stood with his back to the fireplace. 'Guy seems to have his own set of friends, if you can call them that, a set that could never penetrate ours, so it's not surprising that all the other debutantes and young men you know are unaware of his style of life. Ask yourself one thing: he does know a few well-connected families, but do they really accept him?'

'You're just being a snob!' she flashed back.

'I am not being a snob; that has nothing whatever to do with it,' Charles said firmly. 'I don't care who your friends are, within reason. What I don't want to see is you throwing your life away for a drunken lecher!'

'Guy's not a lecher. Let me tell you something; he's never tried to get me into bed and he's done no more than kiss me, and that was almost in a brotherly way. How can you say these things, Charlie? I love Guy. He's the most amusing, interesting and wonderful person I've ever met, and if he does ask me to marry him, which I think he eventually will, then I'm certainly going to accept.' Looking petulant, Diana flung herself down onto the sofa, her mouth set in stubborn lines.

'Then promise me one thing, sweetheart,' pleaded Charles, 'don't rush into anything. Wait a bit and get to know him better. You'll find out in time that I'm right, you know. I only want you to be happy.'

Sudden tears brimmed Diana's blue eyes and she blinked rapidly. 'Trust me to know what's best for me, Charlie. Don't ask me to give him up. You've no idea how much I'm in love with him . . . how much I want him . . .' Her voice caught and a little sob burst from her throat. 'All I dream about, night and day, is being married to him,' she continued. 'Although I know it would be wrong, and Mummy would have a fit, I'd have an affair with him tomorrow if he would let me, but he's a very moral man and he'd never ask me to do anything wrong.'

'*Moral!*' said Charles incredulously. 'Do you call it moral to pay for the services of prostitutes?'

Diana had recovered her composure and now she spoke spiritedly. 'That's malicious gossip and I refuse to believe a word of it.'

Now, as they sat round the antique mahogany

dining table in the soft light of many candles, Diana knew they were all against her. Mary Sutton looked strained, blaming herself for not keeping them apart from the beginning; Sophie and Charles anxiously glanced at one another from time to time, wondering what their next tactic should be to prevent what they considered was impending disaster; even John looked cool.

They all tried to keep the conversation general and inconsequential but inevitably talk turned to the arrangements for the next weekend, when they would all be together again.

'So we're having a dinner party on Saturday night, and a cold lunch on Sunday,' remarked Sophie.

'That's right,' said Mary nodding. 'And then everyone can play tennis, or swim if it's warm enough, on Sunday afternoon.'

'How many people are staying?' asked Charles.

Sophie started going through their names.

Suddenly Diana broke in, a look of defiance on her face. 'Don't forget I've invited Guy. He's arriving Saturday morning.'

'Oh, good.'

Mary, Sophie, Charles, and even Diana, turned startled faces to John, who was carefully peeling a home-grown peach. He looked up, surprised by their reaction.

'What's wrong?' he demanded. 'Guy's a good chap. We have a lot of laughs when he's here; brightens up the old place I think.'

Charles threw Sophie a despairing look, but Diana gave John a grateful smile. It was nice to

know not everyone in her entire family was
against Guy.

Guy was pleased with the way things were going.
As far as he knew Diana had no idea where he
went or who he saw when he was not with her. His
mother was also sending him more money, although
the pressure on him to return to New York
increased with every passing week. All in all,
everything was working out the way he wanted,
and now as he drove down to Oxfordshire, to
spend another weekend at Stanton Court, his feelings of self-satisfaction increased. He adored the
old house and was beginning to feel quite at home
there. And it wasn't just the ancient stone building
he loved but all that it contained. Within the shell
of its thick walls was an Aladdin's cave of sweeping stairs, panelled halls and gleaming parquet
floors. The richness of the antique furniture and
brocade curtains, the gilt-framed portraits of
Sutton ancestors and the fine porcelain ornaments
and vases, filled Guy with a pleasure that was
almost physical. It wasn't just the trappings of
wealth, he'd been surrounded by those all his life.
It was the ancient heritage, from the suits of
armour on the first floor landing to the family tree
painted on parchment in the hall, that gave a
meaning to everything. This house had stood here
for over three hundred years and generations of
Suttons had added their treasures to it, and he
could sense a wonderful feeling of continuity. Now
that was *really* belonging, he reflected, as he came
down the wide staircase to join Diana's family for

dinner on Saturday evening. He hoped their dinner guests, three local couples Sophie had invited, would like him. Adjusting his black evening tie and checking in the hall mirror that his dinner jacket looked right, he opened the heavy panelled doors into the drawing-room.

They were all there, grouped around the blazing log fire like characters in a Noel Coward play. Mary, Countess of Sutton, in black velvet and pearls, Sophie Sutton in a frilly red silk top and a long brocaded skirt, Charles looking strangely clean without his baggy beige trousers and darned sweater. They were talking to their other guests whom Guy had recently come to recognise as what were known as 'the county set'. Clean-cut men in dinner jackets with hair trimmed short and neat, women in tops and skirts rather like Sophie's, but smothered in jewels. None of which looked as though they came from Kalinsky's, he observed wryly. The diamonds were much too small. Apart from the group, and helping himself to another glass of champagne, stood The Honourable John Stanton. Guy went straight over to him and also helped himself to a drink.

'Nothing like a little shampoo to cheer one up!' exclaimed John in his usual flippant manner. 'Old Charlie's got out the best tonight! Can't think why he wants to impress all these boring old farts.'

Guy chuckled and felt better. John was the only person in this household who accepted him without qualification.

'Who are they all?' he whispered.

'Oh, the Crichtons, and the Donnellys and the

Martins. They're all mad keen on hunting! The only thing I'm interested in hunting for is another drink. Can I top you up, old chap?'

Guy held his glass forward and watched as the minute golden bubbles rose to the surface and popped. Then he joined the others round the blazing fire, feeling like an outsider once again. These people just didn't seem able to accept him.

Only John welcomed him on Friday evenings with a warm smile and genuine pleasure. Next to Diana, who was sweet to everyone, John was definitely the nicest and Guy found himself in deep admiration of him. John was attractive too, with his tall willowy frame, long slender limbs and silky blonde hair. When Guy had first met him he'd been instantly reminded of a famous portrait of Prince Henry, son of King James IV, painted in 1610. Perhaps John was descended from the romantic-looking prince in his doublet and hose and fine lace ruffles?

At that moment he caught sight of himself and John in the long mirror that hung on the far wall. They were the same height, almost the same build, but he was as dark and dramatic looking as John was fair and gentle. Such contrasts, and yet . . .?

'Have another drink, Guy? We're going to have to get pissed to get through this ghastly dinner,' John was whispering in his ear.

Guy grinned back at him.

With care, being married to Diana might just work out beautifully.

Meanwhile, he'd be going up to Scotland for Christmas to stay with a chap he knew whose parents lived in a castle. Then he'd be spending the New Year here with Diana. After the New Year, perhaps, he'd propose to her. He had no doubts that she'd accept him. There was only one hurdle he had to cross, and he wasn't looking forward to it.

He'd have to tell his mother, and she was going to go just crazy with rage.

Chapter Four

The storm exploded with a suddenness that took people by surprise, sending them scurrying for shelter. Rain lashed down furiously, bouncing off ledges and awnings. It swelled on the streets until they looked like grey rivers and sent small torrents gushing along gutters, heavy with eddying debris that blocked the drains.

Francesca, walking down Park Avenue towards Grand Central, looked up and saw the monstrous stalagmite skyscrapers veiled through a curtain of water, their tops obliterated by heavy clouds.

'Damn,' she muttered to herself, as she pulled her coat tighter around her. 'I'll never get my Christmas shopping done if this goes on.' It was ten days to Christmas and she wanted to get a present for Marc.

Heading for West 47th Street, she decided to go to the Gotham Book Mart and Gallery where she was certain she would find something special. Maybe even a first edition. As she sheltered in the doorway of a delicatessen, watching the rain slant past her like a beaded curtain, she made a mental list of the other people she had to buy gifts for; her mother, her friend Carlotta Linares, her classmates at Columbia and, of course, Uncle Henry.

Henry Langham wasn't really her uncle but she had adopted him as such ever since she'd been a little girl. Uncle Henry was worth keeping in with. Especially now, for she was sure he was her way of getting into Kalinsky's. He would persuade Sarah to give her a chance. He would suggest she join the board. Above all, he could teach and guide her as he had her mother seventeen years before.

Soaked but triumphant, Francesca stumbled home two hours later. Tucked inside her coat to protect them from the rain were two books. A leather-bound, gilt-tooled edition of Byron's poems, dated 1873, for Marc, and a biography of Winston Churchill for Uncle Henry. Dangling damply from her arms were a dozen shopping bags, including one from Bergdorf Goodman containing a blue and green silk scarf for Sarah. Well, what else did you give a mother who had everything? She hadn't bought anything for Guy. Airmailing parcels was such a bore, but she'd sent him a card.

'A Miss Linares is waiting to see you, in the drawing-room, Miss Andrews,' the butler informed Francesca as soon as she entered the apartment.

'Oh?' said Francesca, surprised. 'I wasn't expecting her. Perhaps you could bring us some coffee.'

'Yes, Miss Andrews.'

Francesca dumped her parcels on the hall table, fluffed out her hair in the mirror and slipped off her soaked coat. She looked a mess and doubtless her friend Carlotta would be looking immaculate as usual, but it couldn't be helped. Pushing open the drawing-room door she greeted Carlotta warmly.

'Hi! What a nice surprise!' she said, giving Carlotta a hug. 'How are things going?'

Carlotta, dark and petite and neatly dressed in navy blue, shrugged her slim shoulders and patted the coil of her chignon.

'My aunt is driving me mad!' she exclaimed, her Spanish accent pronounced. 'All the time it is "Where have you been?" or "Where are you going?". I tell you, it drives me crazy! If only my family would let me live alone, I would be so happy.'

Francesca smiled. It was always the same with Carlotta. Ever since she'd met her at the opening of a modern art gallery and Carlotta had poured out her heart, she'd had to listen to an endless stream of good-humoured grumbling. Nevertheless, Francesa found herself amused by her friend's dramatic tales and histrionics; none of her college friends talked like that, and with Carlotta she could always be sure of a good laugh. Although they were so different, Francesca treasured their friendship and at times almost wished they'd been sisters. She was also intrigued by stories of Carlotta's childhood, as the fourth child of the Marqués and Marquesa Lorenzo de Carranza Linares, living in the family *palacio* near Jerez in southern Spain, and rigidly brought up.

'My family used to be rich,' Carlotta had explained at that first meeting, 'but now everything of value has been sold: the Velasquez paintings, the silver, even Grandmama's rubies. Papa wanted me to marry when I was seventeen, but I would not!' She made a dramatic gesture with her hands. 'I was supposed to marry someone very aristocratic, but he had no money either! What good was that?' she demanded comically.

'So what did you do?' asked Francesca, fascinated.

'I asked my godfather to pay for me to go to Madrid, to study the history of art. I worked hard, and when my professor said he could get me a job at Sotheby's in New York – *de Dios*! – I jumped at the chance.'

'So what about this aunt of yours? Where does she fit in?'

Carlotta threw up her hands in despair, her long scarlet nails jabbing the air. '*Tia* Juanita! She is an old spinster and she hardly lets me out of her sight, but Papa said I must be chaperoned, otherwise he would not let me come to New York.'

Francesca's eyes widened. 'You mean you're not allowed any freedom? But you're twenty-four, Carlotta! How can you stand it?'

'I escape her clutches when I can,' said Carlotta, enigmatically, and refused to say more.

Now, as Francesca poured the steaming coffee into two large cups, she looked at Carlotta quizzically.

'So, you have the day off?' she asked conversationally, wondering why her friend seemed more driven than usual.

Carlotta gave a deep theatrical sigh and shrugged

again. 'I just couldn't bear to go back to the apartment, with *Tia* Juanita sitting, waiting for me, questioning me about everything.'

'Haven't you got a room of your own you could go to? I frequently shut myself away when Mom's on the prowl.' Francesca had never been invited back by Carlotta, and didn't exactly know where she lived except that it was around 49th Street. Suddenly she understood why.

'I have to share a room with my aunt, and we just have one little sitting-room,' said Carlotta blushing. 'It is all we can afford,' she continued painfully. 'Her money wouldn't keep a cat in food, so I have to pay for everything.'

'Yes, I see,' Francesca said sympathetically, marvelling at how well-groomed and smart Carlotta still managed to look, in spite of being poor. 'Can't your parents help?'

'With three sons to educate, there is no money to spare for me. Besides, Papa is still angry that I didn't stay and marry the nobleman he chose for me. Oh, Francesca! You are so lucky! You have a beautiful home, and a nice mother, and you have money to spend on clothes and nice things . . .' Her voice drifted off.

Francesca suddenly felt embarrassed. She *was* very lucky by comparison; lack of money was something she had never had to suffer.

'Carlotta,' she began cautiously, fearing she might be misunderstood and give offence. 'You'll be getting an invitation to Mom's dinner party on Christmas Eve and I do hope you'll be able to come, and I had planned to give you a silk shirt as a

61

Christmas present – ' she stopped, aware that she was babbling. Then she took a deep breath and continued more slowly.

'What I'm trying to say, Carlotta, is that I'd like to give you a dress instead. Something you could wear to the party.'

'Oh! Oh! Francesca!' Carlotta's face lit up and she flung herself at Francesca. 'How wonderful! A new dress for a Christmas party! And all your friends will be there?'

'Well . . . yes,' said Francesca, slightly startled by Carlotta's reaction. 'Mom always has a lot of people, it's usually quite fun.'

'I can't wait! Oh, thank you, you are so good to me.' Carlotta sat down again, flushed with pleasure.

'Have you a boyfriend you'd like to bring as well?'

For a moment Carlotta's eyes widened and then they narrowed slightly, before she turned her head away and said almost brusquely, 'Of course I have no boyfriend.'

After she had gone, Francesca couldn't help feeling curious about Carlotta. Although they had known each other for six months, meeting for luncheon or perhaps a drink, she knew no more about her than she had done in the beginning. She had no secrets from Carlotta – what was there to hide, anyway? But in so many ways Carlotta seemed to be holding back about her private life. And surely she must have a private life, in spite of her ever vigilant aunt, thought Francesca. On the other hand, maybe she is just ashamed of being so poor, and having nowhere decent to live. Anyway, it was no business of hers, and she was glad she'd at least been able to make her happy by inviting her to the Christmas party.

Sarah's annual Christmas dinner party was beginning. She liked to make it a very grand affair, inviting a few politicians, some leaders of industry, a few society couples and maybe a prominent newspaper publisher. Since her husband's death, Guy had always sat opposite her at the end of the long table, but this year, for the first time, there was no Guy. Painfully and silently, Sarah re-drew her original seating plan, placing Henry Langham there instead. Francesca, she decided, could sit on Henry's left, with Marc Raven opposite her. Carlotta Linares could go on his right. She wouldn't know anyone and might enjoy talking to Marc. On the other side of Francesca she decided to place William Yates, a young man in investments. No doubt her daughter would enjoy talking to him, she thought wryly. On either side of herself she picked a senior member of Congress and the editor of the Wall Street Journal. The remaining twenty-two guests were then arranged in order of precedence, taking care to separate husbands and wives and people who would bore each other.

Sarah took a great pride in these dinners. From the moment guests arrived, stepping into a candlelit hall decorated with great boughs of holly trimmed with hundreds of tiny red glass baubles, they were ushered on a journey of rich enchantment.

In the drawing-room a twelve foot tree, smartly decorated in silver and white only, stood before the coral curtains. Underneath it, packed in silver wrapping-paper and coral ribbons, were presents for the guests, each with their name and a message written on a little silver card in Sarah's own hand.

White-coated waiters were floating around now, with trays of pink champagne and silver platters of choux pastry cases filled with glistening dark caviar, while Sarah stood welcoming everyone. She had chosen a long gown of shimmering silver beading and with it she wore a magnificent ruby necklace and earrings, 'because they look pretty and Christmassy'. She was totally aware she was the best advertisement for Kalinsky's jewellery, which she managed to wear as casually as if it had come from Woolworths. That was her secret. She paid no more attention to a bracelet set with a million dollars' worth of emeralds than she would if it had been made from shells gathered on the beach, and what she wore today, every rich woman wanted to wear tomorrow. She had turned the display of her products into an art form.

After a while the double doors which led into the dining-room were flung open by the butler and there was a little gasp of pleasure from those who had never been to one of her parties before.

This year she had chosen scarlet and gold as her theme and the sight that met her guests' eyes was dazzling. A scarlet taffeta cloth covered the long table, where thirty places were set with gold flatware, scarlet candles in gold candelabra, and Venetian goblets of the same red as stained glass windows, edged with a tracery of gold leaf flowers. Down the centre of the table miniature Christmas trees glistened with gold trimmings.

'Shall we go in to dinner?' Sarah's commanding smile encompassed the room. 'Francesca, show everyone the seating plan.' With a beautifully manicured hand she indicated a leather-bound diagram.

'Okay, Mom,' Francesca smiled. Even her mother wasn't going to get to her tonight. Round her neck hung Marc's present, a single gleaming pearl on a fine gold chain. He had given it to her that afternoon after they had made love and she felt it was a talisman, a shield which could protect her from everyone and everything. Of course Sarah had been furious when she realised Francesca was going to wear it to the dinner party.

'Don't be absurd, dear!' she admonished crossly. 'Supposing people thought it came from Kalinsky's? I went to the trouble, specially, to bring you back something really nice to wear tonight. You're wearing your new dark-green velvet, aren't you?' Without waiting for a reply she continued, 'I've brought a necklace of square cut emeralds, linked with diamonds, and earrings to match. You must wear them.'

'They're much too old for me Mom! There's no way I'm going to wear all that stuff. No, I'm wearing Marc's present and I don't care what you say.' Francesca's mouth was set in a determined line.

'Well, I must say!' cried Sarah. '*That* shows how much interest you have in the company, for all your talk.'

The matter had not been discussed again, and now as Francesca grabbed Marc's hand she was so glad she was wearing his single beautiful pearl. As they entered the dining-room together, he squeezed her hand, and glancing at her he whispered, 'I want to go back to bed with you. How long does this dinner last?'

Her eyes twinkling, she squeezed his hand back. 'Rather a long time, I'm afraid, darling. After dinner Mom hands out all the presents, and then we have carol singers . . .'

'Jesus.' His eyes were boring into hers. 'I don't know if I can wait that long.'

'Let's spend all day tomorrow together,' she whispered. 'Preferably in your bed.'

'If it can't be in yours it'll have to be in mine, I suppose.' He grinned wryly. 'What a way to celebrate Christmas!'

'By the way, do talk to Carlotta. Mom's put her beside you and she doesn't know anyone.'

'You mean that little Latin number? Do I have to? The last time I met her here, she drove me mad with her dramatic manner, and you know how I hate neurotic women, honey!'

'Just this once, darling, and I'll rescue you right after dinner.' Francesca gave him another squeeze and, smiling, slipped into her place between Uncle Henry and the boring investment tycoon.

'So what's Guy doing with himself, these days? It's the first time he's missed this party, isn't it?' Henry asked Francesca as the servants served the first course of turtle soup.

'He says he'd got a lot of things on in England,' she replied non-committally.

'Will he be back soon? Sarah's getting anxious to have him back.'

Francesca kept her eyes down, avoiding his.

'Yes, I know,' she said briefly.

'But you'd rather he didn't come back?'

She glanced up quickly and found Henry was watching her with kindly twinkling eyes. Could she trust him? Henry had been by her mother's side for so many years now, she wasn't sure that he could be trusted not to repeat everything she said.

'If Guy were to pull his weight, it would be fine,' she said carefully. 'But I don't know if we could work together, and I'm determined to join Kalinsky's as soon as I can.'

Henry nodded firmly. 'Yes, you must. You'd be a great asset to us.'

'Mom doesn't like the idea, though. She wants me to get married and settle down and all that sort of thing.'

'Leave her to me.' He smiled warmly at Francesca, remembering the little girl with the big brown eyes and abundant auburn hair who used to visit Sarah in her office.

'Will you really help me, Uncle Henry? It's the only thing I want to do . . . apart from going on seeing Marc,' she added, looking fondly across the table to where Marc sat talking to Carlotta.

'Of course I'll help you.' Henry spoke stoutly.

'But Mom will oppose the idea. She only wants Guy in the company, and although I realise he's her heir, I know there's a part I could play as well.'

'You've got to realise something about Sarah – and I've known her since she was a girl.'

Francesca raised her eyebrows. It was amazing to think anyone knew her mother as a girl.

She asked, 'What is that, Uncle Henry?'

'Well, I know I can speak frankly to you and in confidence.' He took a sip of his chilled Chablis, and carefully replaced the Venetian glass on the scarlet tablecloth. 'I'm afraid she's always been jealous of you. Even more so now, because you've got your youth, health, and great beauty.'

Francesca raised her hand to protest, but he silenced her with a shake of the head, and continued.

'There are other factors to take into consideration, too. She's at a very difficult age for a woman, and I think she often feels tired and irritable, although she won't admit it. The really tricky part, from your point of view, though, is that she is also jealous of you for Guy's sake. You've always been smarter than him, and she knows as well as I do that if you join Kalinsky's Guy won't stand a chance.'

Francesca sat silent for a moment, trying to take in what he said. None of it surprised her, but to have him put it into words clarified the problems she faced.

'Yes. I understand,' she said slowly.

'I'll do everything I can. Not just for your sake, Francesca, but for the sake of Kalinsky's. Your mother was left thirty-five per cent of the shares, and you and Guy twenty-five per cent each. Right?'

She nodded.

'The day your mother retires and hands over her percentage to Guy, which is what she says she'll do, it will mean Guy holds sixty per cent.'

'I understand.'

'And sixty per cent, in the hands of the wrong person, is sixty per cent too much.'

She gazed at him, amazed that he was prepared to be so frank with her.

'And you think Guy is the wrong person?' she asked softly.

'You know the answer to that question yourself, honey,' he said pragmatically.

They talked a bit more about the company, until, out of politeness, Francesca turned to talk to William Yates who, though charming, she found rather boring. At last coffee was announced in the drawing-room, and as they all rose from the table, Francesca sidled over to Marc, longing to be with him again.

'Are you all right, darling? ' she asked, slipping her arm through his and smiling up at him.

'I'm okay,' he replied tersely, without looking at her.

'Oh God, were you that bored? I thought you'd enjoy talking to Carlotta, she is very interested in all the arts you know.'

'So it seems.'

Francesca looked at him sharply. Something seemed really wrong. He was clenching and unclenching his jaw, his face was deeply flushed and his eyes glittered dangerously.

'What's wrong honey?'

'Nothing, Francesca.' He seemed to be about to

say something and for a moment he looked at her despairingly. Then he gave her hand a brief squeeze and, without saying another word, he turned and strode out of the room.

Francesca flushed when she saw her mother's look of surprise, then she heard her say, 'Come and help me give out the presents, Francesca.'

Together they knelt in front of the huge silvery tree, calling out the names of the guests. They were such a contrasting pair, mother and daughter. One so deceptively delicate and fragile-looking, groomed to perfection as if she had been cast in ice; the other as warm and vibrant as a summer's day, with shining brown eyes and rich chestnut hair swept back with tortoiseshell combs.

In a minute the room was filled with a babble of voices as the guests exclaimed with delight as they opened their presents, each carefully chosen by Sarah. There were calfskin wallets and blotters, bottles of the most exclusive perfume, specialised books and gold compacts, silver cigarette boxes for the smokers, gold mascots for the car lovers and equipment for the sportsmen.

When they had finished Francesca rose and looked around for Marc. She was holding the gold fountain pen her mother had bought him from Tiffany's, but he was nowhere to be seen. Suddenly worried that he might not be feeling well she hurried into the hall. Glancing round, she saw him sitting on a sofa just inside the front door. He was huddled over as if he were nursing a stomach-ache. Close beside him sat Carlotta, holding his arm.

'Marc! What's the matter?' Francesca rushed forward, concerned.

He looked up, startled by the sound of her voice, and she noticed his face was very pale. There was a sheen of sweat on his brow and upper lip. 'Are you ill, darling?' she gasped.

With a great effort, as if his legs might give way, he struggled to his feet. 'Honey . . .' He sounded broken, defeated. 'I've got to talk to you . . . something's happened . . . Oh God, I feel terrible.'

'Marc, what's wrong?' Shafts of alarm pierced her mind. He had been working so hard lately and now he seemed to be on the point of collapse.

'Don't worry,' Carlotta cut in softly, 'I'll see him home. He'll be all right.'

'Are you in pain, darling?' demanded Francesca. 'Why don't you come and lie down . . . let me get you some water.'

Marc put his hands to his head and she noticed he was shaking all over. 'Francesca, you don't understand.' Then he dropped his hands to his sides in a gesture of total weariness and looked at her with deep pain in his eyes. His lips moved but he seemed unable to say anything.

'I'll take you home, you need to see a doctor.'

'You can't leave your guests, Francesca.' Carlotta spoke with sudden firmness, planting herself solidly by Marc. 'Make our apologies to your mother and we'll slip away without any fuss. Are you coming, Marc?' Her glittering black eyes looked into his.

'Yes, well, okay, I'm sorry, Francesca . . .'

'Hey! Wait a minute!' Infuriated at Carlotta's

high-handedness she put her arm round Marc's shoulder. 'You can stay here. I'll call Doctor Hertz . . . we've plenty of room – '

Marc pulled away from her with a gesture of near desperation and, as if galvanised into action, strode to the door. 'It's no use, Francesca,' he said, and his voice sounded harsh. 'Are you coming then, Carlotta?'

With a little smile, Carlotta slid her arm through his, and guided him out of the door and into the darkness of the night.

The carollers were giving their all to *The First Nowell*. Their voices rose in familiar harmony, filling the room with sweet nostalgia as the guests sat in a large semicircle listening with rapt and slightly drunken attention.

Francesca slipped into the room and took a seat at the back, her mind in a turmoil. What the hell was going on? And what was wrong with Marc? Was he drunk? Cursing herself for having handled the situation so badly – how could she have let Carlotta take him off like that? – she decided to leave it for half an hour and then call him. If he was really ill, she'd go round to see him whatever her mother said.

The carollers had now launched into *O, Come All Ye Faithful* with great gusto, and as the music penetrated her numbed brain so did the realisation that she might have lost Marc. Already a wild searing pain filled her heart. *How* could he have left her with such violent swiftness?

It was an agonising hour later that the party

started to break up with people drifting off in a euphoric cloud of food and wine and Christmas cheer. Sarah, still smiling graciously, was bidding everyone good night. Francesca stood rigidly miserable in the hall by the 'phone. She'd called Marc's number four times and each time the line was busy.

'Are you coming to bed, dear?'

Francesca started, not realising it was so late and that everyone had gone. 'Yes, in a minute, Mom. I'm . . . I'm just trying to get hold of Marc.'

'At this hour?'

'I think he's ill. He left the party very suddenly and I'm worried about him.' Francesca stood twisting her hands nervously, a frown on her face.

'My dear child, he's perfectly capable of looking after himself. You can't go chasing after him in the middle of the night. Anyway, he left with Carlotta, didn't he? He's probably not ill at all. They'll have gone dancing or something. Leave it alone, for goodness' sake.' With an impatient gesture, all trace of graciousness vanished now her guests were gone, Sarah turned away.

Francesca watched her go with a deep feeling of anger, stung by her deliberately cruel words. Perhaps Uncle Henry had been right. Perhaps Sarah *was* jealous of her.

It was the moment when Francesca called to speak to Marc's agent, Martina Hudson, that she felt real panic close in on her.

'You mean you don't know where he is either?' she gasped. Marc kept in touch with Martina

73

several times a week and it was unlike him, just when he was due to deliver his manuscript, not to have told her what he was doing.

'I haven't heard from him since just before Christmas. I guessed he'd gone away for a few days, but you say you haven't been able to contact him since Christmas Eve?' Martina asked. 'That's three days ago!'

'I know.' Francesca sank down onto her lace-covered bed, her legs suddenly feeling weak. 'I started calling him at his apartment a few hours after he left here but all I got was the busy signal. All night long. It was busy the next morning too and now I'm really scared. What can have happened?

'He's not at his apartment,' continued Francesca. 'And I can't get hold of Carlotta who left here with him, either. I'd go round to see her but I don't have the address. Do you think they could have been in an accident or something? It's not like Marc to vanish without a word.'

'Well . . .' Martina hesitated, 'you could call up the hospitals to check but I really wouldn't worry if I were you. I know what writers are like, Francesca. They suddenly get an idea and they're off in hot pursuit of it.'

'Do you have the address of his parents in Queens? He never gave it to me, but perhaps he's gone to visit them, it being Christmas and all that.'

'No, I'm afraid I don't, Francesca.' Martina was beginning to get a bit bored. It wasn't the first time she'd had a wife or a girlfriend on the 'phone, certain that something dreadful had happened to their loved one, only to find him tucked up in some motel, either with his typewriter or another young lady. 'Look,' she added, 'give me your number, and I'll call you if I hear anything.'

'Thanks.' A moment later Francesca replaced the receiver slowly. Nothing Martina had said had alleviated her anxiety. Shafts of panic now filled her as she imagined him mugged, murdered, lying dead in some downtown mortuary, unidentified because he'd been wearing an unaccustomed dinner jacket and had joked to her that there was no room in his pockets for a wallet. All he had carried was a ten dollar bill and the key to his apartment. And could Carlotta have been murdered too? Images of them lying bleeding on some sidewalk as they waited for a cab outside her apartment filled her mind. Something terrible must have happened, something so frightful that it made her blood freeze. She sat on her bed staring into space for a few minutes, fear immobilising her limbs, numbing her mind. She tried to recall every detail of the dinner party on Christmas Eve. She and Marc had never felt happier and more secure in their relationship. Absently she fingered the pearl he had given her, nestling at the base of her throat. He had given it to her after they had made love that afternoon and she recalled him saying, 'I'm going to go on giving you pearls for the rest of your life because they suit you so.' And she'd smiled at him, choked with emotion, the thought flashing through her mind that Kalinsky's never recommended pearl engagement rings because of the old superstition that pearls were for tears. 'I love you,' she'd said instead, hugging him. Then Francesca frowned.

Something had happened during dinner, but what? He'd only met Carlotta once before and he didn't even want to sit beside her. She trusted Marc too much to even think he'd go off with a girl he hardly knew.

Suddenly she jumped to her feet. Panic galvanised her into action. Grabbing the 'phone, she obtained from the operator a listing for Ravenska Bakeries in Queens. It was worth a try.

'Whatch want?' screeched a female voice when she got through.

'Marc Raven – Ravenska,' stuttered Francesca. 'Can I speak to Marc please. Is he there?'

'Marc no here.' The voice was sullen.

'Er ... when will he be? I mean, is he staying with you?' Francesca was breaking out in a sweat and her hands were shaking.

'Marc no here,' repeated the shrill voice. 'Marc no here for long time. Whatch want?'

'It doesn't matter. Thank you.' Feeling sick, she replaced the receiver. Then she called up all the hospitals and the local police stations. It had been a busy Christmas, with a lot of incidents. Arson attacks, murders, rapes, drunken brawls, drunken drivers, muggers, suicides and quite a few burglaries.

No one had heard of Marc Raven or Carlotta Linares and no one cared. They seemed to have vanished into the frosty night without a trace.

She had one more call to make. If anyone could solve a problem it was Uncle Henry. Dialling his private number at Kalinsky's she was relieved when he answered at once.

'What can I do for you, sweetheart?' he inquired pleasantly.

'Can I come to see you? Can we have a cup of coffee someplace? I don't want to go to Kalinsky's in case I bump into Mom.' Her voice was urgent.

'What time is it now?' There was a pause while he looked at his watch. 'Just on noon. Listen, Francesca, my lunch-time appointment has been cancelled. How about lunch at Caravel at a quarter of one?'

'I'll be there. Thanks a million.'

Dear, wonderful, life-saving Uncle Henry, she thought, as she struggled into a green woollen suit and tied a cream silk scarf at her neck. He hated girls to wear drab clothes, so instinctively she always put on her brightest things when she was going to see him. Not that she really felt like it today.

Henry Langham was waiting for her at his table. One look at her face was enough to make him order drinks immediately. 'You look like you could use one, honey. So what's the problem?'

Quickly she told him what had happened and as he listened he watched her carefully. Francesca was usually the calm type but today she was profoundly upset. She talked fast and her eyes flickered nervously.

'I'll see what I can find out,' he said at last. 'He's got to be somewhere and so has this girl, Carlotta. People just don't vanish into thin air and if you've checked with the police and the hospitals, he can't be in that much trouble.'

'I wasn't really scared – only puzzled – until

this morning when I realised his agent hadn't heard from him either,' Francesca told him. 'I wonder if he was taken ill in the street and someone's taken them into their home? Or could he have lost his memory?' Even as she spoke she knew she was clutching at straws.

'And Carlotta too?' he enquired wryly. 'Two people struck down with amnesia on Christmas Eve? Tell me, sweetheart, what do you know about this girl? You haven't known her long, have you?'

'A few months. I liked her, actually.' Already she realised she was talking in the past tense and it made her shudder. 'I felt rather sorry for her, she had so little money and she was living with what sounded like a bitch of an aunt, a real Spanish duenna.'

'And you say you don't know where she lives? Could she have taken Marc home to nurse him if he was ill?' Henry drained the last of his dry martini and ordered two more.

'Then why didn't she let me know?' demanded Francesca. 'Anyway, I don't think that's what happened. I started calling her on Christmas morning, but there's been no reply.'

'She never asked you back to her place?'

'No, never. But I think that was because she didn't want me to see it. She and her aunt really seemed to be poor, and proud with it.'

The head waiter came over with the menus. Francesca chose a salad, Henry a rare steak.

'It seems to me,' he said thoughfully, as they waited for luncheon to be served, 'that two people have gone missing, not just one. And when it's a man and a woman, that usually adds up to one thing only, I'm afraid, darling.'

'I don't believe it!' Francesca cried vehemently. 'I know Marc. He'd never do a thing like that. It's quite impossible. We really loved each other.' Again the past tense. Her eyes brimmed.

Henry put his hand over hers, and squeezed it sympathetically. 'I believe you,' he said sincerely. 'Marc looked like a real nice guy, and a clever one too. Now Francesca, tell me everything you know about him, and about Carlotta too. Everything you can remember. Then I'll check around and see what I can come up with, though I can't promise anything. I might give the Spanish embassy a call. See what they can find out about Carlotta's family.'

'Thank you, Uncle Henry. I really am grateful and you'll let me know if you find out anything?'

'Sure thing, honey, though you realise it may take time.'

'Of course.'

Francesca walked back to Mayfair House, the cold air chilling her to her bones, the wind stinging her face. There were plenty of yellow taxis speeding by but she had this insane idea that if she kept walking, searching the faces in the street as they scurried past, she might spot Marc, walking along absently as he always did with his arms full of books or manuscripts. She gazed at all the faces, her eyes flickering to and fro until they ached. Every now and then she turned her head to see who was behind her on the other side of the street. A sharp blast of wind caught her breath and sent a flurry of icy snow particles whirling through the air. They seemed to blind her, blurring her vision, until she realised it was the tears that coursed down her cheeks.

At six o'clock the next evening the 'phone rang. Francesca grabbed it, a wild hope filling her heart that it would be Marc.

'Hullo,' she cried, her voice catching.

'Francesca, is that you?'

'Oh, Uncle Henry. Have you found out anything?'

There was a moment's silence on the line that seemed to stretch into the darkness. Then he spoke.

'I'm afraid I've got bad news for you, darling.'

Methodically, Sarah squared up the papers on her desk and privately thanked God the day was nearly over. It hadn't been like this when she joined Kalinsky's seventeen years ago. This deep tiredness. This bone weariness. Then she'd been an energetic woman of twenty-six, thinking nothing of putting in a twelve, sometimes a fourteen hour day. God, how she'd worked then, turning Kalinsky's from an up-and-coming New York jewellers into an international concern, with outlets throughout the world. But now she sometimes wondered how she was going to carry on. Of course, her age didn't help. Those night sweats and hot flushes and the frantic feeling, sometimes, that she was going to kill the nearest person in sight for no logical reason at all. Sometimes she felt as if all the nerves of her body had risen up to the surface, just beneath the skin, and that an invisible key was drawing those nerves tighter and tighter as if she were a clock-work toy. She just hoped there'd never be a sharp ping as one of the nerves snapped.

Beside her lay a design for a necklace she'd approved that afternoon. She picked it up and looked at it again. A flexible platinum linked neck-lace, supple as ribbon, the two ends crossing over in a loop at the base of the throat. From the tapering ends hung large tear-shaped pearls, one white, one black, both half wrapped in filigree platinum. It was fantastic – and she'd suggested they make matching pearl earrings, one white, one black. Pearls from Japan, of course.

A great feeling of loneliness crept over Sarah, as she sat there alone in her magnificently furnished office. Soon she would call for her car to take her home. Then she'd order a light supper on a tray, for Francesca would be sure to be out again. And after that? Watch television? Do some reading? She sighed deeply. A single, middle-aged woman in New York was a misfit. Hostesses were reluctant to invite them to dinner because of the numbers. She herself was too tired to want to entertain much. The trouble was, everyone in her circle had someone. Except her. Someone to go to the theatre with or to a restaurant. Someone to escort them to parties or on trips. That was the price she had paid, she told herself, for giving her life to Kalinsky's. It would have been the same if Robert had lived, although it might have been nice to have someone to talk to now. Of course there was dear old Henry, a good friend and a wonderful col-league but hardly a soulmate. And there was

Francesca. Her mouth tightened. There was something about her daughter that never failed to annoy her; she was so damned pushy, and she hadn't felt she could control her since she'd been a small child. Francesca was also too independent, she told herself fiercely, and too ambitious for her own good. At times she actually felt threatened by her and it was a very unpleasant feeling. Guy had always been her favourite child, so gentle and loving, and now she missed him deeply. He must come back home and take up his rightful position in the company before Francesca usurped it, as she surely would. And he must come back right away. She needed him by her side, and it was the least he could do when she'd held the company together all these years, just for him.

Fretfully, a sudden hot flush rising from somewhere inside her and bathing her in glowing sweat, she pulled a notepad toward her. She would write to Guy. Better than talking on the 'phone. She started drafting the letter. It was important to tell him that his future with Kalinsky's would be glittering. She might even buy him his own apartment. Anything to tempt him back. She was interrupted by the ringing of one of the 'phones on her desk. Who the hell wanted her now? It was nearly six o'clock.

'Yes?' she snapped.

'Hi, Mom!'

'Guy! Darling! How extraordinary! I was thinking about you right this minute.'

'Ah, that's telepathy for you, Mom. So how are you?'

'Wonderful, honey. Just fine.' Suddenly Sarah felt twenty years younger. Her flush had subsided as quickly as it had started and her tiredness had vanished. 'How was Christmas? We sure missed you here, darling.'

'I had a great time! Parties every night. I met half the aristocracy of Scotland and I stayed in a fantastic castle that once belonged to a Scottish king. I'm just in London for a couple of days and then I'm going down to stay with the Suttons at Stanton Court for the New Year.'

'So you said,' remarked Sarah pleasantly. 'That'll be very nice for you, dear.' She thought Guy sounded buoyed up, just as he used to when he was a child and she'd arranged some treat for him. Only it was other people far, far, away who were giving him a good time now. She was filled with a deep jealousy.

'Yeah, it's great. I'm having a fabulous time.'

They continued to chat for a few minutes, each longing to say what they really wanted to say, each too fearful.

' – I'm in the middle of writing to you – '

' – I've got some news for you, Mom – '

Their voices clashed and they both laughed nervously. There was a pause.

'You were saying, dear?' said Sarah, something clutching at her stomach.

'Well, I was just calling to tell you, Mom, that I'm planning to stay over here,' she noticed a high-pitched tremor in his voice, 'because I'm thinking of getting married.'

There was a stunned silence that ate a great hole in the ether.

'Mom? Are you still there?'

Sarah was bankrupt for words. Depleted. Drained, so that the sweat on her back turned to ice.

'Married?' she faltered.

'Yeah! Don't you want to know who she is?' he demanded pettishly.

'Guy ... isn't this terribly sudden? I've been waiting for you to come home, to join the company ... I can't go on much longer like this. I need you here, darling,' she said, the hurt breaking her up inside. How come, she thought wildly, I can be so strong, so invincible when it comes to business relationships, but so terribly vulnerable when it comes to my own son? How could he be telling me all this in such a cruel, insensitive way too? What reason have I to carry on if he's not here beside me to take over?

'Of course you can manage,' Guy was saying in a flattering tone. 'You're a mere girl! Kalinsky's would fall apart without you. You don't need me! You'll be President for the next twenty years and loving every minute of it. You know you will!'

'We must talk about this, Guy,' she said desperately.

'What's there to talk about? Now listen, she's Lady Diana Stanton, and her father was the Earl of Sutton. Her brother, Charlie, is the present Earl and they own Stanton Court. Marrying her will make all the difference to my social standing here,' he added.

'Why can't you marry her and bring her over to

live here? I could buy you a wonderful apartment, or a house if you'd like it better, and – ' but as she spoke she knew she was clutching at straws, because she knew Guy. Once he was set on something, nothing would change his mind.

'But it's not what I want!' he cried childishly. 'For God's sake, Mom, I've wanted to live in England since I was twelve. If you need help in the company, what's wrong with Francesca?'

Sarah didn't answer. She couldn't fight him right now. She felt too shocked, too upset, too numbed with misery. And it would be fatal to start crying. 'I'll write you anyway,' she said at last, trying to get control of her voice. 'I was going to explain to you in my letter anyway about the importance of the future of the company. I'm sure you'll understand when I explain it to you, about how you are the only person who can take over from me, as your grandfather wanted.'

'Well, it won't make any difference. I'm going to ask Diana to marry me over the weekend and then we can get married in the summer. Anyway, Mom, I'll be in touch. Let you know how it goes.' He sounded quite merry again.

'You do that, darling.'

For once Sarah left her desk untidy, the surface covered with a scattering of jottings, notepads, pencils and designs. Blindly she picked up her handbag and walked to the double doors that led to the corridor and the lift.

For the first time in her life she felt totally and utterly defeated.

* * *

Francesca was clenching her jaws until her teeth ached. She couldn't believe, wouldn't believe, what Uncle Henry was saying.

'I'm afraid it's true, honey. I checked thoroughly, put the best people I know onto it, and they've come up with all the details,' he replied. 'I'm afraid there's no doubt about it. Marc and Carlotta flew to Las Vegas on Christmas Day and got married.'

Francesca's mind was spinning in jagged loops, grappling with the impossible. Marc simply couldn't have vanished out of her life like this to marry a total stranger. 'That can't be right,' she cried. 'Why should he have done a thing like that? Only that afternoon he talked about wanting to spend the rest of his life with me. There must be a mistake.'

'It's been carefully checked out, sweetheart,' Uncle Henry said sympathetically. 'My people have even talked to Carlotta's father in Jerez. He didn't only confirm they were married, and apparently he sounded pretty shocked himself, but they've actually arrived at the Linares home and are staying with her parents right now.'

'But why?'

Henry could hear the rising hysteria in her voice. 'I'm afraid, Francesca, that something must have happened at your dinner party, and I don't just mean they fell in love. I think something sinister happened. He was sitting beside her, wasn't he?' Henry tried to recall the scene; Francesca so radiant and happy that night, and opposite her, Marc sitting with Carlotta on his right. 'And they left together as soon as dinner was over, didn't they?'

'He said he felt ill. Then Carlotta offered to take him home. The next minute they'd gone – Oh God, how could I have let him go like that? I was a fool not to have gone home with him myself.' She was making a great effort to keep her voice steady.

'Did he actually look ill?'

'He ... he ... well he looked sort of strange. What do you mean about there being something sinister in this?'

'Could she have had something on him? Do you know of anything in his past that he'd want to hide?' Henry asked.

There was a pause while Francesca racked her brains, trying to remember everything Marc had told her about himself. It didn't add up to much. He made no secret of the bakery in Queens or his humble beginnings. Everyone knew about the rooms he shared with friends in Greenwich – could he have been caught up in some drugs racket? She dismissed the idea immediately. She was sure he had never been into that scene. As far as she was concerned, Marc had been hailed as a brilliant new author with a great future.

'I can't think of a thing,' she said at last. 'He had nothing to hide.'

'Well then, darling,' Henry paused painfully, 'are you sure they didn't know each other better than you realised? What I'm trying to say is, are you sure something hasn't been going on behind your back between those two?'

Francesca didn't have to stop to consider this possibility before answering. 'Uncle Henry, I'm absolutely certain there's been nothing between them. I'll admit Carlotta has always been a bit secretive, but Marc hasn't! I always knew exactly where he was at all times, who he was seeing . . .' Her voice broke and she began to sob. 'We were so close. What am I going to do now?'

The poignancy of her voice made Henry's heart ache for her and he realised in that moment that the little girl he had known for so long had vanished forever. He just wished to God he'd gone round and told her the news in person.

'Work, Francesca. Work is the only thing that is going to make you feel better,' she heard him say. 'Keep up with your studies and as soon as you've got your MBA I promise you I'll have a position for you in the company, just as soon as you're good and ready.'

'Thank you, Uncle Henry. That's what I've always wanted,' she wept, 'but Mom is never going to agree, I'm afraid. She says it's a man's world and I know she doesn't want me there.'

'So you become part of a man's world, sweetheart. You can do it and I'll back you every inch of the way. Don't let your mother or anyone else tell you differently.'

'I won't,' she promised, more to herself than him. But when she hung up, it hit her like a physical blow that she'd have to do it on her own. No Marc with his encouragement and support. No one to come back to at the end of the day. Alone now. But no matter how long it took she was determined about one thing. She was going to find out, somehow, what had made Marc run out on her and marry Carlotta.

Chapter Five

Dusk was descending on the city, and as the lights in Piccadilly and Green Park sprang to life, the chauffeur-driven Rolls Royce nosed gently through the heavy traffic, heading for the Ritz.

In the back Diana clutched Guy's hand, her face alight with excitement. 'Isn't this thrilling? I didn't know I could be so happy,' she cried.

'It's been quite a day, hasn't it?' Guy smiled as if he were amused by her elation.

They had been married earlier that day in the twelfth-century Norman church that stood in the grounds of Stanton Court and afterwards Mary Sutton, with Charles and Sophie, had given a reception for three hundred guests.

For Diana the day had passed like a magical dream. She'd been awakened by the dawn chorus of starlings that nested in the Virginia creeper outside her rose-patterned bedroom, and as soon as she'd remembered it was her wedding day, she had leapt out of bed and run to the window. In the east a pale rosy mist was building slowly into shimmering sunshine and below the grass sparkled with the dew. It was going to be a beautiful July day.

The morning sped past so quickly, as florists and

caterers flooded into the house and all the preparations got under way, that before Diana knew it she was being helped into her ivory satin wedding dress. A lace veil that her mother had worn for her own wedding was pinned to her hair and then the hairdresser fixed the family diamond and pearl tiara in place. As Diana looked in the mirror, she marvelled that the radiant girl looking back could really be her.

Then she was walking slowly up the aisle on Charles' arm, the air around her filled with the drenching sweet scent of gardenias. And Guy, her wonderful marvellous Guy, had been standing at the altar rails waiting for her. He looked so tall, his thick black hair brushed smooth and glossy, his creamy olive face turned towards her, his almost black eyes proud and penetrating. It was the only face she saw and as her eyes met his she knew with an overpowering feeling that she didn't fully comprehend that she had met her destiny. She was oblivious to her mother's strained expression, to the tight forbidding look on Sarah's face. Gliding up the aisle with an expression of total trust on her face, she only knew that Guy was the man she loved more than anything else in the world and, in time, she would prove to everyone just how wonderful he was.

An explosion of rose petals and confetti burst over them as they came out of the church forty minutes later, and from then on it was a whirl of kisses and hugs, champagne and wedding cake, laughter and farewells. Only now, sitting in the car with Guy in her blue velvet going-away coat and little blue feathered hat, was she beginning to realise the full impact of what the day meant. She was Guy's wife now, Lady Diana Andrews. And for the first time since her father had died she had someone to look after her who was truly hers.

Guy had booked a suite at the Ritz for their first night and tomorrow they were flying to Paris, where his green Bentley already awaited them. From Paris they would drive to the South of France for a few days before going on to Italy. From Milan they planned to drive over the Simplon Pass into Switzerland, staying in Lausanne before returning to Paris. Diana could hardly wait. The thought of visiting all the glamorous places she had only ever read about – and with Guy at her side – made her feel as if she were the luckiest girl in the world.

And this was only the beginning of her wonderful new life.

Later, after a light supper of lobster mousse, salad and a bottle of Roederer Cristal champagne, Diana slipped into the bathroom, leaving Guy alone with his cigar and a glass of Napoleon brandy. Trembling slightly, she bathed, then put on one of the delicate nightdresses from her trousseau. It was made of fine lawn, embroidered in white silk and edged with broderie anglaise ruffles slotted with white silk ribbons. Brushing her long hair she gazed at herself in the mirror, as she had done before her wedding. She still looked the same, she thought, disappointed. Young, virginal, expectant. She supposed she wouldn't really *feel* like a grown-up married woman until this night she had waited so long for was over. Surely the greatest experience of all would give her an air of maturity, a knowing look? Candid blue eyes looked back at her wonderingly, longing to know how she would be changed. Then she smiled. It could only be for the better.

Guy lay waiting in the vast double bed and as she came out of the bathroom he looked up, his eyes watching her intently from under his thick black brows. He was wearing pale blue silk pyjamas and in one hand he still held his glass of brandy. She smiled shyly and with a thumping heart walked slowly towards the bed, never taking her eyes off his face. Then his hand reached out and, catching hers, he pulled her towards him.

'You sure look beautiful tonight,' he said, and there was an awkwardness in the way he spoke.

'Do I?' Tremulously she slid down beside him.

Slowly, he placed the half empty brandy glass on the bedside table. 'Well, how does it feel to be a married lady?' he teased.

'I don't know yet . . .' Blushing, she averted her eyes for a moment and then looked back at him.

Guy put his arm round her shoulders and gave her a hug. His voice sounded peculiar. 'Well, I think it's time you found out, don't you?' he asked.

And find out she did.

With a swift twist of his body, Guy bore down on Diana, pinning her to the bed, his mouth pressed hard on hers. Startled, she tried to draw back as his teeth ground against hers, but she couldn't move. Then with a tearing sound she felt her nightdress being ripped as he pulled the delicate fabric from her body with a violent gesture.

'Guy!' she cried, wrenching her head to one side, suddenly scared. He was holding her so tightly her ribs were hurting and she could hardly breathe. He had his hand between her thighs now and he was forcing her legs apart. Pressing her palms against his chest she tried to hold him off, but he was too strong as he thrust his body against hers with force. It's as if we're fighting, she thought in panic.

With frightening ferocity he rammed his hand between her legs, pushing her down roughly onto the mattress, grinding his mouth once more on hers, and he was hurting her, hurting her . . .

'Guy!' she screamed, breaking away from his kiss with all her strength. 'Stop it! For God's sake, Guy! Please stop it!'

Unheeding, he tore into her with a heavy lunge, violently and without mercy, as she lay trapped beneath him. Pain seared through her body as she tried to reject the probing sharp force of his penis, but he held her in his strong hands and she could only lie there trying to shrink back from the agony. She was still screaming when he was seized by a spasm. Then he let out a wild strangulated groan and collapsed on top of her. For a moment he lay still, panting, then with an almost dismissive gesture he rolled off, curled on his side, facing away from her, and closed his eyes.

Diana lay absolutely still for a moment, shocked and stunned. Tears gathered in her eyes. She must get to the bathroom for she felt he had damaged her badly. Moving gingerly, she crawled out of the bed, aware that her beautiful new nightdress was ripped and covered in blood. She staggered across the room to the adjoining bathroom. Once safely inside she locked the door and then sank onto the cool marble floor feeling crushed, humiliated, deeply bruised. She sat crouched like that for a long time until at last, rising slowly, she went over to the bath and turned on the gold taps. What had happened to turn Guy from a loving man into a frenzied monster? Surely it couldn't always be like this? Lowering herself cautiously into the comforting warmth of the water she lay back and closed her eyes. She couldn't go back into the bedroom. That was certain. Supposing he were to try to do it again! The thought made her shudder. Reaching for a wash cloth she gently dabbed at her swollen mouth. She'd sleep on the sofa in their sitting-room . . . but then there was tomorrow. What was she going to do tomorrow?

Half an hour later she crept back into the bedroom, put on another nightdress and looked at Guy as he slept in the soft rosy glow of the bedside lamps. He looked so gentle, almost childlike, as he lay there breathing softly through his mouth. His black lashes lay along his cheek and his hands, in repose, were pale and relaxed. This was the man she loved, the amusing, charming man who had shown her nothing but kindness and generosity. She stood there hesitating. Maybe it would make things worse if she went and slept in the next room. Maybe he would be angry with her as he seemed to have been when he made love to her. She wouldn't be able to bear it if he got angry with her again.

Quietly she got into the big bed and, lying as far away from him as she could, she pulled the pink satin coverlet over herself. For a while she lay there thinking about what had happened, and the pillow beneath her head grew damp as tears of misery and disappointment slid silently down her cheeks.

And this had been her wedding night.

'Francesca, are you sure we've got all the luggage? I can't see my hat box anywhere.' Sarah Andrews stood by the departure desk at Heathrow surrounded by stacks of lizard-skin suitcases the porter was rapidly unloading from a trolley.

'It's here, Mom. And I have your jewellery case.' Francesca leaned wearily against the Pan Am counter and watched with dull eyes as her mother handed over their flight tickets for New York. It was the day after Guy's wedding and she felt shattered. They'd been staying at Stanton Court for the past week and the strain had exhausted them both. Perhaps the worst part for Francesca had been pretending to Diana that Guy was the man she imagined him to be. She's so in love with him, Francesca thought. Her gentle eyes had widened with excitement whenever he came into a room and she had hung onto the string of banalities that flowed from Guy's mouth and laughed at his juvenile jokes. Her innocence! Her naiveté! As Francesca prepared for bed the first night in her peach brocaded room complete with Venetian four-poster bed, she found herself wondering about Diana. Where the hell had the girl been all her life? Guy was a spoiled, self-indulgent parasite, deeply selfish and very self-opinionated. He'd have a child like Diana jumping through hoops in a week; he'd dominate her utterly and all because he had to have his own way. And there she was, drooling over him with pathetic adoration and already fetching and carrying for him. Francesca slid between the fine linen sheets embroidered with the Sutton crest, and wondered how a girl could let herself be such a doormat to any man. She'd done it once, worshipping Marc to the exclusion of almost everything else and all that had happened was that he had kicked her in the teeth. She'd never let that happen again. In future her head would rule her heart and she'd call the tune. No man was going to be allowed to get close enough to her to be able to inflict such pain and hurt. Francesca ground her teeth, almost alarmed at her own ferocity of feeling. God damn Marc Raven! She hoped he'd rot in hell! And now here was this eighteen-year-old girl about to throw herself away on a man like Guy, whose only interest in life was himself.

Francesca tossed and turned in the great old bed, filled with an anger born of hurt and rejection. And she was furious with her mother too. Sarah might at least have had the courtesy to be more gracious to the Sutton family. Francesca quite liked them, especially Sophie with her modern no-nonsense ways. The old countess had started off by being utterly charming, but a few hours with Sarah and her snide remarks about being richer than the Suttons had quickly reduced the two women to clawing cats, scoring points off each other, protective of their young, scornful of their different styles of living.

As the days passed the atmosphere grew worse, and Sarah cornered Guy whenever she could, trying to persuade him to change his mind.

As Francesca was walking through the gardens one morning, she heard angry voices coming from the stone folly that stood some distance from the house, overlooking the valley beyond. Her mother's voice, urgent and intense, carried on the still air.

'. . . and I've hung on to Kalinsky's, sacrificing my personal life and happiness, so that you could work with me and become President one day. You can't throw all that away to marry this girl . . .'

Francesca hurried over to the little temple, anxious to stop her mother before she was overheard by one of Diana's family.

'Hush!' she cautioned them as she entered. 'Someone will hear you.'

Guy and her mother stood facing each other, Guy rigid with anger, Sarah flushed and with brimming eyes.

'Mind your own business,' said Guy shortly.

Sarah ignored her, but she lowered her voice as she continued to plead with Guy. 'Listen to me, darling. You won't be happy here. You don't fit in.'

Guy's eyes flickered over her coldly. 'You're mistaken, Mom. It's you who don't fit in, but then how can you expect to? Your father was only some damned half-Russian immigrant who happened to make a killing selling jewellery.'

For a moment Sarah looked as stunned as if he'd hit her, then her eyes widened, spilling tears, and she flashed back at him: 'Money you apparently enjoy spending!'

Without another word, Guy turned on his heel and strode out of the folly and back in the direction of Stanton Court.

'Come on, Mom. Cheer up,' said Francesca comfortingly. 'You know what Guy's like. Don't let him upset you.'

Sarah drew herself up, annoyed at the critical tone in Francesca's voice.

'I'm perfectly all right,' she said with dignity, turning to follow Guy. 'He doesn't mean it.'

And so the week had progressed, slowly and painfully, with the two families hating each other more each day while Diana, happily untroubled, dreamed of the moment she would become Guy's wife; whilst Francesca, trying to be brave about it, knew now and had done for a week, that it was dreadfully and finally over between herself and Marc. Forever. No longer could she dream of reconciliation, when they would meet and he would sweep her into his arms, telling her it was she he loved, and not Carlotta. Her fantasy that one day they would be together, some time, some place, was finally shattered. She had been reading a newspaper article about him, in which he was being interviewed about his second book, and then, in the final paragraph, it mentioned that he was now a father. 'My son, Carlos, was born last week,' he was quoted as saying. 'So far he is a very good baby, we haven't had a broken night yet.'

The article went on to describe his beautiful wife Carlotta, but with her mind spinning and feelings of nausea rising in her throat, Francesca didn't need a calendar to work out that Carlotta must have been three months pregnant when she married Marc. So, Uncle Henry's suspicion that something sinister had been going on between them was unfounded. It was the old, old story of a man getting a girl pregnant and her forcing him to marry her. But . . . Marc! Francesca's mind reeled in a nightmare of betrayal. Marc had said he loved her and all the time he must have been having an affair with one of her best friends, behind her back.

'Are you coming?' Sarah demanded impatiently. 'We don't want to miss our flight.'

Francesca blinked, her thoughts returning from miles away.

'I'm coming, Mom.' Carrying the jewellery case, she followed her into the V.I.P. lounge. In a few hours she'd be back in New York, back to her own problems, back to missing Marc. Diana and Guy were on honeymoon now. They'd have to sort out their own problems, just as she was going to have to become reconciled to hers.

The string quartet played *Tales from the Vienna Woods*, while elegant ladies in straw hats and middle-aged gentlemen in pale grey suits sat around little tables in the foyer of the Hotel de Paris in Monte Carlo enjoying afternoon tea. The delicate chink of china, the murmur of well modulated voices

99

engaged in small talk and the scraping of violin strings all combined to make Diana feel as if she had stepped into a Somerset Maugham story. The tinkling laugh of a woman with sad eyes, half hidden behind the veil of her little hat, floated over to her. A portly man with a monocle snapped his fingers at a passing waiter. An elderly lady, glittering with diamonds and emeralds, made a stately entrance, followed by her companion. The sickly sweet smell of lilies filled the air and somewhere, just out of reach, she felt an underlying layer of melancholy. Nothing was as perfect as it seemed.

Diana was waiting for Guy at one of the little tables and it was a relief to be on her own for a few minutes. He'd told her he wouldn't be long. He just wanted to enquire down at the harbour about a small yacht that was up for sale. And so she waited, refusing to acknowledge that the sobbing of the violins found an echo inside her. She wondered as she watched the other people in the foyer if they were acting a role, pretending to be jolly, just as she had been doing these last few days.

During the past week, she and Guy had seemed to spend all their days in the car, gobbling up the long, straight, poplar-lined roads for mile after mile as they sped through France. Guy never seemed to want to stop to admire the countryside or explore the towns they went through on their way. Luncheons in restaurants were quick, snatched affairs. Picnics were conducted with frantic haste as if they had a train to catch. It seemed as if Guy didn't dare stop anywhere for long, as if he were running away from something. Each night was spent in a different hotel and each morning they'd be off and away before Diana had finished her breakfast. This afternoon they'd arrived in Monte Carlo and she had been enchanted by the prettiness of the town, with its closely terraced villas edging layer upon layer down to the harbour. The sea was bluer than she had ever imagined and the sun so bright it dazzled.

Diana had tried hard not to think about their first night together. On the third day of their honeymoon Guy had suggested firmly that they should only make love on alternate nights, 'because it was so tiring'! She wasn't sure whether she was relieved or not. It was a dreadful, painful and humiliating experience on the nights they did have sex; he handled her roughly, brutally, showing no consideration for her feelings or cries of pain. On the other hand, the nights he rolled away as soon as he got into bed and fell fast asleep left her feeling spurned and unloved. By the end of the week she had come to the conclusion that she didn't attract him in bed. There was no other explanation. During the day he was affectionate, gently teasing and amiable. At night he seemed angry, resentful, intolerant. He'd also said that her clothes were dull and unbecoming and that she ought to wear something sexier. Diana didn't have anything sexy. She had been taught by her mother to wear simple, classical dresses and suits with neat low-heeled pumps and she wasn't even sure what Guy meant by 'something sexier'. Then she would lie awake for hours cursing the fact that she was inexperienced, innocent, and unable to respond, wondering what another woman would have done in her place. But then another woman, she thought with sudden anger and bitterness, would probably have big breasts, curvy hips and a seductive manner.

It was half past four now. The string quartet were playing *The Blue Danube*. Guy would be back in a few minutes so she'd better order tea from one of the black-coated waiters. While she waited she took some picture postcards out of her neat beige handbag and flipped through them. There was a pretty one of the Casino floodlit at night, surrounded by its magnificent gardens and palm trees. Her mother would like that. Taking the cap off her gold fountain pen she addressed the card in her large round handwriting. Then she wrote: *Having a wonderful time. Weather gorgeous. Going on to Italy tomorrow. Love to everyone. Diana and Guy.*

There was no way she was going to admit to her family that she had made a terrible mistake.

They arrived in Lausanne the following week and drove straight to the magnificent Beau-Rivage Palace which Diana had seen somewhere described as a 'Hotel de Grande Classe'. Guy had stayed there before but Diana gazed in amazement when they first entered the enormous white marble lobby. Tall Doric columns reached up to the high, arched ceiling and heavily carved cornice. Life-size statues were set in niches and the gleaming parquet floor was strewn with Persian carpets.

Gilt wall brackets clustered with oyster silk shades filled the vast area with a warm glow, shining down on the oyster brocade and tapestry sofas and chairs. In the corners and on several low tables stood superb arrangements of flowers.

'My goodness!' she gasped, astonished. 'What a place! Isn't it terribly expensive?'

Guy shrugged. 'It depends what you call expensive. Your monthly allowance from your family might cover one night . . . without breakfast. But don't worry, Diana, you're married to a rich man now, you know.' He strolled over to the reception desk to sign the register.

Diana winced. Was he now going to throw her lack of money in her face as well as her lack of sex appeal? Standing quietly behind him a feeling of deep failure seeped through her. And an overwhelming homesickness. At this moment all she longed for was the warmth and security of Stanton Court and the love of her family.

Their suite was no less magnificent than the hotel foyer, with ten foot high gilt-framed mirrors, Empire furniture, a crystal chandelier that sent sparkling rainbow drops of light winking round the walls and heavy aquamarine silk draperies and upholstery. She went to the windows which reached from the floor to the ceiling and looked down on Lake Leman, spread below like a sheet of darkened glass, broken only by tiny ripples as sailing boats swung gently in the breeze. The mountains, purple and green, rose steeply from the lake, soaring to snow-capped peaks that penetrated the clouds. Below, under the protective walls of the hotel, sweet chestnut and southern fig trees mingled with camellias and mimosa bushes hung with gold.

Suddenly Diana wished they had spent their whole honeymoon here, where the mountains embraced the flowering alpine meadows and the air was tangy with the scent of pine. It would have been so much better, so much more peaceful, than scurrying from place to place, never seeming to actually arrive anywhere.

'What are you looking at?' Guy asked, coming over to join her.

'I was just thinking . . .' she smiled wanly. 'Well, I was just thinking how small we are beside those great mountains over there.'

He shrugged. 'We might come back for the winter sports next year. I suppose you can ski?'

'A bit, but not very well.' Then she added hurriedly, 'We used to ride mostly during the holidays or go fishing in Scotland.'

'Well, you'll just have to learn, won't you?' he said briskly, but not unkindly. 'We could take a chalet for a couple of weeks and Charles and John could come too. And maybe some friends. We could have a great time.'

The thought made her feel better. Things wouldn't be nearly so strange if she had her brothers with her, and Sophie. Dear Sophie, whom she was sure would quickly put Guy in his place if he was unkind to her.

'That would be fun,' she said, brightening.

Later he suggested they go shopping in the town that wound up and down the mountainside. Reluctantly she agreed, wondering what he was going to buy this time. She ought to be grateful, she knew, but his relentless determination to throw out most of her existing wardrobe and buy her new 'sexy' clothes made her feel less confident than ever. If he so hated the way she looked why had he married her in the first place? In the past week he had bought her a slinky black cocktail dress, a beaded scarlet evening dress with a plunging neckline and a long slit in the skirt, a backless emerald green dinner dress and a very revealing white silk dress with a bare midriff and shoulders plastered with gleaming white *paillettes*. She was beginning to feel like a cross between Marlene Dietrich and Mae West and she knew her mother would have been shocked if she'd seen her.

They walked slowly up and down the steep streets of Lausanne, gazing into windows of shops displaying a profusion of fine leather goods, gleaming silks, hand-made chocolates, and dozens of wristwatches. Suddenly Guy stopped in front of a discreetly decorated store front which betrayed little evidence of what lay within. He glanced up at the sign over the door and gave a boyish grin.

'This is it,' he exclaimed, grabbing her by the elbow and propelling her through the brass door. 'I knew it was somewhere around here. I came with my mother years ago when she was on a shopping spree.' He strode in and, following, Diana found herself in an extremely elegant fur shop.

An elderly man in an impeccable black suit came forward, smiling and rubbing his hands.

'Madame, Monsieur?' he enquired in a quiet voice. 'Can I be of assistance to you?'

Guy seemed to know exactly what he wanted. 'I'd like to see a selection of your evening wraps, please. Something in white mink, perhaps.'

'Certainement, Monsieur.' The assistant slid silently away, disappearing through dark velvet curtains leaving Guy and Diana in a rich silent temple of luxury. When he reappeared he was reverently carrying an armful of white mink which he laid on the counter with such gentleness it might have been a child.

Guy picked over the furs silently, holding one up against Diana's face. 'These are too old for my wife. What else have you got?'

The assistant did his vanishing trick again and this time produced a white ermine wrap, the narrow bands of fur rippling silkily as he placed the cape round Diana's shoulders.

'No, I don't like the shape,' declared Guy. 'It's too grannyish. Surely you have something ... younger, more glamorous?'

Diana shuffled her feet in embarrassment. She didn't need a new evening wrap. Her pretty dark blue velvet cape went with everything.

The assistant's cheeks were stained red now and his grey eyes swept up and down Guy. 'I do have some magnificent arctic foxes,' he said, 'but they are single furs, with heads and tails, not a *wrap*.' He accentuated the word coldly. 'Of course, we could link them together so that – '

'Let's see them.'

They were produced. Diana gave a little gasp as

the furs, white as snow and soft as thistledown, were looped and draped around her shoulders, across her throat, trailing down her back.

'Magnificent,' Guy pronounced.

Diana turned to look at herself in the long mirror. Her golden head rose as out of a nest of silky down. 'They're beautiful!' she breathed.

Guy nodded, and while he wrote out a cheque and arranged for the foxes to be delivered later that afternoon to the Beau-Rivage Palace, Diana felt brave enough to look at the other furs on display. Mink, dark and rich as chocolate; sable; crisp leopardskin; smoky blue fox. She sighed deeply. It was rather nice being married to someone as rich and generous as Guy. Life did have its compensations. And he was so good to her at times, so kind, wanting only the best for her. If only . . .

'You can wear it with your new green dress, tonight,' Guy was saying, breaking into her thoughts.

Diana smiled at him. So what did it matter if he changed the way she looked? It seemed to please him so much when she wore the things he gave her, and all she wanted, anyway, was for him to love her and approve of her. That mattered more than anything. His approval. The way Daddy had always approved of everything she did.

As they left the shop she slipped her arm through his.

'Thank you, Guy,' she murmured. 'You're so good to me.'

He looked pleased and led her to a nearby restaurant where they devoured large cups of frothy hot chocolate and cream cakes. And all the while Guy talked cheerfully about his plans for them when they got to Paris. A night at the opera. A trip to Versailles. A stroll around the Louvre. And some shopping for her at Dior and Nina Ricci and maybe Schiaparelli. Diana listened, and felt happy again.

Dinner that night passed pleasantly and uneventfully, as Guy ordered caviar, followed by roast duck in a wild cherry sauce, and then crêpes suzette. He chose two different wines to go with the menu. He seemed in very good form.

For the first time since her honeymoon had started Diana was beginning to feel more relaxed. Her acute homesickness had lessened and it no longer seemed so strange to be alone with a man twenty-four hours a day, touring far-away places. She sipped some more of her wine and met his gaze across the candlelit table, realising for the first time how right John had been. Guy was much more sophisticated than she, much more experienced and very, very worldly. She knew nothing of life beyond the safe walls of Stanton Court where she had been shielded and protected from reality. A flush stung her cheeks as she realised what an awful drag she must have been these past two weeks to a man who expected his wife to be as sophisticated as himself. And how nervous and unresponsive in bed, too! No wonder he was disappointed in her! He didn't want a whimpering silly schoolgirl as a wife. He wanted – and had every right to expect – her to be a woman who could hold her own wherever they went. It was just that everything had turned out so differently from what she'd expected. There seemed to be no joy, no tender intimacy in their relationship, now that they were married. And as for romance – she refused to believe it only existed in books and films.

Taking another sip of her wine, her eyes took on a feverish glitter. It was time she grew up and really became a woman – a woman who would please and satisfy her husband. She smiled at Guy and took another sip as the candle flames danced between them.

'Let's go,' Guy said, rising a little while later. 'We might walk down to the lake before going to bed.'

The sky was ablaze with stars and a breeze, sweeping down from the high peaks that surrounded them, rustled through the leaves and played in the long grass at their feet. Only the faint tinkle of a distant goat-bell came floating towards them across the lake. They sauntered to the waterside, hardly talking but seeming to share such a companionable silence that Diana felt warm and comfortable and loved.

Back in their suite, Guy took off his coat and, flinging it onto a chair, went over to the long window and stood there looking out. Pinpricks of light from the edge of the lake twinkled through the trees, but he seemed intent on watching the activity on the well-lit terrace below where people still sat drinking and talking.

Elated by the wine at dinner and her new-found determination to be mature and confident, Diana went slowly towards him. Tonight, she resolved, I will really try to enjoy his lovemaking. I will somehow respond to his rough passion. I will show him how much I love him.

'Darling.' Coming up behind him she slid her arms round his waist and pressed herself into his back, feeling the round hardness of his buttocks against her groin.

For a second nothing happened, and then he spun round, his eyes blazing.

'I'm going out,' he said abruptly, turning away from her. He picked up his coat and without another word strode to the door.

A second later, it slammed and she was alone.

It had grown colder and the stars seemed crystallised in the black sky. Shivering, Guy hunched his shoulders against the wind and started walking towards the centre of the town. Fool! He ground his teeth savagely. Fucking fool! He'd blow everything unless he got a grip on himself. His pace quickened and plunging his hands deeper into his pockets he tried to quieten the turmoil in his mind. If only he didn't feel so trapped. That was something he hadn't foreseen; but Diana's constant looks of adoration, her cloying sweetness and her childlike expectancy were driving him crazy. That was the trouble with women. First his mother and now Diana, with her romantic notions and stupid fantasies. Why couldn't she be more like – he checked himself, trying to quell an avalanche of memories that spilled into his mind, memories of shared experiences that were so piercingly beautiful they tore the heart and the mind and the guts out of him.

Oh Christ! How was he to continue with this marriage? He raised his chin, black despair swamping him as the wind from the mountains whirled down, slicing icily through his clothes.

Somehow he was going to have to strike a balance as he had originally promised himself. He slowed down, feeling slightly better. Of course it was possible. As soon as this honeymoon was over, life could return to ... well, almost normal. At least he wouldn't be trapped by her side twenty-four hours a day, going out of his mind.

He was in the centre of Lausanne now and the restaurants and bars looked welcoming with their warm lights and activity. What he needed was a drink.

Stopping at the first bar he came to, he entered, ordered himself a large brandy, and took a small table in the corner. God, what was he going to say to Diana? She wasn't a complete fool. Naive and unsophisticated, yes. Innocent and trusting, yes. But if he went on taking out his frustrations on her, she'd suspect something was seriously wrong. Guy groaned inwardly. The frustration was the worst part of it. He'd had several women in the past, sleazy tarts who didn't ask questions but reassured him that he could function normally. But Diana ... with her soft little hands and pale virginal body! He felt angry because she wasn't what he wanted and never could be.

At that moment a young German man, with ash blonde hair and a strong jawline, entered the bar and ordered a beer. He glanced casually in Guy's direction and their eyes locked.

111

Guy felt the old familiar magic weaving through him and he smiled. The young man sauntered over to his table and sat down. Guy took a deep breath and it seemed as if he were shedding the tight constrictions of his new life as a snake sheds its skin.

Of course he could have his cake and eat it – as long as Diana never found out.

Chapter Six

'It's a bit much, Diana!' Charles said crossly. 'It's one thing having you and Guy down here every weekend, but you really must stop bringing all your friends as well. What do you think Stanton Court is, a five star hotel?'

Diana flushed deeply, remaining silent.

'It's not like before the war, you know, when we had sixteen indoor servants, not to mention ten gardeners and all the farm hands. And now that Mama has gone to live in the dower house and John has gone with her, it means Sophie has all the arrangements to make,' he continued, 'with only four maids and an odd bit of help from the village. Now that she's pregnant I don't want her to have so much to do.'

'I'm . . . I'm sorry, Charlie, I never thought. This has always been home to me, where we could invite whoever we wanted, so I suppose I presumed it was all right. You've never said you minded.'

'Well, I do mind. It causes an awful lot of extra work and expense. Sophie and I don't even know these people you bring! Why should we play host to a bunch of strangers every weekend? Hang it all, Di, this is my home now.' Charles began pacing the library, a perplexed and agitated expression on his face.

'I'll talk to Guy, but he's going to be awfully hurt. He loves this place as much as we do.'

'No, he doesn't! He just loves showing it off. It's all part of his aren't-I-rich-and-look-what-an-aristocratic-family-I-married-into performance. If he wants to have a stately home for entertaining then he's going to have to buy one of his own.' Charles dug his hands deeper into the pockets of his baggy trousers and jingled his small change.

A look of horror crossed Diana's face. 'Then I'd never get the chance to come home – er, I mean here.'

'You're going to need a country place of your own in time, though. What will you do when you have children?'

Diana stared at him. She hadn't thought that far ahead. Stanton Court meant home, security, a place where she felt safe and happy. The thought of coming here less often filled her with sadness. And what was she to say to Guy? He'd be furious at Charles' inhospitality and take it as a personal insult.

As if reading her thoughts, Charles came over and put his arm round her shoulders, as he'd done when she'd been a child. 'If it makes it any easier, I'll mention it to Guy. I'm sure he'll understand.'

But as Diana walked into the garden to pick flowers for the drawing-room she knew Guy wouldn't understand at all. And what was more, she'd have to bear the brunt of his anger.

Charles, feeling he could have handled Diana

better, strode over to the farm where one of the cows was about to calf. As he entered the yard, he saw Guy with four of the friends he had brought down for the weekend. They were both rich young couples, Alex and June Bowmaker and Douglas and Marisa Taylor. Alex owned a rapidly growing chain of launderettes, the first to be formed in England, and Douglas was a director of a large printing works. Charles' mouth twitched for a moment as he realised his father would not have had people like them to stay in his day because they ranked as 'trade'. As he grew nearer the group he could hear Guy's voice.

'Of course, there's not as much money to be made from milk as there is from beef,' he was saying airily. 'We've got four hundred head of cattle here and a couple of champion bulls, but I shouldn't be surprised if we don't go over to beef soon.'

'Really? That's most awfully interesting,' said Charles coming up from behind. 'Give us the benefit of your knowledge, Guy.' Charles turned to the Bowmakers and Taylors. 'You see,' he continued with a self-deprecating smile, 'I only spent three years at Cirencester Agricultural College, so I'm most interested in learning the basics of farming from my brother-in-law.'

Guy's face flamed and he shot Charles a look of loathing.

'I'd like a word with you, Guy,' said Charles pointedly. The others drifted off tactfully, and the two men stood facing each other in the yard, bridling with mutual hostility.

Guy spoke impatiently. 'What do you want?'

'This place is not a hotel, and Sophie and I are sick to death of your using it like one. Why should we entertain your friends weekend after weekend? It's got to stop, Guy, and I'd be very grateful if you'd limit your visits to when we invite just you and Diana down to stay,' said Charles.

For a moment Guy looked totally abashed, then he ran a hand over his slick dark hair and said arrogantly, 'You seem to forget I'm a member of this family now! They're Diana's friends as well as mine, and I don't think you've any right to stop her, and me, coming here when we like.'

'This is not a museum,' Charles said curtly, 'to be shown off to every Tom, Dick and Harry. This is my home, Sophie's and mine, and when we decide to open it to the general public, I'll let you know.' He turned on his heel and strode off, leaving Guy scarlet in the face and fuming.

'Things change when you get married, don't they?' Diana sounded wistful as she strolled with her mother through the woods on the estate that afternoon. It was a still, hot day and the tender green leaves barely trembled on the trees. Here and there slanting sunbeams shimmered into a clearing, catching the dancing gnats in their light. She looked up at the towering elms and birches and the great oaks that sheltered bluebells in the spring and suddenly realised she would remember this moment forever. It would be engraved on her mind, this picture of perfection on a summer's afternoon, and she knew she was irretrievably bonded to this place of her childhood. Wherever she was and whatever she did, her heart would be at Stanton.

'Of course things change, darling. In what particular way did you mean?' Mary Sutton asked.

'One is sort of . . . well, more on one's own, I suppose,' Diana faltered, then with a rush she added, 'Mummy, is it wrong of Guy and me to come here every weekend and sometimes bring a few friends with us?'

There was an imperceptible pause before her mother answered.

'You have to remember,' she said gently, 'that Stanton Court isn't my home any more. It belongs to Charles. It belonged to him from the minute your father died, but of course I stayed on until you got married, and by that time Charles was married too. It's his and Sophie's home and soon there will be a baby, and that's the way it should be. You have your own home now, so it's quite fair, isn't it? And John and I have the dower house. To answer your question, darling, I don't think you should come unless they invite you and I certainly don't think you should bring your friends along as well.'

Diana nodded sadly. 'Yes, I see that, but it does feel as if the family is breaking up.'

'Rubbish!' her mother said firmly. 'We don't have to live under the same roof to go on caring for each other! We all have to grow up some time, and stand on our own feet. Do you think I liked leaving the Court after so many years? But, you know, in time one gets used to anything and it was the right thing to do.'

As they came out of the forest and started walking back across the buttercup-filled meadows, Diana saw Charles and Guy in the distance, standing on the terrace arguing. They were glaring at each other, red-faced, and with a sinking heart she knew it meant the balmy days of her childhood had finally come to an end.

Relentlessly, the rest of that Saturday passed, and Diana kept out of Guy's way as the tension steadily increased. If it was the last time Guy was going to be allowed to entertain his friends at the Suttons' expense, he was going to make the most of it. The family watched as he and his friends whipped themselves into a fever of high spirits with champagne cocktails in the early evening and large quantities of wine with dinner, followed by port and brandy. Their voices grew louder, their laughter was shrill, their cigar smoke turned the air blue and Guy was shrieking with amusement at his own juvenile jokes.

'Let's go to the drawing-room and dance!' shouted Guy, jumping clumsily to his feet and knocking a silver spoon onto the floor. 'Who-o-o-ps!' he chortled as it went clattering, 'I knew I shouldn't have worn those earrings!'

His friends screamed with laughter.

'Let's roll back the rug. Come on, everyone.' He started tugging roughly at a Persian carpet, under Charles and Sophie's icy gaze. 'Move back the furniture! Let's do a samba! Have we any samba records?'

'Guy, will you stop it!' Diana whispered urgently.

'Stop what?' he snapped in a loud voice. 'Stop what? I'm only trying to liven up this old morgue! John, put on a record.'

'What's the matter with you, Guy?' She'd never seen him in this mood before and there was something frighteningly wild and out of control about his manner. 'For God's sake, Charlie's getting furious.'

'Oh, shut up!' Guy turned his back on her and, grabbing Marisa, swung her around the room. Everything seemed to happen very fast after that. John put on a record and, as the music pounded out, Diana found herself being whirled around in the grip of Douglas Taylor. John was dancing with June Bowmaker and out of the corner of her eye she could see Alex Bowmaker doing a cha-cha on his own in the corner. Mary Sutton was sitting with Charles and Sophie by the fireplace, grim faced, watching the proceedings. The music grew louder and faster and Diana began to feel slightly sick with giddiness, but Douglas would not let go of her. She hardly noticed what happened next. Guy seemed to be swooping across the room towards her and for a moment she thought he was coming to her rescue, but he shot past and it seemed only a second later that she heard Charles' voice cry out in warning. Then there was a woman's scream, followed by a heavy thud that shook the floor beneath her feet.

For a moment she looked dazedly around her, wondering what had happened. A man's voice cried, 'Oh, my God!' and the music stopped with a hideous scraping whine as someone swiped the needle off the record. Then a stunned silence filled the room, broken only by muffled moans. Sophie was lying on the floor in agony, huddled on her side.

'You bastard!' Charles was yelling at Guy. 'You bloody stupid bastard!' And then he leaned over Sophie, trying to gather her up in his arms.

'What happened?' Diana asked blankly of Marisa.

Marisa was ashen and there was a look of horror and fear in her eyes. 'Sophie slipped,' she gasped. 'Guy pulled her out of her chair and tried to make her dance . . . and she fell.'

'I'll ring for the doctor,' Diana heard her mother say.

'That's no bloody good! She's haemorrhaging,' Charles sounded distraught. 'Send for an ambulance.'

Sophie, lying on the sofa, a crimson stain spreading on the cream brocade, whimpered pitifully, 'The baby . . . Oh, the baby.'

Diana sank, almost fainting, into a chair. Sophie was losing her baby and although it was not directly her fault, she felt deep guilt. She should never have brought Guy into her family. They had been right about him. With a terrible certainty now, Diana realised that she had become a part of some destructive force that would bring unhappiness not only to her, but also to those around her.

Paris hummed with activity as the summer sun beat harshly down on the crowded pavement cafés and tree-lined boulevards. Cars honked their horns and the shrill cry of police whistles pierced the dusty air as the city swirled and ebbed around Diana. She walked slowly up the Champs Elysées, absorbing the heady mixture of sounds and smells and when she came to Fouquet, near the Arc de Triomphe, she decided to go in and have a *café au lait*.

It had been Guy's idea that they should spend the weekend in Paris.

'Let's take a suite at the Ritz!' he said. 'We can go to the opera, dine at Maxims on the Friday night, which is the only night worth going, and do some shopping! What do you say?'

Diana hadn't said much. Guy seemed to have recovered his equilibrium very rapidly after the tragedy of Sophie losing her baby and wanted to be out on the town enjoying himself every night. For Diana it was a different story. She felt trapped and profoundly disturbed, and changed. The events of that night had finally made her see what Guy was really like and she was horrified. She had seen him drunken and feckless, dissolute and weak. No matter how often he had apologised for what had happened, swearing never to get drunk again, she realised she was married to a man who was dangerously destructive. And of course for someone in her position, divorce was out of the question. Her family would never forgive her. She was stuck in a marriage from which there was no escape.

And so she settled into an uneasy truce with Guy. They spent less and less time together, he hardly ever made love to her, but to the outside world they still presented the façade of a happily married couple.

Only one thing has to be decided upon now,

thought Diana as she sipped her coffee and watched the busy Parisians scurry by, I must find something to do with the rest of my life. If I've got to be stuck with Guy, there has to be more to my existence than an endless round of parties and balls. But what could she do? None of her friends had jobs and she certainly didn't feel herself qualified enough to pursue a career, but she had to do something. Silently she cursed her family, especially her mother. It might have worked for previous generations of women to be dependent on their husbands for everything, but times had changed. Diana thought about Francesca, with her burning ambitions, and for a moment she deeply envied her. How nice to know where you were going.

Glancing at her watch, she finished her coffee and left Fouquet. She'd promised to meet Guy in the bar of the Ritz at twelve-thirty. They'd probably go somewhere for luncheon, maybe to one of the fish restaurants on the left bank. Tonight they were guests of the British embassy at a reception given by the ambassador and his wife.

Diana wondered vaguely if Guy had any plans for this afternoon.

Guy pushed his cup of *café filtre* away from him and drained the last of his brandy. It was three o'clock and his mind was working quickly.

'Why don't you go along to Nina Ricci and see their show,' he asked guilelessly, 'and buy yourself something for the Embassy party tonight?'

Diana looked up in surprise. 'But I thought you

wanted to go and see the Mona Lisa in the Louvre?'
she said.

'It'll be too crowded, we'll go in the morning. I
want to browse round a couple of places that sell
old books and you'd find that awfully boring. Go get
yourself a party dress and surprise me tonight,' he
said pleasantly.

'If you're sure.'

'Absolutely. Let's meet back at the Ritz about
six. Okay?'

They walked fifty yards to the left bank of the
Seine and Guy hailed her a taxi. Pecking her on the
cheek, he said goodbye and watched as the taxi
drew away into the swirling mass of traffic.

He glanced at his watch and saw he had at least
a couple of hours to himself. He didn't intend to
waste them. Hailing another taxi he jumped in,
telling the driver to take him to the Rue Scribe. He
knew just where he wanted to go, a little cafe
called L'Oiseau Blanc. He'd been there before and
had always struck lucky. It was a haunt for dancers
and on his last visit he'd picked up a magnificent
looking Italian with muscles like an athlete and the
face of a Leonardo da Vinci angel. Thank God
Diana did as she was told and never asked questions, he thought. So far his luck had held and if he
felt a fleeting regret that she could not satisfy him,
he pushed it to the back of his mind. He was made
the way he was and there was nothing he could do
about it.

Except enjoy these secret hours when he could
get away from her.

*   *   *

In another suite at the Ritz Hotel that weekend, Marc and Carlotta Raven had checked in with Carlos and his nanny.

They had been in Paris for two days and all the while Marc had been itching to drive on to the small château he had rented in the Loire valley for the summer. He had work to do. His next novel centred on the French Resistance during World War II and there were weeks of research ahead of him. He was also sick of hotels, sick of Carlotta's shopping expeditions, sick of meeting the 'right people'. Stubbornly, he threw himself onto the satin covered bed and ripped the tie away from his throat.

'I don't want to go to this party tonight,' he grumbled.

'But we must go! I worked hard to get us this invitation and your British publisher will be there. That is important!' She was putting on her make-up at the dressing-table and the room was filled with the heavy scent of her perfume. 'It is vital we go – don't you want your next book published in Britain?'

'The only thing that's vital is that you should be seen around!' Marc tossed one of his shoes on to the floor. 'Don't give me all that bullshit about I-need-it-for-my-image.'

'Oh, you drive me crazy! Of course you need it for your image!' Carlotta waved her arms expressively, her gold bangles clinking and rattling.

'Will you shut up? You're like some fucking gramophone record.' Jumping to his feet, Marc strode over to where she was sitting, and stood, his feet planted wide, his muscular body rigid with anger. 'I'm a writer, for God's sake, not some show-biz personality. Won't you ever get that into your head? I make a living by sitting at a typewriter for hours each day, pounding out thousands of words. I don't give a shit about going to some crummy party and having to be nice to a bunch of morons who ask stupid questions, like where do I get my ideas from.'

'No, you wouldn't, would you?' she challenged.

Marc flushed and turned angrily away.

Carlotta rose with a theatrical gesture, her dark head held high. 'And who do you have to thank for the fact that your hours of pounding out words, as you call it, has made you so rich and successful?' In moments of anger her Spanish accent became marked.

There was a moment's heavy silence, then Marc spoke.

'You just love throwing that in my face, don't you? Well, remember, I did you a big favour too.' His eyes were dark with anger. 'I'm paying the price for my success every goddam day of my life, so there's no need for you to remind me.'

Their eyes locked, neither giving way, knowing that they had reached the impasse in this endless feud that raged between them. They knew too much about each other to be friends and yet they dared not be enemies.

Carlotta moved swiftly over to the wardrobe where her new black georgette dress was hanging. She had bought it that afternoon at Givenchy and it was going to be perfect for tonight. Marc watched her balefully, wondering how much the dress had cost him.

'I'll wait for you in the *petit salon*,' she said, picking up her silk purse and flinging her new black mink coat over her arm.

'I'm not staying long at this party,' he shouted after her retreating figure, 'I want an early night for once.'

Why couldn't Carlotta have been more his type, he thought as he showered and changed. Gentle and warm, with a soft mouth. That's how he liked them. Suddenly he thought of Francesca again. Now she'd been warm, with her sympathetic eyes, rose-tipped breasts and welcoming moistness that gave him an erection just to think of her. How loving and passionate she'd been. Marc closed his eyes and felt a deep sense of loss. Francesca was a thing of the past and he could never have her again. Not after the way he'd treated her. He'd had to make the choice between becoming a successful writer or staying with Francesca, and with swift violence he'd made that choice. No looking back now. He finished dressing and went to join Carlotta in the next room. She had to be his life now.

And all because he wanted to be the richest and most acclaimed author in the world.

The British embassy in the Rue du Faubourg St Honoré was alive with activity as guests flocked through the ornate wrought iron gates and across the courtyard into what had originally been a small palace built in the eighteenth century.

Sir George Anstruther, the ambassador, stood in

the doorway of the famous *salon vert*, greeting his guests with apparent pleasure, a performance he had perfected over the years, no matter how boring the company.

'I'm so glad you could come,' he said warmly to Marc and Carlotta, as they were announced by the footman. 'I gather you're staying in France for a bit?'

'We've taken a place in the Loire,' gushed Carlotta, 'a beautiful little château. Marc is starting on his new book soon and there is so much research to be done and . . .'

'Are you writing this book or am I?' Marc turned to look at her and his eyes were cold.

At that moment, Lady Anstruther came bustling forward, a short plump woman in a flutter of printed chiffon.

'Good evening, Mr Raven, Mrs Raven, come and meet some of our other guests,' she cried, leading them towards a group of people in the centre of the room. Introductions performed, she shot off again at great speed, chiffon pennants flying.

Marc turned to a beautiful young woman on his left who was wearing a clinging blue silk dress and a spectacular necklace of sapphires and pearls.

'I'm afraid I didn't catch your name?' he asked, by way of making conversation.

'Diana Andrews.' She gave a little smile and, indicating the tall dark-haired man beside her, added 'And this is my husband, Guy.'

Marc nodded. Since he'd started writing he'd cultivated a trick of summing up people in a flash. A sort of mini character study. Guy he took to be

127

ambitious, conceited and ruthless. A man who had probably never done a day's work in his life. Then he looked at Diana. She came from a good background but was very inexperienced and probably naive, yet there was something proud about the way she held herself, an inborn sense of dignity. He also suspected she'd made a great mistake in marrying this man who stood so arrogantly by her side. They looked an ill-matched couple.

'Do you live in Paris?' Marc asked them conversationally.

'No, London,' Guy replied shortly.

'Ah . . .' Marc noted the faint American accent. 'So you're American?'

Guy looked at him in a bored fashion. 'I'm half American.'

'How nice for you,' replied Marc drily. He smiled at Diana. 'But surely you're English?'

'Yes, my family come from Oxfordshire.'

At that moment Lady Anstruther brought over another couple. 'May I present Sir Pelham and Lady Ponsonby,' she beamed. 'Sir Pelham is over here for a NATO meeting.'

Everyone shook hands again. Sir Pelham was a well known political figure and a member of the British government.

Guy, Marc noted, latched himself on to the Ponsonbys with an unexpected burst of enthusiasm. So I'm right about him being pushy, thought Marc. He turned back to Diana again. There was something about her that fascinated him.

'What are you doing in Paris . . . do you travel much?' she asked politely.

'Yes. Mostly doing research.'

'Research? Are you a scientist?'

Suddenly Marc realised she had no idea who he was. 'For my books,' he said, amused. 'I'm over here to do some research into wartime France.'

'Oh, how awful of me!' She turned bright pink. 'Of course, Marc Raven! I remember reading *Unholy Spectre*. We all read it at school.'

'Thank you. I really appreciate that.' His smile was wry. 'Now tell me about yourself, what do you do?'

The blush still lingered on her cheeks. 'There's nothing much to tell really. We live in London and go out quite a lot. Sometimes we go to the country at weekends . . .' A shadow fell across her eyes which Marc longed to fathom.

'And what does your husband do?'

Diana paused for a moment. This strange, rugged-looking man was making her feel jittery and she wasn't sure whether he was laughing at her or not.

'Guy's family own Kalinsky's, the jewellers.'

The shock hit him like an unexpected karate chop. Christ! Why was he so bloody bad at names? Francesca had mentioned her brother, Guy, a hundred times. For a moment the room blurred and then swam sharply back into focus.

'Can I get you another drink?' he stammered.

Diana looked down at her full glass and then enquiringly up at him. 'No thank you.'

'Well, if you'll excuse me . . .' He glanced at his own glass, which was also brimming with

129

champagne. 'I don't really like this stuff. I'm just going to see if they have any whisky.'

A moment later Diana found herself alone.

Towards the end of the party Marc saw Diana again, talking to a middle-aged woman. The silk of her dress clung seductively to her small pointed breasts, straining over her nipples. Her long slender thighs curved beneath the fabric of the skirt, and he was filled with a sudden longing. She was warm and gentle and her mouth was soft. He could feel the ache in his groin.

Then he caught Carlotta's eye watching him, and he knew she'd guessed what he was thinking.

'Ha!' Carlotta scoffed, flinging down her mink coat as they entered their suite. 'You didn't score tonight, did you? That silly little English girl wasn't interested in you, was she? Oh, don't look at me like that, Marc. I'm not a fool. I know you lust after other women, I see it in your eyes, but I'm not going to let you do it in front of our friends!' Carlotta's accent had become heavily Spanish in her excitement. 'What do people say?' she demanded. 'They say, there goes poor Carlotta, married to that dreadful man who strays like some dog, and she such a good wife to him.'

'Have you quite finished?' This was a re-run of the fight they had after almost every party and Marc was sick of it.

'No, I not finish!' She ripped off the Givenchy dress and stood there, terrifyingly tantalising in black satin and lace lingerie with black suspenders and silk stockings.

'You don't know how lucky you are, having me,' she cried. 'All those stupid little girls you run after, you think they can give you a better time than me? You belong to me!' Moving swiftly, she came and stood before him, her full breasts rising and falling, her dark eyes glittering. 'You forget eh? You forget how much you need your little Carlotta?' Then she put her arms tightly round his waist, whilst her thigh slipped between his legs and moved slowly backwards and forwards – she raised her face and flicked her tongue along his neck, behind his ear and then along the line of his jaw, while he stood there, still trying to resist her. Suddenly she released the tight pressure on his waist and, pressing her thigh against his groin, felt him harden and become erect as the blood pulsed into his penis.

'Stop it . . .' he groaned.

'But you like it,' she whispered huskily, undoing his trousers and drawing him out. With skilful hands she stroked him, cupping his balls and squeezing them gently, drawing him out until he was rigid. He looked down at himself and watched her slim fingers encircle his shaft. Then he groaned again as the heat and the tension built up inside him, sending waves of excruciating sweetness through him so that he thrust forward, buttocks clenched, terrified now that she would stop.

Raising his hands, he put them on her shoulders and pressed her down until she was kneeling before his parted legs. Then he watched her taking him into her mouth. Suddenly he was aflame as searing waves of exquisite agony surged through his penis, making him bend forward in a spasm. Burying his hands in her long silky hair, he pressed her head to him, feeling his tip against the back of her throat, and all the while she was sucking him deeply. Then she moved slightly, so that her tongue was circling and flicking him, driving him crazy, burning him up, teasing him unbearably. He thrust forward again, feeling his climax beginning, straining to release the fever of excitement that was consuming him.

A hoarse roar broke from his throat. 'Now . . . Oh, God . . . now!'

A second later he was exploding in a wrenching frenzy that seemed to drain all the juices from his body.

'You see how much you need your Carlotta,' he heard her say, as she rose and kissed him fully on the mouth.

Marc was down in the foyer of the Ritz early the next morning, settling his bill. He was anxious to be off to the Loire to start his research and he just hoped Carlotta and the nanny had nearly finished the packing.

As he waited for his receipt, he saw Diana coming out of the lift, alone.

'Good morning,' he said, going forward and shaking her hand.

She looked startled for a moment, and then a friendly smile spread across her face.

'Good morning. How are you?' she asked.

'Great. We're leaving in a few minutes. When are you off?' Suddenly he noticed her eyes, more blue and clear than they had looked last night, and the soft curve of her mouth, painted with pale pink lipstick.

'After lunch. Guy wants to do some last minute shopping.'

Marc smiled drily. 'He should get together with my wife, that's all she likes to do. So you're flying back to England are you?'

She nodded, her eyes never leaving his face.

'Well ... it's been nice meeting you,' he said lamely, feeling an unexpected pang of regret that there wasn't time to get to know her better. 'If you're in the States, look us up. We're based in New York, like your husband's family,' he added awkwardly.

'That would be nice.'

Was it his imagination, or was her look lingering and regretful too? Marc couldn't be sure, and at that moment Guy appeared from the lift and joined them.

'Well, I'll say goodbye,' said Marc, still looking at Diana, his eyes sweeping over her slim figure and long legs.

'Goodbye,' she said softly, and he could swear she could read his thoughts.

Guy gave him a formal nod of the head, said, 'Come on, Diana,' and they moved together towards the elegant black wrought iron and glass doors of the Ritz.

Marc watched them go, seeing Diana's blonde head receding into the distance, and suddenly he felt an unaccountable stab of loss, as if the sun had been swallowed up by a cloud. But then she turned and glanced backwards over her shoulder to where he stood. Marc waved, a sad salute to a paradise lost, and she raised her white-gloved hand and waved back. There was something child-like in the gesture. Then Guy pushed her forward and she was lost to him.

Chapter Seven
1951

Francesca clutched her notepad and pen, hardly able to contain the excitement she felt. After only eighteen months working at Kalinsky's, she was actually being sent to London to help organise a new branch they planned to open in Bond Street. She was to fly over the following week to have meetings with the architect and the decorator, and her happiness would have been complete if there hadn't been a fly in the ointment to spoil it for her.

She was supposed to work on the project with Guy.

'If he won't come back to New York, to work here, at least he can still be a part of the company by setting up an outlet over in London,' explained Sarah as Francesca and Henry sat in her office listening to her plans. 'You will work under him, Francesca, remember that! I am merely letting you go so that you can see the decorators do a good job. Guy will be too busy for that sort of thing,' she added dismissively.

'What exactly is Guy going to be doing?' asked Francesca carefully.

'Hiring a manager, office staff, an advertising and publicity agent,' Sarah said briskly. 'And then he'll have to set up a workroom. Initially we'll be supplying the jewellery from over here.'

Francesca caught Henry's eye in a warning glance. She knew he was thinking exactly the same as her: Guy would get bored half way through and somebody else would have to clear up the chaos. Apart from which, from what they'd heard since he'd married Diana, only Sarah's offer of a lot of money was making him condescend to go into 'trade' in the first place. Reports from mutual friends told of him dividing his time between social climbing on a grand scale or being seen in sleazy haunts without Diana.

'That's about it, then,' said Francesca, rising. 'I'll let you know how we get on.'

'Remember, Guy's in charge. I'm hoping once he's opened up Bond Street he'll want to come back here, so don't go upsetting him, Francesca,' Sarah reminded her.

'Me?' Francesca put on an expression of mock horror. 'Little me? As if I would, Mom!'

Henry made a spluttering noise which he hurriedly turned into a cough, and rose too. 'I think you're in for an exciting trip,' he said drily.

'I'm sure I am,' replied Francesca, not looking at him.

The black taxi drew up with a shudder and stopped, its diesel engine throbbing throatily, outside 16 Eaton Terrace.

'That'll be two shillings and sixpence, luv.' The driver was a burly Londoner with a jovial face.

136

He'd been regaling Francesca with his views on the government, the royal family and the latest results of the cricket match at Lords. Amused, she handed him two half-crowns.

'Thanks. Keep the change.'

'Ta, luv. Enjoy your visit.'

She glanced up and down the rows of pretty houses which had the air of restrained opulence that spoke of old money. They were all painted glossy white with shining black doors and brass knockers. Manicured window boxes provided splashes of colour and clipped bay trees stood stiff as sentries on the marble doorsteps.

There was no doubt about it, Diana and Guy had good taste. Pressing the bell, Francesca waited a minute before the door was opened by an elderly butler.

'Good evening, Madam,' he said gravely, ushering her into a small hall where large, gilt-framed mirrors and blazing crystal lights gave the impression of space. Francesca followed him along a corridor which led into the drawing-room and there was Diana coming forward to meet her with hands outstretched in welcome.

'Francesca, how lovely to see you.' They kissed each other politely on the cheek.

'It's good to see you, too.'

'Come and sit down.' Diana indicated a sofa by the window overlooking the paved garden. Francesca glanced round the room, taking in the stylish decor that seemed to bring the garden into the house. White walls and pale-yellow curtains and upholstery gave it the atmosphere of a summer's day, while high vases of flowers filled the room with fragrance.

'It's good to be in England again,' said Francesca, settling herself on the sofa, 'though I'm worn out from the journey.'

'Wouldn't you rather stay here instead of the Dorchester? There's plenty of room.'

'That's very sweet of you, Diana, but my comings and goings are going to be so erratic, I think I'd better stay put. And how is everything with you and Guy?' she added, trying to hide the shock she felt at the change in Diana, whom she hadn't seen since her marriage. Where was the English rose beauty, the smooth shining hair and simple classical clothes? Diana, she noted, still had a childlike quality about her and an obvious eagerness to please, but her face looked drawn under the heavy make-up and there were dark shadows under her eyes. The most startling change, though, was in her clothes. She was wearing a scarlet jersey silk dress, more suited to a woman of forty, with black silk stockings and black, high-heeled shoes.

'Are you very busy?' Francesca felt awkward. It was hard coming to terms with this new look.

'Oh, very,' Diana gushed, 'I can't tell you! Dinner parties, three balls last week, cocktail parties every night. We entertain a lot too. I'm absolutely exhausted.'

She doesn't sound exhausted at all, Francesca observed. She sounds like a little girl who is strung out after too much excitement and is thoroughly over-excited. Her eyes glittered feverishly and she was waving her hands about a lot. Francesca wouldn't have been surprised if she'd burst into tears any minute.

'Where's Guy?'

Diana gave her a startled look. 'Out somewhere . . . He should be back soon. Now let me get you a drink. What would you like?' She fluttered over to the drinks table.

'Orange juice if you have it. I've got to have dinner with our designer tonight and I want to have my wits about me.'

'Guy's been hectic too, engaging staff . . . and everything.'

Francesca detected an effort on Diana's part to sound loyal.

'I'm looking forward to seeing who he's got. That is one of my reasons for dropping by to see you both this evening. Will he be back soon?' she asked.

Diana handed her a glass of fresh orange juice, but Francesca noticed she herself was having gin and tonic.

'I expect so,' she said vaguely. 'Now tell me more about yourself – it must be nearly two years since we last saw you.'

Francesca nodded. 'Well, apart from joining Kalinsky's, with a lot of help from Uncle Henry in persuading Mom I could do the job, I've also moved into my own apartment . . .'

'Aren't you lonely?' Diana cut in appalled. 'I'd hate to live on my own.'

'I love it!' said Francesca. 'If you'd lived with Mom as long as I have, you'd be thrilled to be on your own. It suits me, too, as I'm working so hard.'

'But do you want to go on working forever? I

mean, wouldn't you rather get married and have a proper home?'

Francesca shot her a penetrating look. It was on the tip of her tongue to blurt out, 'And be like you? An unhappy social butterfly?' but she stopped herself in time.

'Not right now,' she said instead. 'I need to be free to follow my career – to make Kalinsky's the greatest.'

'Don't you even have time for boyfriends?'

A sudden sharp pain clouded Francesca's face, making her hesitate before answering. Memories of Marc, even after all this time, came flooding back, hurting her deeply. How long does it take to mend a broken heart? she wondered.

'I go out with a few people, but no one special.'

At that moment Guy arrived, suave and elegant in a pale grey double-breasted suit that contrasted attractively with his dark hair and olive skin.

'Hi, sis,' he greeted Francesca casually, as if he'd seen her just a few days before. Then he went to the drinks tray. 'There's no lemon, Diana,' he said crossly.

Jumping to her feet, Diana rushed over to see for herself.

'I told you there was no lemon. Why don't you check these things? Bentley!' he called out for the butler.

Flushed and crestfallen, Diana returned to her seat muttering, 'I was sure there was some lemon on the tray.'

'Well, it's not the end of the world,' Francesca laughed.

'What exactly are you doing in England, Francesca? I thought this was supposed to be my operation,' said Guy, sipping his freshly poured martini and taking a seat between the two women.

'Don't worry, Guy,' she assured him with sarcasm, 'I'm not here to steal your thunder. Mom merely wants me to make sure the decorator does what she wants.'

'I could have done that.'

'She thought you'd be too busy, engaging staff and things.'

Guy shrugged. 'That's all taken care of. Bloody boring too. It's the last time I'll ever do anything for the company, it's not really my scene, and Mom's paying me a pittance for all the work I've put in.'

'She hopes it will inspire you to come back to the States and become a director,' said Francesca with total honesty. 'Aren't you going to?'

'Not on your life! My future's here, in England.'

Francesca tried to hide the wave of relief she felt. Ten minutes in the same room as Guy and she knew they would never be able to work together.

'Will you be on the site tomorrow morning?' she asked. 'I'm going along to see if everything's on schedule.'

'Tomorrow?' Guy made a grimace and rose to refill his glass. 'No. I've got other things to do tomorrow.'

'Fine!' Francesca closed her mouth tightly, anger bristling up her spine. This was typical of Guy, she thought. It's exactly what Uncle Henry and I knew would happen.

She arrived at the large new showrooms at nine-

141

thirty the next morning to find the architect and
Anthony de Beaumont, the designer, deep in conversation. Structural alterations had been carried
out and now the first of the blue watered silk wallpaper was going up.

Francesca looked around approvingly. The
sketches for the showroom lay on a trestle table
and she went over to have another look at them. It
was certainly going to be one of the most spectacular jewellery showrooms in Bond Street and she
felt a tremor of pride at the thought that this was
her family's firm.

At that moment a middle-aged man in a crumpled dark-blue suit paused at the street door for a
moment, seemed unsure of where he was, and then
decided to enter.

'Can I help you?' Francesca strode forward and
found herself looking into a pair of bloodshot
bleary eyes. Whisky fumes blasted her in the face
and the man staggered slightly.

'I think . . .' she said, trying to usher him out,
'that you've come to the wrong place. I'm afraid
we're not open for business yet.'

'Er . . . who are you?' He stared at her
uncomprehendingly.

'I'm the owner of this shop. Would you mind
leaving?' She drew herself up to her full height and
tried to look imperious.

The man gave a weak giggle. 'You're not the
owner. I know the owner,' he burbled.

'I am the owner,' said Francesca firmly.

'What's . . . what's your name,' he slurred, stag-
gering again.

'Andrews,' she said coldly, regarding his purple mottled face with distaste. If there was one thing she hated it was drunks and this one took the biscuit.

'Andrews. Thatsh right! Guy Andrews. But you're not Guy Andrews. I know Guy Andrews. He's a great friend of mine.'

'And who are you?' cried Francesca shocked.

'I'm Ernest Marsh. The new manager here.'

'Francesca must be stopped, Henry. She's upsetting everyone.' Sarah Andrews leaned forward anxiously, resting her elbows on the polished surface of her antique desk.

It was nine o'clock in the morning and she had asked Henry Langham to come to her office before they went to the board meeting of Kalinsky's at nine-thirty.

Francesca had only returned from her trip to London the previous evening but Sarah had taken a call from Guy and he had outlined what had been happening.

'We'll be hearing her report at the meeting, won't we?' Henry asked in a soothing voice. He had to be careful these days, striking just the right balance between mother and daughter. He must continue to support Sarah but at the same time it was important that Francesca be allowed sufficient scope for her undoubted talents.

Sarah examined her perfectly manicured nails, which were painted a dusky pink today. The huge fifty-five carat diamond on her left hand sparkled fiercely.

'I don't like her interfering in matters that don't concern her.' Her voice was as hard as the diamond. 'She was sent to London to check up with the architect and designer of the Bond Street operation. Nothing else. From what I hear she took the law into her own hands and behaved reprehensibly.'

'How sure are you of all this? Have you heard first-hand?'

'I believe what Guy had to say!' she cried. 'One thing is for sure, I'm not letting her go back. I shall go over myself for the opening and make sure nothing goes wrong this time.'

Henry watched her hands splayed on the desk top and wondered how a woman with such toughness and ruthlessness could have the slim hands of an innocent girl.

'Have you any other reasons for not wanting her to go back?' he asked softly, a sudden flash of intuition making him ask the question.

Sarah darted him a quick glance. In that second her eyes revealed a surprising vulnerability.

'I don't want her seeing Guy again.'

Henry's face broke into lines of surprise, making him look more rugged than ever. 'Why?'

Sarah gave a quick impatient sigh and her mouth tightened. 'It's obvious she's making Guy feel that Kalinsky's is going to be hers one day. I believe she's doing everything she can to stop him coming over and I'm sure she's trying to turn people in the company against him. He as good as told me so himself on the 'phone last night.'

Henry said nothing, but it sounded to him as if

Guy was up to his old tricks again. Even as a child he'd always managed to make everything look as if it was Francesca's fault and not his.

'I wish we'd never let her join Kalinsky's,' Sarah continued, 'I knew it would lead to trouble. We've got to get Guy to come back.'

'How are you going to do that?' Henry's tone was blunt now and he was getting annoyed. Sarah was being absurdly prejudiced against her daughter and the last thing he wanted was to see Guy at the helm, lording it over all of them. 'If Guy wants to stay in England, how the hell are you going to get him back?'

'I'm going to London myself next time.'

'And you plan to talk him into returning?' Henry sounded sceptical.

'I'm not going to say a word to him about returning.'

'So, just what are you going to do?'

'Henry, my dear, you're being a bit dense this morning, aren't you?' She smiled almost coquettishly. 'What do you think appeals to Diana most in life? Why do you think she pursued Guy until he married her?'

It was on the tip of Henry's tongue to say he couldn't imagine, but he thought better of it. 'You tell me,' he hedged instead.

'Money, of course! What else? Out of the top drawer she might be, but the Suttons have no money and that young lady sure likes to spend. I had to increase Guy's private allowance the other day because of her extravagances. It's always the same with people who've been poor. The minute they get their grubby little hands on cash they go wild.' She took a gold compact out of her handbag and scrutinised her face sharply.

'You do surprise me. I've always thought of Diana as a rather quiet little thing. What does she spend it on?' Henry asked artfully.

Sarah shrugged her shoulders and closed her compact with a snap. 'How should I know? However, I have a plan. What was it you taught me in business, Henry? Aim for someone's weakest spot and you've got them by the balls. Well, I've learned, haven't I?'

Henry for once was lost for words as he watched her open her briefcase and place some documents in it. 'People have to lead their own lives,' he said at last. 'If Guy doesn't want to live in New York and work for the company, I think it's a great mistake to try to force him. He'll be unhappy and so in the end will you.'

'Nonsense.' She rose briskly, straightening the skirt of her black suit and buttoning up the fitted jacket. 'He'll be perfectly happy once he's settled in. After all, it was his grandfather who started Kalinsky's and it's only right he should become President when I retire.'

'And Francesca?' Henry's question hung in the air between them like something tangible.

Sarah walked over to the panelled doors that led to the boardroom, then paused to turn and look at him.

'Oh, she can go on having fun in the public relations department or something. It's time she was married anyway. Are you coming, Henry?

We don't want to keep everyone waiting, and don't forget I expect your full support at this meeting.'

Silently, Henry rose and went to follow her into the boardroom.

That morning Francesca got up an hour earlier than usual, feeling slightly nervous. She knew she was in for a grilling from the board, and she wasn't particularly looking forward to it. Her mother was watching everything she did these days, waiting for her to make a mistake, take a wrong decision or just get plain bored. She could also feel the hostility in Sarah's eyes when she did something right. A look that said *I wish it was Guy, not you, who was working here.* She couldn't win and if Guy came back she knew she was finished. Her mother would have her out quicker than greased lightning. Meanwhile she would go into this morning's meeting with guns blazing, ready to stand by her own convictions. She knew she had done the right thing, the only possible thing.

She showered, washed her hair, and then put on a simple white Chanel suit, edged with black braiding and worn over a black silk shirt. Kalinsky's gold and pearl chains and earrings would go beautifully with it. Lastly, she selected black, high-heeled lizardskin shoes and handbag. The effect was stunning. She just hoped her performance would match up to it.

When Francesca arrived at the Fifth Avenue showrooms she went straight to the lift that took her to the tenth floor boardroom, a large panelled room with windows down one side and an oil portrait of Howard J. Wayne on the far wall. On another wall hung a delicate pastel sketch, dating from 1900, of Howard's mother, Katerina Kalinsky, after whom he had named the company and to whom Francesca bore a marked resemblance. The sketch was the only gentle thing in the room. A large mahogany table ran down the centre and round it stood a dozen maroon leather chairs. Set apart from the others at one end was a larger chair with arms: the President's chair. The formality of the room struck a chill. Jokes were never cracked at meetings. Liberties were never taken. Agendas were rigorously adhered to and all remarks had to be addressed through the chairman.

When Francesca breezed in, a radiant and smiling figure bursting with vitality, the assembled company turned to look at her, then one by one they smiled and there was a welcoming chorus of 'Good morning'. Even the most staid directors found themselves warming under the influence of her personality.

'Good morning,' she returned their greetings, her eyes sweeping over the assembled company, wondering which of them would still wish to be friendly when the meeting was over.

Down one side of the table sat Walter Jarvis, a shrewd banker who had been a director for nearly twenty years, Max Ditzler, an investment tycoon, Clint Friedman and Tony Staver, both working directors, and beside them Craig Greenwalt, a retired property dealer. On the other side were

Sylvester Brandt, a retired stockbroker from Wall Street, Sean Richmond, who had made a fortune in cosmetics, Morris Ayotte and Dan Winthrop, who were also working directors. Between them they held fifteen per cent of the stock.

Francesca took her seat between Morris and Dan and opened her briefcase. The others watched curiously, as if she were a magician about to produce a rabbit out of a hat. Then she placed her report on the table in front of her, trying to control the faint shaking of her hands. It would never do to let them know that inside she was quaking. My God, she prayed silently, I hope I've done the right thing.

'Good morning, gentlemen.'

Ten pairs of eyes shot to the double doors that led to the President's office. The atmosphere chilled.

Sarah had made her entrance.

She stood, an elegant figure in her black suit, her head raised arrogantly, daring them to challenge her authority. Silently she walked to the head of the table with Henry by her side.

'Very well, gentlemen,' she said frostily, 'as we are all present, shall we begin?'

So far she had not even acknowledged her daughter's presence.

'Item three,' Sarah announced at last. Item one on the agenda had dealt with the proposed mark-up on pearls imported from Japan. Item two had been a lengthy discussion on the advertising budget for the coming year. Now it was time for Francesca's report on her trip to London and everyone was looking at her in a friendly and relaxed way. It would be a bit of light relief to hear about the choice of paint and fabrics for the Bond Street showrooms, and what sort of furnishings and carpeting were planned. Only Sarah stared straight ahead at some invisible object on the opposite wall, her face an inscrutable mask.

'I must tell you, gentlemen,' Francesca began, 'that what I found in London shocked me deeply. My brief was to go and discuss the renovations and redecorations for Bond Street. That turned out to be a straightforward matter, the details of which I will come to in a minute.'

Clint Friedman and Morris Ayotte were frowning now, listening to her closely, and there was an awakening tension in the room.

'Whilst I was over there, I happened to meet the newly appointed manager, Ernest Marsh. I was so shocked by what I found that I took it upon myself to have a look at the rest of the newly appointed staff,' said Francesca steadily.

They all stared at her solidly, and she knew what they were thinking. She was young and inexperienced, and they were doubting her ability; she could read it in Max Ditzler's and Morris Ayotte's faces.

'Ernest Marsh,' she continued, ticking off her fingers, 'is an alcoholic. His deputy is totally inexperienced; his last job was in a man's clothes shop. As for the other assistants they are totally unsuited to a job where expertise and personal appearance are of vital importance to our image.'

Max, Morris and Clint Friedman turned sharply to look at Sarah, then turned back to Francesca.

'So what's going on?' thundered Max.

Francesca looked him straight in the eye.

'I fired the lot of them! But don't worry, gentlemen, I have found replacements who come to us with the highest references and a lot of experience.'

There was a stunned silence. She felt calm now. Let them make their judgements. She knew she had done the right, the only thing, to avert a disaster that could have ruined Kalinsky's reputation in the United Kingdom. She had acted, in fact, exactly as her mother would have acted under the same circumstances. And if it made Guy look bad . . . she tightened her lips. The company had to come before everything.

Sarah's voice cut like a rapier across the still room. 'I will take charge of everything concerning the London outlet now. There is no need for you to interfere any further in this matter, Francesca.'

Rebuffed, Francesca flushed and gathered up her papers. 'Very well. Here are the details of the new employees,' she said coldly, handing them down the table to her mother.

'Item four on the agenda,' snapped Sarah.

It was obvious to Francesca that the matter was not going to be further discussed. It was Guy who had caused her mother this embarrassment but it was she who was going to get the blame.

Half an hour later, Francesca was back in her office, still seething. A minute later her door opened and Henry Langham came into the room.

She glanced up warily. 'What can I do for you?'

'I know how you must be feeling, honey,' he said gently. 'You did a great job over in London and I'm sorry you're not going to be allowed to finish it.'

'You might have stuck up for me, Uncle Henry,' she protested.

'I talked to your mother before the meeting. She already knew what you'd done, but I refused to be drawn into it until I had heard all the facts from you. Don't worry, I'm going to talk to her now and put her right about a few things, but I don't think she'll budge over going back to London herself.'

Francesca looked up at him in amazement. 'How did she know what I'd done?'

'It seems Guy called her and told her. I believe Marsh went to him and kicked up a helluva fuss about being fired. Hoped Guy could reinstate him, I suppose,' Henry replied.

'Typical!' Francesca exclaimed. 'Guy must have loved every moment. Anything to get me into trouble.'

Henry sat down heavily in the chair facing Francesca's desk and gave her a fond smile. 'The leopard never changes its spots, Francesca, but as my old grandmother used to say, there are more ways of killing a cat than choking it with butter.'

Francesca tried to suppress a smile. Henry was always full of well-worn platitudes. He had one for every situation.

'So, what should I do?' she asked.

'You're bright, ambitious and very beautiful,' he told her. 'With that combination you can't fail. But let me give you a piece of advice. If you want to succeed, handle your mother with more diplomacy.'

'What about her handling *me* with more diplomacy?' Francesca demanded. 'Christ, Uncle Henry, she treats me like a child. It gave her the greatest satisfaction to put me down in front of the board. Why doesn't she consider my feelings for once?'

'Because your mother is a very complex woman. We don't always see eye to eye, but she has kept control of Kalinsky's for twenty years, sometimes under great difficulties, and you've got to hand her that. You must also remember she's not as young as she was and now she feels threatened by you.'

'By me?' Francesca repeated in amazement. 'Why should she feel threatened by me? She's President, and she's got control, as you've just seen. I only got into Kalinsky's by the skin of my teeth and with a lot of help from you.'

'Sarah feels threatened by your youth. She's afraid you're going to take over, and she's got a right to be afraid. I think you will take over, maybe sooner than you think, but it won't help if you antagonise her. A beehive cannot have two queens.'

Francesca laughed outright this time. 'Uncle Henry, you kill me! In a minute you'll be telling me "a stitch in time saves nine"! So what do you suggest I do about Mom? As I see it, the real trouble is she wants Guy here, not me.'

'You're going to have to think of ways of cooling it without holding back on any plans you may have for the company.'

153

Francesca leaned forward earnestly, her face determined. 'The thing is, I want to be in complete charge, eventually. I don't want Guy messing around here in his usual amateurish way, causing trouble. I know I can take over from Mom one day and build up the company until it is number one in the world. It's all I've ever wanted to do. Is that so wrong, Uncle Henry?'

'It's not wrong at all, honey, and I know you're capable of doing it. You've got time on your side and you can outwit Guy any day if he does come back. I'm just advising you to curb your impatience, be tactful and try not to rub Sarah up the wrong way.'

Francesca gave a deep sigh. 'I know you're right. It's just that there's so much to be done, and all the time Cartier and Tiffany's are streaking ahead, and so are a lot of other jewellers. We don't have the time to pussy-foot around. I want to get on with everything now.'

'I know you do and I can understand that.' Henry heaved his large frame out of the chair. 'I've got to go and see Sarah now, but let's have a meeting in a couple of days. We can talk through some of your ideas and I'll be happy to advise you on how to get them agreed by the board. Softly, softly, catchee monkey,' he added.

'Thank you, Uncle Henry.' Francesca rose and walked with him to the door of her office. 'You're an angel.'

But as she sat down at her desk again, a worried frown puckered her brow. No matter what he did, it was obvious Guy could do no wrong in Sarah's eyes. He had been exposed as a lazy fool, content to hand over the running of the Bond Street show-rooms to a bunch of unsuitable cronies, and yet Sarah was blaming her for interfering!

God help us all, thought Francesca, if Mom manages to persuade him to return.

The rich, the exalted, the titled and the famous converged on Kalinsky's for the opening of the Bond Street showrooms. Sarah, chic in a white Dior dress and glittering with sapphires and diamonds, stood near the entrance as chauffeur-driven limousines swept down Bond Street to deposit the celebrities at the elegant bronze and glass entrance to the showrooms. Photographers clicked and flashed as Maria Callas, the Begum Aly Khan and Elizabeth Taylor stepped under the pale blue awning, on which the company's logo, the capital letter K, was embossed in gold.

Under the dazzling new chandeliers and blue watered silk tented draperies, white coated waiters served champagne in crystal glasses and caviar on silver platters against a background of brightly lit showcases, blazing with millions of dollars' worth of jewellery.

A Sultan walked round with bored dispassion, he could afford to buy the lot; foreign royalty, long deposed and robbed of their treasures, wondered if Kalinsky's could be persuaded to lend them pieces from time to time; English peeresses glanced surreptitiously at the case of tiaras and mentally compared them with their own, while wives wondered what they could wheedle out of their husbands and mistresses looked forward hopefully to Christmas.

Diana wore a magnificent emerald and diamond collar which Sarah had insisted she borrow from stock for the night. She gazed around, bemused by such massed wealth and vulgarity. Guy, on the other hand, did not try to hide his boredom. A glass of Dom Pérignon in one hand, the other casually stuck into his trouser pocket, he stood around as if it was beneath his dignity to be anything other than a blasé guest at such an obviously commercial event.

It was towards the end of the evening that Sarah cornered Diana.

'As you know, I'm going back to the States in a few days,' she said, smiling warmly and tucking her arm through Diana's, 'and I've got a little present for you, darling. Can I come over to your place some time tomorrow? Perhaps in the afternoon?'

Taken aback by her sudden friendliness, Diana mentally recoiled. The last time she had seen Sarah had been at her wedding to Guy, when she had been distinctly frosty.

'Yes, of course,' Diana responded automatically. Guy might be rude to his mother but she was sure there'd be trouble if she was. 'Come for tea. I'm afraid Guy will be out playing tennis.'

'I know,' Sarah cut in hurriedly. 'That's fixed then. I'll look forward to it.'

At four o'clock the next afternoon Sarah arrived, bringing with her a deep square black leather suitcase which was carried in from her car by what looked like a security man.

'Let's go right up to your bedroom, honey,' she said enthusiastically. 'I want to show you what's here and then you can choose.'

A few minutes later Diana watched, astounded, as Sarah pulled out the velvet lined drawers of the case, revealing a dazzling array of jewellery. Necklaces, bracelets, earrings and brooches blazed with brilliant-cut black, pink, blue and canary yellow diamonds, blue and yellow sapphires, aquamarines as clear as a summer's sky, amethysts as dark as Parma violets and emeralds that glowed like tiger's eyes.

'I never gave you a proper wedding present,' Sarah said smoothly, 'so I want you to pick out something you'd like.' As she spoke she took from a drawer a delicate concoction of gold 'ribbons' and diamond flowers, intricately woven into a necklace of twirls and lovers' knots. There were matching chandelier earrings of diamond flowers held in golden bows that quivered like tiny bouquets.

'They're beautiful!' gasped Diana, as Sarah fixed the clasp at the back of her neck, 'but I couldn't let you give me anything as valuable as this.'

'Nonsense. You're Guy's wife and you should have splendid jewels. You can have the emerald collar you wore last night, if you like, but look at everything I've got here first.'

Sarah laid out some more jewellery. A ruby pendant set in gold; a black opal necklace, edged with diamonds; rings set with large rectangular diamonds; a brooch made of diamonds, rubies and sapphires and shaped like a peacock. And all the while Sarah continued her sales patter.

At last she came to a *belle époque* diamond necklace, a sparkling lacy collar set with eight large solitaire diamonds and hundreds of tiny ones.

'Here are the matching earrings,' said Sarah softly.

A minute later a waterfall of brilliant stones hung round Diana's neck and from her ears, the diamonds bursting into tiny white-hot flames of light.

'There's no doubt about it, Diana, this could have been made for you. Look how perfectly it sits round your neck, showing off your shoulders. And the earrings, with your blonde hair ...' Sarah made it sound so sensuous that Diana felt an unaccustomed wave of physical pleasure sweep through her. The jewellery really did enhance her beauty.

'It's the most beautiful thing I've ever seen,' she breathed, 'but honestly, it's too much, I can't let you ...'

'Not another word, honey. I'm truly delighted you like it.' Sarah gave a mellow laugh and started putting the rest of the jewellery back in the case.

'I don't know how to thank you,' Diana went on, looking at her reflection in the dressing-table mirror.

Sarah draped herself elegantly on the chaise-longue, drawing on her cigarette through a long jade holder.

'How I wish you and Guy would come to live in the States,' she said in wistful tones. 'My dear, with your title – and beauty of course – you could be the toast of New York! I could give lovely parties for you and introduce you to everyone. Oh, Diana, you could both have a wonderful life!'

'You're very kind,' said Diana, catching her mother-in-law's reflection in the mirror, 'but, honestly, I don't think Guy wants to leave England. He's been here so long, he practically sees himself as an Englishman. He loves it here.'

'I must talk to him.' Sarah's tone was both complacent and dreamy. 'He could buy a beautiful brownstone on Park Avenue, and then there's our private plane for flying to our home in Palm Beach at weekends . . .' her voice trailed off, suggestive of delights that defied description.

The necklace lay cold and heavy now round Diana's neck, weighing her down like a shackle. She suddenly felt trapped between Guy and Sarah, as if she was a pawn in their constant battle of wills.

Sarah stayed on, determined to see Guy as soon as he returned, and it was half past six before she and Diana heard him coming in. Drinks served, Diana excused herself and went to her bedroom, saying she had to start getting ready for a dinner party they were going to.

Alone in the drawing-room, Sarah spoke in her gentlest voice, softly persuading him to return, promising him everything he wanted: a house, a car, more money, and the position of Vice President.

Guy sat listening quietly, his eyes flickering thoughtfully around the room from time to time, his expression implacable. At length he spoke.

'I can see all the advantages,' he said slowly, 'But there are a few problems to be solved first.'

'What sort of problems, honey?'

He leaned forward confidentially, and whispered. 'I don't want the staff to hear, but we are rather in debt. It's Diana's extravagance, you know. It's killing me. I went to the bank yesterday, trying to raise a loan but you know how it is . . .' He shrugged and looked down sadly at the carpet, a move guaranteed to have the effect he wanted.

'Oh, my darling boy! I *knew* you were making a great mistake marrying that girl. I gave her some jewellery today, because I want us to be friends, but if she's spending all your money . . . How much do you need?'

Guy did a quick calculation, trebled it, and said glibly, 'About a hundred thousand dollars.'

'Right.' Sarah's voice was practical now. She was getting down to business. 'I'll write you a cheque for a hundred thousand dollars now; then, will you put this house on the market, wind up all your affairs over here, and come to New York as soon as you can?'

'It might take a month or so, this is the wrong time of year to put a house on the market.'

'Okay. Let's say three months from now you'll be arriving in New York.' She had written out the cheque, but was waiting for his answer before signing it.

Guy glanced at the cheque and the tantalisingly poised pen. 'Okay,' he said. 'It's a deal.'

*　　*　　*

The board meeting had nearly come to an end. Sarah's glowing account of the party in London had drawn nods and grunts of approval from everyone present, with the exception of Francesca, who had heard it all, several times, since her mother's return.

'We have now come to "any other business" on the agenda,' Sarah concluded brightly, looking round the table. 'Has anyone got anything else they want to discuss?'

There was silence.

'Very well then. I have an announcement to make.'

The directors looked at her with polite expectancy. Francesca caught Henry Langham's eye but his expression suggested he knew no more than her. Perhaps Sarah's success in London had fired her with so much enthusiasm that she planned to open showrooms in other capital cities? Francesca's mind raced. Maybe her mother had pinched one of her brilliant ideas to promote Kalinsky's and was going to present it as her own? Francesca clenched her fists under the table and braced herself for battle. She was not, however, prepared for what came next.

'I am happy to tell you that we'll shortly be having a new Vice President,' Sarah announced.

Francesca's heart gave a great lurch. Henry turned sharply to look at Sarah. Up to now he was the company's Vice President, and if he were to be superseded it could only mean one thing. Sarah confirmed it for him.

'I wish to announce that Guy is returning to New

York as soon as he has tied up a few loose ends in England, and he will be joining Kalinsky's as joint Vice President with Henry Langham.'

Bloody nice of her to let me know, thought Henry, and glanced at Francesca. The blood had drained from her face, a feeling of crushing disappointment overwhelming her. She and Guy would never hit it off, never agree on policy, and of course Sarah would always back Guy without question. Even if it eventually hurt the company. Francesca's days at Kalinsky's could be numbered.

'I hope you will all join me for a small celebration in my office,' said Sarah, gathering up her papers. 'The future of the company is now ensured as a family concern. An Andrews will be at the helm when I am gone.'

She left the boardroom, and the others turned and looked at each other. No one said a word. Although most of them would support Sarah's wishes to have her son in the company, they all knew that Guy was capable of bringing about its ruin.

'I never thought he'd come back,' Francesca whispered to Henry.

He looked at her, still in shock. 'I never thought she'd pull it off, either,' he said slowly.

She glanced at him quickly. 'You knew she was trying?'

Henry nodded. 'Let's go to her office and make it look good. We might learn some more.'

'I don't know that I want to, Uncle Henry.'

He patted her shoulder comfortingly. 'Don't let

this get you down, honey. The battle hasn't even begun yet.'

Sarah had arranged for champagne to be served but most of the directors stuck to club soda. They had work to do, they needed to close ranks to ensure they presented a united front. They all knew what Guy was like. He would start manipulating Sarah from day one and none of them would have the power to stop him.

No one spoke very much, but Sarah did not seem to notice. Like a young girl, she flirted with Max Ditzler and Sean Richmond, whilst pointedly ignoring Henry. It was obvious he had already taken sides but for once she didn't care. He might have supported her in the early days but she wouldn't need him now that Guy was coming back. In future Guy would be her champion, her confidant, her right hand.

Francesca worked until late that night. She wanted to get as many of her plans as possible agreed to before Guy took up his position. Her mother had said he'd be over 'within the next three months'.

A lot could be achieved in three months.

Chapter Eight

Guy would be arriving in two months' time now, and Francesca wanted to get as much done as possible in case he countermanded her plans. Gathering up her papers, she went along to the Promotion Department. Her ideas needed knocking into shape and this was the moment to consult the experts.

Glen Casile had been in charge of Public Relations and Promotions for a couple of years, and to Francesca's joy he was young, enthusiastic and welcomed new ideas. They'd always got along well and she found his freckled face, half hidden behind thick glasses, and jovial manner very reassuring. His assistant, Rita, was a ball of fire too. Francesca breezed into their office.

'Hi, you guys! Can you spare half an hour? I've got some ideas I want to go over with you,' she said, seating herself facing Glen.

'Great! Want a cup of coffee?' Glen asked.

'Please. Black, no sugar. Now!' She placed her papers on the desk. 'Wait until you hear this!'

Rita placed Francesca's coffee beside the papers, her grey eyes twinkling merrily. 'Come on! Tell us!'

'Well,' Francesca smiled at their eagerness.

'First of all, I think we should hand pick half a dozen leading socialites, and offer to lend them our jewellery for special occasions, as long as they say it comes from Kalinsky's.'

'Like Mrs Warburg Williams III,' said Glen, 'she's in *Town And Country* every month!'

'And Mrs Karl Darro and Posy Cohen and Maizie Seigler,' cut in Rita. 'Boy, they'd love it!'

'The only thing that worries me is whether the insurance people will be happy,' said Francesca.

'Sure,' Glen assured her. 'They can have the same cover as you do when you borrow our jewellery.'

Francesca laughed. 'Do you think they're going to like the clause which says the insurance won't pay up if the wearer is drunk when it's lost?'

Glen shrugged. 'When are half these women sober? It's a normal policy, Francesca. How about lending stuff to some of the film stars too, while we're at it?'

'Hey! Why not? What's Elizabeth Taylor doing next?'

'I'll find out,' said Rita, making notes, 'but why should she want to wear our jewellery? She's probably got loads of her own.'

'I think we can get around that,' said Glen thoughtfully. 'Find out the name of the producer of her next film. Then I'll go to him, and tell him there's a gold watch or a piece of jewellery in it for him personally if he instructs wardrobe to get her jewels from us, fully insured! In return for a credit and some publicity stills, it's cheap at the price. Anyone would jump at it.'

'Great idea,' agreed Francesca. 'Going back to our socialites, why don't we offer them a percentage of any jewellery sold through them?'

'You mean if Posy Cohen were to bring in her best friend from Nebraska, and she bought a diamond necklace, we'd give Posy a percentage of the sale?' Glen asked.

'Right! Other companies do it, why shouldn't we?' Francesca replied.

'Get out your social register, Rita! It's going to come in useful at last,' he laughed.

'How about contra-deals, with magazines?' asked Francesca suddenly. 'You know, we'll take so many pages of full colour advertising, if they'll feature our stuff on the fashion pages?'

'That comes under the advertising department, but I'll find out what the position is,' said Glen. 'It's certainly a good idea. What else have you up your sleeve?'

'Sponsorship for sporting events, especially tennis. Gold watches for all the champion players, worldwide, that sort of thing.' Francesca looked up from her *Projects* file. 'When are the next Olympics coming up, by the way?'

'I'll check,' said Rita, still busily making notes.

'Now, I've had a *really* good idea, something you could get enormous press mileage out of!' Francesca drew out some more papers, covered in her neatly typed notes, and handed them to Glen.

'I think we should start a "Young Kalinsky" range. More and more girls are earning their own living now, and wanting to buy their own jewellery.'

Rita raised her eyebrows comically. 'How much are they earning, for God's sake? Our prices start at three thousand dollars for an itsy-bitsy rope of pearls, with such tiny diamonds on the clasp you can't see them! What are we going for, hookers?'

Francesca burst out laughing. 'You've got the point! No young woman, unless she was a hooker, could afford our present prices. I want us to stock a whole new range, starting at five hundred dollars, maybe even less, for the young woman who has a reasonable income.'

'Interesting,' Glen observed, looking alert.

'I think we should have fine gold chains,' continued Francesca, 'with the optional addition of a single pearl or diamond pendant; then we could have gold earrings, triple banded Russian rings in three shades of gold, fine bangles and scarf pins.'

'Incorporating our logo, a simple K?' suggested Glen.

'Maybe,' agreed Francesca. 'Well, what do you think? Are we in business or are we in business?'

'Wow! I think it's great,' breathed Rita. 'Do you think Mrs Andrews will go for all these new ideas?'

'I hope so. I'll get Henry Langham to put them forward. He's very persuasive as far as my mother is concerned, and I'd like to get them through quickly.'

They were all silent for a moment, each in their own way wondering if things would change when Guy took up his position as Vice President. Only Francesca knew, and right now she wasn't saying.

'I wish we could do something sensationally different, though,' she said thoughtfully, as she finished her coffee. 'Something that would have far-reaching effects for Kalinsky's. I don't know about you, but I'm bored to death with all the classical and conventional designs we have. You know, the three rows of graduated pearls and the diamond clips.'

'There is someone I'd like you to meet,' suggested Glen slowly. 'He's a way-out designer, born in Tulsa, but trained in New York, Paris and London. He only returned to New York a few weeks ago, and I'd like you to look at his stuff.'

Francesca leaned forward, instantly interested.

'What's his name? What are his designs like?'

'He's called Serge Buono, and I'm telling you, Francesca, you've never seen anything like his jewellery. Nobody's ever seen anything like it!'

'Have him call me, will you, Glen? You really think we could use him?'

'I think he'd put Kalinsky's light years ahead in the market! He could revolutionise design as we know it.'

'Then I'd definitely like to meet him.'

As she went back to her office her heart was thudding with excitement. Serge Buono and his designs might just be her secret weapon in consolidating her position in the company before Guy arrived.

Francesca liked the look of Serge the minute he walked into her office carrying his portfolio of designs. Tall, well-built, with a beard the colour of bottled honey and eyes as blue as an untroubled sky, he strode forward with an easy grace, his hand outstretched.

'Come and sit down,' said Francesca when she had greeted him. 'I've heard a lot about you.' It was Glen who had filled her in on Serge's background and shown her references from the companies in Paris and London where Serge had trained over the past eleven years as an apprentice making jewellery. She'd also learned that he had lived frugally all those years, saving every penny in order to buy the materials to make up his own designs.

Serge placed his portfolio on the table between them and smiled at her expectantly.

'You started out as a painter, didn't you?' Francesca asked, 'what made you decide to go into jewellery design?'

'I was walking down Fifth Avenue, on my twenty-first birthday, actually,' he said grinning, 'Feeling a bit bored with art school after two years, when I noticed the window display in Cartier. It was amazing! All those wonderful coloured stones and that beautiful workmanship; it really inspired me. By the time I'd looked in the windows of Tiffany's and Van Cleef & Arpels, I was hooked. I knew exactly what I wanted to do with my life. I wanted to interpret jewellery in a totally naturalistic way. After all, stones and precious metals come out of the earth, so I wanted to link them back to the earth. Let me show you.'

He leaned forward eagerly and, opening his case, revealed a stack of designs done in pen and ink and watercolour.

Francesca started going through them slowly, her eyes wide with amazement, as Serge continued talking.

'I began to see things differently from that moment on,' he explained. 'Dew on the grass in Central Park transformed itself into this bracelet; see, I've used spikes of emerald, scattered with tiny diamonds. Now, this crystal pendant, inset with pale blue diamonds – I got the idea for that by watching raindrops form on a windowpane.'

'They're brilliant,' she breathed, and there was awe in her voice. 'Has anyone else seen your designs yet?'

'I showed them to a few people in London, but they thought they were too unconventional,' he said, shaking his head. 'No one was prepared to take the risk of marketing them. They said I was way ahead of my time.'

'That's exactly right! You are! And that's precisely what I'm looking for!' she exclaimed.

Serge continued to show her more of his designs and there was barely suppressed excitement in his voice.

'I get a lot of inspiration from the effect of water, whether it's still or moving. I like to try and capture water falling and splashing on rocks, as in this necklace of platinum and aquamarines, or spraying from a fountain, like these diamond earrings. There's something so wonderfully mobile about water; it changes continually, and the lights in it change. I want to bring that fluidity to jewellery. I hate static stuff,' he added without apology.

Francesca nodded, cheeks flushed. The way he

expressed himself sent a frisson down her spine and she knew she'd found what she'd been looking for. Maybe in more ways than one. She liked the way Serge's eyes crinkled in his tanned face when he smiled, she liked his powerful but sensitive hands, and most of all she liked the way he seemed to be on exactly the same wavelength as her. If her mother could be persuaded to take him on, she would build him up as a 'star' designer, fresh from Europe, a real find. She could see it now: a collection of jewellery by Serge Buono of Kalinsky's.

'Have you got some samples of your work, made up?' she asked.

'Yes, quite a few pieces. I didn't bring them with me today because, frankly, I didn't think you'd be interested once you'd seen the drawings.'

'I'm more than interested. I'm going to set up a meeting, within the next week, so bring everything with you then,' said Francesca warmly. 'I very much hope we can work together.'

He was regarding her with open admiration now, relaxed in the knowledge that she liked his work.

'I hope so, too,' he said sincerely. 'You really are quite a lady. Smart, and beautiful with it.'

Francesca found herself blushing as the magnetic attractiveness of this man hit her. She rose swiftly and went over to her desk. In a funny sort of way he reminded her of Marc; the same strength mingled with sensitivity; the same enthusiasm mingled with creativity; and the same charm. She caught her breath, deciding any relationship she might have with Serge in the future was going to be

172

totally professional. There was no way she was going to make the classic mistake of falling twice for the same type of man. There was no way she was going to let herself be hurt again.

'I'll call you to tell you when we're holding the meeting,' she said, trying to keep her voice steady.

He had come over to her desk and was standing, his feet apart, his hands in his pockets, looking down at her, smiling.

'I'll look forward to hearing from you, and to seeing you again,' he replied softly.

A week later Serge was arranging his jewellery at one end of the table in the boardroom. He and Francesca were awaiting Sarah's arrival to approve his appointment, and she felt a mixture of excitement and nerves. It meant so much to her to have him join the company and she desperately wanted Sarah to make him feel welcome too. Serge had been in her mind all week and now, as he stood beside her, her hands were shaking. He looked so handsome in his pale grey jacket and dark trousers, and she couldn't help wondering if he already had a girlfriend.

'Do you like this?' he asked, breaking into her thoughts. He held up one of his most delicate designs, a spun gold necklace set with aquamarines and pearls, depicting dragonflies hovering in flight around the throat.

'It's exquisite,' she gasped. 'It looks so fragile.'

He laughed. 'It's very strong, really.' He laid it on the table and picked up another necklace. 'This is my favourite one, though.'

Francesca leaned forward, her shoulder brushing his, to examine what looked like a quivering waterfall of platinum and diamonds. Strips of the metal, some rough textured, some gleaming smooth, hung at different lengths, intermingled with various size diamonds, falling from a collar that looked as smooth as water slipping over a ridge of stones. The slightest movement made it sway like a mobile, flowing with life.

'It would suit you,' he said, looking searchingly into her face. 'It goes wonderfully with your colouring.'

Francesca gazed up at him, transfixed by the blue of his eyes. 'Does it?' she murmured.

At that moment Sarah, followed by Henry, walked into the boardroom, shattering their moment of intimacy.

Francesca introduced Serge and then stood aside to let him show them the pieces.

'They're magnificent!' Henry pronounced stoutly, having already been briefed by Francesca. 'They're so avant-garde they could revolutionise jewellery design in the future.'

Sarah was examining both the painted designs and the examples closely. 'They're so revolutionary they could frighten our normal customers away!' she said crisply. 'Remember, as in fashion, the media go crazy about anything new, but the customers still prefer to buy the conventional stuff.'

'I'm not suggesting we abandon the triple rows of pearls with the diamond clasp,' interjected Francesca, trying not to sound sarcastic. 'I merely suggest we do some of these pieces as a new line, and I propose we launch them with a show linked to modern art. Imagine an exhibition showing Serge's jewellery, alongside a Picasso, a Matisse, maybe a Henry Moore sculpture! We could tour the world with it. It would be sensational and – ' here she paused and looked at her mother, knowing her next suggestion would appeal ' – it would be very good for Kalinsky's image to be seen to be taking a serious interest in the arts.'

'Mmm.' Sarah's mind was working quickly. That would be a prestigious move.

'We could start off at the Whitney Museum,' suggested Henry.

'And give a big reception to launch it with strong media coverage,' added Francesca. 'I think people are going to go for these designs in a big way. This is the jewellery of the future and we'd be the first company to promote it.'

Sarah rose with a gracious smile. Francesca waited with bated breath. Suddenly she wanted them to have Serge's designs even more than new showrooms in far flung capitals. It would help, though, if they had Sarah's blessing.

'I think if we can combine this new stuff with our traditional designs, it might be a good idea. But remember, Francesca, I don't want anything gimmicky. We have a reputation for producing very fine classical pieces and they are the pieces that sell. However, an exhibition . . .' Her voice tailed off and Francesca and Henry looked surreptitiously at each other and Henry gave the faintest nod.

It was the nearest they'd ever get to securing Sarah's approval.

Serge Buono was now a part of the company.

When Serge asked Francesca out that evening to celebrate, she hesitated before answering, torn between her desire to see him again and the warning bells that rang in her head. She couldn't bear the idea of getting hurt again; the very memory of how she'd suffered when Marc left still haunted her at times. And then she had to think about Kalinsky's. Serge was going to be the most important element of the new image she hoped to create and if she got involved with him, and then it went wrong, it could affect the company badly.

'Well, I'm not sure,' she said.

His blue eyes bore into hers; friendly, very kind and very understanding, as if he knew what was going through her head.

'Just a little dinner,' he said reasonably. 'If you like Chinese I know a wonderful restaurant on Canal Street. Their prawn and sesame toast is a dream, and they do General Sho's Chicken in the traditional way. You'll love it.'

Francesca smiled, unable to resist his charm. After all, she told herself, what's a dinner date between two adults who are going to be working together. It would look churlish to refuse.

'That would be lovely. I'll look forward to it.'

Serge's face lit up. 'I'll collect you at eight o'clock. Will that be okay?'

'That will be fine.'

During dinner he told her about his parents, still

living in Tulsa, and his married sister who had three kids. It was obvious to Francesca that family life and having roots meant a great deal to him.

'And what about you?' he asked at length. 'Your father's dead, isn't he? Glen told me there was just you and your mother, and a brother who lives in England.'

'Yes,' said Francesca quietly. Then she looked across the candlelit table at him and she knew instinctively that this was a man she could trust. It was the first time she had confided to anyone about Sarah and Guy since the time when she'd poured out her heart to Marc, so long ago, and it surprised her how easy it was to talk to Serge. It was as if she'd known him for years.

'So you see,' she concluded, 'I'm not thrilled about Guy coming over to be Vice President. I think Mom looks upon him as some sort of surrogate husband, you know. He was always the favourite and she's been determined, for years, to have him working alongside her, so she can keep him tied to her apron strings.' There was no bitterness in her voice, just a flat acceptance of how things were.

'The trouble is,' she continued, 'both Henry and I know that it's not going to work. Guy will throw his weight around, not because he knows the business, but because he'll think it his right, as son of the President. He's capable of creating chaos; I'll tell you what happened in our London shop some time. What I want to do is push through my ideas and consolidate my position before he arrives.'

They talked about Sarah and Guy for a little

177

while longer and then Serge asked her the question she'd been dreading all evening.

'And what about your private life? No husband? No boyfriend?'

She clenched her fists under the table, amazed that it still hurt to talk about it.

'No, no one, not for some time, that is,' she said awkwardly, realising that Serge was watching her closely.

'Well, neither have I,' he said, smiling easily, breaking the tension. 'Do you like going to shows or concerts?'

Francesca nodded, thankful the moment was over.

'Great.' His hand reached lazily across the table and touched her elbow. 'We unattached New Yorkers have to stick together! What's good on Broadway at the moment?'

Francesca felt herself relax as he steered the conversation back to generalities. And as the evening progressed it struck her that maybe she had nothing to fear from Serge. Nothing to fear if she allowed herself to fall in love with him. He's not like Marc when you get to know him, she told herself. Marc had a ruthlessness about him that was quite different to Serge's natural ambition. And she would swear that Serge was someone you could *really* trust.

When he dropped her off at her apartment, he leaned forward and kissed her gently on the mouth; an undemanding kiss, but one that suggested sincere affection. She kissed him back warmly and felt good. Maybe, at last, she was ready to put away her fears and give herself to a man again, with love and trust and confidence.

The next morning she arrived at her office feeling elated. If Guy was coming back, well, she was ready for him. She felt stronger than she'd done in ages, and she knew it had to do with Serge. Together they'd sweep Kalinsky's to the top and even Guy wouldn't be able to stop them.

On impulse, she decided to call Diana in London. She might as well find out exactly when they were arriving, and anyway she had a feeling that Diana could be a useful ally. She might even find out things from Diana which could prove useful.

What her sister-in-law had to say left her stunned.

'But we're not coming to New York! What made you think we were?'

Francesca drew in her breath sharply, her mind reeling. 'Mom told us all that Guy was returning to become Vice President! She's full of plans. I don't understand.'

There was a pause on the line. 'She did try,' admitted Diana. 'She had a go at me, and then she talked to Guy, the evening before she left here. But I knew she'd never be able to persuade him. We're definitely not coming.'

'Then why did she make this big announcement? Everyone in Kalinsky's is expecting him. Mom actually said he'd be arriving about six weeks from now. Are you sure he didn't agree?' Francesca was thinking rapidly. Supposing Guy hadn't told Diana of his plans!

'I'll ask him when I see him tonight, but I'm certain you've got it wrong,' said Diana, doubt creeping into her voice. 'There's another reason why I'm sure we're staying in London too. I haven't been awfully well and the doctor doesn't want me to travel . . .'

'Oh, Diana, I'm sorry. Is it serious?' Francesca cut in.

She heard a soft giggle on the line. 'Actually, it's still a secret, but I'm pregnant.'

'Wow!' Francesca gave a shriek. 'That's terrific news! When is it due?'

'In the middle of February. It was a great surprise, I hadn't actually thought . . .'

Francesca could sense her sister-in-law's embarrassment and wondered why it had been such a surprise. Didn't one usually hope to get pregnant if one was married? However, this made it a whole new ball game. Maybe Guy had changed his mind about coming to New York because of the baby.

'Does Mom know about the baby?' Francesca asked suddenly.

'No, and, er, I'd rather she didn't, at least not for the present. I've had a rather bad time and the doctor was afraid I'd lose it, so we want to wait a month or so before we tell everyone, especially your mother, Guy says.' She gave another giggle. 'I think he's afraid she'll come to London again if she knows.'

Francesca laughed understandingly. 'Will you call me back when you've checked this out with Guy?' she asked. 'I really want to know what's happening around here.'

'Of course I will, but I'm sure you've got it wrong.'

'Me, and all the directors of Kalinsky's,' said Francesca drily. She replaced the telephone thoughtfully and buzzed through to Uncle Henry on her intercom. She wouldn't tell him about the baby, but she urgently needed to discuss this new turn of events.

'Could Mom be bluffing?' she asked, as she settled herself on the sofa in his office a few minutes later.

'What would be the point?'

'To put me off my stride? To undermine my confidence and block my schemes?'

'Hardly,' he said reasonably. 'If she'd wanted to do that, she'd have told you privately, she wouldn't have made a public statement. Hell, it's even been in the newspapers!'

'Then is Guy double-crossing her, or Diana?'

'You might just be able to turn all this to your advantage,' Henry said thoughtfully. 'Don't tell anyone what Diana said, and as soon as you hear from her we'll go into action, one way or another.' A slow smile crossed his face as he thought about the possibilities. Sarah had gone too far this time, as far as he was concerned, and appointing Guy as a Vice President behind his back was a humiliating act of treachery. If he could help Francesca turn things around, he would do so.

'What can we do?' Francesca asked.

'Let's find out all the facts first,' he said firmly. 'Remember, "where's there's smoke, there's fire".'

Diana lay propped up in bed on a mound of white linen pillows, watching as Guy got ready to go out to dine. The doctor had said she was to have bed rest for at least another two weeks in case she miscarried, but it had not stopped Guy from going out every night, sometimes not returning until very late. At least he was pleased about the baby and for that she was glad. A baby would certainly give more meaning to their marriage, make it seem a more bona fide relationship, but she knew that in the long run it was not going to be enough. She had to find herself something useful to do with her life and as soon as the baby was born she was going to give it serious thought.

'I heard from Francesca today,' she said suddenly.

'And what did she want?' His words were clipped, but his manner was much more friendly these days.

'She says your.mother's been telling everyone you're going back to New York, to become Vice President of Kalinsky's.'

To her surprise he threw back his head and roared with laughter. 'God, really? How very funny. I've really got her wound up, haven't I?'

'Well, did you say you'd go?'

'Of course!' Guy laughed again. 'Is she getting the office next to hers done over for me? What did Francesca say? I bet she's not looking forward to the return of the prodigal son.'

'But we're not going, are we?' she demanded.

'Diana, by the time she'd given you that jewellery and I'd borrowed a few thousand dollars from her as well, I had to say *something*!'

'So Francesca was right! We are going to live over there?' Her face was pale.

'No, of course we're not! God, you're as stupid as she is, believing I'd leave all I've got here to go and be her bloody slave over there,' he cried impatiently. 'Nothing would induce me to go.'

The colour returned to Diana's cheeks as she leaned back, overwhelmed with relief. 'Hadn't you better let her know?'

'No.' His tone was malicious. 'It won't do her any harm to run around in circles for a bit, getting all excited.'

'But that's cruel! How can you do that to your own mother?'

'When you know my mother as well as I do, the answer is, quite easily,' he said. 'I'm off now and I may be late, so make sure you stay in bed and rest.' He gave her a brotherly peck on the cheek and a minute later he was gone.

When Diana called Kalinsky's the next day she asked to be put through to Francesca.

'We're not going to New York,' she said succinctly. 'Apparently Guy's been stringing your mother along, having got a lot of money out of her first.'

'Thanks. That's all I wanted to know,' said Francesca.

Francesca and Henry sat in his office the next morning and although she was not in complete agreement with what he was suggesting, she was beginning to realise she'd have to be as ruthless and single-minded as her mother if she was going to succeed.

'So you know what you have to do,' Henry said.

She nodded. 'I don't much like this, Uncle Henry. It makes me feel I'm stooping to Guy's level but I suppose it's the only way.'

'It sure is, Francesca, and I'm with you all the way. Okay?'

'Yes. Is Mom in her office now?'

'She is.'

'Right. I'll go and see her right away.' Francesca went into her mother's office looking more confident than she felt. She didn't usually deal in the dirty tricks department but this was an exception and her one chance to pull off a coup that could alter her entire future.

Max Ditzler and Sarah were deep in conversation when she arrived, but they broke off in midsentence, exchanging knowing looks before returning her greeting.

'What is it you want?' asked Sarah, the look of triumph that had been in her eyes for weeks still lingering. 'Max and I have a lot to discuss.'

'I realise you're busy,' Francesca's tone was sympathetic, 'that's why I wondered if you'd like my help in getting the next door office ready for Guy? He'll be here in just over a month, won't he? It doesn't give us long.'

Sarah looked doubtful for a moment, then she nodded slowly. 'Well, you could supervise the redecorating, I suppose. And see to the finishing touches. I want it to be really beautiful for Guy; comfortable, bright and warm, you know.'

'I know,' agreed Francesca. 'Have you had anyone submit designs?'

'Of course. Roberto Pala has been to see it

and he promised to send me some sketches.'

'Okay, Mom, I'll call him up and see what he suggests. Don't worry about a thing. I'll make sure the new Vice President's office is second in magnificence only to yours,' said Francesca, rising and smiling. 'Have you heard when Guy's actually arriving?'

Sarah seemed to falter for a second, then she squared her shoulders and spoke strongly. 'I haven't been able to get hold of him for the past week because he's been so busy. He has a lot to see to, selling his house and so on, but I expect him in five to six weeks.'

'Great!' Francesca strode to the door. 'That gives me time to make sure everything is ready.'

'Thank you, Francesca.' There was a grudging note of respect in Sarah's voice. Then she turned back to Max, her daughter forgotten.

For the next week Francesca and Henry lobbied the other directors in secret, with the exception of Max Ditzler; he was too close to Sarah. Clint Friedman and Tony Staver were invited to drinks at her apartment, and as they were both working directors, they were not difficult to persuade. Neither were Morris Ayotte or Dan Winthrop, who had also worked in Kalinsky's for several years. They had heard enough about Guy, especially his efforts to set up the Bond Street branch, to make them want to back Francesca. Walter Jarvis, a shrewd banker, also promised his support, and so did Sylvester Brandt and Sean Richmond, who had admired Francesca's efforts to get the company moving forward from the beginning. Together with Henry they owned only fifteen per cent of the shares but they were powerful men whom Sarah would not wish to cross. Especially Walter Jarvis, whose bank had recently loaned Kalinsky's something in the region of six million dollars towards their expansion schemes.

The scene was set and Francesca was anxious to get things moving.

'Can't we go into action this week?' she asked Henry.

He considered the matter, gazing at her thoughtfully as he did so. Never in his life had he met a young woman with such strong determination and courage. It took guts to do what she was doing, and ruthlessness too. Unwittingly, Sarah had been her tutor by her own example – but Sarah wasn't going to find it palatable when she was eventually faced by her own creation.

'Timing is of the essence,' he said slowly. 'Choosing just the right minute to strike.'

'Do we tell her privately, or let it all come out at the next board meeting?' asked Francesca.

'If we tell her privately she might try to sabotage everything. A board meeting it will have to be, although that will cause her great pain in public. I don't think it can be avoided though,' he replied.

Francesca rose from her desk and went to look at the stark Manhattan skyline, suddenly feeling a pang of sadness.

'What a pity it has to be like this,' she said, and there was regret in her voice. 'If only Mom had, well, sort of acknowledged me as Guy's equal, then none of this would have happened. We wouldn't have to resort to these games. Mothers shouldn't have favourites!' she added with sudden vehemence. 'If I ever have children, I'll treat them exactly the same, whether they're boys or girls.'

'So, when are we going to do it?'

Francesca returned to her desk and looked at her diary. 'We have the next board meeting at ten-thirty on Tuesday,' she said in a low voice. 'How about then?'

'Fine.' Henry sounded confident, almost as if he were looking forward to it. 'We'll be ready.'

'I hope it will be all right. What will I do if it all goes wrong, if Mom gets wind of what's happening?'

'Don't worry, Francesca.' Henry gave her an encouraging smile. 'Nothing ventured nothing gained,' he added.

In spite of her worry, Francesca couldn't help grinning.

On Monday evening Serge took her to a concert at Carnegie Hall and afterwards they went back to her apartment for supper.

'Are you all right?' he asked her gently as they settled down to coffee and brandy afterwards. 'You seem tense.'

Francesca bit her lip and shot him an anxious glance. 'If you must know, I'm scared silly . . . No, not what you think!' she added quickly, seeing his startled look. 'It's something that's happening at the office tomorrow, at a board meeting.'

'I'm glad to hear it's nothing to do with me,' he

said, grinning. 'I don't usually frighten women to death!'

She laughed, grateful for the look of understanding he was giving her, grateful also that it didn't look as if he was going to probe any further.

'I could never be scared of you, Serge,' she said softly.

He caught her hand and held it tightly. 'I'm glad of that, honey.'

Their eyes locked and held in a long minute of mutual searching, and in that moment she knew for certain that he felt about her the same way as she felt about him.

'Francesca.' Serge was saying her name, over and over. 'Francesca, Francesca . . .' His voice was husky now and she felt a deep tremor sweep through her as he leaned forward and put his arms round her. Then his firm lips and silky beard brushed her face before he clamped his open mouth over hers and kissed her deeply.

She was melting in his arms, her breasts aching for his touch, her groin suffused with a sudden piercing desire for him. Slipping her arms round his neck, she pulled him closer, returning his kiss ardently, wanting him so much it hurt.

Slowly, he undid the buttons of her silk shirt and, sliding his hand inside, cupped one of her breasts, his thumb revolving gently round her nipple. Then he was kissing her neck and as she gave a gasp of pleasure, he dropped his mouth and sucked her tenderly.

'Oh! Serge, darling . . .'

He looked up, and his eyes were glittering with a longing that was as great as hers.

'Let's go to the bedroom,' he muttered, closing his eyes for a moment as if the sight of her, flushed and naked to the waist now, was more than his senses could bear.

They rose, clinging to each other, and Francesca's legs felt so weak that he half carried her until they reached her kingsize bed. Then he undressed her, bit by bit, kissing each part of her golden body until she lay before him, trembling with longing and anticipation. He undressed quickly, revealing a tough muscular body with broad shoulders and slim flanks. His pubic hair was honey coloured too, she noticed, and his shaft thick and strong. When he came to lie down beside her, he laid a sensitive hand on the flat of her stomach and, although he pressed gently, her muscles jumped and contracted convulsively.

'It's been so long . . .' she whispered.

'I know, my darling, I know,' he said, understanding. She had told him about Marc during one of their evenings out together and he knew her fears.

'I promise you you'll never regret this,' he whispered now, letting his hand slide down her stomach to where she was already pulsing with hot passion. 'I love you, Francesca. I fell in love with you from the first moment we met. You are everything I always dreamed of finding in a woman. My woman,' he added, moving down, until his tongue was where his hand had been, licking and sucking her so that she pressed down on him, her swelling and ecstasy sending quivers through her body. When she could bear it no more, she rolled gently to one side and, changing positions, dropped her mouth onto him, taking his flaming tip into her mouth, feeling it throb beneath her touch.

He was nearing breaking point, she could feel it by the way he was stiffening, and when he seized her shoulders and spun her round, so that she was lying beneath him, she knew that the moment when they would become one was imminent.

At his first thrust she was flooded by a sense of rapture so strong that she clung to him, giving her heart, her mind, her very being to him. It felt so right. Her mind was singing – *this is a man I can trust, a man I will always love.*

With deepening ardour, and fierce plunging, he brought her to a point when she felt consumed by passion, lifted high and carried along on a torrent of emotion so complete and so utterly fulfilling that she let out a cry, before lying spent beneath him. He cried out too then, climaxing gloriously within her, filling her with himself and his joy and his triumph.

They lay still for a long while afterwards, talking quietly and lovingly, and then Serge traced a pattern with one finger around the base of her throat.

'I'm going to design a necklace for you.' His voice was still thick with spent passion. 'And it will only be for you. No one else will have one like it.'

'What will it be like?' she asked softly.

'Gold hands, linked together, forming a circlet; tiny gold hands, and the ones in the centre will hold a perfect drop diamond,' he said, still tracing with his finger.

'Linked hands, for eternity?'

'For eternity,' he whispered back.

The next morning Francesca was up early. This was it. The moment she had been longing for yet dreading ever since she'd heard Guy wasn't coming back. Only thoughts of her night with Serge quelled the shaking of her hands and the thumping of her heart. Dressing with care, she arrived at the office and an hour later joined the directors in the boardroom.

Sarah sat serenely at the head at the table while everyone went through the usual things on the agenda, including passing a decision to move the workrooms to bigger premises on Twenty-Ninth and Seventh – nothing world-shattering. Francesca sat tense and rigid, not looking at Henry, while her mother controlled the proceedings quietly, locked in her own world of believing what she wanted to believe. All the directors that morning seemed to be in a mood to acquiesce to her wishes. She liked it that way. Everyone in agreement, her power absolute.

They had got to 'any other business'.

Henry cleared his throat, squared up the papers in front of him and leaned forward, while Francesca's heart thumped so loudly she was sure the others must hear it.

'May I put forward a proposal, Madam President?' he asked formally.

'Of course, Henry. What is it?' Sarah asked, smiling at him in a relaxed way.

Francesca felt a momentary stab of guilt. Her

mother was about to walk right into it and in a few minutes her dreams would be shattered. But Francesca had dreams too, dreams she intended to fulfil, so she just had to exploit this opportunity. If Guy hadn't been a profligate liar none of them would be on the brink of pulling off this coup in the first place.

'We are all looking forward to the appointment of a new Co-Vice President,' Henry said in measured tones.

Sarah's smile broadened.

'As a company,' he continued, 'certain resolutions have been passed to accommodate this appointment and the press, of course, have given us some excellent coverage. All most advantageous to Kalinsky's because a story about a member of the family joining the company lends a nice sense of continuity. Clients will like the feeling that there will always be a member of the Andrews family at the helm.'

Sarah bowed her head graciously in his direction, liking what she heard. Francesca, sitting rigid in her chair, did not raise her eyes. She fixed them firmly on her gold fountain pen as her fingers smoothed the shining surface.

'Nothing must be allowed to upset that valuable image of continuity we have created and so, along with the news I have to give you, I am happy to say I can also offer a solution.'

Ears pricked up. Eyes swivelled sharply in Henry's direction. Sarah seemed suddenly to grow old. Francesca looking up, at last, felt her cheeks suffused with heat.

It was with the hard slam of an axe splitting wood that Henry delivered his next words. Short and sharp. Guy would not be returning to New York and he proposed that Francesca should be made Vice President instead. Only Max Ditzler and Sarah looked shocked. Sarah's face became deathly pale and the skin, tucked and trimmed by too many face-lifts, became stretched so that she looked like an empty mask.

'Motion seconded,' cried Sean Richmond.

There was a chorus of ayes, from Morris Ayotte, Dan Winthrop, Sylvester Brandt, Walter Jarvis, Clint Friedman and Tony Staver. All the directors Francesca and Henry had been wooing at private meetings during the past month, tempting them, one by one, by letting them see, secretly, all her plans for the future of Kalinsky's.

'It seems the "ayes" have it,' said Henry.

An hour later, when the excitement had died down, Francesca slipped into her new office and went and sat behind her new glass-topped desk. She'd done it! With advice and help from Henry she'd achieved what she'd set out to do. Vice President of a company that was going to become the biggest and most successful jewellery corporation in the world. It might take her years to achieve all she wanted for Kalinsky's and she had no illusions that it was going to be easy, but she had her youth, her health, and ambition that would take her as far as she wanted to go. And I'm going all the way, she thought, as she looked round the beautifully appointed room, taking in the brilliantly coloured modern paintings and sophisticated furnishings. The office she'd supposedly got ready for Guy! Then she smiled, remembering the day her mother had sent her off to ballet class because an office was no place for a little girl. Well, that little girl had grown up and now she was going to show them all what she could do.

Chapter Nine
1954

'I'm flying to the States tomorrow,' Guy announced at breakfast. Diana, spooning cereal into Miles's mouth, looked up, startled.

'Oh! Why are you going?'

Guy hadn't been to New York for nearly two years, not since the terrible fight he'd had with his mother for breaking his promise to return to join Kalinsky's.

'There are some things I have to see to,' he replied curtly.

Diana raised her eyebrows and said nothing. Guy never told her what he was doing these days. At that moment Miles yelled for his orange juice and, grabbing his mug, she held it to his lips.

'How long will you be away?'

Guy shrugged. 'For as long as it takes. I don't know. Maybe a couple of weeks.' He rose from the breakfast table and patted his small son on the head. 'He's dribbling, Diana.' Then he left the room without another word.

Diana lifted Miles out of his highchair and put him on the floor to play for a while before she shut herself in their study. She had recently turned it into an office, from which she had started to organise gala nights in aid of charity as a way of filling in the long hours when she was on her own.

Her next project was a ball in aid of Cancer Research. Alone in her office twenty minutes later, having handed Miles over to his nanny, Diana reached for the telephone and dialled the number of the Grosvenor House Hotel, which boasted the largest ballroom in London.

'Have you any dates available during the second week in June, for a ball for eleven hundred people?' she asked, as soon as she got through to the banqueting department.

After a pause the banqueting manager came on the line. 'Is Friday any good? I have that night free.'

'I'm afraid not. No one will go to a party on a Monday or a Friday, and of course the weekend's no good. I really need midweek,' she explained.

'It's possible Wednesday the fourteenth will be available. There's a provisional booking, but I can let you know later on today.'

'Thank you. I'll look forward to hearing from you.'

Diana made a note on her pad, praying they could have the fourteenth. Until it was confirmed, though, she was unable to get on with all the other arrangements, like booking the band, ordering the decorations and arranging for a Toast Master to be in attendance. At least she could get her lists together and the stationery designed. Her next call was to a graphic designer whom she relied upon heavily.

'Anne? This is Diana Andrews. Would you have

a free moment to discuss the designs for stationery and ticket application forms for another function I'm doing?'

'I'd love to. What have we got this time? A Golden Ball? Or a Bluebird Ball?' Anne joked.

Diana laughed. She always insisted on having a theme and they'd had some amusing times trying to think up ideas.

'What about a Flamingo Ball?' she said. 'Have everything pink: tablecloths, candles, flowers, the invitations and, of course, pink champagne.'

Anne sounded impressed. 'I like it! I could do a design of flamingos on all the stationery. Would you go as far as having pink food, too?'

'If I can persuade the chef at the Grosvenor House to co-operate! I also know a place where I can hire life size gold flamingos, which we could group in a sort of pink grotto in the centre of the dance floor!'

'Diana, you really are amazing! It will look fantastic! How do you plan to sell all the tickets?'

Diana gave a deep and heartfelt sigh. 'The usual ghastly way – signing hundreds of letters to everyone I know, forming a committee and getting them to sell tickets too. That's the bit I hate! It's one thing organising a private party for someone, when you're given a budget and you can get on with it. It's quite something else having to sell all the tickets, sell all the sponsored pages in the souvenir brochure, and collect hundreds of prizes!'

'I believe you! Why do you do it?' Anne asked.

'Until I get established I'm taking on everything.

I really want to build up my business into a sizeable company,' said Diana, hoping Anne wouldn't probe further. Anne was a friend and a colleague, but Diana liked to keep her private affairs to herself, and trying to earn her own living so that she could be independent of Guy was still a very private affair as far as she was concerned.

The next morning Guy was up early, his crocodile luggage stacked in the hall, the chauffeur waiting to drive him to the airport. He was on the 'phone in the study when Diana came downstairs and she heard him talking to someone in a low intimate voice.

'I'll call you as soon as I land, darling,' he was saying. 'Yes, I know. I'm going to miss you too, but I'll be back in two weeks. Yes. Goodbye, darling.'

The stillness of her presence made him spin round as he replaced the receiver. Diana was standing in the doorway, her face expressionless.

'I hate the way you always listen to other people's conversations,' he snapped, pushing past her into the hall.

'I came down to see you off,' she said with dignity, controlling her anger. She'd presumed he saw other women, but he'd never made it obvious before and she certainly hadn't been aware of the fact that he might be having a serious affair with someone. She coldly watched as he checked his wallet for flight tickets and passport.

'Okay, I'm off. I'll see you in a couple of weeks,' he said casually as he went down the front door steps and got into the car.

A minute later it glided away in the pallid morning sunshine and Diana shut the front door, overwhelmed with relief that she would have the house to herself for a while.

After luncheon, which she had in the nursery with Miles and his nanny, she decided to go out shopping. It was when she got to Truslove and Hanson, the popular bookshop in Sloane Street, that she stopped in her tracks and stood staring into the window. In the centre was a display of a new publication and the bold design of the jacket and the name of the author made her go in, on impulse, and buy a copy.

It was a novel called *Temptations*, and it was by Marc Raven.

That evening, as soon as she'd kissed Miles goodnight, Diana curled up on the deep sofa in the drawing-room and began reading. When it grew dusky outside, Bentley came in to turn on the lights, and later he brought her supper on a tray. The grandfather clock in the hall chimed midnight and the room grew chilly, but still Diana read on. Finally, as a creaking orange dawn streaked over the domes and spires of the city, she turned the last page and slowly closed Marc's book.

She sat still for a long time, rapt in thought, feeling naked and exposed. How had Marc known? There was no way, during their brief meeting in Paris, he could have perceived the deepest secrets of her soul, and yet here she was, in black and white, a character called Helen who had all her feelings, her hang-ups, her vulnerabilities and her weaknesses. It was her story too. The tale of a beautiful young woman caught up in a disastrous marriage to a cruel and vindictive man from whom she could not escape without causing a scandal and risking social rejection.

All that day Diana went about in a state of limbo, the tiredness from a sleepless night bringing in turns feelings of light-headedness and unreality. But Marc's book had impressed her deeply, not just because it was beautifully written but because it seemed like a blueprint for her past, her present, and perhaps her future, for Helen had finally left her husband for someone else and found happiness.

Going to her desk, she wrote him a brief letter of congratulation, wondering if he'd remember who she was. He probably got thousands of letters each year but she didn't care. Not knowing where he lived, she carefully copied the address of his publishers onto the envelope and left it on the hall table for Bentley to post.

The dining-room table was set for ten. Sarah had ordered the best silver and crystal to be used and in the centre, a large bowl of yellow calla lilies echoed the gilt of the Sèvres china.

'A dinner party tonight? Oh, God!' Guy groaned. 'I'm tired after the flight, Mom, why did you have to go and fix a party for tonight?'

Sarah smiled indulgently, thankful to have him home. The quicker their last fight was forgotten, the better. She shouldn't have tried to push him and it had probably been unwise of her to try to bribe Diana with diamonds. This time she would be more careful. She wouldn't ask him the reason for his unexpected visit and she wouldn't ask him why he'd come alone. In fact she wouldn't go into the office for the next few days, nor would she even mention the existence of Kalinsky's.

'It's not a party, darling. Just a few of your old friends who are longing to see you again.'

Guy flung himself onto the sofa and frowned. 'I have to talk to you. There are important things I want to discuss.'

Sarah's heart skipped a beat. Did this mean he was actually thinking of coming back? Taking a deep breath, she said smoothly, 'Fine, honey. Would you like some coffee?'

'Thanks.' Languidly, he lit a cigarette, the smoke quickly casting a blue haze over her cream and coral drawing-room. They chatted for a few minutes, while the servant brought in coffee set on a silver tray and placed it in front of Sarah.

Guy wasted no time in getting down to business.

'I need to consolidate my position in England. Although I've been married to Diana for nearly five years, her family still don't seem to accept me. Apart from her youngest brother John, that is. I need to do something that will put me on a level with them.'

Sarah looked at the discontented line of his mouth. 'The Suttons are a boring family, why do you bother with them?' she asked.

'Because it isn't just them. They are representative of the whole social set-up. Charles and Sophie get invited to Buckingham Palace garden parties and Mary is quite close to the Queen Mother now the King's dead. All their friends are either in the House of Lords or equerries to the new Queen. I've never even got to meet royalty! I think it's a conspiracy, I think the Suttons are trying to keep me out of sight,' he added petulantly.

'Why is it so important?' Sarah asked. 'I've never even seen the royal family, except on film at the coronation last June. What does it matter, Guy? Surely money and power are more important than being part of some antiquated social system?'

He shook his head, frustrated by her lack of understanding.

'I've got to belong,' he stressed. 'I'm sick of always being an outsider. However,' his face brightened, 'I've been secretly working on a plan for a couple of years now and with any luck I'll be a part of the political scene in Britain within a few months!' He leaned back triumphantly and regarded Sarah.

She looked at him blankly. 'How do you mean? What are you going to do?'

'Well,' Guy leaned forward again, savouring the moment with relish. 'Some time ago I made friends with someone called Reginald Bulmer. He's an old man and he's been Conservative Member of Parliament for a county, not far from London, called Wessex East. He's retiring due to ill health in a few months and I have been chosen as a candidate by the local selection committee to stand in his place at the coming by-election!'

'You've . . .! But why?' Sarah gasped, appalled.

'I've just explained why, Mom. Don't you see what it means? And I've got an excellent chance of winning. Wessex East is a very safe Conservative seat and the selection committee were very impressed with me.'

'But you don't know anything about politics!'

Guy gave a snort of irritation. 'Neither do half the people in the House of Commons! All I have to do is agree with all their policies. I studied their last manifesto, the one they issued just before the last general election, and I memorised it until I knew it by heart! It was no sweat. I had to spend a weekend in Hastings, with seven other possible candidates, being grilled night and day by the selection committee, and I got through with flying colours! After all, Sir Winston Churchill had an American mother and a British father, and look at him now!' Guy's shoulders moved with a swaggering gesture, while Sarah stared at him, bereft of words.

'You seem to have gone into this pretty thoroughly,' she said at last. 'What does Diana think of the idea?'

'I haven't told her about it yet,' he said breezily. 'There's only one snag. I more or less told them I was buying a house in Wessex East. It's important to live in the constituency, to look after local matters and be available to the people who voted for me,' he added with a touch of defiance.

'But you have a house in London, and that's where Parliament is. Why do you have to buy another house?' She was feeling quite ill with shock and the dawning realisation that if he went ahead with this crazy plan, he'd never come home.

Guy spun round and looked at her with fury. 'For God's sake,' he snapped. 'If I'm supposed to be representing the people of Wessex East in Parliament, I'm going to have to bloody well live in their county! It would look awful if I never even went near the place! I've found the house I want. It's a Georgian mansion called Wilmington Hall, with two hundred acres of land, a lake, woods, everything.'

This is the bottom line, thought Sarah. Somehow I've got to prevent this happening. If ever she needed to use her powers of persuasion, it was right now.

'You could have a brilliant political career, darling, I think it's a very good idea,' she said. 'You've got a lot to offer and you're handsome. That's always a vote catcher. I'm sure you could be really successful.' She watched as her words flowed over him; it was like watching a cat being stroked. Then she clapped her hands, as if suddenly inspired. 'Why don't you go into politics here? We could sure do with a few bright young representatives for the Democratic party. Listen, I've got dozens of contacts, I know a lot of senators, I could find out exactly how you could . . .'

Guy turned red with anger. 'Mom!' he exploded. 'Will you never understand that I don't want to live here? I want a high position in Great Britain. Do you realise that as a Member of Parliament I'd be fêted everywhere? I'd get to know the Prime Minister, all the top people who run the country, and get to go to Buckingham Palace! It's a different world over there, you know.'

Sarah sat still and silent, disappointment washing over her in drenching waves. She had lost her beloved son, not only to a wife and another country thousands of miles away, but to a social system she thought both old-fashioned and foolish. And there was nothing she could do except hope she could make him feel guilty at deserting her and Kalinsky's. To stop him now was going to be impossible.

'I see,' she said slowly. 'You've made up your mind. What more is there to discuss?'

'Buying Wilmington Hall. Doing it up. Furnishing it with antiques. I need at least four million dollars, Mom.'

The voice on the other end of the 'phone was instantly recognisable. Rich, warm and vibrant. Diana felt her heart thud as she pressed the receiver to her ear.

'It was really nice of you to write,' Marc Raven was saying. 'I'm over here to promote *Temptations* and I got your letter this morning. Can we meet?'

'Yes . . . yes, of course. Why don't you come for drinks?'

'Great. This evening okay? Around six-thirty?'

'That would be fine.' When Diana replaced the 'phone she found she was shaking. Recollections of his penetrating eyes, his broad muscular shoulders and the way his words seemed coated in rich honey, came back to her.

He arrived at her house on time, just as the grandfather clock was chiming the half hour. Bentley showed him into the drawing-room where

Diana waited, her blonde hair cascading about her face, her dark green velvet suit emphasising her slender figure. He had an impression of clear blue eyes, a warm smile and a scorching blaze of emeralds. Spoils, no doubt, from Kalinsky's. She offered him a drink and he chose whisky, neat. Then she sat on the sofa opposite him, sipping champagne.

'I really loved your new book,' she said with sincerity.

'I'm glad.'

He obviously didn't want to talk about himself. Gradually he began to draw her out, surprised that she now had a small son, glad also that Guy was away. By the end of an hour they were talking as if they had known each other all their lives.

'How are you fixed this evening?' Marc asked suddenly.

For a second Diana paused, then she smiled. 'I'm not doing anything.'

'Then let me take you out to dinner. I know an excellent little French restaurant in Chelsea. I discovered it on my last visit and it's the only place I know, outside Paris, where you can get *cassoulet Languedocien au confit d'oie*, done the proper way.'

'That sounds lovely, I love goose,' she replied, laughing.

Together they left the house and Marc hailed a passing cab at the end of the street. The restaurant turned out to be intimate and candlelit, and as they were shown to a table in a discreet alcove Diana experienced a sense of adventure. It had been a long time since she'd last seen Marc, but she'd often dreamed about meeting him like this and her pulses were thumping.

Marc ordered for them both and selected a fine bottle of Mouton Cadet. He was attentive and seemed interested in everything she had to say and, without realising it, Diana found herself talking to him as she had never talked to anyone else. She told him about her childhood and the death of her father; she talked about her family and her marriage to Guy, and about how much she loved Miles.

'I'm very like your character Helen, in *Temptations*,' she said at last, with a self-deprecating little laugh.

'You mean you don't rate yourself very highly?' Marc asked bluntly.

Diana flushed, taken aback. 'Oh, well, I don't know. I hadn't really thought about it like that.'

'For some reason, perhaps to do with losing your father, you seem prepared to settle for what you can get when it comes to a man,' he said earnestly. 'You don't have to tell me you're unhappily married. I spotted it right away. I think you have a father complex.' Marc spoke so seriously she felt inclined to burst out laughing. What was this? Extra-curricular analysis?

'You miss your father so much, you're searching for him in your relationship with your husband. Longing for the same unconditional love and approval that, in fact, only a father can ever give,' he continued.

'You're making something simple sound most

awfully complicated!' she said. 'I fell in love with Guy when we met, he fell in love with me, and so we got married. Simple as that! Lots of marriages don't work out the way they're planned.'

Marc sipped his wine thoughtfully. 'Agreed. The point is, you were eighteen at the time. Why didn't you wait a bit, see if you met someone else? A beautiful woman like you doesn't have to marry the first man who asks her.'

'I loved him,' she replied, realising she was talking in the past tense. 'Anyway, marriage has to be forever!'

'Does it?' His eyes bored into hers, searching out her secrets, challenging her to be honest with herself.

'Of course. No one in our family has ever been divorced. It would be looked upon as a disgrace. The family would be really upset.'

'But you say your family never approved of Guy. Are you sure you're not just afraid to admit they were right about him all along?'

The arrow reached its mark. He was making her see things she didn't want to see. 'Guy can be very kind and generous,' she said, 'And he loves Miles. Nothing is perfect in this world, Marc, and I'd be stupid to believe otherwise.'

Marc's smile was tender. 'You're right of course, and there's nothing stupid about you. You're the most beautiful and fascinating woman I've ever met. Your beauty you must already be aware of, but do you know why you're fascinating?'

She shook her head.

'To me, as a writer, you're like a tale that hasn't yet been written; a lovely blank sheet of paper that demands to be filled with a story that has depths and unexpected facets, a mystery to be solved.'

Something stirred deep in Diana, a strange feeling that here was a man who could make that story unfold and lead her to parts of herself that were buried so deep she could barely imagine what they were like.

As the evening progressed they talked about other things, poetry and music and art, but every now and again he would bring the conversation back to her, subtly making her realise that there were areas of life into which she'd never ventured.

It was only when she asked him about himself that he clammed up. By the end of the evening she only knew the bare framework of his life. Yes, he'd been born and brought up in New York. Yes, his first book had been *Unholy Spectre* and yes, he was married to Carlotta and they had a small son called Carlos. Diana concluded he must live a very jet-set life, with his flat in New York, houses in the Catskills and Hollywood, and a yacht called the *Sania*, which was at present moored at St Tropez on the Riviera. But there were no personal anecdotes and nothing to help her understand him as a man.

At last they left the restaurant and he dropped her off at Eaton Terrace on his way back to the Dorchester.

'Can I see you tomorrow? Lunch, perhaps?' he

asked, standing close to her as she opened her front door.

Diana didn't hesitate. 'Tomorrow would be perfect.'

Luncheon the next day, at the fashionable Mirabelle in Mayfair, extended to a stroll up Curzon Street and then a short walk in Hyde Park where the sun shone merrily on the dancing leaves and the breeze whipped up a healthy glow in Diana's cheeks. Once he caught her hand and held it for a minute and the strength in his fingers sent an unexpected tremor through her. Another time he placed his hand in the small of her back and she felt as if her legs were melting. Strange thoughts were stampeding through her head, driving her on to she knew not where. They were impossible to resist, and so was he.

When Marc suggested they go back to the Dorchester for tea, she agreed. A wonderful feeling of euphoria was sweeping her along like a roller coaster now and she couldn't remember when she'd last felt so happy.

His hotel suite was a typical mixture of contrived good taste and impersonal furnishings, except for a pile of books and papers. He called room service and ordered tea, and they sat on the sofa and talked, but more disjointedly now, as if their minds were on something else. The flow of their previously easy conversation became stilted, almost self-conscious and awkward, and Diana found she was stammering.

At last Marc stretched out his hand and, taking hers, held it tightly and firmly.

'Diana,' he said softly.

She looked into his eyes, almost fearfully, but what she saw in them was everything she had ever wanted from Guy.

'Diana,' Marc repeated, and then he leaned forward and kissed the soft and tender mouth he'd remembered from their first meeting in Paris. 'Oh, my darling,' he whispered, and his rich deep voice was filled with despair and longing. 'I want you more than anything else on earth.'

Diana felt Marc's kiss, gentle at first and then increasingly passionate as she slid into his arms. Then his tongue was searching for hers, locking them together with such intensity that she felt as if he were overflowing with molten heat. The pressure of his mouth and the weight of his body were irresistible, his hands, stroking her tenderly, not to be denied. She lay in his arms submissively, trusting him, responding to him, as inside she became suffused with swelling desire.

Slowly and carefully Marc undressed her, willing himself to go slowly, fighting against the building up of forces that would soon become uncontrollable.

At last she lay before him, pale and delicate, her rose-tipped breasts hard and erect, the gentle movements of her hips telling him her desire was becoming as great as his. Carrying her to his king-size bed, he laid her on the satin cover and kneeling beside her flicked his tongue over first one nipple and then the other, before tracing a fiery trail down across her stomach, tasting the sweetness of her flesh, smelling the perfume of her skin.

He heard her moan softly as she reached up and put her arms around his neck, her blonde hair fanning out on the pillow, her mouth half open and moist. He heard her murmur his name.

Swiftly he ripped off his clothes and lowering himself onto her, covered her face and neck with lingering kisses as she arched her back beneath him, moulding her body to his. The pressure inside him mounted with such sweet pain that he groaned aloud.

'Oh, God, Diana . . .'

In answer she wrapped her long legs around him and held him close while he probed her wetness, gently at first, and then on a rising surge, with such wild plunges that she rocked beneath him, crying out with great gasps as if she could hardly breathe. He wanted to possess this wonderful creature, to make her his, to carry her with him to such heights of ecstasy that they would both go mad. In a final frenzy of passion he gave the deepest plunge of all, throbbing and exploding inside her with a wild drenching expulsion of his juices. Then she gathered him tightly into her very being, making him a part of herself, holding him strongly and possessively so that he drowned in her.

They lay together afterwards for a long time, close and safe in each other's arms. At last Diana turned and looked into his eyes with a strange expression.

'I never knew it could be like that,' she whispered huskily.

'You've never been made love to before, my darling.'

'But I . . .'

'You've been fucked, sweetheart. There's a world of difference,' he said softly.

Smiling, she pressed herself closer and knew she'd found what she'd been looking for.

A way out.

Chapter Ten

Francesca brought her fist down with a thump, making the things on her desk quiver.

'You're bloody impossible, Guy!' she stormed. 'You've the cheek of the devil! You come over here, thinking you're the future goddam Prime Minister of England, and when Mom refuses to finance your little fantasy you come to me!'

'You can afford it, Frannie. After all, you've got the job that was supposed to be mine at Kalinsky's and instead of behaving like a fishwife you should be glad! Call this payment for my getting out of your way! You always were an ambitious bitch. Well, now I'm asking to be paid for giving you the opportunity.'

Brother and sister glared at each other for a moment, then Francesca jumped up and started pacing round her office.

'You chose not to come back, remember that! And if I played dirty, you played far dirtier. At least I didn't build up Mom's hopes. All I did was get myself appointed in your place, and since I've been Vice President I've increased our profits by sixty-two per cent.' She paused, then added angrily, 'So that makes your stockholding more valuable and that means you're getting more interest from your shares. Where am I supposed to find four million dollars to give you, anyway?'

Guy glowered silently, seeing his vision of Wilmington Hall and a glittering future slipping away.

'There must be a way! Why can't I borrow from the company? For Christ's sake, Kalinsky's is worth millions!' he cried.

'Mom says excess profits are to go towards future expansion and for once we are in complete agreement.'

'Surely my being in the House of Commons would be useful to Kalinsky's? It would add prestige to the company.'

Francesca laughed incredulously. 'Guy, you're living in cloud cuckoo land. Rich Arabs and Lebanese princesses couldn't give a fuck what you do. They don't even know who you are!'

'Then what am I supposed to do?'

'Oh, stop whining and go finance your own crazy schemes,' she snapped. 'I can't help you and Mom won't. Anyway, if you have to live in – where is it? – Wessex East, you don't have to live in a mansion for God's sake. In fact you might be taken more seriously in politics if you bought a small house, one that you could afford to buy without help.'

'Don't tell me what I should do,' Guy shouted. 'You've been against me from the beginning because you've always been jealous of me. You're a scheming little bitch and you want everything for yourself.'

'Yes, and I'm prepared to work for it!' she cried hotly. 'You've always wanted everything handed you on a plate. Mom spoilt you something rotten, which wasn't your fault, but it's time you grew up now and stood on your own feet.'

'We can't all be as aggressive as you,' he said spitefully, 'you're so fucking butch.'

'Well, I'm glad one of us is!'

Guy's face flamed with fury. 'What do you mean by that?'

Francesca shrugged, knowing she'd hit where it hurt.

'I wasn't born yesterday,' she replied evenly, 'even if Diana was.'

With a muttered oath, Guy charged out of her office, slamming the door behind him so that the room rocked.

It had been the most miserable week Sarah had endured for a long time. Guy wasn't speaking to her and he and Francesca were fighting like a couple of alley cats, making the atmosphere heavy with hostility. Henry Langham was carefully avoiding getting involved just when she could do with his support, and on top of everything she felt so tired it was an effort to get up in the morning.

Brimming with self-pity, she wondered how her children could be giving her such a hard time. Francesca had always been ruthless, of course, but Guy . . . What had made him change so? Could that stupid little wife of his be behind this sudden crazy desire to get into politics and buy a mansion? Sarah nodded to herself. That had to be it. Diana had been after their money from the beginning, and now of course she wanted a house to compete

217

with her brother, and a husband in a prestigious position. It put Sarah in a deep dilemma. If she gave Guy four million dollars she was sealing her own fate; he'd never come back. On the other hand, if she continued to refuse she'd be widening the present rift between them – she even ran the risk of losing him altogether.

With uncharacteristic weakness, she locked herself in her pink marble bathroom and wept as if her heart would break.

'Could you do something for me, Guy?'

Sarah and Guy were lunching at the Colony, and her manner was subdued. She was trying to resign herself to him taking up a career in England but her disappointment ran so deep, not to mention the loss of face in front of all her directors, that she found it hard to keep her composure. He still wanted her to give him four million dollars and he was nagging her day and night about it, but she steadfastly refused. It would be like condoning his desertion.

Guy's manner was offhand. 'What is it?' He was working his way through a dish of veal stuffed with goose liver, and didn't want to be distracted.

'I've got some things I'd like you to take back to England for me. There's a necklace for a client and some stones they want in Bond Street. They won't take up much room in your hand luggage and, frankly, it's the safest way of transporting small pieces.'

'Okay,' he said with reluctance. 'I thought I'd go to Palm Beach for a week and then fly back to

England at the end of the month. Is that time enough?' He sipped his glass of Burgundy and then dabbed the corners of his mouth with the linen table-napkin.

'Yes. The necklace is for one of our most valued customers, Princess Mouna. I don't think she's in any hurry for it, so a couple of weeks or so would be fine. I'll inform the Bond Street manager you'll drop in the stones around the same time.' Sarah watched him carefully, hoping to see a spark of interest in his face, but there was none. The jewellery business had been the centre of her world for over twenty years now and she found his lack of enthusiasm incomprehensible.

'I might join you in Palm Beach,' she said suddenly with a bright forced smile. 'It would be good to get away for a few days, and goodness only knows when I will see you again. I just wish you'd brought Miles on this trip with you.'

Guy grimaced. 'He's too young and it would have meant bringing Diana and the nanny as well. This was meant to be a purely business trip, you know.'

'Is that the only reason you came to see me?'

He recognised the dangerous edge to her voice. In a minute she would be flushed and her eyes brimming. Christ, he thought in disgust, how I loathe women who cry. 'Now, don't start, Mom,' he said warningly, irritated as well by her suggestion of coming to Palm Beach with him. He wanted a break, from his mother, from Diana and Miles, but most of all from his eternal public role as a straight married man. There were parts of Palm Beach where he could be lost for days in blissful anonymity, where young men were cheap and the nights could be an endless round of drinking and fucking.

'I haven't made up my mind about going to Palm Beach yet,' he said quickly, 'So don't make any plans.'

Sarah got the message. He didn't want her there. He probably wanted to swim and sunbathe and sleep, and perhaps he wanted the odd girl on the side as well, she thought. Well, it was only natural. That was what being a young man was all about.

'I won't make any plans,' she said evenly. 'Now, if you don't mind, I must get back to the office. There is a lot of work to do.'

Guy's eyes narrowed, recognising the barbed insult directed at him. He shrugged. 'I'd let Francesca do the hard stuff if I were you. God knows, she's aggressive enough.'

Sarah didn't reply. Kalinsky's didn't belong to Francesca and never would. It was up to her to run the company, and there was still time for Guy to change his mind, especially if she denied him the money he wanted.

Guy walked briskly away from the Colony, anger and frustration pounding through his head as he covered the distance between Fifth Avenue and Central Park. Why should he pour himself into the mould his mother had created for him? For that matter, why should he be the loving husband Diana wanted, or the respectable married man society demanded? He wanted to be himself, and as he ground his teeth savagely, he wondered what was

220

so wrong with that? It wasn't even as if he was asking much of life. His family were rich, so they should give him what he asked for. It was his inheritance. He wanted to live in England, so why the hell should he live in America? He preferred men, so why should he have to pretend to be interested in women? Round and round it all went in his head, the reasons justifying his feelings and actions, the excuses for neglecting his wife and hurting his mother. After all, nobody had forced Diana to fall in love with him. The injustice of it all, the knowledge that he'd be made to feel a freak if his private desires became public, showed in the strain on his face. Right now he hated the world and all its phony hypocritical values. And he hated women. Especially those who hemmed him in with their demands, like Sarah and Diana. Most of all, he hated Francesca. She was dangerous and she knew the truth about him, of that he was now certain. He was also as certain as hell that she was not going to give him the four million dollars either.

Slowly a plan began to form in his mind that might involve him pretending to be in Palm Beach when in fact he wasn't. It was dangerous and could land him in real trouble, but he *had* to buy Wilmington Hall. He *had* to raise the money and if his family wouldn't give it to him, he'd find another way.

Diana stretched lazily, a wonderful feeling of well-being rippling through her satisfied limbs. Marc lay beside her, his strong brown hand flung carelessly across the sheet, the fingers open and

221

relaxed. She watched him as he slept, the rugged face gentle in repose, the thick black lashes resting on his cheeks. She leaned over him, her long golden hair falling forward framing her face, the softness of her breath waking him.

'Good morning, my love,' he murmured, a smile coming to his lips.

'Good morning, darling.' She traced the outline of his mouth with her finger, loving its sensuality and carved strength.

This was their third night together in his suite at the Dorchester, three nights of arousal, passion and fulfilment. A loving that was both tender and tumultuous. She had never realised it was possible to be as happy as this.

'Did you sleep well?' Marc propped himself on his elbow as his eyes took in the loveliness of her face, the long line of her neck and the curves of her small breasts.

Diana smiled and nodded gently. 'What shall we do today?'

'Have breakfast first, I'm starving!' he cried with a grin, reaching for the bedside 'phone. He ordered a full breakfast for himself and a continental breakfast for Diana.

'After breakfast I'll call home to see if Miles is all right,' Diana remarked, slipping into a dressing-gown. She'd told Bentley and the nanny she was staying with friends for a few days.

When she got through to Bentley, half an hour later, he spoke with his usual gravity.

'There is a message for you from Mr Andrews, m'lady,' he informed her.

Diana's heart gave a lurch. 'Yes?'

'I explained you were away for a few days, staying with friends, m'lady, and he asked me to tell you he will be staying in America longer than anticipated.'

'Oh!' For a moment Diana was thrown, wondering what Guy's reaction had been on being told she was away. But Bentley was correct, formal and also very discreet, so she merely asked, 'Did he say for how long, Bentley?'

'I gathered that protracted business negotiations might last another two weeks at least, m'lady.'

'Another two weeks!' Diana echoed his words, the dazzling prospect of two more weeks of freedom filling her with elation.

'Fine. Thank you.' She hung up as Marc strolled out of the bathroom, a blue towel slung low round his hips.

'Everything all right, darling?'

'Fantastic, Marc. Guy's going to be away for another two weeks! Isn't that marvellous?' She rose up on the bed, kneeling, her face flushed and her hair tousled.

With a leap, Marc jumped onto the bed, rolling her over, laughing as he tickled her.

'That's marvellous!' he cried. 'I've got you all to myself now.' Playfully he grabbed her ankles and, as she shrieked with laughter, blew hot breath on her toes as she wriggled beneath him.

'Stop! Oh, stop!' she giggled, 'I can't bear . . . Marc!' His breath was fanning her legs now, coming higher. She slid her hands round his body and started tickling his ribs.

'Dreadful woman!' he said, grabbing a pillow and pretending to smother her. 'I'll teach you to tickle me!'

Together they frolicked around the large bed like a couple of children until Marc suddenly turned serious as he seized her, his mouth clamped over hers, and swiftly and skilfully pinned her under him, entering her powerfully, filling her with himself until her giggles turned to shuddering gasps of pleasure. With gathering momentum, their bodies became locked in thrashing unison, until the room was filled with their cries, as she drew the last drop of his juices from him.

When it was over, she was sobbing, her face awash with tears, her mouth trembling, shattered by the intensity of her own emotion.

Marc held her tenderly, cradling her in his arms, as if she were a child. 'God, I love you, Diana,' he said huskily.

She clung to him. 'I love you too, you'll never know how much.'

They lay together for a long time, utterly at peace, completely content. Then Marc stirred, his face alight.

'I've had the most marvellous idea,' he said. 'The *Sania* is moored at St Tropez, why don't we fly down to the South of France and spend a week cruising around?'

'Could we?'

'No problem. I've got one more magazine interview this afternoon and then I'm free.'

'What about . . .?' She couldn't bring herself to mention his wife.

Marc grimaced. 'Carlotta? Oh, damn Carlotta.' He suddenly looked ugly with anger and bitterness. 'Carlotta can go fuck herself for all I care. But I'll put a call through to New York and tell her I've got more work to do over here.' Springing out of bed, he reached for his navy blue towelling dressing-gown and grabbed the 'phone. 'I'll also put a call through to the captain to tell him we're coming and I'll book our flights for late this afternoon. By tonight, darling, we'll be floating under the Mediterranean stars.'

Chapter Eleven

Francesca ordered the car to drop her off on Seventh Avenue and 28th Street. 'I'll walk the rest of the way,' she said to the chauffeur.

For security reasons she never took the limousine right up to the door. The fewer people who knew where the workrooms were the better, because that was where millions of dollars' worth of stones were made up into jewellery by a staff of skilled designers, craftsmen and apprentices. She walked quickly and purposefully, her elegant cream suit covered by an inconspicuous raincoat. In her hand she carried a brown paper bag. To the casual observer it might have contained a pound of apples. It held, in fact, ten perfect square-cut emeralds worth two million dollars, wrapped in a silk scarf. As she approached the dilapidated building which also housed a fur manufacturer, a leather goods machine factory and a debt collecting company, she glanced up and down the street. Reassured that she had not been followed, Francesca entered the building and got into the rickety old lift. With a shudder it creaked into action, taking her to the fifteenth floor. When she got out she turned left and walked down a short corridor at the end of which was a heavy metal

door which bore no name sign. Pressing the buzzer
of the intercom, she waited until a man's voice
crackled over the loudspeaker.

'Yes?'

'Orange-pineapple-melon.'

The password for the outer door was changed
every week.

'Come in,' rasped the disembodied voice.

The door erupted into a series of buzzing noises
and she pushed it slowly open. An inner door faced
her, equally heavy and unmarked.

'Virgo-Leo-Aries.'

The password for the month. Experience had
taught them they couldn't be too careful. Only
three months ago Goldblum's had suffered heavy
losses from their workrooms when a gang had
rented offices in the next building. Working over a
weekend, they had drilled through the wall, carefully disguising the hole by plastering a strip of
matching wallpaper over it in Goldblum's foyer.
When the staff arrived on Monday morning, the
robbers pounced through the wallpaper, trussing
up everyone and demanding the combination of
the safe at gunpoint. Five million dollars' worth of
diamonds and sapphires had been stolen.

The inner door was opened and Francesca
stepped into the large workroom, beyond which
were other smaller rooms for polishing and buffing
the metals, first with sandpaper buff sticks and
then with calico or fine cotton mops, using tripoli
wax and rouge compound. Francesca usually tried
to avoid going in there because the smell of
ammonia and detergent, used for cleaning dirty
metals, made her eyes sting.

228

Her favourite place was the workroom itself where eight craftsmen shared thick round wooden benches in which half circles had been cut out to form a niche in which they sat. Leather 'aprons' nailed to the half circle caught fine metal droppings as the gold and platinum was skilfully shaped and soldered with old-fashioned gas jets. Francesca found the atmosphere of this room fascinating; it was the real throbbing heart of Kalinsky's, where a design on a sheet of art paper became transformed into the actual thing. She glanced around her now, interested to see what was going on. Dave, their master craftsman who had been with them for eleven years, the first four and a half of which he'd been an apprentice, was completing work on a pair of cuff-links and four shirt studs. They were square, made of platinum, each set with nine rubies the colour of pigeon's blood, in a symmetrical design. Dave was using a fine handsaw to cut the gold for the actual links.

'Good morning,' Francesca greeted him. 'Those look wonderful,' she marvelled, in genuine admiration. They were a special order for a Texan oil millionaire who had also commissioned Kalinsky's to make him identical sets in rubies and also in emeralds.

'Thanks, Miss Andrews,' Dave beamed, hardly looking up from his intricate work. Round the other side of the brightly lit bench, Hank, another long-time employee, was drilling holes through pearls by hand. There were fifty-six to do and, using a bow drill, it was going to take him a long time.

'Isn't it amazing,' exclaimed Francesca, 'in this day and age, methods of making jewellery haven't changed in the last two hundred years, and are unlikely to change for about another two hundred years!'

'We have got an electric drill,' laughed the workroom manager who was hovering by her side, 'but we only use it for inferior or cultured pearls.'

Francesca nodded in agreement. Every single piece of jewellery that Kalinsky produced was of the highest standard of workmanship. She edged eagerly down the room, the smell of hot charcoal blocks, gas jets and melting gold filling her senses, until she came to Serge.

He looked up at her. 'Hi, darling. How do you like this?'

In his hands lay an eighteen carat gold collar inspired by an ancient Olympic wreath. He had fashioned oak leaves entwined with acorns made of pale milky opals and pearls. The necklace could have been made two thousand years ago and yet it was futuristic in concept.

'I've only got to do the clasp and then it's finished,' he said.

Francesca looked down at him, thrilled.

'It's fantastic!' she enthused. 'Actually I've come in to check on the necklace we're making for an Arab princess. I've brought along the emeralds for it,' she rattled the brown paper bag. 'And I wanted to see you, of course.'

'Couldn't you wait until tonight?' he chided jokingly in a whisper, so the others wouldn't hear.

Francesca gave him the faintest wink. 'Tonight

never comes soon enough,' she whispered back.

His eyes met hers and held them in a moment of intimacy, then she smiled. Serge had been living with her for over two years now and it had made all the difference to her life. For the first time ever she felt secure, confident in his love. There was only one thing that cast an uneasy shadow over her happiness. He wanted them to get married and she wanted to retain that final independence that had always meant so much to her. Marriage would alter that feeling of freedom which ultimately allowed her to do her own thing, and marriage would inevitably mean having to have children. Right now, she didn't want either. There was still so much to do if Kalinsky's was to become a major international company and now that she was Vice President she wanted to be the one to do it. Ambition was spurring her on, challenging her to reach greater heights and, in spite of Serge's pleas, she remained adamant. She wanted things to stay the way they were.

Once he'd said, 'But I wouldn't hold you back, Francesca.'

'I know, darling,' she'd replied and added, 'but I'd be holding myself back. Once I get married I'm sure I'd get all broody and domesticated, and that would undermine my work. Please let's just go on as we are.'

Serge had looked sad and she'd wondered why marriage meant so much to him. After all they lived together, looked after by her housekeeper, and that, as far as she was concerned, was as far as she wanted to be committed.

Handing over the emeralds to the workroom manager, she gave Serge another smile and turned to leave. Yes, she thought as she left the building and made her way back to the office, I'm right not to get married yet. However wonderful Serge is, work still comes first.

The *Sania* was moored alongside a row of yachts in the harbour at St Tropez when Diana and Marc arrived. The captain and crew greeted them with drinks and a supper of fresh lobster and quails' eggs stuffed with foie gras, set on a table on deck, before Marc showed Diana to their stateroom. Then he gave orders for them to sail at sunrise.

That night, as they lay in the silk-sheeted bunk, the waters lapping gently round the *Sania's* hull, Diana felt as if she was dreaming. She didn't want to, couldn't bear to, think about the future. Marc was married and so was she. They each had a child. But at this moment she felt so strong with Marc lying beside her, she was sure she could face the trauma of a divorce and all it entailed with her family. But what of Marc? Was he prepared to leave his wife for her? She knew so little about his private life; she didn't even know how long he'd been married. Snuggling closer to him, she forced her mind to concentrate on the present, on this glorious loving man in whose arms she now lay, his dark head resting on her breast.

Tomorrow they would set sail and she would leave behind all the unhappiness of the past few years. This would be a hedonistic holiday, the pleasures of the flesh would overrule the caution of the mind. She would swim in the clear waters, sunbathe on deck, eat all the delicacies the *Sania's* chef could conjure up and spend all her nights loving Marc. As if aware of her thoughts, he pulled her closer, wrapping his legs round hers.

'My darling,' he whispered.

'Oh Marc, Marc . . .' Her heart was dying for love of him, her body ached with yearning. 'Oh, take me darling, take me. . . .' As the moon rose cool and clear above the dark waters and the *Sania* rocked gently on its moorings, she experienced a love she had never known existed.

It was five days later when the captain came to Marc, his face flushed and his mouth tight.

'I have Mrs Raven on the ship-to-shore line, sir,' he said stiffly.

'What the . . .?' Marc looked up sharply, noticing the captain's annoyance. 'How the hell did she know where I was?' he demanded.

'I don't know, sir, except that she seemed to have heard from someone who was staying on another yacht in the harbour. If I may say so, she was extremely abusive to me.'

'Hell and damnation!' Marc, his face like thunder, strode along the deck to the radio operator's room, leaving Diana sitting alone on deck.

He was back in five minutes, his black eyes sparkling dangerously, his hands shaking with rage.

'She's found out I've got someone on board,' he said without preamble, 'and she says she's catching the next plane to Nice. She'll be here by tomorrow morning.'

Diana sprang to her feet, alarmed. 'What shall we do?'

He turned away and leaned on the rails, silently looking at the distant coastline of France.

'Marc! What shall we do?'

'Jesus Christ, that bitch will be the death of me,' he growled fiercely. 'I'd give anything to be rid of her. It's you I love, Diana. I wanted us to be together forever, sharing our lives, but now . . .' His voice drifted off in despair.

'Why can't we be? I'm prepared to leave Guy for you, why can't you leave her for me?' Her blue eyes, bewildered with shock, looked searchingly into his.

He shook his head slowly, like a lion in pain. 'There are things about my marriage I've never told you . . . or anyone. Reasons why I can't leave Carlotta, why I'm bound to her hand and foot. Oh, Christ!' He spun round and kicked one of the deck chairs with such savage force that it went slithering up against the rails. Then he took Diana into his arms and held her close. There were tears in his eyes.

'I can't bear to hurt you like this, darling. You've been through enough already with that husband of yours and I really hoped we could always be a part of each other.'

'I don't understand, Marc.' She was trembling now, seeing her happiness shattered, her dreams disintegrating. 'We love each other! All she could do is sue you for divorce.'

'She could do much worse than that. Much, much worse.'

'How? What could she do?'

Marc stiffened, and his face became grim. 'We'll have to sail for the mainland right away,' he said, ignoring her question. 'We should be in port by six o'clock this evening. I'll have to get you on a plane at Nice tonight. For your own sake, I want you away from here before she arrives.' He pushed her gently away and went to find the captain. A black rage scorched through his brain, and all the while he was thinking, *God damn Carlotta, God damn the hold she has over me, and God damn her for screwing up my life for the second time.*

There was so little time to say goodbye. Diana, in shock, watched one of the stewards as he packed her cases, her stomach tied up in the old familiar knot of nerves. Marc was angry and agitated by turns, snapping at the crew, his rugged face set in deep lines of unhappiness. As they neared St Tropez, Diana stood on deck with him, the impact of what had happened just beginning to sink in. She saw a commotion on the quay side and several flash bulbs going off.

'That can't be . . .?' she cried in alarm.

'No. It's some starlet going shopping,' he replied, morosely.

'When will I see you again, Marc?' she asked in a quiet voice.

There was a long silence before he replied. 'God knows, but I'll find a way.' He turned agonised eyes to her. 'But will that be enough for you, my darling? It doesn't seem fair to you, but I'm afraid it's all I have to offer.'

'Oh, Marc.' Diana took his hand in hers and held

235

it tightly. 'I love you. Please don't let's say goodbye – I couldn't bear it, darling. We must be able to see each other again, surely?'

Marc took her in his arms and held her as if he could never let her go.

'Somehow, I promise, we'll be together again. I don't know exactly when . . .' his voice caught.

'I'll be waiting, darling,' she whispered through her tears.

As soon as the *Sania* was moored, they rushed down the gangplank and into a waiting car, running unnecessarily as if that would help ease the pain.

The journey to Nice airport took two hours and as they followed the coastal road the setting sun cast flickering golden lights on to their faces. They drove through avenues of trees, barely speaking, but Diana kept her hand on Marc's knee and from time to time he clasped it with his. And yet there were a thousand things that should be said, she thought. The trouble was, neither could find the words.

It was all bustle at Nice airport; people departing and people arriving, trundling trolleys loaded with luggage, babies in push chairs and running toddlers. Officials wandered about looking suspiciously at everyone and long lines of people waited to check in. Above it all a hollow voice, from the loud speakers, made announcements in spectral tones. Marc fixed everything for her and before she had time to get her bearings, he was gently guiding her to the departure gate.

A wild voice inside her wanted to cry out at the

injustice of their being torn apart like this, but it was caught inside her like a captive bird, struggling to find expression, and all she could manage was a strangled sob.

Marc took her in his arms.

Something inside her was choking her, robbing her of breath.

He kissed her gently and with a lovingness that was killing her slowly.

'Goodbye, my darling.' The words were wrenched from him.

Mute and blinded by tears, she looked back at him. There weren't words for a time like this.

'Why can't I collect this Arab princess's necklace from your office, and the loose diamonds at the same time?' demanded Guy. 'Or I could pick them up from Mom? I'll be going to the office to say goodbye to her, in any case, on my way to the airport.'

'Because we have a foolproof system for bringing jewellery from the workrooms straight over to the showroom, down below, where it is checked in,' said Francesca curtly. 'On the ninth and tenth floor we don't have the security for that amount of stuff. Why are you being so difficult?'

'Why should I bother myself with all those assistants in the showroom, when it would be much easier to pick it up from you?' he insisted.

'Okay, okay. Have it your own way. God, you're so lazy. And whatever happens, don't leave your hand luggage lying around. Everything's insured, but the Princess will be waiting for her necklace and it would be terribly embarrassing if it got stolen.'

'What kind of fool do you take me for?' he stormed. 'It's damned kind of me to go to all this trouble anyway.'

They were having drinks in Sarah's apartment, waiting for her to join them. It was Guy's last night in the States and she'd insisted on having a farewell dinner.

As far as Francesca was concerned the sooner Guy went back to England, the better. His brooding manner was beginning to undermine her and Sarah was looking more haggard by the day. He'd been spending a lot of time at head office, snooping around whenever Sarah was out, going through her papers. Just what the hell is he looking for? Francesca wondered.

'I'm practically getting armed guards to keep an eye on these,' Henry had said one morning, tapping a pile of ledgers on his desk. 'In fact, I've arranged with the company bank to keep them in their vault for the time being.'

'Sales ledgers? What on earth for?' asked Francesca. 'They're of no interest to anyone except the Accounts Department, and there are easier ways of finding out how much we make than ploughing through a lot of ledgers.'

'If these ledgers were ever to fall into the wrong hands and become public knowledge it could bring disaster to kings and emperors, sultans, princes and several presidents, not to mention some of the richest businessmen in the land,' he said, with a touch of pomposity.

Francesca gave a shriek of laughter. 'Uncle Henry, don't be so absurdly dramatic! It would be very indiscreet of us to let these become public knowledge, I grant you, but how could it hurt anyone?'

'These don't only contain a record of each item of jewellery sold and how much it cost. They also have the name of the person who purchased the item, and the person for whom it was intended. Get it?'

Her face was a study of amazement. 'You mean if a married man comes into Kalinsky's and buys something for his mistress you find out who she is?'

'Most of the time it's unavoidable. The recipient may come in to choose the designs, be fitted for a necklace or ring, and sometimes we've had to deliver it personally.'

'I never knew any of this! Why didn't you tell me?'

'I would have done in time. It's one of the things your mother insists is kept secret. You'd be surprised at some of the names in these books.' He flipped through the pages. 'Two presidents in the past ten years, an enormous number of senators, judges, people in high places and some company chairmen you probably know. And that's just in the United States! You should see the documentation from our European branches. Half the titled nobility seem to keep women on the side and there are one or two dukes who are extremely generous. We have the listings of all the jewellery the Duke of Windsor bought for Mrs Ernest Simpson, over twenty years ago, when he was still King Edward VIII. Now if that had become known before he abdicated, it would have toppled the throne of England.'

'My God. I had no idea. What happens if there is a mix-up, and the wife gets the jewellery by mistake?'

Henry chuckled. 'That happened once, here on Fifth Avenue. The wife of a well-known man came into the shop and as soon as the assistant, who was new, heard her name he said, "Oh, the piece of jewellery your husband has ordered for you is ready." '

'What happened?'

'We had to let her have it, and then get on to the husband to tell him what had happened. The poor sod had to pretend he'd meant it as a surprise for her.'

'Wasn't he angry?' Francesca leaned forward, intrigued.

'That's an understatement, but this is where your mother has always been very clever in creating good will. She instructed the showrooms to let him choose another piece of jewellery, with our compliments, for his girlfriend. Of course it worked. He's been one of our best customers ever since.'

'No wonder you're keeping those ledgers under lock and key. Anyone unscrupulous could have a black-mailing bonanza with all that information,' she said thoughtfully.

'Exactly.' A worried frown flickered over Henry's brow. 'I only hope I'm not too late. I only thought about getting them out of here and locking them away last night.'

Neither had mentioned Guy by name, but they each knew what the other was thinking.

The long shadows crept with stealthy fingers across the well-kept lawns and already a pale challenging moon hung above the trees, ready to claim the night.

Diana sat in the window of her old bedroom at Stanton Court, absently watching the peacocks strut below. A week had gone by since her hasty return from France, a week in which she'd been grateful that her family had asked no questions. Down the corridor Miles and his nanny were sharing the nursery wing with Charles and Sophie's new baby, Philip.

Guy, thank God, was still in America. It was enough to have to cope with the deep sense of loss she felt, without having Guy snapping round her heels like a bad-tempered dog. Since she'd said goodbye to Marc she'd hardly slept and deep shadows dug into the skin under her eyes. All she could keep asking herself was when would she see him again? The memory of his face and his voice ground deep into her mind, torturing her at night as her body cried out for his. But she did not try to suppress her memories; by going over their time together, again and again, she could keep him alive within her. Each day she hoped the 'phone would ring, but all that happened was she picked up a copy of the *Daily Mail* one morning and read that Marc Raven was cruising around the Greek islands with his beautiful wife, Carlotta, and his son, Carlos.

At that moment there was a tap on her bedroom door and Sophie slipped into the room, her face as cheerful as ever.

'I've just had Francesca on the telephone,' she said, coming to join Diana on the chintz window seat. 'She was trying to contact Guy and she thought she might find him here.'

Diana regarded her with apathy. 'But he's still in America.'

'He left New York four days ago. Francesca says he was supposed to fly direct to London, but she's called your house and Bentley said he had no idea when Guy was returning.'

'I don't know where he is. What does she want with him?'

'Apparently he was bringing some jewellery back from the States and the Bond Street branch are panicking because they haven't received it.'

'I don't have to speak to Francesca, do I?' asked Diana. 'There's nothing I can tell her.'

'Don't worry. I've dealt with it all. Like to come for a walk? It's a nice evening.' Sophie got briskly to her feet.

'I don't think so, thank you. I thought I'd go and play with Miles before he goes to sleep. Is Mummy coming over for dinner this evening?'

'Yes. John's off somewhere though. An art exhibition in Oxford, I think. See you later then, darling.' Sophie pecked her on the cheek. Something was obviously wrong with Diana and she was longing to ask what it was, but her sister-in-law's dignified manner forbade questions.

A thousand miles away the *Sania* cut through the waters like a razor through whipped egg-white. A storm was getting up and the foaming sea churned around the bows, spuming over the deck and rocking the yacht as it sliced its way from the coast of Greece and out to sea.

Marc and Carlotta sat in the stateroom, glaring at each other. She had been on board for a week now, fizzling with fury and demanding to know what had been going on. She had brought Carlos with her.

Marc shrugged, refusing to talk.

'So who was she?' demanded Carlotta shrilly. 'How dare you have a woman on board the minute my back is turned?'

'She was a friend,' he said dully, 'so mind your own business! You don't own me, you know.'

'Oh, no?' She arched her fine black brows sardonically. 'I can ruin you any day I want to, Marc, so don't you forget *that*! I have told you before I will not tolerate you having women, especially on board, where the crew know what's going on. It is humiliating for me. Now, what was her name?'

'There's no good your going on about it,' said Marc. 'She was a friend and I've no intention of telling you her name, because I know what you're like. The minute you find out you'll make life hell for her, and that's the last thing she needs.'

Her scarlet mouth snapped closed for a moment, while she gathered another burst of energy before launching another salvo. 'You can't treat me like this!' she stormed. 'You are a pig! A dirty rotten pig! I don't care what you say, I'll find out who this bitch is and I'll make her pay!' The stateroom door slammed and he found himself alone.

The *Sania* began vibrating and bucking as the wind whipped up the sea and the violence matched Marc's mood. Another day, cooped up with Carlotta, would drive him crazy. He buzzed the captain on the intercom.

'Let's get the hell out of this,' he cried. 'Make for the nearest port. I'm flying home.'

A minute later Carlotta walked in, her mouth tight with anger.

'What the hell do you want to go home for?' she cried. 'I have only just arrived! This silly storm will soon pass! This is a good opportunity to start your next book.'

'I might as well be miserable in New York as here!' he yelled back at her. 'And fuck my next book! I've sacrificed enough in my life to be a fucking writer! I've had it.'

'But I want to sail to Marbella. I want to visit my family! And I want to find out the name of the woman you had on board!' she screeched.

'You can do as you fucking well like! I'm going home,' Marc yelled back.

Francesca faced her mother across the antique desk in Sarah's office, her face pale with worry.

'Then where the hell is he?' she demanded. 'How dare he vanish like this with all those jewels? Even his wretched wife doesn't know where he is!'

'You're being hysterical, Francesca.' Sarah's voice was cool. 'Guy has probably just stopped off somewhere on his way back to London.'

'Such as in the middle of the Atlantic?' Francesca couldn't keep the sarcasm out of her voice. 'Really, Mom! It's irresponsible of him, to say the least, to do a disappearing act when he's got the Princess's emerald and diamond necklace with him, not to mention half a million dollars' worth of loose diamonds in his pocket.'

'If we have anything to be concerned about it's Guy's welfare. If he's safe then the jewellery is safe too. Don't get in such a panic, he'll turn up soon.' Sarah straightened the papers in front of her.

'And what do I say to the Princess if she calls and asks where her jewellery is? "Oh, I'm sorry, Your Highness, but my brother has taken it on vacation with him!" For God's sake, this is serious!' Francesca started pacing round the room, imagining the repercussions if their richest client didn't get delivery on time.

'Everything's insured, so stop being absurd. Have you set up the photographic session for the new catalogue?'

'Monday morning. Ten-thirty,' Francesca replied automatically, her mind still on Guy.

Back in her own office she buzzed Henry.

'Can I see you for a moment?'

'Sure. Come right along.'

Henry's face was thoughtful as she explained the situation to him.

'So where can he have gone, Uncle Henry?'

He shrugged. 'Paris, Rome, Munich, Antwerp, Amsterdam?' He cocked his head to one side. 'I'd put my money on Munich or Amsterdam.'

'For what reason?'

'There's a good time to be had in those capitals, I'm told, for someone of Guy's persuasion.'

Shocked, she looked at him. 'I didn't know you knew about Guy,' she said slowly. 'I'm sure Mom doesn't.'

'Then it's better to keep it that way. I knew from the time he was a small boy.'

'Really?'

'Sure. It's my bet he's stopped off to have himself a little fun on his way home. I just hope the stuff doesn't get stolen.'

'God, so do I.' Francesca looked concerned. 'It's the Princess I'm worried about. She's our best customer. I don't want anything to happen to offend her.'

Princess Mouna had been a customer of Kalinsky's for several years. The favourite daughter of Mohammed Al-Thamir, ruler of Sharifa, she had been indulged since childhood and given everything she wanted. Sharifa, a small state in the Persian Gulf, possessed a giant oil field with no less than thirteen billion barrels of proven reserves of Arab light grade crude oil. Ruled by the Al-Thamir family who lived in a mock Georgian palace on the shores which jutted out of the Arabian peninsula into the steamy shallow waters of the Persian Gulf, it formed a theocratic state, governed by the strict laws of the Quran.

Mohammed Al-Thamir himself, a stern and sadistic man, was well into his seventies and the father of thirty children. He would not tolerate modern alterations to his laws. Thieves still had their hands cut off. A mere sip of whisky earned a severe lashing. Adultery was punished by stoning to death.

Princess Mouna grew into a very beautiful young woman, full blown, dark eyed and passionate. When she became of marriageable age, following the time honoured Bedouin traditions, her father arranged for her to marry her cousin Hisham, Sharifa's Minister of Defence. The fact that he was fat, unattractive and in his sixties did not disturb Mohammed Al-Thamir at all. Hisham would provide for Mouna in a right and proper way and indulge her love of shopping. They had townhouses in London and Paris, a hunting estate in Austria, and they travelled widely. Mouna spent money like water and one of the things she loved most was jewellery.

And it was to her Mayfair house that Guy made his way. He was ushered into a large gloomy room, heavy with dark drapes and ornate furniture. A servant told him to wait and presently Princess Mouna entered, a voluptuous figure with smouldering eyes.

'Princess,' said Guy rising, 'I have brought you your necklace.'

He handed her a fine leather case, embossed on the lid with a gold K.

She glanced round the room quickly, as if to make sure they were alone, then she opened the case. On the dark-blue velvet lining lay the necklace: ten priceless emeralds and a hundred and eighty diamonds weighing a total of 39.4 carats, set in platinum.

'I expected you sooner,' she said shortly.

'I came as soon as I could.'

She gave him a darting look, closed the jewellery case with a snap, and glanced round the room again.

'All right, Princess?' Guy asked.

'All right,' she muttered. Without another word she rang for a servant and a moment later Guy was ushered out.

His next stop was Kalinsky's in Bond Street.

'Here are the stones,' he said casually, taking a flat packet out of his inner pocket, on the front of which all the details were written in tiny handwriting.

'We expected these ten days ago,' remarked the showroom's general manager, opening the packet and reaching for his loupe. Holding it to his eye, he picked up a diamond, seeing it magnified ten times. Then he examined the others. His long drawn-out breath was almost a gasp.

'Magnificent. Pure white. None of them is drawing colour.' He turned to Guy. 'That means none of them have a yellowish brownish tinge,' he added.

'I know what it means,' Guy snapped. 'Okay? Satisfied?'

'Yes, thank you, Mr Andrews.' The atmosphere in the showroom was distinctly chilly. Reverently, the manager put the stones in the safe.

A minute later Guy was in Bond Street again, hailing a taxi.

'Take me to John D. Wood in Berkeley Square.'

When he arrived he strode into the estate agent's elegant offices and went up to a young man sitting behind a cluttered desk.

'I wish to purchase Wilmington Hall, near Kelvedon, in Wessex East,' he said.

Chapter Twelve

Back at the Eaton Terrace house, Guy lost no time in making several telephone calls before Diana returned with Miles from Stanton Court later that day.

The first was to the Conservative Party headquarters in Wessex East, confirming the date when he would start canvassing for the by-election. Then he called his bank, Child and Co., in Fleet Street, asking them to reserve a safe deposit box for him.

'A large one, I have a bulky package to leave,' he added. He 'phoned his tailor in Savile Row to check if the three new dark blue pinstripe suits they were making for him were ready, then he called Lobb's in St James's to ask for a repeat order of the black lace-up shoes they always made for him. He also called Ivan's in Jermyn Street to make an appointment to have his hair cut.

Guy saved the most important call to the last, as a child saves the cherry on top of the cake. He spoke in a low voice in case any of the servants were around.

'I'm back! Can you talk? It's wonderful to hear your voice too, darling. Yes, I've missed you very much. Yes, I know, but everything's working out wonderfully well! All my plans are falling into place . . . a VERY successful trip to the States . . . Yes, it really won't be long before we can be together all the time . . . Oh, I can hardly wait either! Can I see you tonight? The usual place, about ten-thirty? I'll be there, darling.' Quietly he replaced the receiver and a smile of anticipation and pleasure spread across his face.

At dinner that night Guy and Diana faced each other over the silver-laden surface of the highly polished dining-table.

'So those are my plans,' said Guy at last. He had been talking to her throughout the first and second courses while Bentley hovered at a discreet distance. 'I want a life in politics – you've always said I should have an occupation – and a large house in the country.'

'But why politics, Guy? You've never shown any interest before. Have you the qualifications?'

Guy shrugged impatiently. 'It's no sweat. I've read up the Conservative Party manifesto and when I repeated it back to them, word for word, at the selection committee, I came out on top! With my money and position they're jolly lucky to get me, especially as Wessex East is a tinpot constituency. Of course it appealed to them when I said I was buying a house in the area . . . We shall have to entertain a lot, all the local big-wigs, you know.'

Diana did know. She and her family had many friends who were in Parliament, and it was not the easy road to automatic success that Guy seemed to presume. Something else puzzled her. She knew roughly how much money Guy received in interest from his stock in Kalinsky's and she also knew Sarah gave him a large private income, but none of it amounted to enough even to buy Wilmington Hall, pictures of which Guy had just shown her, far less furnish it.

'Isn't this all going to cost a lot?' she asked.

Guy looked at her in surprise. There'd been a time when Diana had been far too naive and innocent to question what he did.

'Mom's paying for it all,' he said airily.

'Really?' Diana looked at him doubtfully. 'I am surprised. I mean, it puts paid to your ever returning to live in America, doesn't it? That must have upset her.'

Guy waved his hand dismissively and continued to expound enthusiastically about his future while Diana found her mind wandering as she thought about her own future. Since returning from France she had become convinced she must leave him. Falling in love with Marc had changed everything and even if they had no future together, now that she knew what love was she could never settle for anything less. She'd be better off on her own, she reflected, than staying with the wrong person. But now was not the moment to walk out. There was Miles to consider, and her business. It was thriving, but she wasn't earning enough to support herself yet. She'd have to bide her time. And meanwhile here was Guy bombarding her with the details of his grandiose scheme, expecting her to support him in becoming a Member of Parliament and no doubt act as a political hostess.

'I hope you're doing the right thing, Guy,' she said slowly.

Guy flung down his damask table-napkin with a theatrical gesture. 'You all make me sick!' he exploded. 'Why does everyone always put me down?' Jumping up from the table he stormed to the door, nearly bumping into Bentley who, realising there was about to be a fight, was trying to make a quick exit himself. 'I'm not staying here to listen to your bitching. I'm going out.'

Diana finished her dinner and her glass of wine calmly. It was not the first time Guy had walked out on her and it wouldn't be the last, but then with any luck she'd be able to leave him one day soon, and it would no longer matter. She smiled to herself. Since meeting Marc, she no longer cared what Guy did or where he went.

As if by telepathy, Marc called later, when she was already in bed. His voice was as close as if he'd been in the next room.

'I'm back in New York,' he announced and he sounded cheerful. 'I couldn't stand another day of being with Carlotta, so she and Carlos are still cruising on the *Sania*. How are you, my darling?'

'I'm fine, sweetheart. It's wonderful to hear your voice again, I've missed you so much.' They talked for a few more minutes then she told him of Guy's plans, including their buying a country mansion. 'But I'm not hanging around to see the outcome,' Diana added firmly. 'I've got plans of my own.'

'Good girl. The quicker you have some independence, the better. I'm hoping to get away for a few days next week and I'm coming to England. You'll be in town, won't you?'

'I'll be here,' she promised.

They talked for a long time, forging the bonds of love and understanding, companionship and trust, that surmounted even their physical desires. It was after midnight when Marc finally said with regret, 'Diana, I'm going to have to go now. I'd like to talk to you all night, but I don't have shares in the telephone service!'

'I know, Marc. It's been wonderful being able to talk like this. I have so much to say to you and I can't wait to see you next week. Is it safe for me to call you?'

'It's fine for the moment but we'll have to be careful when Carlotta comes back.'

'When will that be?'

'Not for some time yet,' Marc replied.

He was soon to realise he'd been over-optimistic.

'Come in.' Carlotta opened her cabin door, took a quick look along the passageway to make sure no one was watching, and then ushered her visitor in, closing the door quietly behind him. He was a tall young man in his twenties who stood strictly to attention in his crisp white ducks. His pale blue eyes looked insolently at her and his blonde hair was cropped close to his Germanic head.

Carlotta strolled across to the bed, her white terry dressing-gown revealing long, slim, tanned legs. 'So you've thought about it, Ernst?' she asked.

'Ja. I've thought about it,' he replied. 'I will do as you wish.'

'Very good. You won't regret it.' Carlotta lay back against the padded headboard, her black hair fanning out around her shoulders. She stubbed out her cigarette in an onyx ashtray, beside which lay a sealed envelope containing five hundred dollars.

Ernst seated himself stiffly on the nearby chair and continued to watch her arrogantly. His large beefy hands lay loosely clasped on his knee.

'Hurry up then,' Carlotta said irritably, 'I'm waiting.'

'The name of the young woman is Lady Diana Andrews. She comes from London and she is the wife of a Mr Guy Andrews. Mr Raven brought her on board on Friday 21st . . .'

'All right, all right! I'm not interested in that part. What happened when they got on board?'

'They slept in this cabin,' he said boldly. 'They spent a lot of time in here during the day, and were together every night.'

'Did you see anything? Did you see them making love?' There was a sharp edge to her voice and her dark eyes betrayed a mixture of fear and anger.

Ernst didn't bat an eyelid. 'I heard everything,' he replied. 'That was sufficient. They were not discreet.'

'When did she leave?'

'As soon as Mr Raven heard you were flying over from the United States.'

'Would you say the relationship was a casual one? I mean, did they . . .'

'They were very much in love.'

Carlotta swiped the sealed envelope from the

bedside table and threw it at him violently. 'Get out!' she screamed. 'Get out of my sight.'

As Ernst walked down the passageway he could still hear her screams and sobs of rage.

Diana clutched the telephone, her head reeling, the full impact of what she had just heard barely sinking in.

'Are you sure?' she gasped. This wonderful, yet terrible, news was something she had not expected.

'Oh yes. The result of the pregnancy test is positive,' replied Dr Wolfson. 'I thought you'd like to know right away.'

She'd only gone to see him because she had been suffering from indigestion and heartburn. She thought the urine test was just routine. But now he was telling her she was expecting Marc's child! The enormity of it swamped coherent thought. In a daze she heard the doctor ramble on about making an appointment to see the gynaecologist who had delivered Miles, but all the time she was thinking. Guy mustn't find out yet and she must get hold of Marc at once. This would alter their whole future together.

As she said goodbye to the doctor, she did not hear the upstairs 'phone extension being quietly replaced.

The long black limousine swerved to a standstill as it drew up outside the Dakota and as soon as the chauffeur opened the passenger door, the trim figure of Carlotta shot out on to the sidewalk, dragging Carlos by the hand. Volatile looking, in a scarlet suit and matching scarlet high heeled shoes, she did not even glance at the chauffeur as she snapped, 'Bring up the luggage.'

On the fifteenth floor, Carlotta got out of the lift and strode to the door of their apartment, Carlos whimpering by her side, tired from the long flight from Madrid. Marc was in his study, as she had guessed. He was sitting at his desk checking the proofs of his latest book, and a glance at his face showed her he did not welcome her unexpected return.

'Carlotta!' he croaked, appalled.

'Yes, Marc, I'm back.' She stood before his desk, glaring down at him. 'I've been learning all about your romantic activities on board *Sania*. You didn't think you could get away with it, did you? Remember one thing, Marc, you can never leave me, because you know what will happen if you do! But if you choose to go off with someone else . . . then I shall certainly tell everyone all about you. And I shall cite this Diana what-ever-her-name-is in a divorce action!'

Her voice had risen, and Carlos, standing in the doorway, burst loudly into tears as he looked at his parents in fear. Marc's face was deep crimson and his dark eyes flashed dangerously as he bounded up from his seat behind the desk. For a second it seemed as if he were going to strike Carlotta, but as he noticed Carlos, his hand fell heavily and he thumped the desk instead.

'How dare you spy on me!' he cried. 'You don't know anything about Diana . . .'

258

'I do know that you are never going to see her again! Or would you like me to tell your little secret? What would become of Marc Raven, famous author, if I left you?' Her narrow scarlet mouth was drawn back in a sneer now, as she realised she was gaining the upper hand. They were bound together by a shameful secret that allowed him to continue writing, and gave her the riches, position and power she craved. And she knew he was no more prepared to give it up than she was.

'So? You agree not to see her again?' she demanded.

For a long moment Marc remembered the sweetness of Diana, and their days and nights on board *Sania*. For the second time in his life he was having to choose between the woman he loved and his writing, and the pain was unbearable. He shrugged.

'If I stop seeing Diana, it doesn't mean I can ever love you,' he said quietly.

'But you like me in bed and you like the life we have,' Carlotta replied grimly. 'That is all I ask, Marc. Leave Diana to me. If she tries to contact you I will soon get rid of her myself.'

When the telephone rang the next morning, Carlotta pounced on it with the silent venom of a cat after a bird. For the time being she was going to intercept all calls because she knew that sooner or later Diana would try to contact Marc. It happened at noon the following day. From the cut-glass English accent, Carlotta had no doubts who it was.

'Mr Raven is away,' she said succinctly.

There was a hesitation on the line, as if the caller wasn't sure if she was speaking to the wife or a servant. 'When will he be back?' she asked at last.

'I've no idea,' said Carlotta, and suddenly felt herself exploding. *God damn that insipid little bitch. Well, she'd got rid of Francesca. She would get rid of Diana too. All the money, the jet-set life-style, and the reflected glory of being Marc Raven's wife were going to belong to her. God knows, she worked for it.*

'And if you call my husband again, Lady Diana, or whatever you call yourself, I shall tell your husband everything! So keep away from Marc, I'm warning you!' she screeched.

It was four o'clock in the morning, when life is at its lowest ebb and the night holds a thousand mysteries. Marc walked through the rustling darkness of Central Park, looking beyond the trees at the distant skyscrapers, to where myriads of lights still twinkled in a man-made galaxy. Events of great magnitude were happening every second in the city that never sleeps but under the real galaxy above that spread speckled and pale by comparison, the events were of no greater significance than the twinkling of an eye. That is what he told himself. In a hundred years, in a thousand years, in a million years, what happened tonight would be of no importance. Everyone in this lonely city and everything that happened to them would be forgotten. The thought brought him a measure of comfort, for he had just completed the most difficult piece of writing he'd ever had to do. He could have posted the letter in the morning, but he knew that when morning came his resolution would waver and he would delay the inevitable. The letter to Diana, telling her they could never see each other again, would be on its way in a few hours, carried across the Atlantic to England by impersonal hands. Marc tried to imagine her receiving it, opening it, reading the contents that spelled out the end of their love affair, and his blood froze in an agony that was colder than the stars.

Chapter Thirteen

As soon as Diana saw the airmail letter on the breakfast table she knew with a dreadful certainty that it was all over between herself and Marc. Carlotta had obviously seen to that. She hadn't scared Diana with her threats but maybe she'd made Marc feel guilty. Diana's mouth tightened and her hands shook. She must get hold of him and tell him about the baby. It changes everything, she thought in desperation. Besides, he has a right to know.

At that moment she heard Guy's footsteps coming down the stairs. Slipping the letter into her handbag, she grabbed the rest of her mail and excused herself on the pretext that she had to do a lot of 'phoning in connection with the musical soirée she was arranging at St James's Palace in six weeks time. Guy shot her a quizzical look but said nothing. Diana hurried to the study and shut the door behind her, thankful her new secretary, Pamela, had not yet arrived.

She read Marc's letter several times, skimming it at first, then re-reading it slowly, trying to digest what he was trying to say. That it was all over between them was definite, but why? Why, Marc, oh God, why? she thought. Through a blur of tears she tried desperately to find the reason. Several times he said he loved her, truly and deeply, and that she must always remember that. He would always love her. There would never be anyone in his life like her again and it was breaking his heart to have to end their affair. Theirs had been a glorious love, the joining together of minds and souls and bodies that was rare to find. But they could never see each other again, there was nothing he could do to alter the circumstances. To make any contact in the future would bring about his ruin. He wished he could explain what it was all about but she must try and understand . . . and so on and so on. The last line read, 'If you love me as much as I love you, you will never try to see me again. Forgive me for having hurt you like this. Of all people, no one deserves this less than you. Marc.'

Diana never knew how she got through that day.

Pamela arrived and they tackled the mail which included eighty-seven applications for tickets to the concert, a meeting with the florist to decide on the decorations, the advertising to check for the souvenir gala programme, and a hysterical call from the concert pianist who was performing, demanding twenty tickets for his friends, for which he refused to pay, saying it might be a charity night but he had no money. Keeping a grip on herself, Diana worked automatically, barely aware of what she was doing, but, because this sort of thing came naturally to her, making the right decisions and saying the right things.

Pamela left at five-thirty with a cheerful 'See you tomorrow'. Slumped at her desk, exhausted, her back aching, Diana sat gazing into space for a while, searching for solutions that weren't there. The most obvious and convenient thing would be to have an abortion, though she'd no idea where to go to get one. She could expect no help from Dr Wolfson either for he would never co-operate in an illegal act that could get him thrown out of the medical profession. Then there was Guy. If he found out she was having someone else's child . . .! Her mind was reeling with jumbled thoughts, knowing an abortion was the answer, yet unable to bear the thought of destroying Marc's baby. At that moment Guy sauntered into the study, his hands in the pockets of his immaculate grey suit, his dark hair smooth and shining.

'Had a busy day?' he asked casually, as he seated himself on the sofa. 'It's a pity you have to clutter up the study with all your papers but I suppose if it keeps you amused . . .' He shrugged condescendingly, a patronising smile on his face.

Diana collected herself and straightened some of the papers in front of her. 'Yes, it's been very busy,' she said, determined to ignore his goading manner.

'I shall be out for dinner tonight.'

'Very well. I'll tell Bentley.'

Guy rose, a tall towering figure in the small cosy room. Then he walked to the door and turned to look at her.

'Why don't you have an early night,' he said. 'You look terrible. But then you always do when you're pregnant.'

* * *

'What a wonderful night it's been, hasn't it?' exclaimed Francesca, flinging herself joyfully on to her large bed, where Serge lay still fully dressed, dazed by his amazing success. Earlier in the evening Kalinsky's had invited two hundred and fifty people to a champagne reception at the Whitney museum for the private view of Serge's jewellery, shown in juxtaposition with the works of leading modern artists including Picasso, Matisse, Salvador Dali and the sculptures of Henry Moore. Brilliantly staged and lit, the jewellery had drawn gasps of wonder and sheer delight from everyone present and by the end of the evening Francesca realised Serge was a hit. They had invited the *crème de la crème* from their list of rich clients, senators and leading socialites, and some of their richest French and British clients had flown over for the occasion. By the end of the evening Francesca was besieged by wealthy women wanting to buy the pieces. The fashion editors of the glossiest magazines were also stampeding to feature Serge's jewellery in 'natural' settings to enhance its mobile quality.

'I'd like to photograph the dragonfly necklace hovering over a real lake, and as for the waterfall necklace, imagine how wonderful it would look placed in the shallows of a real waterfall!' breathed one fashion editor intensely.

Francesca thanked them all and promised to contact them the next day. Serge, bemused and pleased, stayed close to her side all evening, making her feel it was a team effort.

'It went better than I expected,' admitted Serge.

'It was fantastic!' Francesca crowed. 'Those women were *drooling* over some of the pieces! How are you going to keep up with the demand? And I tell you something else,' she propped herself up on one elbow and kicked off her shoes, 'We've got to take the exhibition to London, or at least your jewellery. Maybe we should have a fashion show. Hey, that would be good! I'd have all the models in slinky black evening dresses and make it a real gala night, with royalty and everything . . .'

Serge let out a long groan. 'Francesca, don't you ever think about anything but work?'

The words chilled her. They were like a rebuke. 'For God's sake,' she cried, 'this is just as much for your benefit as mine! Don't you want to be a success?'

'Of course. Tonight was like a dream come true, but even I'm not obsessed with work twenty-four hours a day.'

Francesca rose from the bed and went over to her dressing-table, unscrewing her diamond drop earrings. 'And you think I am?' she demanded. 'Don't you understand? Kalinsky's is important to me! My grandfather started the company, my mother has held it together for twenty years, and as Guy has no interest in running it, I want to.'

'I understand that, but for your own sake, wouldn't you like to have time to read books, or listen to music? And I'd like us to go to the theatre or opera occasionally, too.' Serge heaved himself higher up the bed and with his hands behind his head, rested against the headboard.

'I'd like that too, darling. It's just that the work

seems to keep piling up . . . and I'm so tired most evenings, but you're right. We should relax more, I suppose.' Francesca looked at him, realising he didn't fully understand her obsession with the business. For all his artistic and technical genius, he was a man who felt very strongly about a private life too. And she wasn't sure she was ready to return that all-consuming love. Being with Serge was the perfect finishing touch to an already fulfilling life; it was not an end in itself.

'The business expansion has to be stabilized before I can indulge in enjoying myself,' she said gently. 'You do see that, don't you Serge? There are great things we can achieve together, but we've got to keep at it right now.'

Serge smiled. 'Admit you love every moment of it though, sweetheart. Talk about Burmese rubies or twenty carat diamonds, and you're fucking *turned on!*'

Francesca threw back her head, laughing. 'Other things do turn me on as well, you know. Like tall, blond, blue-eyed jewellery designers!'

'I'm glad to hear it,' he said, his eyes twinkling, 'but I still think you work too hard. How about a trip, now the exhibition's opened?'

'I'm not sure . . .' her brows puckered, 'I've an awful lot of things to follow up after tonight; this is not really the moment to be going away.'

Serge rose from the bed and came to put his arms round her, holding her close, breathing the perfume of her hair, filled with love for this woman whose elusive quality drove him crazy.

'I want to be alone with you,' he whispered, 'I

want to forget about everyone and everything, except us. Kalinsky's isn't going to miss you for a few days, sweetheart. How about it?'

'I'd love to, you know I'd love to, but it will have to wait a bit,' she said reluctantly. 'You've got important commitments as well, Serge. The promotions department have set up several important radio interviews for you. Tonight has put you in the spotlight, you know.'

He pressed her close. 'I want to make you really mine.'

'I *am* yours, darling. I always will be. You know that.'

Gently, she led him back to the bed, and lay down beside him. She ran her fingers tenderly through his hair and stroked his bearded face, loving him so much, yet wishing she shared his need for total commitment between them. In her heart she knew that her dedication lay in a different direction.

The first thing Francesca did when she arrived in her office the next morning was to look at the newspapers. Exultantly, she read about last night's exhibition and she glowed with pride. Serge Buono was hailed as a genius, an artist who would revolutionise jewellery designs for ever more. It confirmed her feelings of the previous night. They must stage a fashion show in London and it must outshine every show that had gone before. It must be spectacular. They must hold it in a glamorous and exclusive place and royalty must be invited. Whatever it cost, it must be an event that would put Kalinsky's on top of the heap. The first priority was getting a member of the British royal family. Did one just write to Buckingham Palace and invite them? And when should it be held? Suddenly she had a brainwave. She'd call Diana, the very person who would be able to provide all the answers. It was ten o'clock. Three o'clock in the afternoon in London. She picked up the 'phone and asked for the international operator.

'I have a problem,' Francesca said after greeting Diana. 'I need your advice.'

Diana listened carefully. 'Francesca, you'll never get a member of the royal family to attend a commercial show. It would be helping you to advertise Kalinsky's and they never do that.'

'Hell!' cried Francesca, disappointed. 'It would have been such a coup.'

'There is a way round it, though. If you gave a gala benefit night, and chose a charity that has a royal patron, they might come.'

'Diana, you're brilliant! How do I go about finding the right charity and inviting whoever the patron is? Can you help me on this?' Francesca liked the idea. It had been good for Kalinsky's image to be seen to be a patron of the arts and now it would be even better if they sponsored a charity event. The publicity department could really go to town on that. Maybe they could even hold a raffle, and give a lovely piece of jewellery as a prize!

'I can do more than that. I can organise the whole thing for you. I've started a business as a professional event promoter and organiser, and so far I've organised several very successful functions.'

'You have?' Francesca could not keep the astonishment out of her voice. Timid little Diana, wife, mother and socialite, becoming a business woman! What the hell had prompted that? 'Well, er, that's great,' she said, confused.

'I'll send you a presentation,' continued Diana, 'outlining how I suggest it should be organised. I might be able to get you the Guildhall. I can find someone who can stage-manage the whole show, providing models, clothes and everything. We can have an invited audience and charge them for tickets, and of course a souvenir programme for which we can sell advertising space. If Kalinsky's would agree to sponsor the whole night so that all ticket and advertising money goes straight to the cause, then I will present the whole package deal to a suitable charity who, in turn, will invite a royal patron.'

'My God, Diana, can you really do all that? It sounds terrific. When should we hold it?'

'In six to seven months.' Diana sounded competent and knowledgeable and Francesca listened with growing amazement. 'The royal family make up their diaries every six months, and as they've planned all their engagements for the next few months I suggest we go for October or November, when they're back from Scotland. Leave it to me. I'm sure we can work out something.'

'Right. It all sounds great. Tell me, Diana, what made you take up this work?'

There was a long pause on the line and Francesca could sense that the question made Diana uneasy. 'I . . . I just felt the need to do something,' she said at last.

'Well, good for you,' said Francesca warmly. 'I hope you get paid for all this work?'

'Of course. I hope to make a living out of it in time.'

They talked for a few more minutes and then hung up. But for the rest of the day Francesca felt puzzled. Why should Diana want to earn her own living when she was married to a rich man, who for all his faults was at least financially generous towards her? Perhaps the marriage was breaking up and Diana was planning to leave him? And who could blame her for that, thought Francesca wryly.

Diana replaced the 'phone and let out a long deep breath.

'Everything all right?' asked Pamela brightly. She was a jolly nineteen-year-old, proud of her newly acquired shorthand and typing skills, and thrilled to be working for the beautiful but enigmatic Lady Diana.

Diana smiled and looked up from her cluttered desk. Her face was strictly controlled but her eyes looked strained. 'Everything's fine,' she said firmly. 'We're going to do a big gala night for my husband's family firm, Kalinsky's, and all the arrangements are going to have to be perfect because my sister-in-law is a high powered, super-efficient person who doesn't suffer fools gladly.'

Pamela laughed. 'Will she be bringing over loads of jewellery?'

Diana nodded seriously. 'Probably something in the range of several million dollars' worth. Make a note, Pamela, to hire top security guards for the night.'

272

Each day, from half past nine until five o'clock, Diana kept a tight grip on herself, presenting a thoroughly professional and composed face to the world. Her upbringing, which had stressed discipline and control, was coming in useful now. How often had she heard her mother say, 'You must never show your emotions in public, darling, and of course never cry in front of the servants. It embarrasses them.'

Diana was still in her study at six o'clock that evening, although Pamela had gone home. As long as she immersed herself in work, she could hold at bay the clamouring anxieties that were eating into her mind, and the longing for Marc that made her body ache. But soon it would be evening and her self-restraint would weaken as the need to keep up appearances dwindled. It was the uncertainty that was killing her. Guy had not referred to her pregnancy since that night over a week ago and he'd hardly spoken to her since. She knew him well enough to realise that he was probably planning some diabolical revenge, for there was no way the child could be his. They hadn't slept together since the birth of Miles, and she wondered what twisted, vicious scheme he was about to put into action. If he exposed the fact that she was pregnant by someone else, she would face public scandal and contempt. Her family would be deeply shocked and she would be ostracised by society. People would nudge each other and whisper and it would end her hopes of becoming a professional event organiser.

Well, I won't go grovelling to him, she thought

with sudden anger. *He's having an affair with someone, so I could turn the tables on him and ruin him.* But she knew she couldn't. There was one code of behaviour for men and another for women. He'd be looked upon as a Jack-the-lad, while she'd be regarded with scorn and condemned as a bad wife and mother. That was the way society worked. The pressure from public and the press alike would force her to leave London and seek refuge elsewhere.

At that moment Diana heard Guy's footsteps in the hall. He'd been out since early morning and now she braced herself for his return. Straightening her shoulders, she looked at him squarely when he entered the room.

'Good evening, Guy,' she said evenly.

'Hi.' He went over to the cabinet in the corner, where Diana kept the drinks since she had turned the room into an office. 'Want a drink?'

'No, thanks.'

'I've come to several decisions,' he said, a few minutes later when he'd poured himself a whisky and soda and taken the armchair facing her. His face gave nothing away. His dark eyes were impenetrable.

'I don't want any moralising, Guy,' Diana said sharply. 'I may be guilty of having had a lover, but I'm not blind . . . or deaf. I've known for some time you've got someone, too.'

'Is that so? And who am I supposed to be having an affair with, for God's sake?'

Diana shrugged. 'How should I know! It no longer matters to me.'

His eyes swept over her contemptuously. 'So I can see. So who's the father?'

'That's my business. It's all over anyway. He lives abroad so I shan't be seeing him again.'

'He *must* care a lot to abandon you and the baby.' The vindictiveness in his voice grated on her nerves. 'I wonder what he saw in you in the first place.'

Diana's face flamed and she jumped to her feet, wanting to kill him. His superior expression, and the way his mouth curled down at one corner, inflamed her so much that at this moment she wished she had the courage to strike him down.

'Don't you dare talk to me like that! Leave me alone! Get out of my life and leave me alone!' she cried, her voice choked with fury.

Guy took a cigarette out of his gold case and tapped the tip of it with maddening precision. 'I'm about to make you a very generous offer, Diana, so I advise you to shut up and listen. I intend to overlook this gross behaviour of yours and I will support you and this wretched baby providing, and I do mean providing, we appear to remain together as husband and wife. As long as you're not foolish enough to give the game away, no one need ever know. I don't need this sort of dirt in my life and neither do you.'

'It's your future in politics you're thinking about, isn't it? Not me, or the baby, or Miles,' said Diana tightly.

'Of course it is. I'm not going to let you or anyone else get in my way. You can't afford the scandal this will cause if it gets out either, so don't forget it.

And I'll make sure there is a scandal, too. I'll see you utterly disgraced if you're stupid enought to admit the truth.' Suddenly his face took on an almost savage expression and he looked ugly. 'If you stay with me your bastard will have a name and your reputation can remain intact. You really have no option.'

Diana sat for a long moment, trying to deny the truth of his words, but she couldn't. He was right. She'd have everything to lose and nothing to gain if the truth were ever to get out. She also had to think about the baby. How would the child feel, in years to come, compared to Miles who had all the privileges associated with being legitimate? Diana made a swift decision. She would go along with Guy for the time being and that would at least give the baby a name. Then she would insist on a separation, which could be carried out quietly and discreetly without any scandal. A divorce would not be necessary.

'Very well,' she said quietly. 'We will carry on as before, but I do intend to live my own life, Guy. I'm interested in the work I do now and I shall soon want to expand and take on extra staff – but don't worry,' she looked at him mockingly, 'I will not be coming to you for financial support. This is something I intend to do on my own.'

'That's up to you.' He dismissed her work as if it were of no consequence. 'I shall expect you to act as hostess, though, when I entertain politically. A Member of Parliament must appear to have a stable marriage and home.'

'Don't push me too hard, Guy,' she said angrily,

'or I might be tempted to sue you for adultery.'

He laughed harshly. 'You just try it and I'll see you damned in hell.'

Two hours later Guy left the house to go out to dinner, pleased with the way things had gone. He had Diana over a barrel, and now even if she did find out anything about him he could threaten to countersue with a vengeance. He'd have to be more careful in future though. With the by-election only weeks away he couldn't afford to have anything go wrong. He thought about some of his homosexual friends who were being blackmailed; one was even serving a prison sentence and another was awaiting trial for being caught in the act in the lavatory of a railway station. At least, in the past few years he'd been very careful.

The chauffeur dropped him in Curzon Street and he entered the Mirabelle where he was ushered to his usual table in a discreet corner.

His lover was already there, waiting for him.

Chapter Fourteen

Security was the biggest headache on the night of the Kalinsky Jewellery Gala at the Guildhall. At seven o'clock, an hour before the guests were due to arrive, an armoured vehicle drew up to the entrance and out sprang ten armed guards, heavy jewellery cases chained to their wrists. Police escorts blocked the road off for those vulnerable few seconds. Over three hundred million dollars' worth of jewellery was going to be shown that night and everyone was alert to the possibility of a major raid.

Police ringed the building at fifty yard intervals, in a half mile circle, and inside the guards stood watch over the jewellery cases. Mingling with the guests later in the evening would be twelve further security guards in dinner jackets, their eyes roaming watchfully, the revolvers in their pockets ready loaded.

At half past seven Francesca briefed the twelve models. 'You will all come straight from the changing-room and go directly to the long table hidden on one side of the stage by the screen,' she explained. 'Each piece of jewellery will be put on you, you will go out onto the catwalk and do your bit, as we rehearsed this afternoon, and then you will come straight back to this table. Is that understood? No one is to leave this area wearing the jewellery for any reason whatsoever.'

The twelve models, chosen for their height and beauty, nodded, awestruck.

'Good,' said Francesca. 'Don't let anyone waylay you, not even a photographer. Certainly not a guest. It might be a trick in order to snatch the stuff off you. Is that clear?'

The girls nodded again and giggled.

'Great. You've an hour before the show starts so check your hair and make-up, but don't put on the clothes until the last minute. And . . . good luck, everyone.'

'Thank you, Miss Andrews,' they murmured, and drifted back to the changing-room.

'How can you be sure they've handed back every bit of jewellery at the end?' whispered Diana, who'd been checking the seating plan for the three hundred guests.

From her briefcase, which was business-like in contrast with her flowing white chiffon evening dress, Francesca produced a stack of photocopies of each of the pieces of jewellery. 'It's easy,' she said smiling. 'These will be spread on the table and each piece of jewellery will be placed on top of a photocopy of itself. As each girl comes off her jewellery is instantly put back onto the photocopy. If anything's missing at the end of the show, it will be instantly obvious.'

'How simple, but very effective,' exclaimed Diana. 'I imagined each piece would have to be returned to its individual case.'

Francesca shook her head. 'That's too unreliable a method. Cases get pushed and scattered around in the scramble, there's too much rush and excitement for someone not to make a genuine mistake. This is foolproof, and I thought of it myself!' she added proudly.

'Brilliant!'

'Well, I couldn't have done what you've done tonight, Diana,' she said warmly. 'It's fantastic the way you've sold all the tickets, made all the arrangements, not to mention getting a member of the royal family along.'

'I've really enjoyed it,' said Diana, 'and because of tonight, I've been asked to organise about another ten events!'

At eight o'clock the guests were thronging the magnificent banqueting room, anticipation filling the air. At eight-thirty a blaze of lights and a fanfare of trumpets heralded the arrival of the royal guest of honour.

Backstage, doing a final check on the arrangements, Francesca crossed her fingers and looked at Serge, whose honey-blonde hair and beard had been trimmed that morning, and who stood handsome and assured in his new dinner jacket. He returned her smile and, reaching out, squeezed her hand.

The Guildhall and the presence of a royal patron was a long way from Tulsa.

'Diana, you've done a magnificent job.' Francesca hugged her impulsively. 'The evening is going so well – even Mom's pleased, so it must be good.'

Diana laughed, pleased. She had worked very hard to make the gala a success and now, as guests enjoyed a superb champagne supper following the extravaganza, she felt she could relax for the first time that day. Three hundred people had bought expensive tickets for the evening, making several thousand pounds for the charity for crippled children, and the show had gone without a hitch. Twelve models, wearing draped jersey silk dresses designed by Nina Ricci of Paris, had paraded millions of dollars' worth of jewels on the spotlit catwalk, and at the end the audience had given them a standing ovation. The historic Guildhall, in the City of London, had never seen a night like it. Diana took her seat thankfully at the top table, glad to be able to sit down for a while. She was eight months pregnant now, but her deep-crimson draped evening dress made it hardly noticeable, and she looked exquisite with a blaze of rubies and diamonds around her neck and in her ears.

Across the table, which had been placed in a prominent position, the royal guest of honour was talking to Guy and congratulating him on winning the by-election for Wessex East. Diana noticed how Guy was basking in the situation, happy at last at being an accepted member of the establishment. At least, she thought, it is making him an easier person to have to live with. He was at home less and less, and that was a great relief, but when they were forced to be together his manner was more polite and tolerant.

Sarah was sitting on Guy's other side, the proud matriarch besotted with her son and still trying to act as if he were a part of the company. The rest of the round table of twelve was composed of Diana, Francesca, Serge, Henry Langham and some dignitaries from the charity.

An orchestra played softly in the background and, looking across the candlelit table towards Diana, Francesca marvelled that her sister-in-law had made all this happen. It might be costing Kalinsky's a fortune but every penny was worth it in terms of publicity. With a royal guest and the cream of English society present, it would put Kalinsky's on a par with Van Cleef & Arpels and Cartier.

'The television people want to interview me tomorrow,' whispered Serge, squeezing her hand under the table.

'Darling, that's wonderful,' Francesca said. 'I know you're going to get an awful lot of publicity out of tonight. Your jewellery really outshone our usual range. Everyone was going wild about it, and we've had a wonderful turnout from the press.'

'But where have they all gone now?' Serge looked round the vast room. There wasn't a camera to be seen anywhere.

Francesca nudged him surreptitiously. 'They're not allowed to take pictures while a member of the royal family is eating,' she whispered.

Serge threw back his head and guffawed, his trim beard jutting forward. 'Unlike animals in the zoo!' he laughed. 'Is that what Diana said?'

Francesca nodded, smiling. 'If you want to know anything about etiquette, just ask Diana.'

Diana, hearing her name mentioned, turned and smiled at them. 'Everything all right?'

'Great,' said Serge. 'It must have been very hard work, setting this all up and getting all these people here tonight. You're not just a pretty face, are you, Diana?'

Diana gave him a direct look. 'Not any more,' she said quietly. Then she caught Francesca's eye and for the first time felt a bond of understanding between them. She smiled and Francesca replied with the briefest of winks. Neither said anything. Neither needed to.

Suddenly Francesca's attention was caught by someone at another table, and Diana turned to see who she was looking at.

'It's one of our most important clients, Princess Mouna. She must have just arrived,' murmured Francesca.

Serge glanced over too. 'Isn't she wearing the emerald and diamond necklace we made? You remember, you came into the workrooms carrying the loose stones as if they were a bag of apples? Then your mother got Guy to deliver them personally to the princess?'

'That's the one.'

'It's a beautiful necklace,' observed Diana. 'The stones are so large it's hard to believe they're real.'

Francesca nodded. 'They're real all right, all three hundred thousand dollars' worth.'

The announcement in *The Times* was brief and to the point.

'Lady Diana Andrews, wife of Mr Guy Andrews, M.P., has given birth to a daughter.'

Lying in her private room at the Harley Street Clinic, Diana read it with a sense of irony. What a lie for the world to believe! And of course they would believe it. She and Guy were continuing to present themselves as a model couple. Who would believe they shared only a roof over their heads and nothing else? She read the announcement again, wondering if Marc would see it and realise the child was his. It was unlikely. The newspapers had recently reported him to be in Hollywood, writing the film script of his novel, *Temptations*, with Carlotta, as usual, by his side.

If someone had told her nine months ago that she'd still be married to Guy, dividing her time between their Eaton Terrace house, her new suite of Knightsbridge offices and Wilmington Hall, with a new baby, she'd never have believed them. She glanced across at Kathryn whose tiny face was just visible above a pink shawl. Such a beautiful baby, with dark hair just like Marc's. Just like Guy's too. No one will ever suspect anything, Diana reflected.

At that moment the baby gave a whimper and a little hand waved about.

Diana slipped out of bed and, gathering Kathryn in her arms, held her close, nuzzling the down on her head. 'My darling,' she crooned. 'I will always love you, and so will Miles. We'll look after you.'

Guy had only been to the hospital twice in the past week, bringing Miles and the nanny with him, and each time he had oozed graciousness to the nurses. For him the visits had been a public relations exercise but the hospital staff had been overwhelmed by his charm and Diana heard them whispering that he must be the best-looking young politician in the country.

As soon as she was strong enough Diana took the children down to Wilmington Hall with the new nanny she had engaged.

The eighteenth-century mansion would never be home to her, as Stanton Court had been, but she had to admit it was a beautiful old house. Guy had spent a fortune redecorating and furnishing it in perfect style, and the fine antiques and brocaded curtains harmonised beautifully with the Georgian building. There was no doubt about it, Guy had very good taste. Staff were taken on to look after the running of the house and a team of gardeners was employed to restore the gardens and grounds to their former grandeur. Guy, who spent Monday to Friday in the House of Commons, warned her they would have to do a lot of entertaining in the constituency at the weekends and put their gardens at the disposal of the Conservative Party for local fêtes. To Diana it was as if it were a part of her new job; if Guy wanted to foot the bill, she would lay on caterers, florists and everything else that was required to entertain in style. If they had guests to stay, they would be looked after as if they'd checked into a five star hotel. But home to her it certainly would never be.

Then one day Guy, looking very pleased with

himself, told her something that cheered her up a lot.

'You know Charlie always seems to be worried that your brother John doesn't have a proper job?'

Diana nodded. Charlie had never thought John would be able to make a living out of painting watercolours of wild life and he'd been nagging him for ages to do something more secure.

'Well . . .' Guy puffed out his chest and looked self-satisfied. 'I've offered him a job and he's accepted. It will mean he'll be staying with us, here and in London, but you'd like that, wouldn't you?'

'What sort of job? John isn't exactly a whizzkid,' said Diana, surprised.

'As a Member of Parliament, I have dozens of letters to answer, appointments to fix, arrangements that have to be made for me, so I've asked John to become my private secretary.'

'And he accepted?'

'Of course. Your family's delighted too. It'll get him out and about, meeting people, instead of squinting over bunches of flowers all day long.'

'That's wonderful! No wonder Charlie's pleased and it will be lovely having him here. Why didn't you tell me about it before?'

Guy shrugged and jingled the small change in the pockets of his elegant grey flannel suit. 'I didn't want you to be disappointed if he refused,' he said casually. 'So I spoke to your mother first, and then I discussed it with Charlie and Sophie, and finally John accepted. I'm giving him a fair salary and there's no doubt he can make himself useful.'

287

'Well, that's very nice of you, Guy,' she said slowly, thinking how relieved her family must be that John was about to start a serious job. 'When does he start?'

'In a few days actually.'

For the rest of the day, Diana busied herself getting a spare room ready for John, and looking forward, more than she'd admit, to the prospect of having her beloved brother living with them. Although he'd be kept busy by Guy, he'd be an ally, someone she could trust absolutely.

It was Christmas Eve. Thirty people were gathered in the large baronial hall for champagne before dinner. Guy, suave and elegant in a dinner jacket, his black hair smooth, his expression bland, was mingling with his guests, who included the mayor and his wife, several local councillors, a few company chairmen who had their businesses in the area and a smattering of the landed gentry. Diana, her figure restored to its accustomed slimness, glided from group to group seeing that everyone had enough to drink. A fifteen foot Christmas tree dominated the room and garlands of evergreen and holly, tied with scarlet ribbons, decorated the arches and doorways. The champagne flowed, great logs crackled in the fireplace filling the air with the fragrance of apple wood, and through the dining-room doors guests could glimpse flickering candlelight on a long refectory table set with silver and crystal, their appetites sharpened by the aroma of roast partridge.

'You and your husband have done wonders with

this old house,' said the lady mayoress to Diana. 'You must be very happy here.'

Diana switched on her bright smile. 'It's a lovely old building,' she replied politely. 'Our son loves the garden, it's perfect for children.'

'We must congratulate you on having a little girl,' said the mayor, coming up to join them. He was a man in his sixties, owner of a bicycle factory, and deeply impressed by Diana's title. 'Your husband told me he was delighted, always wanted a little girl, he said. We've got six ourselves, three boys and three girls. I expect you'll be having some more, Lady Diana?'

Diana forced a tinkling laugh from her throat. 'It's a lovely idea, but we're both so busy I doubt we'll find the time.'

'Oh, I don't know. I see Guy as a real family man. He takes a lot of interest in our local nursery school, and the children's wing of the hospital.'

Because he knows they're vote-catching interests, thought Diana, amazed that Guy had managed to fool these locals. *But then he fooled me too . . . at the beginning*, she thought.

At that moment Guy pushed past her. 'Where the hell are all the servants?' he snapped, irritated. 'The 'phone is ringing and ringing and nobody seems to be answering it.'

'Shall I go?' Diana offered.

'No, I'll get the damned thing myself.' He charged off in the direction of the library.

'Guy Andrews speaking,' he said pompously into the receiver.

'What the fuck are you playing at, you goddam bastard?' Francesca was yelling down the 'phone.

Kalinsky's, in New York, was in a furore.

'I'll kill that son of a bitch,' Francesca stormed. 'How dare he pull a trick like this?' She was standing in Henry's office, shaking with rage. In her hand she held a letter from the Princess Mouna's lawyer.

'Tell me again what it says.' Henry had been at one of their branches in Dallas for a few days and was desperately trying to catch up on the situation.

'It says, in so many words, that we have sold her a necklace of fake stones, worth only a few hundred dollars! Chunky junk in other words! Can you believe that? I've got our legal department dealing with it right now, but she's going to sue.' Francesca ran her hand distractedly through her hair, and her expression was grim.

'And this was discovered when she went to a jeweller in Paris to have the clasp fixed?'

'Right. They told her the stones were made of coloured glass! Christ, can you imagine? Guy must have had the real stones swapped for fake ones when he disappeared for a week on his way back to London. D'you remember how worried we were, wondering where the hell he'd gone? Now we know how he paid for his country mansion!'

Henry shook his head sadly. 'Yup, you're right. Hell, this could ruin us. We've got to think of a way of compensating the princess and hushing up the affair at the same time.'

'You haven't seen this morning's newspapers, then?'

Henry closed his eyes for a minute and leaned forward, resting his arms on his desk. 'They've already got the story?' He didn't have to ask what the papers said. He could just imagine it. Bold, sensational headlines about an Arab princess who had been duped by an international jewellery company.

'It's the lead story,' Francesca replied succinctly. 'There's something that bothers me about this whole thing, though.' She wrinkled her brows in perplexity.

'Such as?'

'When I saw her at the jewellery gala in London three months ago, she was wearing the necklace. I may not be a gemology expert, Uncle Henry, but I could swear she was wearing the real thing.'

'Humph.' He shook his head sadly. 'They make pretty good fake stuff these days. I wonder where the real stones are now? I'd better get on to our insurance people to see how we stand in a situation like this.'

'What worries me is that although you and I are certain it was Guy, everyone else in the company is feeling uncomfortable in case they are under suspicion. Especially in the workrooms. It's breeding a feeling of anger amongst all the craftsmen and apprentices. What can I do to stop it? I obviously can't just charge in there and say, "It's okay, you guys, my brother is the culprit!" Not just like that. I wish to God I could.'

'Let's take this a step at a time, Francesca, and not lose our heads. We haven't any actual proof that Guy swapped the stones, have we? Of course

291

he denied it to you on the 'phone, but he would anyway. But is there any possibility it could have been someone else? Who do we have that's new in the company?'

'There's no one else it could have been, Uncle Henry. The stones had been verified as genuine when I left the showrooms here, and I took them straight to the workrooms. I never let them out of my sight. When I got there I gave them to Louis Sedelman, and they were either in his safe or being set into the necklace until he himself brought the necklace back to my office here. Then I gave it to Guy.'

'Then there's no reason why the finger should point at anyone else?'

'Try telling that to Mom! I've persuaded her to keep the police out of this because I want to find a way of making the whole thing appear to be a terrible mistake, for the sake of the press. It's better we look inefficient than a bunch of crooks.'

Henry looked sceptical. 'So what can you come up with, for God's sake? We've sold a bum piece of jewellery to some foreign princess, letting her think it's the real thing. I'd like to know how we get out of that!'

'We're going to lie through our teeth to protect Kalinsky's, that's how. I'm going to say we always make a fake copy of original pieces, for reference or for any reason you goddam like, and by some terrible mistake we packed the replica in the jewellery case and gave it to her, instead of the real one.'

Henry's jaw dropped open. 'Jeez, how about that

for imagination!' he gasped. 'We've never made a fake copy of a real piece of jewellery in our lives.'

Francesca shrugged. 'Who's to know? We offer to exchange it for the real one, and then we pray we get away with it. We've got to do a cover-up to protect our good name.'

'How are we going to match up ten more price-less emeralds in order to deliver the "real one"? And what's it going to cost?' he groaned.

'It doesn't matter what it costs to clear Kalinsky's name,' said Francesca.

'What does Sarah have to say about all this? I've managed to avoid her since my return.'

'You'll never believe this, but she's actually told Guy he must fly home at once to clear his name. So far the newspapers haven't linked him with all this, but I don't know how long that will last.'

'Is he coming?' Henry's mind was beginning to reel. Suddenly he felt too old for this sort of thing, and nothing as nasty as this had ever happened in Kalinsky's before.

'You bet he is! Full of self-righteous indignation and martyrdom, too. He's saying I gave him a fake necklace to take back because I wanted to finally discredit him in the company. Oh, Uncle Henry, it's the most God awful mess.' Francesca dropped into the chair facing his desk, suddenly worn out with nervous energy and worry.

'When is he flying in?'

'Not until the end of the week. He says he has to attend an important debate in the House of Commons and can't come sooner.'

'Never would be too soon,' remarked Henry sourly.

Everything was working out as Guy had planned. He had his four million dollars and yet he was not likely to be drawn into a public scandal that would ruin his chances in politics. It had been a risky business from the beginning and he'd had a few sleepless nights wondering if he was going to get away with it, but now he felt reasonably safe. Too much was at stake for too many important people for anyone to dare spill the beans. His name had not appeared in the newspapers at all in connection with the fake necklace. Kalinsky's were, predictably, playing the story down and Francesca was quoted as saying it had all been a terrible mistake, a careless accident, and of course the company were going to get the real emerald necklace to Princess Mouna immediately. None of the media had connected Guy Andrews, Member of Parliament, with Kalinsky Jewellery Inc., and there was no real reason why they should. He had managed to distance himself from the company for a long time now, and even at the Guildhall jewellery gala he had attended as an M.P. and the husband of the aristocratic Lady Diana Andrews, the chairman and organiser of the night, and not as the son of the President of the company.

If Diana suspected anything, she was not saying. They led such separate lives these days that he hardly saw her. He had not even confessed to John what he had done. There was only one more hurdle now and he was convinced he could get over that one too. He had purposely made a point of insisting he pick up the necklace from Francesca's office the day he left for England. He would remind her that she made a fuss at the time, but he was acting as a mere courier, so the blame could not be his. She must have given him the wrong necklace, that was what he would say, and nothing would make him change his story. As for his mother, she would protect him no matter what. He knew she would rather die than let him take the can for anything.

'I have no doubts at all,' said Sarah firmly. 'It was Serge Buono who stole the stones from the workroom and replaced them with fakes. He had the opportunity, the knowledge and the technical ability. It's my betting that when the necklace was finished – and remember there was a delay in getting it to England until Guy came back from Palm Beach – he secretly removed the stones and replaced them when nobody was looking.'

Henry looked at her, appalled. If she was trying to deceive herself she was making a good job of it. But to suggest it was Serge! This was a diabolical move to discredit the one man who had brought enormous success to Kalinsky's in recent months and whom Henry trusted as if he'd been his son.

'You're making a very serious accusation,' he said sternly. 'If you go around talking like that, you're going to have a writ slammed on you for slander before you know what's happened! How can you possibly accuse Serge? Apart from anything else he came to us with the highest credentials. You're crazy, Sarah, if you think he's got anything to do with this.'

'There's no one else it could have been. Why are you trying to protect him, Henry? He's merely someone Francesca produced from nowhere and now he's dragging us all down in this dreadful scandal. I'm not going to hang around any more while you and Francesca mess about. I'm calling in the police.'

'No.' Henry said the word so loudly it resounded around Sarah's office. 'No way, Sarah. We have got to talk to Guy before we bring the police in and hopefully we can keep the trouble to ourselves. We don't want more publicity, and if the police take your wild accusations at all seriously, we'll be in real trouble. Francesca has come up with a very good hand-out story which people are believing. Let's leave it at that.'

'I will not leave it! The culprit must be punished. God, if Serge gets away with it once, he'll get away with it again. Have you thought of that?' Sarah thumped her desk angrily with a small fist.

'But it's got nothing to do with Serge!' Henry thundered. 'Why won't you face facts, woman? The only person who could have got those stones switched is your own blessed son.'

'I won't have you talking like that! One more word about Guy and you're out! He's my son and he would never rob his own family business. If he wanted money he'd ask me for it,' she cried.

'He did, and you refused him,' said Henry drily. 'And yet he went ahead and bought some great mansion and filled it with antiques and paintings. Where did he get the money for that?'

At that moment Francesca hurried into her mother's office, abandoning her usual practice of knocking first.

'Talking about Guy again?' she asked briskly. 'I've just had a call from England that may change everything. It's possible Guy's not involved at all.'

Sarah and Henry gazed at her blankly. Sarah was the first to recover. 'Of course it's got nothing to do with Guy, but what have you heard?'

'An insurance company in London have just told me that Princess Mouna had the necklace insured through them and they expressed doubt about this whole incident.'

'Why? If she showed them our bill of sale there would be no problem getting it insured,' said Henry.

'The point is,' continued Francesca, 'she took it to Burridges, the jeweller in New Bond Street, and had it revalued quite recently. Jewellery is increasing in value at such a rate that it's quite a normal thing to do. The point is, she does have the real necklace. They examined it, and the stones were real.'

There was silence in the room as Sarah and Henry tried to digest this turn of events.

'Then what about the jewellers in Paris, where she had the clasp fixed? Are they on the level?' inquired Henry.

'Absolutely. Experts from our Paris branch have been to see them and they've examined the necklace. It's definitely made of glass,' said Francesca.

Sarah leaned back in her chair and gave a deep

sigh. 'Well, I'm glad we've got that straight, anyway.'

Francesca and Henry turned on her sharply.

'What have we got straight?' Henry demanded. 'The whole thing's more confused than ever. Now we seem to have two necklaces that look identical, but one is real and the other is a fake. It doesn't help at all.'

'Unless . . .' said Francesca thoughtfully, but when Sarah looked at her she shook her head and smiled. 'No, it's nothing. Forget it.'

Outside in the corridor a few minutes later, Francesca turned to Henry, speaking in a low voice. 'I've had an idea, Uncle Henry. Can you get out our sales ledgers, you know the ones with the confidential notes in them covering the last ten years?'

Henry looked surprised. 'Sure. What do you want them for?'

'I have a feeling we might just find the answer. Our London and Paris branches send us theirs at the end of each year for safe-keeping, don't they? I'd like to look at them too.'

'We have them all here. New York, London, Paris, Rome.'

'The New York, London and Paris ledgers will do just fine,' she said.

'Serge, I'm flying to England tomorrow,' Francesca announced that evening, as they dined in her apartment.

'What the hell for?' He looked up, startled, from his plate of lobster thermidor.

'Something quite extraordinary has come up concerning this necklace business, and I've got to keep it under wraps until I can find out more. You're the only person who knows where I'm going.' She held out her glass. 'Can I have some more wine, sweetheart? Thanks. Mom thinks I'm checking out our Los Angeles branch and so does Uncle Henry!'

Serge grinned with amusement. 'What happens if they try to contact you? I'd better say I've had you kidnapped and taken to my mountain hideway . . . where I'm going to ravish you all weekend!'

They both burst out laughing and Francesca murmured, 'If only you were! There's nothing I'd love more. After these last few days of hell, I could do with a bit of ravishing!'

Serge raised his glass. 'I'll drink to that, my love. But seriously, do you have to go to England?'

She nodded. 'I've got to get to the bottom of this business. It's caused enough disruption as it is and I'm anxious to get it cleared up.'

'You're putting your work before everything again, honey.' Serge helped himself to salad and pushed the bowl over to her. 'When are *we* going to come first?'

'Oh, Serge, you're not being fair! I'll only be gone a few days, and this is important.'

'Everything to do with Kalinsky's is important, as far as you are concerned,' he said drily and his eyes had suddenly lost their twinkle. 'You've been away on a lot of trips this past year. Are you ever going to want to settle down, have a baby, live a more normal life?'

Francesca let out a sigh. 'Honey, you know how it is. And this crisis over the necklace hasn't helped. Do try to understand that my life *has* to be divided into two halves; one with you and one with the company.'

Serge leaned forward and refilled her wine glass.

'Is it ever going to work out for us?' he said, almost sadly.

'It will work out if you let me have breathing space, darling.' She didn't want to lose Serge; he had brought warmth and happiness and love into her life and she loved him deeply, but she had a career also, and that meant a lot to her. She wasn't going to admit, even to herself, that it might mean more.

'Sure. I understand you need some space, but I'd like us to marry one day and have a family. I'd like us to be a real couple, but right now, being married to you would be like being married to the President of the United States!' He gave a wry smile.

'That's why I want us to stay the way we are,' she exclaimed. 'You can't really want to marry me as things stand?'

'Of course I do . . .,' he said slowly, looking tenderly into her eyes, 'but I realise you're not ready yet. You've got mountains to conquer before you're ready to become a wife and mother.'

'And you'll wait for me?' she asked, suddenly anxious. A voice in her head was saying I love him, I need him and I want him around forever, but another voice was clamouring, you love and need your work too.

'As long as your hair is auburn and your eyes dark brown velvet,' he joked gently. 'So, you'll be back within a few days?'

She took his hand in hers and squeezed it tightly.

'I promise.' Guy would be arriving in New York on Friday morning and it was imperative she get back before then. 'Serge, as soon as this business is cleared up, let's go on a trip. Bermuda or somewhere. You're right, we don't get away enough on our own. How about it?' A note of quiet desperation had crept into her voice. She must try and strike a balance between Serge and Kalinsky's. She must make him feel important to her. 'Isn't that a wonderful idea?' she added coaxingly.

He leaned across the table and kissed her mouth with tenderness. 'It's the best idea you've had in a long time,' he said.

Francesca was waiting for Guy at the arrivals gate at Idlewild Airport when he landed on Friday morning. He looked tight-lipped and angry when he saw her and his first words were icy.

'What are you doing here?'

'The car is waiting for us,' said Francesca, smoothly. 'I thought we'd better talk before you see Mom.' She strode elegantly towards the car, a striking figure in a strong amethyst woollen suit, her lapel sparkling with one of Serge's designs, a diamond basket filled with amethyst violets with emerald stems.

'I've nothing to say to you,' snapped Guy, as he supervised the loading of his Louis Vuitton luggage into the boot of the car. 'Haven't you done enough damage already? You try to involve me in a dirty trick that is supposed to disgrace me, especially with Mom, and you end up having to make a public apology on behalf of the company and making a complete ass of yourself.' He flung himself petulantly into the back of the Lincoln Continental and stared moodily out of the window.

Francesca glanced at his averted profile, amazed at his gall.

'I was in London on Wednesday,' she said conversationally.

Guy's only response was a slight raising of the eyebrows and pursing of the lips.

'I went to see Princess Mouna.'

His head shot round and he looked at her with eyes like dark daggers. But still he didn't say anything.

'We had a very interesting conversation,' Francesca continued. 'It seems you paid her a brief visit when you were supposed to be in Palm Beach!'

'I was in Palm Beach,' said Guy defensively.

'But not for the whole ten days,' rejoined Francesca. 'You slipped over to London and put a little proposition to her, didn't you?'

'The fucking bitch!' exploded Guy. 'I'll kill that goddam fucking cow!'

Francesca continued as if she hadn't heard.

'You frightened the wits out of her by threatening to reveal to her father that she'd bought a lot of jewellery and expensive gifts over the years for her lovers, didn't you? You found it all in our ledgers and you used that information to blackmail her, knowing that under the strict laws of the Quran her father would order her to be killed for having committed adultery. Not stoned to death, of course,' she added sarcastically, 'that is only for the peasants. She'd merely have been taken out and shot, all nice and clean.'

Guy remained silent, his jaw clenching and unclenching.

Francesca continued. 'She broke down and told me everything and I felt very sorry for her. She was a mere child when her father arranged for her to marry her sixty-year-old cousin. And so she took lovers, meeting them in the afternoons when everyone thought she was out shopping, taking suites at the Dorchester in London or La Tremoille in Paris under an assumed name. And then she would buy them gold watches and jewelled cufflinks at Kalinsky's, to be delivered to the man in question, which is how we have all the records. Confidential records which you used to scare her so much that she agreed to buy your silence by giving you four million dollars, in cash, to be paid in four instalments, which you no doubt put straight in a bank safety deposit box. Am I right?'

Guy had begin to shake; great tremors swept over him and his face looked almost black with rage.

'I'll kill that whore . . .!'

'And that wasn't all, was it, Guy?' Francesca's voice was soft as silk now as her words continued relentlessly. 'You came up with another little idea, didn't you? One you hoped would raise even more money. You told her you would be bringing her emerald and diamond necklace over to England in ten days time. You also told her she would be receiving an exact fake replica, delivered by a courier, from Amsterdam, a few weeks later. Right? Are you still with me, Guy?'

His fists were clenched on his knees like tight weapons of bone and sinew.

'You wanted to discredit me because you were afraid I'd ruin you publicly by revealing what I know about your private life,' she continued calmly. 'You were also greedy. But then you were always greedy, weren't you, Guy? You always snatched the last cookie, the best toy, Mom's attention . . .'

'I will not sit here and listen to this filth,' he shouted suddenly.

Francesca's voice cut across him like a sharp knife slicing butter. 'I haven't finished,' she said icily. 'You got this wretched Princess Mouna to agree to take the fake necklace to a jeweller in Paris for a minor repair so that it would be discovered the stones were glass. Then the plan was for her to sue Kalinsky's, get me disgraced, and whatever recompense she received was to be split fifty-fifty between you.'

'Stop the car!' yelled Guy to the chauffeur. 'If you think I'm going to sit here while you . . .'

The limousine, if anything, gathered speed as it made its way through the grimy suburbs of New York.

'He has instructions not to stop until we arrive at Kalinsky's, so you can save your breath,' said Francesca calmly. 'It's pointless making a scene. I

304

have a letter signed by Princess Mouna in which she agrees to drop all charges against us and to go along with my story about her getting a replica necklace by mistake. I, in turn, have guaranteed that no one will ever know about her lovers. We are also going to give her a valuable piece of jewellery as compensation for breach of confidentiality. The information in those ledgers is sacrosanct and you damned well knew it. You have abused every privilege you ever had; you have disgraced me, Mom, the company and its good name, and I am going to make sure you never get a chance to do it again.'

Like a rising storm, Francesca's anger was gathering momentum. Held in check until she had all but demolished him, years of resentment and dislike were bursting the banks. She was shaking too now, and feeling slightly sick. This was her brother, her own flesh and blood, and yet she was determined to ruin his future in the company because Kalinsky's meant so much to her. But, she reminded herself, Guy had been bent on destroying her too. Sibling love never had existed and never could exist between them.

'I have one more thing to say before we arrive at the office,' she said, and her voice suddenly sounded tired. 'And this is the bottom line, Guy . . .'

When they arrived at Kalinsky's Francesca led the way to her office on the tenth floor, with Guy following defiantly, his head held high. They had struck a deal. Francesca would not tell anyone what he had done and in return he was to sell her his twenty-five per cent stock in the company.

'I will tell Mom everthing, if you refuse,' Francesca had warned him, as they drove into Manhattan. 'And I mean *everything*, Guy. But if you let me buy your stock, and you keep out of the company in future, I will merely say the princess had a copy made herself to lessen the risk of travelling abroad with the real thing, and that it was all a stupid mix-up. Mom will be happy to let the whole thing drop if you appear to be in the clear and we give her a reasonable explanation. And if you don't talk, the princess certainly won't either. We'll inform the insurance company it was all a mistake, and as far as the newspapers are concerned the story has become yesterday's news.'

'Meanwhile you will hold the majority of shares,' Guy's voice had been filled with scorn and loathing.

'Meanwhile I will hold the majority of shares,' Francesca repeated, quietly. 'It's no good looking like that, Guy. You brought this whole thing on yourself. It was all yours once. You could have been President of one of the leading jewellery companies in the world, but you played into my hands. You've damned well given it to me, on a plate, gift-wrapped! So don't try and pretend that you're heartbroken about being out of Kalinsky's.'

'I'd like to know how I'm supposed to manage without the income from my shares,' he said bitterly.

'You still get a large private income from Mom, and presumably you get paid as a Member of Parliament? Even Diana seems to be earning her own living. You might, for once, just try to live within your income instead of like a multi-millionaire playboy.'

'Oh, fuck off and die!'

Francesca turned to look at Guy's averted profile. 'Well, here we are. It's up to you. I'll get you out of this, in return for your shares, or you face serious charges for fraud with intent to rob.'

Guy gave her a look of pure hatred. 'It seems I don't have a choice.'

'Good. The transfer documents are in my office. You can sign them before you go to see Mom.' At that moment it struck her she was becoming exactly like Sarah.

As they came out of her office fifteen minutes later, Henry came lumbering down the corridor, breathing heavily. 'I must talk to you, Francesca,' he said, pointedly ignoring Guy.

'Why don't you go ahead and see Mom?' she said to Guy. She could trust him not to spin Sarah some fantastic yarn now. She'd got him over a barrel and he'd signed over his shares. It was obvious he was deeply aggrieved but there was nothing he could do about it. When Sarah found out Francesca owned his shares, she was to be told that as a Member of Parliament he was not allowed to have any business connections because of conflicting interests. That, Francesca reckoned, would keep her quiet.

'What's the matter, Uncle Henry?' she asked when they were alone.

'Serge has been arrested for stealing the emeralds.'

'He's *what*?' Her head was reeling. The morning with Guy had been a terrible strain and now it was assuming the proportions of a nightmare. 'Why the hell has Serge been arrested?' she yelled. 'What's going on around here?'

'Your mother contacted the police and told them it was Serge. She's suspected him from the beginning and he happens to be the only person in the company who is new and had the opportunity and the expertise,' Henry said, grimly. 'The circumstantial evidence against him is bad.'

'But ... oh Jesus! This is terrible! I've spent the whole week finding out what's happened and it's got nothing to do with Serge. And now I've given my word to Guy that I'll stay silent...'

'Why, for God's sake?' Henry looked appalled.

'In return for his twenty-five per cent shareholding,' said Francesca hurriedly. 'I'd better get on to the police myself and sort this whole thing out.'

Henry gave a long low whistle, and gave her a look of awe mixed with cynicism. 'Well, you've really done it, haven't you! You realise you only need one more share and you can take control of the company?'

'I know.' Francesca felt a hot flush creeping up her neck to her cheeks. 'Do you think it is very underhand of me, Uncle Henry? But Guy provided me with the opportunity and I'd have been a fool not to take it. After all, it hurts him less to sell me his shares than to have to face arrest. This way he can fly back to England, his reputation spotless and intact, so that he can pursue the life he's always wanted.'

'Oh, I get the point, and I'm not criticising you, honey. I'm just saying you're one hell of an opportunist.'

'I've had to be,' she said, 'and I haven't finished yet. I'm hoping you'll sell me that one extra share, from your five per cent, giving me that magic figure of fifty-one per cent!'

'Which would mean your mother could be pushed out,' he said thoughtfully.

'Yes, it does.' Francesca looked at him steadily, no longer the innocent, serious little girl who'd first been brought to the office by her nanny, but a young woman who'd learned a lot in a very short time and whom nothing was going to stop now.

'Let's get this present business wrapped up first,' he said gently, feeling a sense of loss that the little girl had gone forever. 'I'll get on to the police and say we wish to drop charges against Serge as the situation has resolved itself, and you'd better get up to your mother's office and see what Guy's up to.'

The meeting in Sarah's office was protracted and painful. Sarah did not believe a word of the story that the Princess herself had had a replica of the necklace made and had got it confused. She probed and prodded ruthlessly, sweeping aside Francesca's explanations, convinced something was being kept from her. Guy was the first to break. Cornered, as Sarah questioned him and Francesca, he suddenly jumped to his feet, pushing his chair back violently, his mother's insidious delving hitting him on a raw nerve.

'Oh, fuck this goddam fucking business!' he shouted, his face scarlet with anger. 'I'm sick of the whole bloody lot of you! All right, I *did* get the necklace copied but it was Princess Mouna who wanted to sue you and get damages.'

'But *why* should she want to do that, Guy?' demanded Sarah sternly. 'She's been one of our best customers. We've never had any trouble with her before.'

Francesca looked down, keeping silent. She was going to keep her side of the bargain and not even her mother was going to induce her to tell the whole story now.

'Do you realise the position you've put me in?' continued Sarah, looking at both of them. 'I've called in the police and told them I suspected Serge Buono. Now it looks as if I'm going to have to apologise to the wretched man! How could you let this happen, Francesca?' she added accusingly.

'I wasn't to know you could possibly suspect Serge,' replied Francesca, coolly. 'I was more interested in the Princess's activities.'

'But it doesn't add up,' persisted Sarah, 'and I'm going to get to the bottom of this affair if it's the last thing I do!'

'It's all your bloody fault, Mom,' Guy shouted. He looked like a frightened little boy now, caught doing something dreadful by his mother, his basic weakness of character revealed in his trembling hands, his black eyes glittering with unshed tears.

'You've never given me anything I wanted,' he

continued, his voice shaking. 'You never wanted me to live in England. You disapproved of me marrying Diana. You only gave me extra money when I got into debt and needed it. You've been a selfish, self-centred old woman who always wanted your own way. I've never wanted to work here but would you listen? You nagged me, day and night, to come and work for this lousy fucking company, and all you've done is to try and tie me to your apron strings. You've never loved me, Mom, you just wanted to keep me by your side, not having a life of my own, fulfilling your fantasies. Well, I'm sick of it. You wouldn't even give me the money to buy a house in the country when I told you I wanted to go into politics. You've deprived me of everything I've ever wanted, Mom. It's your fault that I had to get it my way.'

Francesca looked from Guy's vicious face to Sarah, who looked like a death mask, her red-rimmed eyes stricken. Sickened, Francesca rose and turned away, unable to witness the naked destruction, limb from limb and sinew from sinew, of mother and son in a bloodbath from which neither would ever heal. She heard Guy telling his mother what he had done with an almost defiant pride. It was all Sarah's fault now. And Francesca's. Between them they had driven him to such lengths in order to raise the money to buy a house. It all came spewing out in a torrent of vindictiveness, and Francesca was reminded of a cornered animal, mad with fury and convulsed with rage.

The tears were trickling down Sarah's cheeks

now and with a pathetic, childlike gesture, she wiped her eyes. 'Guy, how can you do this to me?' she said brokenly. 'I love you, honey. I've always put you first in everything. You're my son, everything I've ever done has been for you. Please don't say these dreadful things to me. I'm sorry for not letting you have that money for your house, but . . .'

Francesca turned on her mother, a shocked look on her face. 'Mom!' she said, 'Mom, how can you apologise to him! You've nothing to blame yourself for. Guy's behaved in an utterly unforgivable way, and here you are, grovelling before him. For God's sake, you don't have to take this shit from him.'

'You're a fine one to talk,' Guy snarled. 'Do you know what she's done, Mom? Do you? She said she wouldn't tell anyone about my part in the necklace affair if I sold her all my shares. Well, I don't care! I've done it now and I'm glad to be rid of you and the company. You two can get on with it now. You fucking well deserve each other.'

'Is this true, Francesca?'

Francesca met her mother's eyes with honest directness. 'Yes, it's true. I'm prepared to give my life to the company, to do everything I can to see it prosper. As you have done, Mom. It's obvious Guy has never been prepared to take an interest. All he's ever wanted are the profits. You can rely on me to put Kalinsky's before anything else.' Then Francesca made a sudden decision. She had planned to get Henry to sell her just one of his shares which would put her in the position of being able to topple her mother out of the President's chair, but now the sight of Sarah, utterly broken

312

and devastated by Guy's cruelty, filled her with sudden compassion. That one extra share could wait for a while.

'Don't worry, Mom. Henry and I will be happy to continue to fly the flag for Kalinsky's as joint Vice Presidents.'

That same night, as Francesca lay in bed with Serge, she tried to explain to him what had happened.

'I'll never forgive myself for your getting involved with the police,' she said mournfully. 'I nearly *died* when I heard you'd been charged and arrested. Mom really went over the top this time.'

Serge still looked grim from his day's humiliating experience. 'If it hadn't been for you, d'you know what I'd have done?'

She looked at him questioningly.

'I'd have walked straight out of Kalinsky's the moment I was released, and I'd have told your mother what she could do with her damned company. And then I'd have gone along the road and offered my services to Tiffany's.'

'I don't blame you for feeling like that, honey. I can never forgive her for what she's done to you. God, it makes me sick! She's prepared to put the blame on anyone rather than let her precious son take the can.' Francesca angrily plumped up the pillows behind her head, and leaned back again. 'Not even the police imagined you were guilty, until she pointed the finger.'

'Where's Guy now?'

'Gone back to England, thank God, saying he'll

313

never speak to any of us again. Can we be that lucky?' She gave a wry smile.

Serge chuckled, in spite of his chagrin. 'We deserve to be, after all he's put us through,' he remarked, 'but right now I could kill him. How did your mother take his confession?'

Francesca nestled down in the bed and snuggled into his side. 'She's pretty shattered, but she's a tough old bird. She'll get over it.'

Serge turned on his side, and started kissing her neck softly. 'And do we get our trip to Bermuda now?' he whispered.

'You bet your ass we do!' replied Francesca, flinging her arms round his neck.

In her apartment in Mayfair House, Sarah sat with Henry, drinking brandy late into the night. Over and over again she reiterated the same questions. How could her children have treated her like this? All she had ever wanted was for them to be happy and successful, and now they had wounded her deeply. How could Guy have turned into a criminal? And why was Francesca so devious?

Henry drew a deep breath and looked across the richly cluttered drawing-room to where Sarah sat on a cream velvet sofa. They'd been friends for over twenty years now and in spite of their differences he'd always been honest with her. In spite of his damning words there was deep compassion in his voice.

'The thing is, my dear,' he said slowly, 'the children you finally get are the children you deserve.'

*   *   *

314

The next day Sarah summoned her lawyer. She had decided to change her will. Riddled with guilt that she was to blame for the way Guy had turned out, and filled with anguish at their estrangement, she told her lawyer she wished to leave her entire estate to her son.

'I feel so terribly sorry about what has happened,' she explained. 'It is really my late husband's fault, of course. If he hadn't insisted Guy be educated in England none of this would have happened.'

The lawyer said nothing. He had handled Sarah's affairs and her father's before her, and he knew you didn't cross an Andrews. Privately he thought she was being unfair to Francesca.

As if she sensed his disapproval, she continued, 'I feel bitter towards Francesca. She behaved very badly, tricking Guy out of his stockholding in Kalinsky's, and I blame her for the fact he didn't want to return and work here. She has been jealous of him ever since she was a small child and no matter what I did it was Francesca who made him feel unwanted here.'

'So your estate is all to go to Guy,' said the lawyer, making notes. 'Your own stockholding in Kalinsky's, the New York apartment, the house in Palm Beach, all the furnishings, paintings, silver, *objets d'art*?'

Sarah nodded.

'And your jewellery, Mrs Andrews. What about your own personal collection of jewellery?'

'That is to go to Guy too, with a request that it should be passed on to his daughter, Kathryn,' she said firmly. 'I am also going to increase his personal allowance as from next month.'

That evening she wrote to Guy, telling him of her intentions, hoping it would bring forth some loving response. He was her only son, after all, and in spite of everything there was no one in the world she loved more.

Book Two
1970

Chapter Fifteen

Diana took the bend at thirty miles an hour, revving the engine of the Jaguar as the drive straightened out ahead of her and the overhanging avenue of oak trees flickered past. Ahead lay Wilmington Hall, its mellow Queen Anne brickwork bathed in bright morning sunshine, a drooping marquee and the wilting remnants of last night's ball still in evidence on the lawn. Bedraggled tablecloths and scattered gilt chairs filled the terrace and the place had the desolate flat air of the morning after.

This was the first time she'd been back for fifteen years and she'd had to steel herself to make the journey, as if to prove that the past held no terrors for her. Fifteen years had passed since that afternoon, when she'd given a children's party to celebrate Miles's fourth birthday, and she'd discovered something so dreadful that it had changed the course of her life. It had begun so happily, too, with the great dining-room decorated with balloons and streamers, a marvellous spread of all the things children like best to eat, and an entertainer, who was going to give a Punch and Judy show after tea. Twenty-three children arrived in their best party clothes, escorted by mothers or nannies, and Miles had greeted them with solemn good manners as they pressed gifts into his willing hands. Little Kathryn, wearing a primrose yellow organdie dress, had viewed the proceedings with lively interest, as she tried to cram chocolate cake into her tiny mouth.

'I don't know how you do it!' gushed a mother to Diana, as she surveyed the jolly scene.

'Diana's so brilliant,' enthused another. 'Don't you ever get tired of arranging parties, as you do it all the time?'

'I enjoy it,' Diana replied simply. 'No two parties are ever alike and children's parties are particularly fun, especially when it's your own children.'

'Well, I think you're jolly clever. I could never go to all this trouble,' remarked a third.

Diana was glad Miles's birthday had fallen on a Saturday, so that Guy had no excuse to stay away. He might be a rotten husband but when he saw the children . . . even Kathryn . . . he put on a good performance of being the loving father, especially if other people were present. This, she felt, was important to their sense of security. In time, both Miles and Kathryn would come to realise what Guy was like, but if she could postpone that day as long as possible, she hoped it would help them to grow happy and adjusted.

Guy had come down from London that morning, with John, bringing with him a train set, coloured bricks and a pair of roller skates. Miles had been thrilled, and now, as Diana supervised the tea, Guy was seeing to the re-arrangement of the drawing-room furniture in readiness for Punch and Judy.

Strains of *The Teddybear's Picnic* drifted from

the record player as, tea ended, little faces and hands were being wiped, endless trips to the bathroom were made, and children and parents bustled into the drawing-room to take their places.

Diana heaved a sigh of relief. Peace would reign for at least another half hour. Wandering into the hall, where it was cool and peaceful, she sat down on an oak carved chest to enjoy a belated cup of tea. The black and white marble floor gleamed in the sunshine that came pouring through the high windows above the sweeping curve of the oak staircase. A bowl of yellow roses, placed on a drum table in the centre, were undisturbed by prodding little hands.

It's a nice house, she thought absently, and I've done my best with it, but it's not home. Not like Stanton Court. It's Guy's place; a perfect setting for his political entertaining, his new image as country squire, Member of Parliament, upholder of old English traditions and respectable family man.

At that moment she noticed that the oak-panelled door under the curve of the staircase was open a couple of inches. Quickly she sprang to her feet. That door was supposed to be kept locked, especially when the house was full of children, because it led down to the wine cellar and the steep twisting stone steps were dangerous. She was just about to close it when she heard a slight scraping sound coming from the dark depths below. She paused and listened. There it was again, followed almost immediately by what sounded like a low moan. As she peered down she saw a light was on.

'Oh, my God,' she muttered, under her breath. If

any of the children had gone exploring after tea, the cellar was a death trap. The ancient stone floors were uneven, there were odd steps up and down and in places the wine racks stuck out at angles, sharp-edged and lethal. If a child attempted to climb about they could bring racks and bottles crashing down on top of themselves.

Clutching on to the rough stone walls with one hand, Diana started to descend into the cobwebby dimness, taking the steps one at a time. Above, from the drawing-room, the Punch and Judy show could be heard in full swing. 'Send him to prison!' screeched the puppet. 'Yes, yes,' chanted the young audience.

Diana continued down, hearing louder moans now coming from the depths below, while the puppets and the children screamed in unison, from above, 'Send him to prison!'

Diana paused, trying to accustom her eyes to the semi-darkness, peering in the direction of the noise, terrified of finding a child hurt or injured. Then she froze, immobilised by shock. It wasn't children, playing hide-and-seek or sardines. It was Guy and John, pressed up against the wall, locked in what looked like a struggle. Wild groans sprang from their throats, and as the puppet's voice filled Diana's ears, she realised that Guy and John were not struggling in conflict, but were locked together in a violent act of sex.

She had struggled against enveloping waves of horror and nausea as she retreated back up the steps, but not before Guy had glanced up and seen her standing there. She tried desperately to control herself as she fled up to her bedroom, hoping no one would see her. But when the party ended, and the children and their parents trooped into the hall to thank her, it took the greatest act of will not to show that she was filled with rage and anguish and despair. The moment she almost broke down was when one of the children's fathers came to collect his wife and child. He was such a kind looking man, normal and slightly dull, but with a wild rush of feeling, Diana wished with all her heart that he was her husband.

She had left Wilmington Hall, with the children, that night. All she wanted to do was get away from Guy and protect them from the consequences of his relationship with their uncle. For that reason, and that reason only, she had promised Guy and John that she would never speak to anyone about what she had seen.

Now, fifteen years later she was thankful she'd kept silent. The law had changed, in any case, after twelve years, making homosexuality between consenting adults legal, and Miles and Kathryn had grown up, presuming that incompatibility was the reason for their parents' separation. There had been no divorce. Guy had bought himself a flat in King Charles Street, near the Houses of Parliament, while she had stayed on with the children at Eaton Terrace. John, for appearance's sake, took a flat in Chelsea which he never used but which served its purpose, and publicly he was Guy's secretary, an arrangement which was acceptable to society at large and which drew no suspicion. Privately their affair continued to flourish.

Wilmington Hall remained a setting for Guy's work in the constituency, which was more flamboyant than useful but had been sufficient to allow him to retain his seat at each General Election. The image of do-gooder and upholder of law and order settled on his shoulders as comfortably as a cloak and he blossomed under the high regard of his colleagues as a garden will bloom under the gentle rain that falls from heaven. If he and his wife were 'incompatible' it was a matter for sympathy and not judgement. He appeared to adore his children, with whom he was frequently photographed, and even the most critical remarked on how nice it was to see he and the Lady Diana conduct themselves in a friendly and civilised fashion.

From Monday to Friday he sat in the House of Commons, catching the Speaker's eye with remarkable success if he wished to say something, and his speeches on educational reform were clear and lucid. Each Sunday he attended Matins at the village church near Wilmington Hall, each Christmas he gave a party for the mayor and councillors and all those who supported him in Wessex East, and each summer he lent his grounds for the local fête. Once a year he also gave a ball for every useful contact he had made in London, whether in Parliament or in the world of high finance, and the delicious irony that it was Diana's company, Event Organising Ltd, who arranged all these functions did not escape him. Not that Diana organised them personally. Her highly trained assistant, Patricia, was in charge in every detail, from hiring marquees and bands to arranging caterers, florists and the printing of the invitations. Needless to say, Event Organising Ltd did not give him a discount for their services.

Last night he'd held his annual ball for four hundred guests and Miles and Kathryn had come down from London for the occasion. As Miles hadn't yet passed his driving test, Diana had decided to collect them. Guy and John, she knew, would have left at dawn for an important debate in the House, and she hoped that one more look at Wilmington Hall would wipe out those lingering memories of an afternoon that had seared her mind and still haunted her in the private stillness of the night.

'Hullo, Mummy!' Kathryn came running down the stone steps as Diana parked her car in the drive. At seventeen she had the wild beauty of a gypsy; dark haired, dark eyed and creamy skinned. Taller than her mother and with a curvaceous figure, she looked older than her age but childhood still lingered in the soft roundness of her cheeks and the fullness of her mouth. As she hugged Diana, the tall slim figure of Miles came bounding from the house. Strong, fine featured and dark like his sister, he'd inherited his mother's natural dignity and thoroughbred manner. Standing together in the drive Diana amusedly compared them to a highly bred racehorse and a spirited little Shetland pony.

'Hullo, Mum!' Miles hugged her too, as if to prove his loyalty really lay with her and not Guy.

'Hullo, darlings. Did you have a good time? Was the party fun?' Diana asked, as she walked with them into the house, her fists clenched secretly in her pockets, her mind forcing her not to look at the door that led to the cellar.

'Smashing!' announced Kathryn. 'I wish you'd been here. The Prime Minister came, and there were lots of photographers, and the Home Secretary asked me to dance.'

'Oh, stop showing off, Kathryn,' Miles said in a bantering tone. 'You should have seen her, Mum, dressed up like a dog's dinner, flirting with all those boring old M.P.s.'

Kathryn swung round, her eyes sparkling with indignation. 'And what about you? Bowing and scraping and calling everyone "Sir"! He even called one of the barmen "Sir", by mistake, Mummy.'

Diana laughed and put her arms affectionately round them. 'Shut up, you two,' she chided. 'Are you packed? I want to get back to London.'

'Aren't you going to stay for a bit? You haven't been here for ages,' said Kathryn.

Diana still stood in the hall, her back resolutely turned on the cellar door. She glanced through the open doors into the dining-room where servants were still clearing away after the ball, but all she saw was twenty children, in paper hats, laughing and singing *Happy Birthday To You*, as a four-year-old Miles blew out the candles on his cake.

'No, I have to get back,' she said, keeping her tone light. 'I have a surprise for you at home and it's a surprise that won't like to be kept waiting. Fetch your cases and I'll wait for you in the car.'

She turned and walked swiftly through the front door, her chin held high, her eyes fixed on the garden beyond.

There were some things that even the passing of time couldn't obliterate.

Francesca waited in the drawing-room at Eaton Terrace, flipping through *Country Life*. The country pursuits and interests of the English upper classes riveted her. Who could possibly be interested in broken down barns, even if they had been built in 1700? Or the fact that talking to a cow caused it to yield a greater quantity of milk? She turned to the small fashion section where tweed and wool dominated, then she closed the magazine. Kalinsky's jewellery definitely wasn't a part of *Country Life*.

Glancing at her wristwatch, a superb design by Serge of gold and lapis lazuli, she realised Diana and the kids would be back from Wilmington Hall in a few minutes. Enough time to compose herself and present them with her usual cheerful smile and all-successful image. Enough time to plan what she would say when they asked about Serge. Diana would enquire after him, in her usual polite way, and Francesca was going to have to reply cheerfully that everything was fine. It struck her as lucky that she and Diana had never been on really intimate terms, for that would prevent her sister-in-law enquiring further. Their friendship had grown over the years, but it was based on mutual respect and liking. Diana admired her for the ruthless driving qualities that had made her the youngest Vice President of the largest jewellery company in the world. Francesca admired Diana because she had dragged herself up from being a social butterfly into a woman who owned her own thriving business. Event Organising Ltd was minute compared to Kalinsky's, but it was a one-woman achievement and in terms of advancement Diana had actually achieved more, considering the start she'd had. Beyond that, the only thing that bonded them together was the existence of Guy, about whom they never spoke, as if it was a subject they both preferred to ignore. Diana had never told her exactly why she and Guy had separated and Francesca had never asked. By the same token, Diana had never questioned her about why she had never married Serge, although they had lived together all this time. They respected each other's privacy and the unspoken nature of their relationship forged deep trust between them. As Uncle Henry had once told Francesca, the quickest way to wreck a friendship is to know too much about the other person. And anyway, Francesca reasoned as she rose from the sofa in Diana's pretty drawing-room and went over to look out of the window, everything would come all right between her and Serge again.

The trouble was her job caused her to travel frequently, visiting outlets in all the major cities, and when he heard she was planning to go to Europe for two weeks, he had become deeply angry. In a way she could understand his feelings; he was stuck in the design and workroom section of Kalinsky's day after day, while she jetted all over the place, having what looked like a good time. She made a wry face. Being on the road, living out of suitcases, and waking up in a different hotel room every few days was anything but glamorous. On the other hand, she told herself, Serge should understand by now. Seeing that all the branches throughout the world were running smoothly was part of her job. It was childish and maddening of him to get angry. Then she shrugged. When she got back to New York she would suggest they relax together a bit more, take in a few theatres and dinner parties; go on holiday. It had worked before. Surely it would work again?

At that moment the front door slammed and she could hear voices in the hall. A second later Miles and Kathryn, led by Diana, came into the drawing-room.

'Aunt Francesca!' shrieked Kathryn joyously. 'Mummy said she had a surprise for us, but I never guessed it was you.' She flung herself at Francesca, hugging her.

'What a lovely surprise,' said Miles, kissing her on the cheek.

'Hi, kids! Hi, Diana.'

'I'm sorry we're late getting back from Wilmington. The traffic was hell. Have you been waiting long?' Diana asked.

'Only a short while. I've been catching up on *Country Life*!'

They both laughed. Life in the country was definitely not Francesca's style.

'Who'd like a drink before lunch?' Diana asked.

'I've got presents for you all,' Francesca announced a few minutes later.

'Wow!' Kathryn's dark eyes lit up with excitement. Miles tried hard to assume an air of grown-up nonchalance.

Francesca unzipped a large Gucci bag and took out some packages. They were wrapped, as all Kalinsky's packages were wrapped, in pale blue paper, held in place with a cream seal bearing the embossed K in gold.

'Your grandmother was in a wildly extravagant mood when she picked out these things for you,' laughed Francesca. 'I just hope to God you like them.' She handed one to Miles, another to Kathryn, and with an almost undetectable wink to Diana, handed her the third. They both knew Diana's had been chosen by Francesca, for Sarah had made a point of ignoring Diana's existence since the separation from Guy. Again, by an unspoken understanding, it was agreed between them that it was better Miles and Kathryn didn't realise this.

For Kathryn there was a pair of earrings, exquisite diamond flowers with a sapphire in the centre, and for Miles a set of pearl shirt front studs. When Diana opened hers, she found a snakeskin appointment book, combined with address book and wallet. Its corners were bound in eighteen carat gold, the silk lining of the hard covers embossed with the letter K.

'It's beautiful,' Diana exclaimed.

'I hope you like it,' said Francesca. 'It's part of a whole new range we're marketing. Blotters, cigarette boxes, handbags, small luggage. I decided it was time to expand our interests. We're going into the perfume business next year, with gorgeous

Lalique glass bottles, and the stopper will be a gold K.'

'Wow,' gasped Kathryn for the second time.

'Mom's having a fit, of course,' said Francesca. 'She still thinks we should be majoring on three rows of graduated pearls with a nice clasp.'

Diana laughed. 'In spite of the sensational success of Serge's designs? They've revolutionised everyone's concept of jewellery.'

'You bet,' Francesca's tone was succinct. 'But then you know Mom.'

Over lunch, Francesca listened with interest as Miles told her what it was like up at Oxford, where he was studying economics.

'I'm taking my A levels in three months time,' said Kathryn cheerfully. 'I've no idea what I'm going to do with myself, after that. I really want to get a job. An academic career doesn't appeal to me at all.'

'Well, I have an idea, if your mother agrees,' said Francesca.

Diana raised her eyebrows enquiringly, trusting her sister-in-law not to suggest something too outrageous.

'How would it be if you came over to the States for a vacation in the summer, after sitting your A levels? You could stay with me in my apartment for a bit, and I know your granny would love you to stay with her at Palm Beach for a while, when she goes there on vacation. There are masses of young people there and you could have a ball.'

'Oh! Oh, wow! I'd love that. Mummy, I can go, can't I?' Kathryn's face glowed and she was almost trembling with excitement.

'Well . . .' Diana teased, and seeing Kathryn's face falling, she laughed. 'Of course you can go, darling. I think it would be wonderful for you.'

'Then that's settled. Mom will be thrilled to have her beautiful granddaughter stay with her,' said Francesca.

'Can I go to your workrooms and see Serge designing?' Kathryn asked eagerly. 'And can I go to your offices and can I look at all the jewellery?'

Francesca smiled at her indulgently. 'Well, if your father didn't show any interest in the business, it's certainly been passed on to you. You remind me of myself, when I was your age.'

Diana felt a slow flush creep up her neck and she looked away. If heredity was anything to go by, Kathryn should really be a budding writer by now.

When the telephone rang later that afternoon, Bentley, more decrepit and lugubrious than ever, announced it was Mr Guy Andrews calling for young Mr Andrews.

'I wonder what he wants,' said Miles, dashing out of the room to the 'phone in the study. He was back in a few minutes, his face alight with obvious pride.

'Guess what?' he cried. 'Dad's just been made Minister of Public Enterprise. The Prime Minister is announcing the appointment this afternoon, and Dad's giving a party this evening in his flat, to celebrate. He's asked me.' Then he faltered, and looked embarrassed. 'But he hasn't asked Kitty,' he added, calling her by the nickname he'd used when they'd both been small, and which he only used now if he felt sorry for her.

'I don't mind,' said Kathryn stoutly. 'I'll stay with Mum.'

When Miles and Kathryn went off to Regent's Park to play tennis, Francesca brought up the subject of Kathryn not being invited.

'Does Guy have favourites?' she asked bluntly. 'It would be history repeating itself if he does. Mom always put him before me and to this day I think it's unfair for a parent to love one child more than the other.'

'I suppose he does,' said Diana, sounding vague, 'But frankly Kathryn doesn't mind. She's never been as close to Guy as Miles has and on the whole she thinks what he does is pretty boring.' She hoped she sounded convincing. You never knew with Francesca. She was very shrewd and couldn't be easily fooled. They'd never discussed Guy in any detail, but she obviously realised he was a homosexual. What Diana didn't ever want her to realise was that Marc Raven, world famous author, now a multi-millionaire, was Kathryn's real father.

Francesca's apartment was dark and empty when she returned home after her two weeks in Europe, and in a heart-stopping moment she knew Serge had gone.

The place had a deserted hollow feeling about it that filled her with fear and dread. Frantically she ran from room to room, hoping for some miracle; she would find him asleep in bed; or lazing in the bath. Perhaps he was fixing himself something in the kitchen? Her housekeeper, emerging from her own quarters, greeted her morosely and confirmed, in halting tones, that Mr Buono had indeed packed his things and left the previous week.

Rising panic engulfed Francesca as she wondered what to do. It brought back memories of the fearful night Marc had vanished. Oh God, had Serge found someone else? Had he finally got tired of hanging around while she put the company first? She glanced at her watch. It was nearly ten o'clock at night, so she couldn't contact him at work. What could she do? Certainly not call her mother.

Pouring herself a strong vodka and tonic, tears of abject misery flowing down her face, she cursed herself for having blown it.

The sapphires lay spread on a sheet of white waxed paper; pale ones from Ceylon, darker ones from Burma and the very darkest blue and the most valuable, from Kashmir. There were also a sprinkling of almost jet-black sapphires, imported from Australia and Bangkok and the least valuable. Serge placed them one by one, with a pair of tweezers, onto a drawing he had done of a brooch, securing them in place with plasticine. With infinite care and a steady hand he adjusted one or two of the smaller stones, then leaned back and studied the effect. When it was made up the brooch would resemble a perfect blue iris, set in white gold. The effect would be three-dimensional and the individual petals, backed with tiny coiled springs, would quiver in a life-like way when the wearer moved.

'This is ready to be made up, Jim,' he called to

the workroom foreman. 'I'd give it to Phil to do.'

'Okay.' Jim came over to Serge's workbench and for a few minutes they discussed the technical problems of setting the stones with a fine milgrained edge instead of the traditional claws which would show.

'Fabergé, eat your heart out!' marvelled Joe, picking up the design with care. 'Are you letting me have the design for the coral necklace this afternoon?'

'Nope.' Abruptly Serge got to his feet. 'I've had enough for today. I feel lousy.'

'Nothing serious, I hope?'

'Nothing I can't handle,' said Serge briefly. He walked slowly out of the busy workroom and into the private office at the far end. Reaching for the 'phone, he dialled the number of Sarah's private office at Kalinsky's.

'Sarah, I've a favour to ask you,' he began without preamble. 'I've got to get away for a while, have you any objection to my going to Europe for a break?'

There was a moment's silence, then Sarah spoke. 'If you wanted to go to Europe why didn't you go with Francesca? Didn't she get back last night? I hope she did because I'm expecting her in the office this morning. The work is piling up.'

'This has nothing to do with Francesca,' he replied evenly. 'I just feel a need to get away.'

'For how long, for God's sake?'

'I don't know. Don't worry about my work. I'll be sending in my designs, with full instructions. Jim and Phil can look after everything.'

'What's the matter, Serge?' She sounded deeply irritated. 'I'm warning you, there is a clause in your contract with us that says if you leave Kalinsky's you are not allowed to work for any other jeweller for five years.'

Serge was filled with a deep weariness. 'This is a personal matter, Sarah. Some people do have personal lives, you know. We're not all like you and your daughter who put work before everything else.'

'There's no need to be rude. Some of us are professionals. We don't go off on some whim when there's work to be done. Have you discussed this with Francesca?'

Serge evaded the question. Let Francesca explain the situation to her mother if she wanted to. 'Out of courtesy to you, as President of Kalinsky's,' he said heavily, 'I am calling to inform you that I shall be away for a while, but that the design department will not suffer in my absence. Okay?'

There was a click and the line went dead. Serge looked at the silent receiver and replaced it slowly. What a bitch, he thought, and if he felt a pang of remorse at walking out on Francesca, because she was getting like her mother, he put it quickly out of his mind. Maybe Francesca couldn't help being tough and independent, maybe she was unaware she was emulating Sarah. Whatever it was, he knew he couldn't handle it any longer.

For once, Francesca was late getting to her office. Jet lag and insomnia had kept her brain buzzing until five in the morning, and then she'd fallen into a deep uneasy sleep, only waking up at ten o'clock when her housekeeper, slightly anxious, had brought her a cup of coffee. She drank it slowly, painfully aware of the empty space in the bed beside her, missing the sounds of Serge having a shower, talking on the 'phone, sharing breakfast with her. She tried to be philosophical, telling herself this was a temporary split. She'd go to the workrooms later today and persuade him he was being childish, she'd make him see they were happy the way they were. Who needed marriage anyway?

The first thing she saw on her desk was a memo from her mother. It was short and to the point.

'Did you know Serge had left for Europe? I want to talk to you as soon as you get in.'

It wasn't even signed. Just a hand-scrawled note on a sheet of blue paper marked 'The President's Office'.

Francesca put it to one side, numb with shock. Then she put a call through to the workrooms and was informed he'd already left and he hadn't said when he'd be back. So that was that. She leaned back in her swivel chair and gazed blankly round her opulently furnished office. She'd have to stall for time before seeing Sarah, the one person she couldn't face right now. Quickly she opened her briefcase and jammed into it the various reports her secretary had left for her to study. She'd take them home and work on them there. Today was going to be a day when she had to be alone.

* * *

337

Later that night she was still going over the various reports, having informed her secretary that she was at home catching up on work and was not to be disturbed. She told her housekeeper to say she was out if anyone called, and that meant her mother too. As the day passed and she became absorbed in her work, she was able to push thoughts of Serge to the back of her mind. A lot had been happening in her absence. Security needed tightening up in the Madrid branch. It was a firm rule that showroom doors were to be locked at all times, whether customers were in the shop or not. Closed-circuit television on the entrance must be operative to record all comings and goings. Only one piece of jewellery at a time was to be shown to a customer. And yet the previous week a man, purporting to be a German industrialist, had got away with a bracelet, two rings and a pair of earrings valued at a hundred thousand dollars, before the bewildered staff could gather their wits. Francesca made a note to call the manager, Paulo Rodriguez, and ask him what the hell he was playing at.

Then there was the problem they were having with fake replicas of their distinctive wristwatches being produced in Tokyo and Hong Kong. The copies were almost impossible to distinguish from the real thing, even down to the famous K in gold on the clock face. China and Japan were exporting them in great quantities all over the world, for a mere two hundred dollars. Who was going to bother with the genuine article at six thousand dollars?

Suddenly Francesca wished Uncle Henry hadn't

retired. He always seemed to know how to handle tricky situations and she wished she could talk to him right now. Not only about the company, but about Serge. On impulse, she grabbed the 'phone, hoping he hadn't already gone to bed in his new house in Stockbridge.

'Why hullo there, honey,' he said when she got through. 'It's great to hear from you.'

'Uncle Henry, I'm sorry to call so late, but I really need to see you. Can I fly down to Stockbridge tomorrow? I need your advice.'

'Sure, I'll be glad to see you. How's everything going?'

'Not so good. I've got problems at work . . . and Serge has left me.'

'Left you?' he repeated, surprised. 'Really left you, I mean, for good?'

Francesca hesitated. 'I'm not sure. He's gone to Europe. No one seems to know when he's getting back.'

'Had a lovers' quarrel?'

'Something like that.'

'Don't you worry, darling. He'll be back. A little trip might do him good. Remember what they say – "Absence makes the heart grow fonder".'

'Uncle Henry, I love you,' said Francesca, smiling to herself. 'I feel better already.'

She lay awake for a long time that night, thinking about Serge and Kalinsky's. Since Henry's retirement she'd been the sole Vice President, while Sarah clung on to the Presidency, refusing to let anyone make major decisions without her permission and often over-ruling Francesca. It was a situation that couldn't go on much longer. With the ever-growing competition from other jewellery companies, cheap copies of one of their best lines coming from the Far East, and now the defection of Serge, Francesca felt it was vital to have someone strong running the company. And someone strong in the right way. Sarah's strength was now petty and narrow, more concerned with the window display on Fifth Avenue than a robbery in Madrid. Like a little bird in her couture clothes and a blaze of jewels, she pecked and scratched at trivia, still blaming Francesca for the fact Guy had never come back, still bitter that her daughter had tried to take his place.

Francesca sat up in bed and turned on the lamp, her mind alert and working rapidly. She now owned fifty-five per cent of the stock of Kalinsky's, thanks to Henry who had sold her his shares when he'd retired six months before. She could gain control any time she wished, though Sarah didn't realise it. The point was, was she ruthless enough to oust her mother at last and be done with it?

Sarah had always sworn that nothing but death would prise her hands from the rudder. She was Kalinsky's now that Guy would never come back. At times Francesca believed her mother would rather see the company sink into oblivion than let her take it over.

Then there was the question of Serge. She had to persuade him to come back. He was as much a part of Kalinsky's as she was. Together they had built up the design section into an unrivalled position.

Surely he couldn't let all that go because she didn't want to get married?

Both problems have to be solved, she thought, as she turned out the light. My taking over complete control and getting Serge to return.

In the sudden darkness she hoped she had the ability to do it.

Three days later Francesca was back in her office, refreshed and restored by Henry's quiet common sense and string of homilies and platitudes. There was something deeply comforting about him, especially when he assured her that Serge would soon come running back.

'Hell, sweetheart, he's loved you for over fifteen years, and because he loves you he wants to marry you. Can't blame the guy for that!' he added, the twinkle in his eyes undimmed by the passing years. 'I expect he's already realised it was a mistake to put on the pressure. He'll be back soon as if nothing had happened.'

'I hope you're right. I do love him, and I can't imagine life without him. It's just the thought of marriage that makes me feel trapped. I'm afraid I won't be my own person any more.'

'You'll always be your own person, Francesca, no matter what you do with your life. I think this has more to do with the hurt you suffered from that writer, Marc Raven. He was your first love and that's always the most painful. On a subconscious level, a part of you is afraid of getting hurt again, though God knows why with a guy like Serge. You'll never find a better one.'

341

Francesca gave a little laugh. 'Did I come to you for psycotherapy, Uncle Henry? Now, what am I going to do about Mom?'

Once again, as in previous years, they worked out a strategy. The time had come for Francesca to seize power.

Now, seated at her desk, she rang for her secretary so they could go through the morning's mail. One of the envelopes was marked 'Private and Confidential'. The handwriting she knew as well as she knew her own.

'That will be all for the moment, Rita,' she said abruptly, her hands shaking. Her secretary quietly withdrew, wondering what was wrong.

Serge's letter was brief. He would be away for several months touring Europe so she would not be able to contact him. He would have his designs couriered to the workrooms on a regular basis so she need not worry that production would slow down. He did not even wish her well or send her his love. As tears gathered in her eyes, she stuffed the letter in her handbag. It looked as if she'd turned him down just once too often.

The board meeting was the shortest Francesca could ever remember, the element of surprise catching Sarah off-guard. All along Sarah had been under the illusion that Francesca owned fifty per cent of the stock, having bought Guy out. Her own thirty-five per cent, left to her by her father, was not as impressive a share, but it kept her safe from ever being out-voted. The remaining fifteen per cent was owned by Henry Langham, Max

Ditzler and Clint Friedman. She would remain in complete control for as long as she wanted.

'I'm afraid your figures are inaccurate,' said Francesca, trying to keep her voice steady. 'I have owned fifty-five per cent for the past six months. The transfer of the extra five shares went through when Henry Langham retired and sold them to me – to use how and when I liked,' she added quietly.

Sarah's face turned grey so that her blusher lay on the surface of her skin like bright pink powder. Her mouth tightened and she looked down at her bejewelled hands as they lay, tightly clenched, in her lap. The silence in the boardroom was tense and for a moment Francesca wondered if her mother was going to cry, and she was filled with a pang of pity. What she was doing was a terrible thing, taking away from Sarah the one thing that had motivated and sustained her for nearly forty years. With a feeling of dark premonition Francesca realised exactly the same thing would happen to her one day. She'd be sitting in the President's chair, thinking she was in control for a long time to come, and then someone younger, fitter and more able to cope would kick that chair from under her. And she too would have to surrender the reins of power, hand over the company that had been her life, relinquish everything that she'd held dear.

Francesca opened her mouth to speak, but no one would ever know what she'd been about to say. Sarah had risen with dignity, her head high, her hands gripping the edge of the mahogany table.

'I don't think we need prolong this meeting,' she

said in a thin voice. 'Gentlemen, it has been my pride and my pleasure to guide Kalinsky's from the relatively small company it was when my father left it to me to the giant corporation it is today. I have given my life to the company but maybe now I should hand over that privilege to someone else. I will spare you all the embarrassment of voting on the issue of who should be the next President. I resign, as of now.'

Without another word she turned and walked slowly out of the boardroom, a proud lonely figure, leaving all she had cared for behind.

At that moment, Francesca had never felt so dreadful in her life.

Chapter Sixteen

The sun sparkled blindingly on the wings of the jumbo jet as it taxied down the runway of Kennedy Airport. On board, Kathryn was clutching her hand luggage, hardly able to contain her impatience. Two whole months in the States lay ahead of her. Aunt Francesca was waiting to meet her and show her the delights of New York, and after that there'd be Palm Beach. She'd had a letter from her grandmother saying that although she was not very well herself, her friends had rallied round and now there were lots of young people for her to meet and lots of parties to go to. She hoped Kathryn was going to enjoy herself. Enjoy herself? She was already enjoying herself and she hadn't even got off the plane!

'Kathryn, honey!' Francesca came rushing forward as soon as she got through the arrivals gate and swept her up in a big hug.

'Oh, Aunt Francesca, isn't this wonderful!' Her large round eyes looked dazzled as she was led to the waiting Lincoln Continental.

'I'd like you to do me just one big favour on this trip,' Francesca was saying with a teasing smile.

'Yes, what? Anything!'

'Could you bear to call me just Francesca?' She

glanced across at her niece. 'Now you're as tall as me and a very sophisticated young lady, you're making me feel about two thousand years old with this "Aunt" business.'

Kathryn roared with laughter. 'That's Mummy. She always insists I call you "Aunt". I still have to refer to Charles and Sophie and John as "Uncle" or "Aunt".'

Francesca's mouth twitched. To call John 'Aunt' might be more appropriate than Kathryn realised.

'Let's go straight to my apartment,' said Francesca quickly. 'Maybe this afternoon you'd like to accompany me to the workrooms. I have to go there in any case, and it would be a chance for you to look around.'

Kathryn's cheeks turned pink with pleasure. 'I'd love that,' she said fervently. 'Will I see Serge actually making some jewellery?'

'I'm afraid not.' Francesca's face tightened and her eyes looked suddenly strained. 'Serge is in Europe at present.'

'Oh!' Kathryn was silent for a moment and then impulsively she asked, 'Aren't you together any more?'

There was a pause and Francesca seemed to be choosing her words with care. 'I think he needed a break, he'd been working very hard. I expect he'll be back . . . in time.'

'Wow! You must miss him.' Kathryn looked at her sympathetically, and Francesca realised how refreshingly open and naive her niece was.

'Yes, I miss him,' she replied, 'but we've been so busy there's hardly been time to stop and think.

Since I became President I've been rushed off my feet. The next thing is the Paris exhibition. I've still got a lot of work to do for that.'

'You lucky thing.' Kathryn's voice was heavy with envy. 'You have such a fascinating life. I'd love to do what you're doing.'

'Seriously?' Francesca looked at her questioningly.

'Yes, really. Do you think I could ever get a job in your Bond Street showroom? I wouldn't mind what I did, hoover the floors, clean the glass cases, anything just to be there,' she ended dramatically.

'If you're that interested, I think we can find you something more amusing than office cleaning,' exclaimed Francesca. 'Anyway, see how you feel when you've found out a bit more about the business. It's not enough to just love pretty jewels, you know. It's big business, and pretty cutthroat at that.'

Kathryn's eyes were solemn but her voice sounded excited. 'I can imagine that. Can I see your office too? And watch what you do? I promise I won't get in the way.'

Francesca looked at Kathryn and remembered a little girl in red shoes, begging to be allowed to stay in her mother's office so that she could see what went on. 'Of course you can, darling,' she replied warmly. 'It will be nice to have you around and, time permitting, I'll explain all the things we do as I go along.'

'Fantastic!' enthused Kathryn. 'I can hardly wait.'

Kathryn took her tour of the workrooms

seriously. She was allowed to weigh diamonds on the new electronic eye machine and watch gold being transformed into 'white' gold by being rhodium plated. She tried her hand at a giant fly press which, when screwed down, had a pressure of five tons for pressing and flattening metals, and she was allowed to compare the difference between Siam rubies which were a blacker red than Burma rubies, which were a blueish red.

'I could stay here forever,' she said at last, her eyes resting on a dome-shaped sapphire ring, that Francesca was taking back to the Park Avenue showrooms. 'This is an enormous sapphire!'

'It isn't really,' Francesca explained. 'It's a layer of sapphire topped with a crystal dome, known as a doublet. We do triplets too. It works equally well with other stones, like emeralds.'

'Wow! There's so much to learn!'

Francesca sprang to her feet, remembering all the work she had to do back at the office. 'Okay, let's go. You can look around the showrooms when we get back and feast your eyes to your heart's content.'

Kathryn was allowed to spend the rest of the afternoon in the showrooms examining pieces of jewellery, one at a time as security rules dictated. She had never enjoyed herself so much in her life. Fiery black opals, blue diamonds, pale grey pearls and yellow sapphires, made up into necklaces, bracelets, earrings and rings, were laid out before her on a black velvet pillow. Nothing was too much trouble for the President's niece. Halfway through the afternoon, the manager was called to the 'phone and when he came back he was smiling broadly.

'That was Miss Andrews, calling down from her office. Your aunt wishes you to have something special as a gift,' he said. 'She suggested you might like this.' From a locked drawer he produced a ring and placed it in front of Kathryn.

It was a square cut emerald, slightly raised, and mounted on a little hillock of small diamonds. Kathryn picked it up reverently, gazing into its cool yet fiery depths, overwhelmed by Francesca's generosity.

'If you press that little gold knob at the side . . .' the manager suggested, still grinning.

Cautiously, Kathryn pressed the gold button and the emerald sprang open like the lid of a box, revealing a tiny Kalinsky watch, the Roman numerals marked in fine gold.

'Oh!' she gasped. 'I've never seen anything so exquisite!'

He nodded. 'Miss Andrews got the idea for it a couple of years back. We find they're very popular.'

'For the woman who has everything, I suppose?' said Kathryn.

'For the young lady who has everything,' he agreed, liking her very much.

'Oh, thank you, and I must go and thank her. How do I get up to her office?' Kathryn gathered up her things, flushed with excitement.

'I'll get someone to take you up.'

It was Kathryn's first real experience of what a day in the jewellery business was like and she enjoyed herself so much that during the following weeks she asked to be allowed to spend as much time as she could in either the workrooms or the various offices.

When she finally left for Palm Beach to join Sarah for the remainder of her stay, Francesca called up Diana to tell her how Kathryn's trip was going.

'I think she must take after my mother and me,' she joked. 'She's riveted by the business, unlike Guy. She's even more interested than I was at her age. Who knows, Diana? Kalinsky's may be run by another Andrews after I'm gone. After all, it is in her blood.'

Diana, on the other end of the line, stayed silent. If Guy's family were so fond of Kathryn and were going to give her the opportunity of a wonderful career and inheritance, she would never ruin the girl's chances by revealing the truth.

'So how is your father, Kathryn?' They were the first words Sarah uttered when her granddaughter arrived. 'Is he well? I miss him so much, you know. Tell me all he's doing.'

Sarah had aged greatly since she'd resigned from Kalinsky's. Her once sharp eyes now had a smokey look, and sometimes her footsteps faltered. Her hands trembled slightly as she fiddled with her long Kalinsky chains of gold linked with pearls and she quavered on about her beloved son until Kathryn felt ready to scream. Kathryn had never felt close to Guy and she was not prepared to spend all her days closeted with her grandmother in a stuffy, over-furnished room, while Sarah reminisced and probed with awkward questions.

'He's fine,' said Kathryn flatly, wishing to change the subject.

'I wish he'd come and see me,' Sarah continued. 'Tell him to write to me, dear. I call him up sometimes, but he never seems to be in.'

'I'll tell him. Can I go for a swim now, Granny? It's so awfully hot . . .'

Sarah looked disappointed. Oh well, she thought, the child is young, and there is this evening to look forward to when I can show her all the snapshots of Guy when he was a boy. 'Run along, dear. You'll find everything in the pool house. There may be some young people out there already. My next door neighbours have some friends of their son staying, and I've said they can use my pool as it's bigger than theirs.'

'Thanks, Granny.' Kathryn kissed her swiftly on the highly rouged and withered cheek and shot out into the garden where the large blue pool looked cool and inviting.

'Hi! I'm Oliver. You must be Kathryn.'

Kathryn looked up, startled, into the dark eyes and suntanned face of a young man who was standing by the edge of the pool, rivulets of water running down his athletic and muscular body. She had never seen anyone so amazingly healthy looking in her life. The boys back in England were pale and puny by comparison.

'Y-yes, I'm Kathryn,' she mumbled.

'I reckoned you must be.' He had a lazy American drawl and his smile showed even white teeth.

'I'm staying with the Rosenthals, next door, and I came over to cool off after tennis. It's more peaceful here. I hope you don't mind?'

'Of course I don't mind. Granny said I might find some people out here. Hang on a second while I change.'

Five minutes later she emerged from the poolhouse in a sky-blue bikini that revealed her long slim legs, pointed breasts and small waist. Oliver's appreciative eyes swept over her as he swam slowly towards her. With a perfect dive, she entered the pool and came up beside him, grinning at the sheer joy of finding herself floating in the cool clear waters.

'Isn't it great!' she cried, flinging her head back so her long dark hair spread out around her, fanning on the gentle ripples.

'Race you to the end,' he said.

'You're on.' Side by side they swam the length of the pool, Oliver reaching it a second before she did.

'And back again?' he suggested.

'Okay.' Kathryn found it harder going on the way back, and when she finally reached the end she clung to the marble rim, panting.

'I'm exhausted,' she gasped, laughing. 'Let's go and sit down.' She hauled herself out of the pool and led the way to some blue and white striped and padded sun beds.

'So tell me about yourself?' Oliver was looking at her with penetrating eyes that seemed to caress her body and she liked the way his full mouth turned up at the corners.

'There isn't much to tell. I'm nearly eighteen, I

live in London and I hope to go into the jewellery business. Granny has asked me to stay here for a few weeks and then I'm having a final week in New York with my aunt before I return home. What about you?'

'I'm trying to get into films or television. I'm just here on vacation because Hollywood's pretty dead at this time of year.'

'You live in Hollywood, then?' Kathryn eyed him with renewed interest. Of course she should have guessed. He *looked* like a film star. 'Should I have heard of you? What's your other name?'

'Power. No, I haven't done anything you would have seen me in. Just a few pilots for television series. I hope I'll get a break one day.'

'Oliver Power,' she repeated slowly. 'Well, I'll look out for you! Wow, isn't it hot? I'm going to get myself a cool drink. Can I get you anything?'

'Coke, please.'

As Kathryn walked over the hot stones to the bar in the poolhouse she had a feeling that her stay in Palm Beach was going to be even more fun than her visit to New York.

Two weeks had passed; two weeks of long, hot, lazy days that stretched into languorous, balmy, star-studded nights, during which Kathryn moved slowly and wonderingly, her senses heightened, her body aware of strange feelings she had never had before. Oliver had become the pivot of her existence, and when he was not by her side she experienced a lonely ache and a longing that drew her nerves taut and kept her awake at night. It was with bitter-sweet agony that they met and parted during those days, Kathryn having to spend a certain amount of time with Sarah, and Oliver, who had extended his stay with the Rosenthals, having to fulfil his role of polite houseguest. But whenever possible they slipped away together, to go swimming or walking, or just to sit and talk quietly by the ocean's side, where the surf whispered along the sandy shore and the breeze rustled in the palm trees.

The joy of discovering shared interests kept their conversation flowing easily, as if they could never hear enough about each other and, shyly holding hands, they discussed their favourite music and films and books, finding their tastes so similar it seemed more than coincidental.

'Don't tell me you're crazy about John Donne, too!' exclaimed Kathryn, as they walked back from the beach one day. 'He's positively my favourite poet, but everyone at school *hated* him!'

Oliver smiled at her, and quoted.

'Twice or thrice had I loved thee
Before I knew thy face or name . . .'

Then he blushed furiously, looking straight ahead.

'That's from *Air and Angels*, isn't it?' cut in Kathryn hurriedly, to cover the sudden flush of embarrassment she felt. 'Doesn't it go on:

So in a voice, so in a shapeless flame,
Angels affect us oft, and worshipped be?'

He nodded, and then he squeezed her hand. She looked up at him out of the corner of her eye, and was filled with an intense desire to kiss the flat plane of his tanned cheek. He slipped his arm round her waist, pressing him to her side, so that she could feel his hip against hers, and a molten heat swam through her veins, making her heart throb almost painfully.

That evening she spoke on the phone to Diana.

'I'm longing for you to meet him,' she told her mother. 'You've no idea how wonderful he is.'

'Tell me about him, darling,' Diana asked, a flicker of anxiety crossing her mind. She, too, had been eighteen when she'd fallen in love with Guy.

'His name's Oliver Power and he's an actor, but not a penniless failed one. I think his family's rich anyway. He's twenty-two . . .'

'Who are his family?'

'The Powers, I suppose!' Kathryn giggled. 'Mummy, I hope you're not going to be snobbish or anything like that.'

'Of course I'm not,' said Diana indignantly. 'I'm just interested. So you're staying with your grandmother another week and then you're going back to New York?'

'Maybe . . . but I'd like to ask Granny if I can stay on a bit longer while Oliver's here. He doesn't have to get back to Hollywood for another fortnight.'

'Well, if you're not outstaying your welcome, that's fine.'

'Thanks, Mummy. I'll talk to you soon.'

'Goodbye, darling.' Thoughtfully Diana hung up the phone. How quickly children grow up, she thought sadly, remembering Kathryn as a small child. Soon she and Miles will leave home forever, and for a moment she felt a deep pang of regret that the days of their innocence and youth were coming to an end.

Later that night, as they walked slowly along the beach, Kathryn could sense a different and fragile tenderness in their manner towards each other. For the first time there was a tension between them that was tingling and heavy, laden with something she didn't understand. Her body felt keyed up and uncomfortable, her breasts tender and her insides moist. When they reached a secluded part of the beach they stopped and stood under the boughs of an over-hanging tree which shrouded the sand in darker shades of night. Standing close together, they looked out to sea and saw the fiery silver trail of reflected moonlight on the calm waters.

Then he turned to kiss her, finding the corner of her mouth in the darkness, before she turned her head, and his lips met hers, gently and tenderly at first, until his tongue entered her mouth, searching, probing, flicking the tip of her tongue, exploring the gentle moisture as her tongue gradually began to respond to his. As the breeze rippled round them, they stood for a long time like that, until her body ached with growing longing and she began to tremble.

'Kathryn . . .' her name seemed wrenched from his throat. He held her tighter.

'Oh . . . Oh, Oliver . . .' Her voice was like the murmur of the sea, lost on the wind.

'I love you, I love you so much,' he said in a rush.

For answer, she buried her face in the smooth warmth of his throat, and her fingers stroked his dark hair where it rippled and curled at the nape of his neck. She felt swollen and wet inside now, crazy to have him touch her where she was most sensitive, hurting in her need for him. She could feel him, hard against her stomach and he was trembling too. She was no longer shy and embarrassed, her need now too great.

'Can't we . . .?' she faltered in a husky voice.

Without a word, he gently pulled her down so they were kneeling, facing each other on the deep soft sand, and, very slowly, he slipped down the thin shoulder straps of her dress. With tentative fingers, as if he were touching a work of rare art, he stroked her breasts, draining the last of her strength and her will to do anything but respond. Then he gradually pulled her down so that they were lying together, his legs wrapped around her yielding limbs. For a while they clung together, as if Oliver was holding back, reluctant to make the final move that would bind them as one, then Kathryn lifted her head, as if to search his face.

'I want you,' she said at last, and there was urgency in her voice.

'Oh, God, I want you too . . . but are you sure?'

'I'm sure,' she whispered.

The moon swam behind a solitary cloud as if to shield the lovers from the night, as nervously at first, and then with mounting confidence, Oliver took her with one swift stroke, his kiss muffling the first sharp cry of pain she uttered, his arms holding her tightly, helping her to match her rhythm to his, until with a gasp and spasm, he lay spent and panting on top of her.

A little while later he spoke. 'Are you all right, honey?'

Kathryn pulled his head down to her breast. 'I'm fine,' she murmured softly, and then a little later, 'I wish we could spend the night together . . . the whole night.'

'One day we will,' he promised, 'nothing can part us now, Kathryn. We'll be together for always.'

Alone in her bed that night, Kathryn dreamed that a large black monster flew out of the sky and whipped Oliver away, high above her, so that he was beyond her reach.

Francesca was working late in her office, trying to clear her desk before flying to Paris the next day for the highly publicised jewellery exhibition Kalinsky's were holding at the *Musée des Beaux-Arts*. A hundred unique pieces were going on show, demonstrating the history of the company which was celebrating sixty years in business. The glossy catalogue lay before her, printed in French and English and heavily illustrated. It was going to be an impressive exhibition, and years had gone into acquiring, through auctions, many of their original pieces. They had even managed to secure the first important jewel they had ever made; a gold buckle, commissioned by the last Tzar of Russia, set with cloudy green chrysoprase, pale watery moonstones and rubies. Then there were elegant Edwardian hair ornaments, studded with gems, Art Nouveau necklaces and dangly earrings made of jade and glittering jet, through to the stylised diamond clips so favoured in the 'fifties. Representing the 'seventies were some of Serge's finest designs, collars and bracelets and brooches that breathed life into the very stones so that they seemed like a part of nature.

Art magazines throughout the world had featured the forthcoming event, which was tipped to take Paris by storm, before moving on to London prior to a triumphant return to New York. Kalinsky's advertising and promotional departments had poured money and effort into publicising the exhibition, and Francesca was delighted with the results. There couldn't be anyone in the main capitals of the world who hadn't now heard about it. Cartier, Van Cleef & Arpels, eat your heart out, she thought as she looked at the catalogue again. This really put Kalinsky's at the top of the heap. They now had branches in nineteen countries, stretching from Tokyo to Monte Carlo, San Francisco to Marbella. They had two thousand employees worldwide, and the promotional budget alone was over three million dollars a year.

Temporarily satisfied, Francesca swung gently in her Italian leather swivel chair, looking around at what had once been Sarah's office but was now hers. Gone was the Louis XV desk, the fragile French chairs and fussy lamps, the heavy curtains and delicate *objets d'art*. In their place she had imported from Rome the sharp crystal facets of Fabian's lucite furniture so that desk, console and coffee tables and clear fluted columns displaying crystal and gilt lamps in the shape of miniature palm trees, seemed to float, transparent and gleaming, above a carpet of pale Kalinsky blue. The white silk walls, displaying a collection of modern art, completed the airy modern atmosphere. It suited Francesca to perfection.

Letters signed and papers attended to, she went methodically through the contents of her slim brief-case, checking her passport and flight tickets for the next day. Her secretary had booked her on Pan Am Flight No. 847, departing from Kennedy Airport for Paris at 1400 hours. Her seat number, in first class, was 3 D. She thanked God for an efficient secretary. Now there was only one more thing to do before she left the office for the night.

'Put me through to Mrs Andrews in Palm Beach,' she told the girl on the switchboard. Diana had called her earlier, asking who this young man was that Kathryn was seeing. As she'd never heard of him she said she'd ask Sarah, though she felt her sister-in-law was making a fuss about nothing. So Kathryn has a boyfriend, she told herself. So what? Surely Diana wasn't getting like the old Countess of Sutton, who Francesca thought was a terrible snob.

'Hi, Mom,' she greeted Sarah breezily when she got through. 'How's everything?'

'Fine.' Sarah's voice was stiff and chilly as usual.

'And how's Kathryn?'

'She seems to be enjoying herself, not that I see much of her but that's typical of the young,' Sarah replied, grudgingly.

'How is she getting on with the boyfriend I heard

about? Do you know anything about him? Diana was asking me today, but I don't know him.'

Sarah exuded indignation. 'I don't think we need worry about Oliver Power. After all he's staying with my great friends the Rosenthals, and they're not in the habit of entertaining undesirable young men.'

'No, I didn't mean that. I think Diana just wanted to know who his family is.'

'She's probably more interested in finding out what his family's worth,' corrected Sarah. 'He's a very nice, polite boy and you can tell Diana that Kathryn will come to no harm while she's under my roof.'

'Of course not.' Francesca suddenly felt too weary to start a fight. 'I'm off to Paris in the morning,' she added conversationally.

'So I gather from everything I read. I hope you haven't been spending too much on advertising for this jaunt.'

'It's not a ...' began Francesca, and then stopped. What was the point? She had called to ask how Kathryn was and that was all. 'I'll call you when I get back next week, Mom. Take care of yourself.'

'Goodbye, Francesca.'

As she gathered up her handbag and files, she realised nothing would ever change.

Six blocks away in the Dakota, Carlotta Raven was supervising the last of her packing, glad to be getting out of the city. Marc had been on board *Sania II* for ten days now, cruising around the

361

Mediterranean while she supervised the redecoration of their apartment, and she was anxious to join him. He'd never lost his wandering eye but he was at least safe from the clutches of other women while on board his yacht. The crew had been hand-picked by her, with orders to report back on any women who might be invited on board, and Marc knew it. So far, apart from a few indiscretions, she'd managed to stop him having any serious affairs since his run-around with Lady Diana Andrews.

Now that Carlos was twenty-two and leading his own life, Carlotta was free to pursue her interests, namely hanging on to Marc and spending his money. Marc called her a shop-aholic. She called it buying necessities. He said she was never satisfied with what she had. She argued that she was a perfectionist and that she had to dress well for his sake. Marc said she was obsessed with their apartment. She strenuously denied this, saying they had to have an impressive home in their position.

Carlotta felt maddened at times. He should be grateful to her for all she had done for him, but all she got was his resentment. Well, she was off to Paris tomorrow to buy herself a new wardrobe at Yves St Laurent, Dior and Chanel, and there wasn't a damned thing he could do about it. If it weren't for her he'd have been washed up years ago anyway.

Placing her jewellery case by her luggage, ready to be taken down in the morning, she sat on the wide satin-covered bed and checked her flight tickets. New York to Paris. Wednesday, 18 June. Pan Am Flight No. 847, departing 1400 hours. Her seat in first class was already booked . . . 4 D.

She stretched languorously, looking forward to this trip, and wondered if she wouldn't get herself a new fur coat as well. After all, if one was going to Paris specifically to shop one might as well do it properly.

Kathryn awoke early and decided to go for a swim before breakfast.

Out by the pool a pale sun cast long opaque shadows on the ground and the air was fresh and sweet. Breathing deeply, she swam a length, letting the cool water flow silkily over her limbs. Then she climbed out and sat on the mosaic surround, her feet dangling in the water. She'd had another terrible dream that night and she still felt disturbed by it. This time, the large black monster had swooped out of the sky, and had gripped her with long sharp talons and carried her high above her grandmother's garden. She'd tried to scream and on the ground below she'd seen Oliver, yelling at her to come back – but she couldn't answer, no words would come from her throat, and as the monster rose up and up Oliver had become smaller and smaller, until he was just a dot on the landscape below.

Kathryn closed her eyes, still affected by the vividness of the dream. What could it mean, she wondered? She never dreamed as a rule, and she had nothing on her mind to induce such nocturnal horrors. In fact she'd never been happier in her life. Oliver would be coming over after breakfast and they were going sailing again, and tonight they were attending a party given by the Rosenthals.

Springing to her feet, she slipped into the house, wrapped only in a beach robe. The delicious aroma of coffee filtered through the air from the kitchen, mingling with the perfume of lilies that filled the living-room vases. Feeling good, Kathryn pranced through the hall and then stopped dead in her tracks and gave a gasp. Sarah was sitting on the stairs, clinging to the rail, her face grey.

'Granny!' Kathryn sprang forward and crouched beside her, seeing with alarm that her grandmother's mouth had a strange blue tinge to it, and her hands were blue too. She seemed to be having trouble breathing and her eyes were filled with fear.

'Granny ... Oh God! Dorothy! Dorothy, come quickly,' Kathryn yelled and a minute later Sarah's personal maid came running down the stairs.

'Madame!' she cried, appalled, but already Sarah had slumped sideways, her eyes closed and her body slack.

Chapter Seventeen

The first thought that hit Francesca when she awoke was that she was going to Paris without Serge. They'd always taken major trips together, combining business with pleasure, but this time she'd be going alone.

A wave of depression washed over her as she got out of bed and slipped into her white satin robe. Paris wouldn't be the same without him. They usually had a suite at the Ritz and managed to find time to eat in a few good restaurants and slip into the Louvre, if only for an hour. As she showered her feelings of unease and dejection increased. What was she so suddenly afraid of? In the past few months she'd got used to being without Serge, she told herself angrily as she rubbed her legs in a circular movement with the loofah. In fact, her life was working for her just as she'd wanted it to. She'd built up Kalinsky's so that it now had a turn-over of a thousand million dollars. She'd become its President. She had a fabulous apartment, fully staffed, wonderful clothes and furs, and of course the pick of the finest jewels in the world. She was a highly respected business woman whom everyone looked up to, and she'd worked hard to achieve it all. And now she was off to Paris to launch a terrific and exciting exhibition that would further enhance the reputation of her company. So why the hell, she muttered under her breath as she dried herself vigorously, am I feeling as wobbly as a twelve-year-old going off to summer camp alone for the first time?

The hairdresser came to do her hair at ten o'clock. Her maid finished her packing and placed her cases just inside the door of her apartment by eleven o'clock. At noon the car arrived to take her to Kennedy Airport.

At twenty minutes past twelve the telephone rang, and Francesca's maid answered it.

'Can I speak to Francesca Andrews?' asked a frantic female voice.

'She's left for the airport, Madam.'

'Oh, God. . . .' The voice gave a desperate sob. 'I . . . I must get hold of her. How can I get hold of her? It's a matter of life and death!'

'Perhaps her office can contact her at the airport, Madam. I'm afraid I don't even know which flight she's on.'

'Okay, I'll try. If she should contact you for any reason, can you say it's her niece, Kathryn. Tell her to call her mother's house in Palm Beach . . . s-something terrible has happened.'

Carlotta swept into the V.I.P. lounge at Kennedy Airport and ordered a large vodka and tonic. Flying still made her nervous, even after all these years, and New York to Paris was a long flight. She glanced at her gold Cartier watch. It was twelve thirty-five. She was much too early, but she thought that if she sat quietly, engrossed herself in the new copy of *Town and Country* and perhaps had a couple of drinks, maybe even a tranquillizer, she would have calmed down by the time she boarded the plane.

Her thoughts were disrupted when the tannoy burst into action and a spectral woman's voice made an announcement.

'Calling Miss Francesca Andrews! Calling Miss Francesca Andrews! Will Miss Andrews please report immediately to the Pan Am enquiry desk.'

Carlotta listened for a moment and then shrugged. She hadn't seen Francesca for over twenty years and she wasn't really interested.

'I'm still trying to get hold of Francesca!' Kathryn's face was pinched and white and her eyes were brimming with tears. 'Oh, Oliver, I'm scared. I wish I knew what to do.'

Oliver put his arms around her, holding her comfortingly close. 'It'll be all right, honey. They'll catch her at the airport. You've done all you can.'

An hour earlier, the medics had arrived and Sarah had been lifted on to a stretcher, given oxygen, injections, and borne gently away in the waiting ambulance.

'Don't worry,' the doctor had told Kathryn reassuringly, 'we'll take her to the hospital and she'll get the best treatment there is. She's had a heart attack but it may not be as severe as it looks.'

With a mournful wail, the ambulance drove off.

Nearly two hours later, Kathryn still had not been able to get hold of Francesca. 'I think I'd better get hold of Daddy,' she said suddenly. 'He could be here by tomorrow and if Granny . . .' She couldn't finish the sentence.

'Hey, there, lots of people have coronaries and get over them,' said Oliver, stroking her back gently. 'She's going to be just fine, darling.'

'If only Francesca were here.'

'Don't worry. She will be. Meanwhile why don't you call up your parents?'

Kathryn dried her eyes. 'Yes. I'll ring Mummy and get her to tell Daddy.'

'Wouldn't it be better if you told him yourself?'

Kathryn shook her head. 'I don't really get on all that well with my father. I'd rather talk to Mummy.'

As she went to pick up the 'phone, it rang piercingly, startling her.

'Hullo?' *Oh please God don't let it be the hospital saying granny's died*, she thought.

Kathryn grabbed the 'phone and, with her heart pounding, held it to her ear. A minute later a look of relief filled her face and she gave a deep sigh. 'Oh, thank God they got hold of you before you flew off, Francesca. Can you get back here as quickly as possible? Granny's ill . . . I think it's a heart attack,' she blurted out.

'Where is she?' Francesca's voice sounded tense.

'They've taken her to the Burton Foundation Hospital. I think it's quite near here.'

'I know it. I'll get a flight to Palm Beach right away. Can you arrange with Sarah's chauffeur to meet me at the airport and I'll go straight to the hospital?'

'Okay. I'm so glad we caught you in time . . .

368

before you took off for Paris,' Kathryn repeated fervently.

'So am I, honey. I'll call you from the hospital after I've seen Mom. Are you on your own?'

'Oliver's here.' Kathryn felt better. Francesca was coming to take control of the situation and Oliver was holding her hand as if he'd never let it go.

When she'd hung up, Oliver took her in his arms and held her close. 'I told you everything would work out all right, didn't I?' he said, comfortingly.

She nodded. 'I feel much better now Francesca's on her way. I'm sure it'll all be okay now.'

But that long day was not yet over.

Carlotta knew that something was dreadfully wrong. A minute before, the quiet routine activity on board the Boeing 747 had been violently disrupted by shouting and a woman's scream. From the exclusive seclusion of First Class, she and the other eleven passengers strained over their shoulders to see what was happening back in the tourist cabin, but a stewardess was standing blocking the entrance, her body taut and rigid. Coarse male voices came nearer, yelling in a language Carlotta didn't understand, and then she saw the stewardess pushed to one side with a violent shove as a tall man with swarthy skin and blazing dark eyes thrust his way up the aisle and swung round to face them. He was wearing a smart cotton suit and a pale blue open-necked shirt. In one hand he held a revolver, in the other, with studied nonchalance, he jiggled a hand grenade.

'You stay in your seats,' he shouted in broken English. Carlotta caught his eye and, with a reckless gesture, she straightened her shoulders, raised her chin and stared back at him defiantly.

'You, woman,' he screamed. 'You lean forward, hands on your ankles . . . You stay like that.'

The passengers stared at him blankly, numb with shock. But Carlotta understood and a wave of cold fear clutched her heart. The man was a terrorist and this was a hi-jack.

The terrorist swiftly slipped the grenade into the left hand pocket of his loose cotton jacket and, leaning forward, grabbed an elderly woman sitting in the front row by her hair. 'Down!' he yelled, forcing her head between her knees.

One by one the other passengers crouched forward, dropping their hands to their feet, too terrified to do anything else. Reluctantly Carlotta did the same.

'You!' The terrorist turned his attention to the stewardess who was standing, pale and uncertain, by the entrance. 'Which is Francesca Andrews?'

Diana stayed at her desk until late that night, checking and re-checking the arrangements for the following day. She was organising a sponsored polo match at the Guards Club, Windsor, and with a thousand people expected there was a lot to see to. Prince Charles was playing, and several members of the royal family were attending. Luncheon in a marquee preceded the match, followed by tea and then a champagne reception afterwards. Badges had been issued, car parking facilities arranged. Caterers, florists, a brass band and photographers had all been organised, and score cards printed. All she prayed for now was a fine day. But if the worst came to the worst, she had arranged to hire five hundred umbrellas, which they could hand out.

She glanced at her watch, then switched on the television to watch the weather forecast for the next day. A minute later, she sat slumped on the sofa, her hand clamped over her mouth, her eyes staring in horror at the screen.

'. . . A Pan Am Boeing 747, bound for Paris from New York, has been hi-jacked in mid-air by terrorists who are thought to be from the anti-American Arab Liberation Front. Within two hours of take-off, the terrorists, four men and a woman, were holding the three hundred and fifty passengers and a crew of thirteen, at gunpoint.'

The BBC announcer paused, glanced at his notes and continued: 'Radio contact with the pilot, Captain John Kilroy, confirms that the terrorists are demanding that the plane be re-routed to the island of Malta, although it is feared they may not be carrying sufficient fuel on board. Among the passengers is Francesca Andrews, President of Kalinsky Jewellery Incorporated. She is thought to be their chief hostage and we have heard from Arab sources that they are demanding five million dollars in return for the safe delivery of Miss Andrews and the other passengers. The plight of those on board is as yet unknown, but they have been in the air for four hours now and it will be many more hours yet before they reach their new destination. Six Britons are reported to be among the passengers. We will be bringing you up-to-date reports . . .'

Diana didn't wait to hear any more. Reaching for the phone with shaking hands, she dialled the number of Sarah's house in Palm Beach.

'I'm afraid your mother's heart has been rather badly damaged by the coronary,' the doctor told Francesca. 'We are monitoring her all the time and of course she is in intensive care, but it will be a few days before we can be sure how things are going to go.'

'Can I see her?'

'Just for a moment, and don't be too alarmed by all the tubes and drips – they're routine in a case like this.'

Francesca's stomach contracted as she walked along the corridor to her mother's private room. Hospital smells had always filled her with a sort of nervous dread and now as she approached the room she wondered fearfully what she would find.

Mom looks so small, was her first thought. A tiny frail body festooned and imprisoned with wires and tubes and an oxygen mask covering her ivory face. She looked so tiny and helpless, and yet this was the woman who had ruled a giant company like a despot less than a year ago. Francesca found herself wrenched with pity. Kalinsky's had been her mother's life as it was now hers – it should have been a shared bond, a shared love, and instead there had been nothing but animosity between them and deep jealousy. Hot tears stung her eyes and at that moment she hoped with all her heart that her mother would recover so that they might one day try to understand each other.

'She needs rest now,' whispered the nurse sympathetically.

Francesca nodded, unable to speak.

When she returned to the waiting car the chauffeur was listening to soft music on the car radio. Suddenly it broke off and an announcer's voice cut in.

'We have a newsflash.'

A minute later Francesca had turned pale, a sense of disbelief making her brain reel. She had been so absorbed in her mother's collapse she had not been aware of the events of the last few hours.

It was reported that she was to have been the chief hostage on the hi-jacked flight to Paris, but that it had now been discovered she had cancelled at the last moment.

It was also reported the terrorists were now holding Carlotta Raven, wife of the rich and famous author, as their chief hostage in her place.

The stench inside the aircraft filled the air like a fetid miasma. Carlotta lolled sideways in her seat, racked with pain and exhaustion, trying to control the terror she felt. She was going to die. It was just a matter of time. When the terrorists had realised Francesca was not on the flight they had turned the full focus of their attention on her.

'You Marc Raven's wife?' demanded Riva, the young female terrorist, as she guarded the first class passengers. She had long straight greasy hair, a fanatical face and a gun gripped tightly in her bony hand. She turned to one of the armed men and they jabbered together for a few minutes. Carlotta watched them stealthily with mounting panic. She didn't need to understand their language to know they were planning to use her as a substitute for Francesca.

The girl swung back to Carlotta. 'Your husband plenty rich!' she spat. 'He give money to our cause!' Her eyes gleamed and in that second Carlotta knew she was doomed because Marc would not give money for her release. He would ignore their pleas and the irony of it was that he would be forced by the American government to ignore their pleas, because one did not give way to threats of this kind. In fact he would be glad, at last, to be rid of her.

The second irony also hit her with force. She was standing in for the very woman who had once been her friend. How long ago that seemed, when she had used Francesca to get to Marc. Well, she thought, through the jumbled panic of her mind, I wanted money and respectability, position and power, and I got the lot, even if it meant walking all over a friend and blackmailing Marc into giving me what I wanted.

A frightened sob escaped from her throat. *I don't want to die. I want to see my beloved Carlos again. I want to go home to mama and papa in Spain*, her mind shrieked.

The plane had landed an hour before, and whilst one of the terrorists stayed in the cockpit with the crew, trying to negotiate their terms over the radio, the others guarded the exits. The tension was mounting; they shouted commands at each other from time to time, and then a shot rang out, whistling through the air. There was a sharp cry and one of the passengers slumped into the aisle, blood gushing from his head.

The terrorists were keeping their latest promise . . . to shoot a passenger every hour until their demands were met.

Diana turned on her bedroom radio the next morning while she got ready to go to the polo match. She was anxious to hear more news about the hijacking, though once she'd heard Francesca was not on the flight it had become another of the world's remote but horrific tragedies.

The announcer's voice was charged and strained. '. . . the hi-jacked 747 has been forced to land in Malta in the early hours of this morning. The terrorists, who are thought to be heavily armed, are keeping all three hundred and fifty pasengers as hostages on the plane and conditions on board are thought to be very tense. According to security forces on the ground, the pilot has signalled from the cockpit that no one is to come near the aircraft. Several shots have already been heard and the terrorists are making new demands. Their original plan was to hold Francesca Andrews, president of Kalinsky's, the multi-million jewellery company, to ransom. When it was discovered she was not on the flight after all they turned their attention to another passenger, Mrs Carlotta Raven, wife of the bestselling author, Marc Raven, who is reputed to be worth twenty million dollars. They have carried out their threat to shoot one of the passengers every hour unless their demands are met, and several bodies have already been thrown from the plane onto the tarmac. It is understood . . .'

Diana sat immobile at her dressing-table as the full implications of this new turn of events thudded through her brain.

The *Sania II* moved forward gently on the lilting waters of the Mediterranean and Marc lay on deck sunning himself. The morning had gone badly. He'd awoken with a hangover, and when he sat down at his typewriter to work on the final chapter of *Blue Moon* he'd been unable to string two words together. Irritated and frustrated, he went up on deck and ordered a campari and soda. Maybe another drink would soothe his mind and calm his spirit. Carlotta would be joining him in Capri in a couple of days and that, he supposed, was the cause of his sudden depression. At least she hadn't been on the ship-to-shore 'phone since she'd left New York, using it to link her to him like some fucking umbilical cord, he thought with a burst of anger. He loathed the way she monitored everything he did, feeding and starving him of his life's blood as she thought fit, burying him forever in a dark womb of possessiveness from which he could never kick his way to the outside world and freedom.

He had drifted into a light doze when a hand tapped him gently on the shoulder and looking up he saw the captain gazing down at him.

'I'm afraid I have bad news for you.' His manner was direct and unemotional. 'Your wife is being held hostage by Arab terrorists on board a hijacked plane in Malta. They are demanding you give them five million dollars for her release.'

'Jesus Christ!' Marc jumped to his feet, a look of total disbelief on his face. 'I don't believe it! What the hell's happened?'

'I only know what the airport authorities in Malta told me, sir. Three hundred and fifty passengers are being held in the plane, on the tarmac, and they won't release your wife or any of the others, until you promise to give them the money.'

Marc shook his head slowly as he looked at the captain with glazed eyes. 'I've no choice, have I? Radio back that I agree and find out how they want the money, when, and where. And change course. We'd better get to Malta fast.'

'Yes, sir.'

Three hundred and fifty passengers ... including Carlotta! Marc sank slowly down on to his deck chair and drew in a long breath. The enormity of the situation hit him forcibly. And so did the knowledge that the American government would not allow him to help. One did not meet the demands of terrorists, but at least his promise of five million dollars might give them the necessary time to mount a rescue campaign.

Kathryn and Oliver walked slowly back to the house from the tennis court, their arms about each other.

'Let's have a swim before lunch,' Oliver suggested.

'Good idea.' Kathryn felt relaxed and happy. The news of Sarah had been much better that morning, and Francesca had promised that they could all have lunch by the pool as soon as she got back from visiting her mother in the hospital.

'I wonder if there's any more news on the hijack. . . . what a miracle Francesca wasn't on that flight. It must be terrible for all the others.'

'I know.' Kathryn shook her head, trying hard to imagine the horror of being held at gunpoint, for hours and hours, in a stifling hot plane.

'Shall we have a quick look at the television to see what's happening?'

'Okay.' Together they entered the beautifully cool house and switched on the set in a corner of the living-room.

A quiz show was in progress, the hysterical participants clapping their hands and jumping up and down like a bunch of performing seals.

'I'll switch channels,' said Kathryn. The picture flicked and there it was! The Boeing 747, stranded and isolated on the hot dusty tarmac, looking like a great glittering dead object. There was no sign of life anywhere and apart from the distant airport buildings it might have been the Sahara Desert in a shimmering heat haze. The television camera must be some distance away, thought Kathryn, because even when it zoomed in to get a closer look the plane still seemed to be a long way off. There was something terribly chilling about the deserted runway and as she vaguely wondered what the three huddled bundles were on the ground near the wheels, the voice of the announcer filled the calm tranquillity of the living-room.

'The terrorists are carrying out their threat to kill a passenger every hour until their demands are agreed to. Three bodies have so far been thrown out of the plane, and you can see them on the left of your picture. The terrorists say they will shoot anyone who comes near the aircraft to attend to the victims.'

'Jesus!' muttered Oliver.

'How can anyone behave like that!' gasped Kathryn. 'Surely there must be another way for them to . . .'

'Sshhh!' interrupted Oliver, suddenly going tense.

'. . . The terrorists are reported to be demanding five million dollars for the release of their main hostage, Carlotta Raven, wife of Marc Raven . . .'

'Jesus Christ!' yelled Oliver, jumping to his feet. His eyes bulged and there was a white line around his mouth.

'What's the matter?' asked Kathryn, startled.

Oliver pointed a shaking finger at the television which was still showing the grounded plane, quivering in the heat.

'Carlotta Raven!' his voice croaked. 'That's my mother!'

The authorities were holding an emergency meeting at an office in the terminal building at the airport in Malta. Linked by 'phone to the White House in Washington and the Foreign Office in

379

London, they were deciding what the next step would be. Marc Raven had contacted them and said he was willing to pay the ransom but they had told him that it was against all policy to meet terrorists' demands.

'We must wait until nightfall and then we must mount a commando attack on the plane,' said the senior official. 'The British Navy, anchored in Valletta, have trained anti-terrorists and ammunition on board. They have offered their services. It is the only way.'

There was consternation among the group. 'It could be a bloodbath,' said one flatly.

'Not if we trick the terrorists,' said another. 'We will tell them that we have agreed to their demands. If we can fix it with the pilot we can get them to speak by radio to Marc Raven himself. He's still on his yacht, but he is on his way here and we haven't as yet told him he cannot be allowed to supply the ransom money. It might satisfy them if they think the money is on its way.'

'Supposing it goes wrong?'

'It's already going wrong. They've shot three people so far.'

And so it was decided. At ten o'clock that night anti-terrorists supplied by the British Royal Navy were to enter the plane and overpower the terrorists.

'What do you mean, she's your mother?'

Oliver was trying to get hold of Marc on board *Sania II*. He had already booked himself a flight to Europe, hoping he could land at Gozo, and then maybe get a helicopter, or at worst a boat, over to Malta. He looked distracted as he grabbed Kathryn's hand.

'My parents are Marc and Carlotta Raven. My real name is Carlos Raven, but I didn't want to succeed in the movies just because of my father's name,' he said hurriedly. 'I was always over-shadowed by his fame. Changing my name was the only way of getting out from under.'

'Why didn't you tell me before?' Kathryn was intrigued. She'd read a lot of Marc Raven's books at school, though the teachers would not have approved, and she thought his tales of scandal and adventure in high places were fascinating.

'I didn't think it was important, although I'd have told you in time . . . like when I ask you to marry me,' he said, suddenly looking shy.

'Oh, Oliver!' Kathryn flushed deep pink with pleasure.

Oliver kissed her swiftly. 'I'll ask you properly when this nightmare is over. I've got to get to my mother now. Christ, I hope it's going to be all right. Listen, darling, I've got to hurry or I'll miss my connection in New York. Can you get hold of my father for me? I'll give you the number on his yacht. Tell him I'm on my way.'

Through his tenderness to her she could feel the anxiety and horror he felt. 'Of course, darling.'

In a flurry, he dashed back to the Rosenthals' house, packed a small case, explained what had happened and then came back to say goodbye to Kathryn. Everything was happening so fast and the whole drama seemed so unreal; he had kissed her goodbye and was gone before she realised she might not see him again for days.

As Francesca was still at the hospital visiting Sarah, Kathryn settled herself before the television set, watching for newsflashes on the latest developments of the hi-jack that was rocking the United States with horror. And to think that Oliver . . . or should she call him Carlos now? To think that it was his mother who was being held as the main hostage!

The television was showing a soap opera now and, bored, Kathryn decided to call Diana in England. Just wait, she thought, how amazed Mummy is going to be when she hears that my boyfriend is actually the son of one of the world's most famous authors!

Sarah lay, frail and birdlike, in a deep sleep. The doctors had told Francesca that if she continued to make good progress she would recover, but that it would take a long time. And in future, she'd have to be very careful.

Sitting by her bedside, Francesca watched the sleeping figure, longing to talk, make some close contact. But the eyes remained shut, the face closed off and distant.

'She needs rest more than anything,' the doctors said. 'She must be kept very quiet, and no talking. But I'm sure it is a comfort for her to have you here, even though she is asleep most of the time.'

Francesca hoped that was true. Twice a day she visited the hospital and sat by Sarah's bed as the instruments around her bleeped a regular rhythm.

It was nearly time to go home now. Francesca stretched, her back aching from the uncomfortable hospital chair, a feeling of enormous tiredness weighing her down. The past couple of days had been so traumatic, first with Sarah's heart attack, and then the realisation that if she'd caught that flight to Paris she could have been at the mercy of a bunch of crazed terrorists. She felt drained and empty and could hardly believe that it was Carlotta who had taken her place. Francesca hardly liked to admit it to herself, but it really did look as if fate had designed this whole incredible, macabre incident.

At that moment a shadow fell across the instruments by Sarah's bed and, thinking it to be a nurse or a doctor, she looked up, smiling. Her expression froze and her heart started beating wildly as she looked into a dearly beloved and familiar face.

'Serge!' she whispered.

'Hullo, Francesca.' He laid a strong hand on her shoulder and his blue eyes gazed questioningly into hers. 'How are you?'

'Oh . . . Serge!' She rose and flung herself into his arms, all the strain and anxieties of the past few days bursting the banks of her self-control. Silently she wept into his shoulder, realising how much she had missed him in the past few months. 'I . . . I thought I'd never see you again,' she said brokenly.

'I was waiting for you in Paris,' Serge said softly, stroking her hair. 'I was going to tell you then that I couldn't live without you, and that I was a fool to go off like that.'

'No, no, darling, you weren't! I was a fool to let

you go.' She clung to him, loving the familiar feel of his arms around her, drawing deep comfort from his presence.

'I'm sorry about Sarah. How is she?' He looked down at the still figure, keeping his voice low.

'I think she's going to make it.'

'That's great. And what about this hi-jack? I nearly went out of my mind when I first heard you were on the flight.'

'I know. The last few days have been hell. Let's go, Serge. Visiting time is over.' Francesca dried her eyes quickly and gathered up her things. 'You know I've got Kathryn staying – she was visiting Mom when all this happened.'

'Yes, I heard. In fact the newspapers have been giving out the details of all the goings-on in your family for the past few days.'

'They have? I didn't know. It's been such a crazy time I've lost track of everything.'

Together they left the Burton Foundation Hospital and got into the car. On the way back to Sarah's house they were silent, a deeply companionable silence as if words weren't necessary. They were together again, and when Sarah was better they'd resume their life in New York, living, loving and working side by side. Francesca wondered if Serge would ever bring up the subject of marriage again, and a part of her hoped he wouldn't. She still liked things the way they were. Her hand slid across and she rested it on Serge's thigh. He turned quickly and gave her a loving smile. Francesca smiled back.

It was enough for the moment that he was back.

* * *

Kathryn heard the crunch of Francesca's car on the drive and rushed out of the house to greet her, bursting with news. She stopped short in her tracks when she saw Serge, and then a delighted grin appeared on her face.

'Hullo!' she beamed.

'Hi, darling.' Francesca got out of the car quickly, and Kathryn could see she was looking pleased. 'How's it going? Where's Oliver?' She glanced round, expecting to see him at Kathryn's side.

Kathryn's face fell and her eyes looked troubled. 'The most extraordinary things have been happening,' she blurted out.

As they all walked into the house, Serge still holding on to Francesca's hand, Kathryn explained that Oliver was really Carlos Raven and that it was his mother who was the main captive on the plane.

'Dear God,' said Francesca, sitting down suddenly. It had been the impending birth of Carlos that had forced Marc to leave her and marry Carlotta, and now that son was a grown man, and in love with her own niece. Serge looked at her anxiously, knowing the whole story. 'What an incredible thing,' she said at last.

'Yes, isn't it,' said Kathryn innocently. 'Fancy him being here with me, while his mother is being held in your place as a hostage.' She shook her head wonderingly, then she frowned. 'But something awfully odd has happened as well.'

'What?' said Francesca.

'Well, you know how Mummy always wants to

know who everybody is? I mean, the moment I have a new friend the first thing she asks is, who is their family? I think it's a bit snobbish myself. Well, anyway, she's asked both Granny and me, several times, who Oliver is, and frankly I couldn't care less. So today, when he told me he was the son of Marc Raven, I thought she'd be so pleased that I called London to tell her.'

'And . . .?' Francesca was looking puzzled too. Why should it matter, she thought! Diana had never known about her affair with Marc. It had been too painful to talk about at the time, and later it didn't seem important.

'She freaked out!' cried Kathryn. 'She went absolutely crazy. Said I must come home straight away and that I was too young to get involved.'

Francesca stared at her blankly. Surely even Diana couldn't disapprove of Kathryn going out with the son of such a rich and famous man?

'I don't understand it,' Francesca said finally. 'Oliver's a really nice young man.'

'Could you talk to her, Francesca?' Kathryn pleaded, looking distressed. 'Tell her how nice he is. And she must have heard of his father – everyone's heard of Marc Raven.'

'I'll see what I can do,' promised Francesca. 'What's the latest news about the hi-jack?' She turned to the television which was still switched on.

'Everyone's still being held. The plane's been sitting on the runway for thirty-six hours now,' said Kathryn, 'And they've killed five people so far.'

*   *   *

The interior of the plane was in complete darkness and only the distant lights from the terminal buildings outlined the rows of huddled passengers. The air, thick with the stench of sweat, urine and faeces, entered the nostrils and lungs sickeningly. The silence, solid and heavy, was palpable with tension. Earlier in the day flies had got into the plane, attracted by the smell of drying blood, and now they buzzed angrily in the darkness, swooping and diving in maddening circuits round and round the cabins. An occasional waft of air came from the open exit doors near the front of the aircraft, and when it did the passengers tried to catch it, gulping and sniffing and marvelling that they had never before appreciated something as ordinary as fresh air.

First class passengers had been herded at gunpoint into available seats in tourist class, lumping the privileged and the under-privileged into one block of terrified humanity, welded together by a communal desire to survive.

While one of the terrorists remained in the cockpit with the captain and crew, acting as spokesman and trying to negotiate by radio their demand for five million dollars, the other three stood and watched the passengers and air stewards.

Rifles poised, their eyes flashed to and fro with animal watchfulness. Only the girl, Riva, seemed to be relishing the situation. With her gun held in her slim brown hands and her black hair thick and matted on her shoulders, she held her head arrogantly, her eyes flashing with fanatical self-righteousness. The Cause was all that mattered, and she was prepared to die for it. She regarded the passengers as scum, especially Carlotta. She deserved to die. Anyone who lived like a parasite deserved to die. She eyed Carlotta's jewels and expensive clothes with contemptuous hatred. She would take pleasure in killing her personally, even if her capitalist husband did come up with the money.

Carlotta, squeezed into row M between a fat business man from Chicago and a middle-aged spinster travelling alone, carefully avoided catching Riva's eye because there was something she recognised of herself in the young woman – fleeting remembrance of a ruthless girl, desperate to claw everything she could out of life. Riva at least had a cause she believed in with a passion she was ready to die for, and with a stab of shame Carlotta was aware that all her desires had been self-motivated. She had wanted the world for herself and now Marc was not going to come to her rescue. He was going to let her die here with all the others in this stinking metal shell.

She closed her eyes as despair swamped her, trying to blot out even the darkened outlines of the other passengers. Then she heard someone cursing softly behind her. Strain and fear and suspense were reducing most of them into a kind of dull stupor; others were hanging on to their self-control by substituting anger for panic.

One of the terrorists began to get jumpy as the whispered cursing continued. Saliva formed into a globule in his gullet and he swallowed nervously.

'Shut up!' he yelled to no one in particular. Then

he lit a cigarette, his hands shaking, his eyes sunken hollows in his skull from lack of sleep. With an oath one of the other terrorists pounced on him, grabbed the burning cigarette out of his mouth and ground it with his heel on the floor. They argued furiously.

I wish they'd kill each other while they're at it, thought Carlotta.

On the outskirts of the airfield, under cover of a black Mediterranean night, fire engines and ambulances moved quietly into place. Everyone spoke in whispers, fearful their words might carry across the deserted runway. No headlamps or torches were used. Engines were turned off as soon as the vehicles were in position.

The anti-terrorists were about to spring their attack with military precision.

In single file, crawling on their bellies along the runway, a line of SAS commandos approached the aircraft from behind, out of the line of vision of anyone on board. Their faces were hidden by black woollen balaclava helmets. Their hands were blackened. They slid with stealth, watching for any sign of activity on board the silent plane. Foot by foot they edged forward, until at last they were under the silver fin of the tail which towered above them like some monster fish. Then they spread out into a fan, under the aircraft, the whole exercise choreographed to the last move and carried out in complete silence.

They carried ropes and stun bombs as well as knives and revolvers. They crept their way outwards from under the plane, the open exits now just visible above them, black gaping holes in the darkness. The plan was to lob stun bombs with deadly accuracy into the exit doors where two of the terrorists stood guard. They would be knocked off their feet and literally stunned for up to two minutes. In that time the commandos had to scale up the ropes which they would have flung over the wings, enter the aircraft and overpower the five terrorists.

It wasn't a perfect plan, but somehow it had to work.

Carlotta awoke with a start. She'd dozed off momentarily, overcome with exhaustion and the putrid atmosphere, but suddenly she felt petrifyingly alert. Something was happening – something had awakened her. Opening her eyes cautiously she looked around. The plane was still in darkness. The night was still silent but it was a different silence from before. This silence ached with a premonition of disaster and prickles of fear sprang out on her arms. The atmosphere now pulsated with some unknown terror and glancing over at Riva, who had raised her rifle, she could tell by her outline in the darkness that her head was raised like an animal scenting danger. A second later all the lights in the aircraft sprang on in a blinding blaze, dazzling everyone.

Carlotta blinked, trying in that instant to accustom her eyes to the brilliance, but suddenly automatic gunfire sprayed the interior, bullets spitting and ricocheting round the enclosed space, whipping through the air with a deafening roar. Smoke and flames filled the cabin as the stun bombs crashed through the door. Screaming passengers slumped in oozing wells of blood. Some ducked on to the floor, others panicked and rushed the exits, struggling to release the emergency chutes, fighting to escape the horror.

In the distance Carlotta was aware of sirens wailing from the outer darkness, hurtling towards the aircraft, before the staccato bursts of gunfire inside the plane deafened her completely. A group of passengers scuffling and struggling their way up an aisle to get to an exit were mown down by a hail of bullets in a screaming bloody mass of humanity, and the smell of fear became stronger than all the other smells. Carlotta saw a man hit by a bullet in the neck. A fountain of blood sprayed the air with a thousand ruby droplets, raining down on her face and arms, splattering her dress. Women screamed as they tripped over the body of a stewardess which lay across an exit. Someone at the back of the crowd pushed violently forward in a frenzied attempt to get out, so that a group of passengers, still struggling to release the emergency chute, tumbled out of the plane and fell twenty feet on to the tarmac below, their screams echoing eerily above the other noises.

Riva, her face resolute and as cold and composed as carved marble, pulled the trigger of her gun with more specific care than her compatriots. She aimed at the well-dressed, the rich, the privileged. Then across the smoke and chaos, she caught Carlotta's eye, and for a long moment they looked at each other. Dark eyes met dark eyes, frozen in time, primeval with pure hatred. Then Riva raised her gun and fired.

Carlotta felt something hot and stinging enter her chest, and as she looked down helplessly she saw a torrent of blood flowing and spreading like a river before her.

A stunned world heard with shock the outcome of the hi-jack. Two hundred passengers had escaped, but a hundred and fifty had been killed in the carnage that took place on the Boeing 747 when the terrorist in the cockpit had suddenly panicked. He thought he saw movement on the ground, coming from the direction of the terminal building, and he commanded the captain to switch on all the lights in the plane. It had been an illusion brought on by hours of strain and lack of sleep, but it had been enough to throw the other terrorists into a frenzy of panic and before the commandos could make their planned attack, mayhem had broken out.

All the terrorists perished, along with their chief hostage, Carlotta Raven.

Chapter Eighteen

For once, Diana and Guy were in agreement.
Kathryn must return to London immediately.

'But we mustn't tell her the real reason,' said
Guy pompously. 'We'll *all* be in the shit if she finds
out her sainted mother's a whore!'

'Don't you dare talk to me like that,' said Diana
with cold fury. 'I loved Marc. It was not some
shoddy affair, like all yours have been. How many
men have you slept with over the years, Guy? Two
hundred? Five hundred? A thousand? Not to mention my brother, John, who for some bloody reason
still seems to love you!' She was shaking with rage
now, as much from anger at Guy as from the horri-
fying implications of Kathryn's affair with Marc's
son – her half brother.

'At least I haven't been spawning children all
over the place,' he shot back, furiously. 'Being gay
is an accepted part of life and no one thinks anything of it these days.'

'I don't think an exposé of your private life
would actually help your political career,' she said
sarcastically.

'All the more reason for us to shut up about
Kathryn not being my daughter, and don't put on
this moral attitude with me, Diana. It's your

fault that we're in this mess now, not mine.'

'If you'd been a proper husband I might not have even looked at Marc Raven,' she retorted.

'Diana, this is getting us nowhere.' Guy suddenly sounded defeated. Protecting his image as a respectable Member of Parliament and Minister of Public Enterprise was what mattered most to him now. So far there had not been a breath of scandal surrounding his long term separation from Diana, and he intended to keep it that way.

'We've got to think about what we're going to say to Kathryn,' said Diana, interrupting his thoughts. 'Neither of us is blameless in this affair, but what reason are we going to give for forbidding her to see Carlos again?'

Guy shrugged. Miles and Kathryn were Diana's affair. She'd been responsible for bringing them up and now he'd leave it to her to unravel this situation . . . just so long as he was protected!

'I think we should tell her she's too young to get involved,' continued Diana, 'And frankly, I think that is a valid point. She's only eighteen, and I think she should see a bit more of life. I'll have to think of something to keep her occupied.'

'What about bringing her out? Why don't you give a big ball for her at Wilmington Hall?'

Diana could see his mind working to his own advantage as usual. Having a society ball at Wilmington Hall for his debutante daughter would attract a lot of media attention and give Guy an opportunity to appear not only the high-powered politician but also the devoted father.

'I'll think about it,' she said shortly. 'The first

thing is to get hold of Francesca and tell her to put Kathryn on the next plane home.'

'I'm sorry, darling, but your mother, and even Guy, are adamant you should go home,' Francesca said regretfully.

Kathryn looked at her forlornly. She wanted to stay on so she would be here when Carlos got back. He'd called her to say he and Marc were taking his mother's body to Spain to be buried in the Linares family plot just outside Jerez, but after that he wanted to fly back to Palm Beach to see her. He had sounded so broken up by his mother's death that it upset Kathryn deeply. She'd promised to wait for him, knowing Francesca wouldn't mind how long she stayed.

None of them had expected Guy and Diana to forbid the relationship to continue.

'Listen, Kathryn,' said Serge gently, for he understood how she felt and thought Diana's behaviour was ridiculous. 'Why don't you fly home now and talk to your parents? These long-distance 'phone calls are a hopeless way of communicating. Explain to them how you feel and how you're not proposing to do anything crazy like rush off and marry Carlos this minute, and then perhaps they'll understand. They might let you come back.'

'I so wanted to be here when he returned.'

'I know you did, honey, but Carlos is a very sensible young man. He'll understand. It's only natural, when you think about it, that your mother and father should feel protective towards you. You're just eighteen and you've fallen in love with a young man they've never even met. They're bound to be anxious until they find out what he's really like.'

Francesca shot Serge a grateful glance and then she smiled to herself. He was treating Kathryn in just the same kind, tactful way that Henry Langham had treated her at the same age.

'I suppose you're right,' agreed Kathryn reluctantly. 'It's so unlike Mummy though. I can't think what she can possibly have against Carlos.'

Privately Francesca agreed. But then Diana didn't know Carlos's father as she did. Perhaps, she thought to herself, I should call Diana up and tell her what Marc meant to me when I was a girl, but then she decided against it. It would only complicate matters and Diana would wonder why she'd never mentioned it before. It would be better to let Guy and Diana find out for themselves that there was nothing to be feared from Kathryn and Carlos's relationship.

Kathryn packed sadly that night, wondering when she would see Carlos again. The scenes of the hi-jack massacre on television still brought clear images of the horror of it all to her mind, and she felt wrenched with pity for Carlos and his father. The newscasters reported Marc Raven as saying he'd been prepared to give them what they asked in return for his wife and the other hostages, but it had all been in vain. Photographs of a laughing glamorous Carlotta, taken at a party the year before, had been flashed onto the screen and then Kathryn watched a clip of film of Marc Raven being interviewed on his yacht the day after the incident. She had noticed how grim his eyes were and how harsh his voice sounded, almost as if he were angry. Then Carlos appeared standing beside him, his head bowed in grief, his voice tight and choked.

At that moment Kathryn longed more than anything to be with Carlos. The droop of his shoulders, and the line of his clenched jaw expressed such deep sadness, and at the same time such dignity, that her heart broke. She might be leaving for England in the morning but nothing and no one was going to part her from Carlos for long.

Marc poured himself a whisky from the wide-based ship's decanter and looked across the saloon at Carlos who was sitting in a deep armchair, his long legs sprawled before him. Outside, the harsh Mediterranean sun glittered on the blue waters and shone through the *Sania*'s portholes.

'Want a drink?'

'No thanks, Dad.'

Marc walked slowly to the opposite chair and sat down heavily, wondering how much to tell Carlos, or if he need ever tell him anything. They'd never been very close and as soon as Carlos was eighteen he'd left home, changed his name to Oliver Power and gone to Hollywood to try his luck in films. Ignorance is bliss, Marc thought to himself as he sipped his whisky, so why not let Carlos remain ignorant? The past had died with Carlotta. There was no reason to rake it all up now.

The silence between them lengthened, each of them lost in their own thoughts. They were moored on the northern coast of Malta and tomorrow they would fly, with Carlotta's body, to Jerez. Marc would then rejoin the *Sania* and continue cruising for a few more weeks, and Carlos, he supposed, would return to the States.

'What are you going to do now, without Mom?' Carlos asked suddenly and painfully.

Marc regarded him closely for a moment, the question hitting a raw nerve though not for the reasons Carlos would suppose. 'I still have to finish my new book, *Blue Moon*,' he replied. 'After that . . . well, we'll see. I'll probably cruise down to the South of France, have a break, invite some friends to stay on board . . .' Marc's voice sounded tired. It suddenly struck him that his new-found liberty could weigh on him like an unaccustomed burden until he got used to it. He'd been at Carlotta's beck and call for twenty-three years and now that freedom had been handed him on a plate he wasn't entirely sure that he knew what to do with it. He sighed, and Carlos mistook it for sorrow.

'I'm so sorry, Dad,' he said. 'It's worse for you than for me. Mom was your whole life, wasn't she? I've at least got my own career, my own place and my own friends, but I know how much you're going to miss her.' He looked sympathetically across the saloon.

Marc averted his face, feeling a terrible hypocrite. Now he knew he could never tell Carlos the truth.

'You'll be going back to the States, after the funeral, I presume?' he asked, in a low voice.

'Yup. My agent has a couple of films she wants me to go up for and there's also a girl . . . I want to go back and see her.'

Marc eyed him gently, glad that Carlos had a girl. He remembered his own youth and he gave a bleak smile. Young love is a private thing he thought, deciding not to question Carlos, and he suddenly felt very old. Would he ever be able to recapture that wild elation that young love brings? He doubted it. The woman he had hated, but needed, had died in a bloodbath two days before, and because of her he had twice been robbed of loving and being loved. And yet she *had* given him something in return, something that at the time had meant more than anything in the world to him.

The question that haunted him now was, had it all been worth it?

Diana decided that Stanton Court was the best place to hold a family conference. Ever since Kathryn had returned to London she had been withdrawn and unhappy, unable to understand her mother's point of view and unwilling to co-operate in anything. For the first time in years Diana was at her wits' end, and the situation was driving a deep wedge between them. Kathryn couldn't be told the truth. The shock of finding she'd been having an affair with her half-brother would be even more traumatic than finding out that Guy was not her real father. The only way to put an end to their relationship was to stop her seeing him again, and for that Diana felt she needed Charlie's and Sophie's advice and support.

As soon as they arrived on the Friday afternoon Kathryn's cousins, the Honourable Philip Stanton and Lady Charlotte and Lady Lucy Stanton, dragged her off for a game of tennis, leaving Diana alone with Charles and Sophie.

'What's up, old girl?' asked Charles, seeing her strained face. 'Guy been playing up again?' Over the years, Charles had grown into a more comfortably shambling figure than ever. His fair hair was thinning on top and his weather-beaten face was deeply lined with good humoured wrinkles. However expensive his clothes were they never seemed to fit and were usually patched and mended.

'I've got to tell you something, and ask your advice, and you're not going to like it,' said Diana grimly.

Sophie led the way into the drawing-room, and then Charles shut the door, sensing that whatever was coming was probably something none of them would wish to be overheard.

'You said something about Kathryn falling in love with someone in America,' Sophie asked briskly. 'Isn't she rather young for that sort of nonsense?'

In spite of her worry, Diana smiled. How like Sophie to be matter-of-fact and prosaic about the whole thing. Nevertheless, she found her attitude strangely comforting. 'That's what we've got to make her believe,' she said, 'That she's far too young to get involved. The trouble is it's not as simple as that, and I hope you don't mind but I've asked Guy to come here this weekend, so that he can talk to her as well.'

'What's it got to do with Guy?' asked Sophie bluntly. 'He's been a bloody rotten father to both of them, except when it suited him on public occasions, and I don't suppose Kathryn will listen to a word he has to say.'

'We've got to try everything,' said Diana desperately. 'The situation is far more serious than you realise.' Then she told them everything in slow, clear, measured tones, neither asking for sympathy nor expecting it. Charles listened, his blue eyes wide with disbelief, his jaw dropping. Sophie, startled, kept giving little silent intakes of breath.

'So we decided to pass her off as Guy's child,' Diana concluded. 'He threatened me with a divorce that would have dragged us all into a big scandal. That was before I realised he was a homosexual. If that had got out it would have been even worse for Miles and Kathryn! Remember, it didn't become legal until several years later.' She shrugged, and Charles and Sophie found it hard to reconcile the Diana they knew with this self-possessed woman who had loved passionately and suffered deeply, and had kept everything to herself for so long.

'Of all the young men in the world Kathryn had to fall for ...' said Charles, shaking his head, his voice drifting off incredulously.

'I know,' agreed Diana wretchedly. 'And of course when she kept on talking about "Oliver Power" I had no idea he was Marc's son. Neither had Sarah or Francesca. It seems the boy wants to make it on his own in films and that's why he changed his name.'

'You're right about one thing,' Sophie's tone was positive, 'Kathryn has to stop seeing him again, even if we do have to invent a reason.'

Charles looked across the library at Diana, remembering when she'd first fallen in love with Guy and how they'd all tried to put her off marrying him. If Kathryn was as obstinate as her mother they might have to end up telling her the truth. For Diana's sake, he hoped it wouldn't be necessary.

'So when's Guy arriving?' asked Sophie.

'Tomorrow morning.'

'How much of all this, if any, are we going to tell mother?' Charles asked.

Diana considered the question for a long moment. Mary Sutton was getting rather frail these days, content to let events pass her by while she tended her roses and enjoyed the companionship of her grandchildren. It seemed pointless to shatter the few illusions she had left.

'I don't think there's any point in telling her everything,' said Diana. 'We'll just say that Kathryn has got involved with someone and as she's only eighteen we want to put a stop to it.'

'Your Ma was married at eighteen,' commented Sophie drily, 'and so were you. I hardly think that will wash.'

'All the more reason to prevent it,' Diana flashed back.

Guy arrived in time for luncheon the next day, full of self-importance and obviously irritated at not being able to go to Wilmington Hall for the weekend.

'I don't know why we all had to come here,' he said ungraciously as Charles handed him a glass of sherry before luncheon. 'Diana over-dramatising the whole thing as usual,' he added, as if she were not even in the room.

'It's a pretty serious matter,' muttered Charles. 'We've got to think of a way of stopping it before it's too late.'

'Send Kathryn to finishing school in Switzerland,' Guy retorted.

'I've thought of that,' said Diana, 'but how can we be sure she'd not contact him secretly?'

'You can't exactly lock her in her room and guard her night and day,' snapped Guy. 'For God's sake, Diana, be sensible. We just forbid her to see him again. She'll have to obey us!'

The others looked pityingly at him and sipped their sherry.

'I've an idea,' said Sophie, her face lighting up. 'It's obvious that this boy – what's his name, Carlos – has no idea Kathryn is his half sister. Can't we get hold of Marc Raven and tell *him* what has happened? Maybe he could talk to Carlos himself and tell him the truth, and then he'd certainly stop seeing Kathryn.'

'Surely this is not the time to bring all this up, what with his wife being killed and everything?' reasoned Charles.

Sophie suddenly turned to Diana. 'I suppose Marc Raven knows Kathryn is his daughter?'

'He's no idea. We broke up before I even knew I was pregnant,' said Diana painfully, hating every moment of having her affair with Marc talked

403

about like this. It had been the most beautiful and private thing in her life, and she had treasured her memories of their time together. Now it seemed as if that wonderful time was going to become public property!

Guy gave a snort of mocking laughter. 'Trust you to screw it up, Diana!' he exclaimed. 'You couldn't even have one little affair without fucking up everything. I'm telling you one thing, this business about Kathryn is not to lead to any sort of scandal! We've got to hush up the whole thing, and if necessary send Kathryn abroad. If the press were to get hold of the whole story it could ruin me.' His eyes flickered defensively around the room at the others. 'At least I've always been very discreet,' he added defiantly, 'which is more than I can say for you.'

'Now look here,' blustered Charles, going red in the face.

Diana's face had hardened as she'd watched Guy speaking. The sheer hypocrisy of what he'd said reminded her how much she disliked him. With his flashy clothes, smooth hair – dyed, she imagined, for it was still a glossy black – and his bombastic manner, he epitomised everything she now hated in men.

'Trust you to think only about yourself,' she said coldly. 'We are talking about two young lives that are about to be ruined unless we can stop them seeing each other. Carlos is still writing to Kathryn and I imagine she is writing back. Without them knowing the truth, we have to think of a way of putting an end to their affair.'

'Well, for God's sake, let's do it quietly,' said Guy impatiently. 'Just tell her she can't see him any more. Where is she, by the way? I came down to talk to her and knock some sense into her head, not to have an argument with you lot.'

Charles glared at him balefully and Sophie's mouth tightened. Only Diana, as implacable and cool as ever, looked at him with disdain.

'Then let's get on with it,' she said calmly.

At that moment, Charles and Sophie's youngest daughter, Lady Charlotte, who was just eleven, bounded into the library, her face glowing with excitement. 'Guess what?' she cried.

Sophie ran an affectionate hand over her long blonde hair which was held back by a dark blue velvet ribbon. 'What, darling?'

'Kathryn's just had a telephone call all the way from Hollywood! Imagine! And guess what? It's still in the middle of the night there! Isn't she lucky!' The child's voice echoed with envy at her cousin's good fortune. 'I wish someone would ring me from Hollywood,' she added wistfully.

'I think the next call we're all going to have is the gong for luncheon,' quipped Sophie swiftly. 'Come along, everyone. Charlotte, sweetheart, call Kathryn and Philip and Lucy will you?'

'Okay.' Charlotte went skipping away, yelling their names at the top of her voice.

'We'll have to talk to Kathryn tonight,' Diana murmured urgently as they all trooped across the hall to the dining-room.

'Don't worry. I'll sort her out,' said Guy dismissively. 'You just need to be firm with the girl.'

Diana gave him a withering look. 'Fat lot of experience *you've* had with girls,' she remarked drily.

Lunch was a tense affair, with Kathryn sitting between her cousins, Philip and Lucy, her eyes downcast and her cheeks flushed. The call from Carlos had cheered her greatly. It was wonderful and comforting to hear him tell her how much he loved her, but now she could feel the family's disapproval homing in on her, dissolving the joy she had felt a few minutes before. It all seemed so terribly unfair. She glanced at Guy, who was holding forth at great length about the increasing number of divorces in the country.

'People get married on the slightest whim,' he was saying, 'it's not surprising so many marriages end up on the rocks.'

Kathryn glanced around the table at her mother and Charles and Sophie, and realised Guy was manipulating the conversation round to her and Carlos. Angrily, she took a sip of white wine and at that moment she caught Diana's eye. For a moment her mother looked at her compassionately, remembering how she had felt, sitting at this very table all those years ago when Charles and Sophie had tried to turn her against Guy. Then a pained expression crossed Diana's face and she looked hurriedly away. Kathryn's heart sank. They were all against her, every one of them, even her mother.

Guy was continuing to expound his theory on the reasons for the rising divorce rate as if he were addressing the House of Commons, and Charles was nodding his head and blinking rapidly. Sophie looked stern, muttering something about education being the most important thing for young people to concern themselves with, while Diana tore at her bread roll, a distracted look on her face.

Kathryn felt misery give way to a slow burning anger. I *will* see Carlos again, she told herself. I'll call him as soon as I get back to London after this ghastly weekend. I won't let anyone separate us, and as soon as I can I'll fly back to the States to be with him again. Francesca will help me, she thought. She's not stuffy and snobbish like Mummy and Daddy. Kathryn's anger grew as she considered the injustice of it all, and slowly a plan began to form in her head.

Francesca and Serge stayed on at Sarah's house in Palm Beach after Kathryn left. Sarah was still in hospital but her condition had improved so much that the doctors thought she could be flown back to New York within a couple of weeks. Once back in her apartment Francesca would be able to arrange for nurses to look after Sarah while she herself dropped in on the way back from Kalinsky's every evening.

Now, lying by the pool with Serge beside her, Francesca tried to relax and recharge her batteries before returning to work, but it was more difficult than she realised. She still felt strung out and tense and deeply shaken by the hi-jacking incident. As she lay in the sun looking up at the brilliant cornflower blue sky above, it hit her with a terrible force that this was a day she was not supposed to have seen. If the terrorists had had their way she would inevitably have been gunned down, as Carlotta had been, and her life would have ended abruptly by now, killed in a carnage that had shocked and sickened the world. Grateful to be alive and feel the breeze on her tanned legs, the sweet perfume of the flowers in her nostrils and the warmth of the sun on her back, she turned to Serge, her eyes brimming with tears. If she'd died she'd never have seen Serge again and that would have been the greatest loss of all. The years had flashed past, swallowed up by work and ambitious plans and the heady elixir of success, and she had never, for one moment, stopped to consider how wonderful life was. She had forgotten the beauty of a sunrise over the ocean; she had become deaf to the songs of the birds; the seasons had come and gone as each new year had been born and swelled to summer, only to fade with a golden autumn, and she had simply stopped noticing. Except that it meant buying new clothes to suit the seasons.

Reflecting on all this she watched Serge as he read, her eyes travelling from his strong bearded face and piercing blue eyes to his sensitive hands. She had so much to be grateful to him for and yet she had treated him so casually, and now she felt a pang of guilt. She'd wanted him by her side and yet she'd refused to commit herself. Refused to marry him and have his children. Refused to put him before Kalinsky's. Serge deserved much more, and yet even at this moment she didn't know if she had it in her to give him more. She wanted to, Oh God she wanted to, but something held her back. Fear? Yes, she thought, all sorts of fears: fear she would be hurt again as Marc had once hurt her; fear that marriage and children would get in the way of her forging ahead, hampering her driving ambitions. It struck her with sudden shock that if she had been killed in the hi-jack she'd have had nothing to show for her life but a company whose heart was as cold as the diamonds it sold. Surely there should be more to life than that? And yet there was also the rivalry that had hung over herself and Sarah like a dark shadow. Perhaps if Sarah had welcomed her into Kalinsky's, helping her to realise her ambitions, she might have been less self-seeking and ruthless, might have had more time for a private life, for loving, for marriage. If I had a daughter, Francesca reflected, knowing now that she never would, I would treat her so differently. Of course there was Kathryn. She had become so fond of the girl and had been so thrilled when she'd shown an interest in the jewellery business, that it had already crossed her mind how wonderful it would be to train her so that one day she could take over the company, keep the Andrews family at the helm ... Francesca sat up suddenly and Serge looked up from his book.

'What is it, honey?' he asked gently.

Francesca smiled briefly, a tight weary smile. 'I was thinking about something ... and then I realised I was as bad as my mother,' she said.

Serge raised his eyebrows comically. 'That would be difficult! What were you thinking?'

'I was thinking how wonderful it would be if Kathryn eventually came to live in America, and joined Kalinsky's. She's absolutely fascinated by the business you know, and I could train her, and as I don't have an heir to take over . . .' Her voice broke, and she looked swiftly away and took a deep steadying breath. 'Then I realised I was as bad as Sarah. Planning someone else's life to fit into my own. It's what she tried to do with Guy, and look what happened!'

Serge shrugged. 'The trouble with Guy was that he wasn't interested in the first place. If Kathryn shows genuine interest then I think it would be a good idea.'

'I'm not sure.' Francesca wrinkled her brow in worry. 'Do you know I've just realised something. My greatest fear, my really deep fear, is that underneath it all I'm really very like my mother.' She turned to look at him, her velvety brown eyes suddenly wide with the astonishment of self-awareness and the glitter of unshed tears. 'I'd never thought of it before, Serge. It scares me . . . Do you think I'm like Sarah?'

Serge's mouth tipped up at the corners with amusement. 'Only in as much as you're both highly intelligent, hardworking women. There the resemblance ends. You're gentle where Sarah's harsh. You're compassionate, whereas she really is a ruthless lady.'

'I was ruthless in getting her out of the company,' said Francesca unhappily.

'She asked for that,' Serge replied quietly. 'She really asked for that. If she'd shown any imagination she'd have encouraged you over the years, so it wouldn't have been necessary.'

'I hope you're right.' Francesca plucked fretfully

at the tufts of grass that grew between the flag-stones surrounding the pool. 'It fills me with absolute horror to think I've spent my entire life trying to be different from my mother, only to find out in the end that I'm exactly like her.'

'You've nothing to worry about, darling.' Serge spoke firmly and, reaching across, stroked the firm tanned skin of her shoulder. 'For one thing, nothing would have induced me to live with your mother for over sixteen years, and that's for sure.'

Francesca smiled at him, his calming attitude soothing her. What would I do without Serge, she thought, grateful once more to have him back.

Sunday dawned clear and hot and Francesca was up early, swimming in the pool before breakfast. Later in the morning she was going to the hospital to visit Sarah, and in the afternoon she and Serge planned to go sailing.

At seven o'clock the telephone rang. It was Sarah. She sounded deeply agitated and for a moment Francesca thought she must be ill again.

'I'm all right,' snapped Sarah, fretfully. 'It's Guy I'm worried about. Get over here, Francesca. I want to put a call through to him.'

'Why should there be anything wrong with Guy? Have you heard anything? Is he sick or something?'

'I don't know. I just have a bad feeling . . . like I'm never going to see him again.' The old woman's voice quavered and Francesca realised she was getting hysterical.

'Okay, Mom,' she said resignedly. 'I'll put on some clothes and be right over.'

Serge was still in bed when she went into the bedroom to get dressed.

'I'm sorry, darling, I've got to go to the hospital. Mom wants to see me urgently,' she explained as she slipped into white lace underwear and a white linen dress.

Serge raised himself on one elbow and watched her fondly.

'Is there a problem, sweetheart?'

'She's got it into her head there's something wrong with Guy, and she wants me there when she calls him. She said she has a feeling she's never going to see him again.'

Serge frowned. 'You don't suppose her real worry is that something's going to happen to her, and that's why she's not going to see him again? After a heart attack people can get very scared about their own mortality. Maybe she's afraid she's going to die?'

Francesca slipped into her high-heeled white sandals and then she fixed a gold choker round her neck. 'You may be right. I can't imagine what could be wrong with Guy, and Mom's not the sort of person given to premonitions.' But as she drove to the Burton Foundation Hospital she began to feel uneasy. Suppose Sarah was about to have another coronary!

The sun sweltered down from a blank sky and the air shimmered with heat. God, she thought, how I hate Palm Beach. How I hate this whole wretched summer. It had begun when Serge had left her and then there was Sarah's illness, and the hi-jack, and now just when things should have been

412

getting back to normal, Diana's strange attitude towards Kathryn's romance with Carlos Raven had soured what was left of the summer.

When she got to the hospital she found Sarah sitting up in bed, bright red spots staining her thin cheeks, her hands fidgeting nervously.

'Why did you take so long?' she demanded ungraciously. 'What time will it be in England now?'

Francesca looked at her slim gold Kalinsky watch, and did a quick calculation in her head. 'It must be about seven in the evening – they'll probably be having cocktails.'

'Get on to him for me then – I know something's wrong, I must speak to him.'

'I suppose he'll be at Wilmington Hall as it's Sunday.' Francesca opened her address book to look up the number. 'Don't worry, Mom. Guy will be fine. He's never had a day's illness in his life and I'm sure you're just imagining there's something wrong.'

'Francesca, I *know* there's something wrong!' Sarah's voice had risen querulously and Francesca shot her an anxious look. If she got any more worked up she'd have a relapse.

The servant who answered the phone at Wilmington Hall announced that Mr Guy Andrews was away for the weekend, staying at Stanton Court with the Earl and Countess of Sutton.

'Thank you.' Francesca hung up, puzzled, and flipped through her book for Charles' number. 'Apparently Guy's staying with the Suttons,' she informed Sarah as she started dialling again.

'Oh God, I know something's happened to him,' moaned Sarah.

'Mom, stop it! You'll make yourself ill again! This is nonsense. Why the hell should anything have happened to Guy?' When she had finished dialling the number of Stanton Court she pressed the bell for the nurse. Sarah was rolling her head from side to side on the pillow, and giving demented little whimpers as if she was in physical pain.

Francesca could not get through to the Suttons. The line was busy.

She decided to try again in a few minutes.

Sunday in Oxfordshire dawned grey and misty. The lawns of Stanton Court were wet with dew and the roses, full-blown and blowsy, hung their heads and scattered their petals on the grass.

Charles was out early as usual, pottering around the farm, checking up on a sick calf, glad to escape from the house for a few hours. He hated rows and last night there'd been one hell of a fight, mainly between Kathryn and her parents, but of course he and Sophie had found themselves involved. He shook his head as he pulled a wisp of hay off the calf's neck. The atmosphere in the house was going to be wretched today too, there was no doubt about that, and he wondered what excuse he could think of to absent himself for the afternoon. Thank God Guy was going back to London this evening, but that still left Diana and Kathryn, glaring balefully at each other and not talking. Even his children were taking sides, urging Kathryn to have Carlos as a boyfriend if she wanted to. Charles leaned against the barn door and regarded the little brown calf affectionately. How much nicer animals are than people, he thought.

Diana awoke with a headache and wished she'd never asked Guy to come down for the weekend. It hadn't done a bit of good, and only put Kathryn in a more defiant mood than ever. Feeling tired and desperately worried, she wondered how she was going to get through the day.

Guy, in his room along the corridor, lay in bed, working out the speech he was going to make in the House of Commons in three days' time. He was trying to get a motion through the House to change the law on drunken driving offences, and he knew he had the Prime Minister's backing. He stretched his long frame in the carved four-poster bed and mentally preened himself. Within a few months he was certain he'd be invited to join the Cabinet. At last he belonged; he had a place in society. It had taken him most of his adult life but now he knew he'd made it. An assured place in politics, the respect of his fellow men and, with the help of Diana, he'd managed to maintain a highly respectable image. And no one ever suspected what he was really up to, when he vanished for a few brief hours now and then, in pursuit of his private desires. Really, he thought as he lay there, the world is a very funny place!

Then he got out of bed and went to have his bath.

Not once had he given a thought to the problem of Kathryn and Carlos.

* * *

Kathryn sat at the little desk in her room, once her mother's room, writing to Carlos. The house was quiet. After the fight with her parents last night she was more determined than ever to see Carlos again.

'My Darling Carlós,' her letter began. Somehow she would find a way. He had been so loving on the 'phone yesteray, and in spite of his grief at Carlotta's death his voice had been filled with longing for her. Her heart thumped and hammered when he said how much he needed her, and now as she wrote she felt filled to overflowing with love for him. *I've got to be with him again,* she thought desperately. *I've got to see his face, hear his voice, feel his arms around me. We belong, in a very special way that I didn't know existed.*

Downstairs, she could hear her Aunt Sophie calling to the dogs, and her cousins, Philip, Lucy and Charlotte, arguing over which horses they would ride after breakfast.

It was the beginning of a very long Sunday.

The family sat down to luncheon at precisely one o'clock. Mary Sutton had walked over from the dower house to join them and Charles seated her on his right, where she proceeded to watch her family as they sat around the long table, her eyes taking in everything, her silence strictly diplomatic. Conversation was general and inconsequential; no one wanted a repeat of last night's livid arguments. In any case, in a few hours Guy would be leaving for London so they might as well conduct themselves in a civilised manner, something Mary always recommended. Fights in a family were wounding and useless, and things were often said which were later regretted, she maintained.

To Kathryn, it seemed as if everyone had taken it for granted that she would never be seeing Carlos again. She was to be a good little girl, taking a shorthand and typing course at Constance Spry's school, Winkfield Place, which was situated near Ascot, and after that Diana would give a coming-out ball for her. In time Carlos would be forgotten, and she would marry the son of one of her mother's friends, someone with a nice country house and a bit of money. She would spend the rest of her life in tweeds, walking her dogs and growing roses.

Kathryn shuddered. That was not the life she wanted. There wasn't one thing about it she wanted. What she did want was to go back to America, get a job at Kalinsky's and be with Carlos. She regarded her family balefully from under her thick lashes.

'Is it me, or has it got terribly hot?' Sophie suddenly demanded, flapping her linen table-napkin like a fan before her face.

'I'll open a window, it is rather stuffy,' said Charles, rising and sauntering over to the French windows that led from the dining-room to the terrace which ran round three sides of the house.

'I think there's going to be a storm. I noticed it was getting very oppressive when I walked over here,' remarked Mary Sutton.

'The garden could probably do with a bit of rain,' volunteered Diana, trying to sound cheerful.

'There are dark clouds coming over from the west,' observed Charles, coming back and sitting down. 'We could have one hell of a storm.'

The weather having been fully discussed, a heavy paralysing silence fell upon the table. No one spoke. It was as if they were all listening intently.

Charles glanced at his watch. 'I thought so! Twenty-past two. Angels passing over the house! Isn't that so, Mother?' He smiled at Mary.

'That's what they say, my dear. Angels pass over at twenty past and twenty to each hour. I've always noticed there's a deathly silence for a moment or two at those times, even when there are several people gathered together.'

'What a bloody silly old wives' tale,' said Guy crossly.

But Diana gave a little shudder. It had felt to her more like the spirits of evil passing over the house.

After luncheon had come to an uneasy end, Sophie suggested they have coffee on the terrace. It was still hot, without a breath of wind, but the storm seemed to be holding off. Lucy, Philip and Charlotte had other ideas.

'Let's have a swim, I'm boiled,' said Lucy.

'You can't swim right after luncheon,' Sophie remonstrated.

'Don't worry, we'll sit around the pool for a while first. Coming, Kathryn?'

Kathryn shook her head. 'Not just now. Maybe later. I've some letters I want to write.'

'How about some clay pigeon shooting this afternoon?' suggested Charles. 'It's good practice, and it gets your eye in before the season starts.'

'Good idea,' said Guy. 'Pity I didn't bring my gun down with me.'

'We can lend you one. Let's go to the gunroom. There are several there you can choose from.'

The two men ambled off, their only bond a love of the sport – Charles because he had been brought up to it, Guy because he knew it was a fashionable country pursuit.

Sophie, Mary and Diana settled themselves on the terrace, happy to be left in peace for a while.

They were unaware of the 'phone ringing until Charles put his head out of the library window to say he'd had a call from the farm and the sick calf was worse. He was going over to look at it.

They didn't know that Kathryn had joined Guy in the gunroom, where he was fiddling with a shot-gun. But dimly, through their own conversation, they heard raised voices and Diana's heart sank. Guy and Kathryn were fighting again.

'I forbid you to see him again, haven't I made that clear?' she heard Guy yelling.

The rumble of distant thunder drowned what was said next but then she heard Kathryn's voice, high pitched and angry, screaming at him.

'If you'd ever loved anyone in your life you'd understand. You don't know the meaning of love . . .' The rest was drowned by another rumble, nearer this time.

Diana rose swiftly, but Sophie caught her by the wrist.

'Leave them, Diana.'

'I must stop them, it'll do no good . . .' She was

cut off in mid-sentence by a towering crash of thunder that seemed to make the very terrace tremble beneath their feet and left them almost deaf for a moment. Shocked, she looked at Mary who was rising slowly to her feet.

'We'd better go indoors,' said Mary, shakily.

At that moment they all heard a tearing sobbing sound coming from the hall. Then there was the crash of a door slamming before a prolonged rolling boom of thunder rent the air and blocked out everything. It was followed by more ear-splitting claps and the storm seemed to be exploding right above the house. By the time they reached the French windows to the library, the rain was splattering down. Sheltering inside, the three women watched as a river of water flooded the terrace and swamped the lawns. Streak after streak of lightning split through the sky in a prolonged and violent display, and thunder rattled the windows.

At least, thought Diana, the storm seems to have put a stop to Guy and Kathryn fighting. Apart from the noise outside, it was absolutely quiet indoors.

It wasn't until half an hour later when the summer storm had abated, leaving a trail of desolation among the roses and honeysuckle, that they found Guy. He was lying on the floor of the gunroom, his guts spilling into pools of blood, his face contorted in a rigor of frenzied fear.

Kathryn was missing. And so was Diana's car.

For an hour now Francesca had been trying to get through to Stanton Court. It would be evening in England and she couldn't understand why the line seemed continually busy. Perhaps someone had left the 'phone off the hook. She wouldn't have bothered, but Sarah had become so hysterical that the doctor had given her an injection to sedate her, and now she lay drifting in and out of a light sleep. Whenever she woke she asked the same question: 'Have you got hold of Guy yet?'

Francesca sighed with impatience. What on earth had got into her mother? She'd never been like this before but Francesca knew there'd be no peace for anyone until Sarah was satisfied that Guy was all right.

At lunchtime she left the hospital, promising Sarah she'd let her know as soon as she reached Guy. Serge was waiting for her when she got back to the house. One glance at his face, pale and grave, told her there was something wrong.

'What is it, darling?' She stood before him, looking up into his eyes.

'Bad news, I'm afraid,' he said tightly. 'There's been a call from Diana. Guy's been murdered.'

'He's . . . dear God!' Stunned, her mouth open, she gazed blankly at him.

'There's worse,' said Serge. 'Much worse.'

Her mind was reeling, her thoughts jumping about in disjointed fragments.

'Worse?' she croaked.

'Yes.' Serge put his hands on her shoulders, as if to help her brace herself for the final blow.

'Kathryn's been accused of his murder.'

Chapter Nineteen

Sarah was inconsolable. Guy was dead and she didn't know how she was going to bear the pain. In the split second the bullet had entered his body, she had lost the one person she had loved most of all. Guy had been her life. Everything she had done, she had done for him. The tragedy was that he had not wanted any of it – except for the money.

The tears rolled down her lined cheeks and her mouth trembled. She wished she could be grateful for the forty-five years during which she had loved him so much, but all she could think of were the dark powers that had taken him away.

At least she had made Francesca promise her one thing. Guy's body was to be flown back to the States as soon as the British authorities permitted it, and she would see that he was given a magnificent funeral, placed in the earth beside her father in the family plot at Woodlawn Cemetery.

The doctor came to give her another injection. She wished they'd all go away and leave her alone. She wished she was dead too.

Francesca rose after another sleepless night, haunted by the horror of what had happened. She couldn't believe, wouldn't believe that it was

Kathryn who had killed Guy. She was a gentle girl, without malice, and this had been a savage murder, the gun shot at point blank range, blasting Guy violently to the ground, almost severing him in two. In the morning she and Serge were flying to England to find out what had happened and to offer their assistance to Diana who was distraught. Kathryn, she was told, was being held in custody.

Sarah, too, was causing her anxiety. The doctors had warned her that her mother's grief could bring on another attack and at first Francesca felt she could not leave her, but then she began to realise that her presence wasn't helping either. Sarah didn't want her. She showed her bitterness at what had happened when Francesca visited her at the hospital the day after the murder.

'Why did it have to be Guy?' Sarah moaned through her sobs. 'He was my favourite child . . . I loved him more than anyone will ever know.'

Deeply hurt, Francesca crept quietly away.

When she got back to the house she put a call through to Henry Langham. 'I hate to ask you this, Uncle Henry,' she plunged in immediately, 'but could you possibly come to Palm Beach so as to be near Mom? I've got to fly to England to see to the arrangements about bringing Guy's body home, and although she's getting the best possible care I'm worried about leaving her.'

'Consider it done, honey.' Henry had spoken to Francesca the previous day and he knew this was a traumatic time for her. It would not be the loss of her brother that would grieve her, or even the shock of hearing Kathryn had killed him; it would be the final knowledge of how much more Sarah had cared for Guy than she did for Francesca. Henry understood the twisted workings of Sarah's mind very well. She would be feeling angry that Francesca had lived and Guy had died.

'Is there anything else I can do for you?' he asked.

'Could you keep in touch with the office in New York? I think everything's under control, but I can't think straight at the moment, and if there are any major queries . . .'

'No problem. Leave it all to me. I shall enjoy coming out of retirement for a while, and don't worry about Sarah. She's a tough old bird. She'll pull through.'

'I hope so,' said Francesca doubtfully.

'There's no doubt she's guilty,' said Arthur Kilgour, the Chief Superintendent of Police, as he sat in his office at New Scotland Yard, studying the evidence before him. 'It's an open and shut case.' He was a hardened man in his forties who had worked his way up from the ranks and had a deep dislike for the upper classes.

'Whether it *will* be an open and shut case is another matter,' he added darkly.

'How's that?' One of his colleagues, Bob Bridges, who had also studied the various statements collected in their investigations into the murder of Mr Guy Andrews, Member of Parliament for Wessex East, sounded puzzled. 'There was no one else who could have killed him.'

Arthur Kilgour looked at him askance, his bushy, sandy-coloured eyebrows rising a fraction.

'Ever had to deal with people like the Sutton family before?' he asked.

Bob Bridges hesitated, racking his mind. 'No . . . no, I suppose not,' he said.

'I didn't think so.' He made a grimace, his tone dry. 'Well, let me tell you something. These sort of people cling together tighter than mussels to a rock! They'll go to any lengths to protect their own. They're vulnerable, you see.'

'Vulnerable?' Bob Bridges looked surprised. 'Why should they be vulnerable? They're a grand family – pots of money, high positions . . .'

'That's why! These privileged families are a dying breed. They're hanging on to their way of life like grim death. Have you seen how the press have made mincemeat of them in the last few days? They can't *afford* that sort of bad publicity. Let me tell you something,' Arthur Kilgour brought his fist down on the desk with a thump, as if he was hitting someone. 'They think they can hide behind their titles and their public schools and their stately bloody homes. Well, they can't! They're finished. All those lords and ladies have had it! But do you know what's going to happen? Shall I tell you what's really going to happen? They'll employ the most expensive lawyer in the business and they'll withhold any information that might make this spoilt little brat look guilty. For God's sake, Bob, she's as guilty as hell! So far even they haven't been able to think of a cover up. But they will. You can bet your fucking last penny they will.'

Bob Bridges listened to the diatribe and smiled to himself. The trouble with old Arthur Kilgour, he thought, is just plain old-fashioned jealousy. The chip on his shoulder was positively making him topple over. He shrugged. Why get into an argument? His promotion was more important.

'So what do we do?' he asked casually.

'We make this evidence stand up in court, that's what we fucking well do,' snapped the Superintendent.

Diana sat in the oak panelled office of her lawyer, Mr George Selwyn, in Lincoln's Inn, discussing the defence. Mr Selwyn was a member of the Queen's Counsel and one of the most highly respected and successful members of the legal profession. Charles had told her there was no one better to take on the case.

'We are going to have to plead that it was severe provocation that drove Kathryn to shoot her father,' he said, as he studied the various reports and statements spread out before him on his desk.

'But she didn't do it!' cried Diana. 'Provocation or a *crime passionelle* doesn't come into it! She's not guilty.' She clenched her fists as they lay in her lap, desperate to make George Selwyn understand. There was no way she was ever going to believe that Kathryn had picked up a gun and shot Guy.

Mr Selwyn sighed heavily. He liked Lady Diana and he felt sorry for her. He felt sorry for her daughter too, but the statements, taken separately from everyone who was at Stanton Court that day, were fatally damning.

He glanced down at them, committing them to

memory. The facts were there, and the conclusions were obvious. There was no one else who could have shot Guy.

He ran through them in his mind again, assessing each statement, trying to find a loophole where no loopholes existed.

Mary Sutton, Sophie and Diana had been together on the terrace drinking coffee; Charles had left Guy alone in the gun room to go and answer the phone, and had then gone straight to the farm to see the sick calf. Lucy, Philip and Charlotte had been by the swimming pool and when it started to rain, they'd gone into the pool house to play Scrabble. The servants had been together in the kitchen, having lunch after the Sutton family had finished theirs, and they had overheard a quarrel between Guy and Kathryn. All the outworkers, gardeners, maintenance men and farm hands had alibis to prove they were either with their families or at the local inn.

None of them had seen anything unusual.

There were no signs that anyone had climbed over the twelve foot high wall that surrounded the estate, although the rain had obliterated any possible footprints. It would have been impossible for anyone to have entered via the farm gates because Charles and the farm manager had been pottering around the yard at that time. The facts were clear and damaging.

Kathryn must have joined her father in the gun-room after Charles had left for the farm and as a result of a violent quarrel over her boyfriend, she had picked up a gun and shot him, and then thrown down the gun before running out of the house. Her fingerprints were clearly visible on the weapon.

Finally, the police had ruled out all possible question of suicide. A man could not possibly shoot himself in the stomach with a shotgun, unless he had arms six feet long.

'You see,' explained George Selwyn gently to Diana, 'the evidence, circumstantial or not, is totally damning. Presented with the facts a jury will undoubtedly bring in a verdict of guilty. But, if we go for provocation – under stress because Guy Andrews had forbidden Kathryn ever to see her boyfriend again, that she became distraught, grabbed the gun and fired it without knowing what she was doing – then she stands a good chance of being convicted of manslaughter. And that, Lady Andrews, means a much shorter sentence.'

'Whose side are you on?' demanded Diana furiously. 'You believe she did it, don't you? You actually think my daughter killed him!' The colour had risen to her face and her eyes blazed with anger.

'I work on facts, cold-blooded, unemotional facts. Of course you believe she's innocent. If she were my daughter, I'd believe she was innocent too. But the judge and jury aren't going to listen to personal beliefs. They're going to listen to the evidence that is put before them, and decide accordingly. Believe me, Lady Diana, unless we can come up with some proof that she didn't kill her father it is better to plead provocation, or the fact that her mind was unbalanced at the time. It might be a good idea to get a couple of psychiatrists to talk to her.'

Diana jumped to her feet, clutching her handbag and gloves with shaking hands.

'I won't listen to any more of this,' she stormed. 'We appointed you to prove her innocence! If you're not prepared to take on the case, I'll find someone else who will.' She turned and strode quickly out of his office.

In the street outside she started to shake, so that her legs almost gave way beneath her. For a moment she held on to the wrought-iron railings outside the historic buildings, then she took a deep breath and straightened herself. Even if she had to do it single-handed, she was going to prove Kathryn's innocence.

When Francesca and Serge arrived at Diana's house the next morning, they found her in the study with Miles. She seemed to be bearing up with grim resolution but Miles looked wan, and he kept blinking his eyes, as if in deep confusion.

'Hullo, Francesca, Serge,' he greeted them hollowly.

Francesca put her arms around him and hugged him close. It was obvious to her that he was grieving for his father, but the added strain of Kathryn's case seemed to be edging him to breaking point.

'You two could do with a good long vacation,' she remarked, taking in the blue shadows under Diana's eyes and the tight line of her mouth.

'No question of that, we've got to find a way of proving Kathryn didn't kill Guy,' declared Diana.

'And we *know* she didn't!' cut in Miles. 'But who

the hell did? We've been racking our brains for days now and we haven't come up with anything.' His head was bowed as he clenched and unclenched his hands.

Serge sat on the sofa beside him, a comforting strong figure. 'We'll find a way, Miles. There has to be an answer to all this.' He turned to Diana. 'You've told us everyone's version of what had happened last Sunday, but what does Kathryn have to say?'

Diana spread her hands in a gesture of despair.

'It's perfectly straightforward,' she replied. 'Kathryn admits she and Guy had a terrible fight in the gunroom. She went in there to ask him for some money. I think she wanted it so that she could fly back to America, behind our backs, to be with Carlos. Obviously that's what Guy concluded too! Kathryn says he flew into a terrible rage, threatened to make her a ward of court and practically lock her up at Wilmington Hall! She admits that while he was ranting and raving she did put her hand on Charlie's gun which he'd left lying on the table, but she fingered it idly, without thinking, certainly never intending to pick it up or use it. After all, she's no stranger to guns. She's been going rabbit shooting with her cousins since they were about twelve. Charlie taught her himself! A gun isn't something she would shrink from, do you see what I mean? Oh God, I wish she hadn't touched it though, because it had her fingerprints on it, mixed up with a lot of other prints of course, because Charlie often lends it to guests or one of the family.' Diana drew a deep breath, then continued.

'Guy was fiddling with another gun and then she says the fight got worse. He called her terrible names. She burst into tears, ran out of the house and decided to borrow my car to get her back to London. What she'd planned to do was pick up her passport, borrow some money from a girl-friend and get on a flight to New York, where she was sure you would allow her to see Carlos again. She was packing when the police turned up at Eaton Terrace and arrested her.'

Diana's voice had sunk to a flat whisper and dark hollows showed beneath her eyes.

'Have you thought of getting a private detective?' Francesca asked.

'Not yet. I've spoken to Charlie. He's not too keen on the idea, thinks it might jeopardise our relationship with the police,' said Diana. 'You know, they might get angry because we're doubting their ability. It might go against Kathryn.'

'Rubbish,' said Serge. 'If your police are like ours, who wants a relationship with them anyway? Get in a private eye first thing in the morning, Diana. We've got to get to the bottom of this for Kathryn's sake. Where is she now?'

'They're holding her at Holloway Prison.' Diana shuddered. 'I visited her yesterday and you've no idea what a terrible place it is. Overcrowded, depressing, the poor child's in a terrible state. I'm hoping to get her out on bail tomorrow.'

Miles, who had been listening intently to his mother, leaned forward and put his hand on her shoulder, in a protective gesture.

'Don't worry, Mum, it'll be all right. We'll

get her out somehow,' he said sympathetically.

Diana smiled back at him, their gaze holding in a moment of understanding. Then she looked away. She hadn't been able to tell him that Carlos Raven had telephoned the previous evening, adding to her troubles. She'd told Carlos to get lost; the memory of what she'd said made her feel guilty now. It wasn't Carlos's fault, not any of it, but she hadn't been able to bear the added complication of having him hanging around. It was as vital as ever that he and Kathryn never see each other again and, of course, she hadn't been able to tell him why. She'd have to lie to Kathryn too, if she asked about Carlos.

The knot of lies and deception both she and Guy had perpetrated over the years was getting tangled, tighter and tighter, threatening to strangle them all.

Chapter Twenty

'Silence and be upstanding for the judge,' said a sepulchral voice.

Judge Edward Hughes-Lytton entered the courtroom with the slow dignity of one who knows the strength of his position, and he inclined his grey wigged head with gravity as the prosecuting counsel, the counsel for the defence and the clerk of the court rose and bowed deeply to him. Number one court at London's Old Bailey, the scene of the most infamous trials in history, was about to witness the trial of Kathryn Andrews, accused of murdering her father. Mr Justice Hughes-Lytton settled himself on the podium, his papers spread before him, the folds of his scarlet and black robe and the crisp whiteness of his jabot hiding his lean frame and angular shoulders. It was ten o'clock in the morning and he wished to have a private discussion of the case before he set in motion the irretrievable mechanics of conducting a trial. Soon the vast, oak-panelled room, with its glass ceiling through which the daylight flooded and its stiff highbacked chairs padded with green leather and embossed with the City of London crest in gold, would be filled with people; eager to catch every word as the accused and the witnesses made their statements.

On the judge's right the jury of twelve would fill the two rows of seats on a raised podium, and the witness box stood between them and the judge. High up in the public gallery, on the opposite side of the courtroom, the curious and the morbid, who had been standing outside in line since six o'clock in the morning, would be straining forward, eager for a bird's eye view of the proceedings. Various clerks, barristers, lawyers and policemen, not to mention members of the press, would be taking up seats, adding to the tense atmosphere of this case which was expected to last several weeks.

Four hours earlier Kathryn had been brought to the Old Bailey, and now, in a white tiled cell beneath the raised and oak-panelled dock which was situated in the centre of the courtroom, she waited with two policemen and a policewoman for the moment when she would be summoned to appear. Her face was pinched and pale and from time to time a tremor shook her body as she sat waiting with clenched hands. She had chosen a simple navy-blue dress with a white collar for this first of many long days, and her long dark hair was held back with a navy-blue ribbon.

In the vast corridors of this imposing building, which housed nearly thirty separate courtrooms, the witnesses for the defence stood gathered together anxiously. They were led by Diana who had been much photographed as she arrived at the Old Bailey. With her were her mother, Charles and Sophie, and their son, Philip. The farm manager and several of the Suttons' staff had also been called as witnesses. For the prosecution, several policemen and a forensic expert stood by to give evidence of their findings on the day in question, although it would be a long time before any of them would be required to give evidence.

Discussion over between Mr Justice Hughes-Lytton and counsel, they returned to their papers and reference books at the long tables arranged before them, their grey wigged heads nodding at each other, their black robes adding to the medieval atmosphere of the proceedings. The clerk of the court, also black-gowned and bewigged, rose to his feet, and at a signal eighteen potential jurors entered the courtroom and took seats at the back.

In utter silence Kathryn was then brought up the steps from the cells into the dock, where her guards showed her to a hard wooden seat in the centre.

Opening a wooden box, hollowed out in the centre like a bowl, the clerk of the court then proceeded to pick at random twelve cards out of the eighteen that lay there. Each one bore the name of a member of the potential jury.

At last, the jury was sworn in and the clerk of the court, standing on the floor below Mr Justice Hughes-Lytton, rose and read out the indictment against her.

The case of the Crown v Kathryn Andrews had at last started, six months after that fatal Sunday when Guy had died.

Marc Raven sat on the deck of his 157-foot motor yacht, *Sania II*, and sipped his favourite midday aperitif, a bullshot. The chilled consommé and vodka soothed his stomach, not yet recovered from last night's heavy consumption of brandy, and he began to relax. He was supposed to be on holiday, having a well-earned rest after writing the screenplay of his novel, *Never Look Back*. Instead, thanks to the friends he'd invited on board to keep him company as they cruised in the Mediterranean, it had become a marathon of eating and drinking, parties and sex. Last night he'd hardly slept a wink. The little blonde now draping herself along the teak deck beside him had seen to that. And the previous night it had been the luscious Liza who wore a fine gold chain studded with tiny diamonds round her waist. She had been preceded by Ellie, a remarkable black girl with muscles like a stevedore and she had been preceded by – oh, Jesus Christ, he felt weary. He ordered another bullshot from one of his white-coated stewards.

In spite of all his other homes around the world, Marc looked upon *Sania II* as his haven. The 'crunch' boat he called it. 'When the crunch comes,' he would inform his friends airily, 'there's no place safer than the *Sania*.' He never thought to make it clear whether he was referring to a nuclear war, or the Inland Revenue. The great thing was, he was free of Carlotta, and he intended to enjoy himself.

Today they were berthed in Puerto Banus. Marc liked it here. José Banus, a man of vision and an old friend of Marc's, had designed and built the marina only sixteen years before, but now hundreds of sparkling white buildings edged the waterfront, against a backdrop of southern Spanish mountains. It was convenient too. Malaga airport was only an hour's drive away and if he felt like looking up some old friends, Marbella was even nearer. Best of all, he liked the sophistication of the marina with its restaurants, chic boutiques, and evenings spent drinking with the younger set at the two main bars, Sinatra's and Hollywood's. His was one of hundreds of yachts, but it was undoubtedly the largest, the best fitted and the most powerful. That knowledge added to his sense of pleasure. In the old days he'd have preferred to go to St Tropez, but it had just become one more hellish tourist resort. One day, no doubt, the same thing would happen here, but right now it was good just to let his eyes roam lazily along the waterfront and out to sea, where sailing boats skimmed smoothly over the blue water, their spinnakers making gorgeous abstract blobs of colour on the horizon. His idle thoughts were disturbed by the appearance of two stewards bearing platters of fresh asparagus, a large bowl of caviar set in crushed ice, and a mound of rosy *langoustines*. These were placed on a large round table on deck, protected from the high sun by a yellow and white awning. Bowls of exotic salad and fruit quickly followed and then the chef brought in his speciality, a *mille-feuilles*, its delicate layers of fragile pastry interlaced with wild strawberries and whipped cream. He placed it carefully on the table, checked the other dishes, adjusted the cheese board and glanced over at the champagne, chilling in a great silver ice bucket.

'Are you hungry, honey?' asked the little-girl

voice of the blonde. 'Can I get you something?' Her
hand slid up his bare thigh.

'Later,' he replied tersely. A sudden feeling of
discontent and depression swept over him as he
watched the ritual of luncheon being brought on
deck. It was the same every day. And although the
faces around him changed frequently, they were
still the same faces. Silly, sycophantic and insin-
cere. These people didn't know a thing about him.
They couldn't gauge his feelings. To them he was
the man they had read about in all the magazines:
– the rich, sexy spinner of words who could buy
anything or anyone he wanted. And they were up
for grabs, weren't they? It didn't do the girls any
harm to be linked even briefly with Marc Raven, to
take nice little trips on his yacht and then depart
with a trinket from Cartier. Marc took a swig at his
drink. It was his own fucking fault, but he had
worked so hard for the past twenty-five years,
churning out book after book, seeing most of them
made into award-winning films, amassing millions
of dollars, that he felt he owed himself a spot of
fun. He'd come a long way from his poverty-
stricken childhood in Queens. But now that he had
it all, he wasn't sure if he liked it anymore. He
was winding up as some super sugardaddy. The
thought pained him. Depression, an old familiar
friend from his childhood, settled about him like
cold damp moisture, cramping his stomach and filling his head with black thoughts. He watched as
his guests jostled round the lunch table as if they
hadn't eaten in a week. Liza and Mitzi, arms
around each other – he'd often wondered about

those two; Ellie, Nancy and Mary-Lou, flashing their brown tits in minuscule bikinis; and Vic and Bob – he'd never had any doubts about them. And there was lonely old Tony, a has-been actor if ever there was one, who would go anywhere for a free meal but was a mean hand at poker. All trash. Christ, were these the rewards of world-wide fame and more money than he could ever spend? He ordered a third bullshot morosely, letting himself slide deeper into depression. That was something that never failed him, that creeping paralysis of despair that some said made him the great writer he was, but brought him a certain comfort in its well explored familiarity.

'Anyone listen to the BBC world programme on the radio this morning?' demanded Tony in his actorish voice, pronouncing each syllable as if he had a plum in his mouth.

'No, what's on?' said Marc, not really caring.

'Lovey, you *must* have been following this sensational murder case! The earl's niece who shot her father!' Tony looked shocked, as if Marc had missed out on a presidential election. '*Everyone's* talking about it! Her father was heir to Kalinsky's – he must have been worth millions. Her mother's Lady Diana Andrews – she was supposed to be quite a beauty in her time. You mean you haven't been following the case? It's been a terrible scandal in England.'

Marc sat upright, shocked at hearing Diana's name again. It had been such a long time ago but the memory of their affair was still vivid. Of course he hadn't seen or heard anything of her in nineteen years, not since Carlotta had found out. He didn't even know she'd had a daughter. Then he shrugged – it was such a long time ago, and Diana had probably forgotten all about him by now.

Mr Justice Hughes-Lytton had started his summing up and the courtroom was so quiet a buzzing fly would have sounded like an aeroplane.

Sitting in the dock, dressed in a plain cream suit, Kathryn stared straight ahead, oblivious of the tall, dark-haired young man who sat in the public gallery, a frown of anxiety drawing his well-defined brows together. Carlos Raven had flown over for the last few days of the trial, hoping his very presence might help her as she sat, far below, in the dock. He recognised Francesca, sitting in the seats reserved for witnesses after they had given their evidence. She was with a blonde woman whom he took to be Kathryn's mother, and beside her he thought it must be Miles sitting quietly and anxiously. He'd never forgive that stuck-up Lady Diana Andrews for barring him from seeing Kathryn again, but he'd made up his mind that as soon as this trial was over . . .

Mr Justice Hughes-Lytton was addressing the jury with a sympathetic understanding of their predicament. Who would think, he thought privately to himself, that a beautiful, innocent-looking young girl like Kathryn had murdered her father, and yet he feared it was true. In his long experience as a judge this was one of the most open and shut cases he had seen. The evidence might only be circumstantial, but if the jury brought in a verdict of 'Not Guilty' he'd be surprised. But it was his duty to guide them, to tell them to look at the facts and not be swayed by their emotions, and to that end he now conducted himself.

The jury were out for thirty-six hours, trying to make up their minds. Only Francesca, who had stayed with Diana throughout, Diana and Miles remained, waiting for the verdict. Diana had insisted her mother, together with Charles and Sophie, return to Stanton Court. They were all being besieged by press photographers and the newspapers carried full spreads about Kathryn Andrews and her aristocratic relatives. The strain had become unbearable. It seemed as if the whole world was awaiting the outcome of the trial.

At last the jury shuffled back into their seats. The nightmare was finally coming to an end and in a few minutes they would all know whether Kathryn had been found innocent or guilty.

Diana, clutching Francesca on one side and Miles on the other, felt a mounting panic as she looked at their faces. There was not a smile or a kindly glance between them. The words she had been longing yet dreading to hear now reached her across the packed room.

'Do you find the defendant guilty or not guilty of the murder of Guy Andrews?' asked the clerk of the court.

When the answer came, it hit Diana like a body blow, wrenching cries of protest from her throat, filling her with a rage and anguish that almost sent her out of her mind.

'Guilty, M'Lud.'

In the gallery Carlos Raven covered his face with his hands as the tears streamed down his cheeks.

'Oh, my God.' Sophie let out a long drawn breath. 'Poor Kathryn! This is terrible, Charles. What can we do? What did Diana actually say?'

Charles shook his head bleakly. 'She was distraught of course. She rang me from the Old Bailey but she was crying so much I could hardly make out what she was saying.' He dropped heavily into a chintz covered chair facing his wife in the library. 'And as for Kathryn! Oh Christ, it's awful. I wish I hadn't listened to Diana. I should have been up in London today.'

'She made us promise to stay away, darling, once we'd given our evidence. There was nothing you or any of us could do, and she did fear your being there today would only attract more publicity. You know how she's hated all this dragging the family name down as it is.' Sophie spoke softly and sympathetically, knowing how much it had cost him to stay in the background at a time like this.

'I know.' He passed a weary hand across his eyes. If their name had been Smith or Jones, the story would have only filled a couple of column inches in the newspapers and then been forgotten, but being the Earl of Sutton made him vulnerable. The Suttons had been untouched by scandal in the four-hundred-year history of the family. Until now.

At that moment Mary Sutton came slowly into the room, a shocked expression on her face. She was followed by John who, since Guy's death, had returned to live with her in the dower house.

Charles knew immediately that they had heard the news. Taking his mother's elbow, he guided her gently to a chair, his face pink and puckered with misery.

Mary was the first to speak and her voice was surprisingly calm and strong.

'We must fight this, Charles. We must lodge an appeal at once. It is utterly wicked that Kathryn should be punished for something she didn't do.'

'You're right, mother, of course. Diana's already told me she's had a word with counsel about an appeal. They're meeting in the morning to work something out.'

'Poor child.' Mary's mouth quivered. 'I feel so helpless.'

'We all do,' said Sophie. 'It's a hell of a mess.'

'It certainly is,' said John, in a hollow voice.

Francesca and Diana sat and stared at each other in the drawing-room of Eaton Terrace, too shocked to speak. They'd returned from the Old Bailey an hour before and they still felt numbed by the jury's verdict.

'I just can't believe this is happening,' said Diana at last. She had lost a lot of weight during the past few months and her elegant clothes hung unbecomingly on her.

'I wish to God we could find out who *did* kill Guy,' said Francesca for the umpteenth time. 'I suppose there's absolutely no way it could have been suicide?'

'No way at all. Besides, why should he want to? He loved every minute of his wretched life. What is so strange, and what went against Kathryn, is the police saying they're sure Guy was shot by someone he knew, because there was no sign of a struggle.'

'But *who*?' cried Francesca. 'That's the terrible thing. There was no one else about!'

They had gone over the whole thing a thousand times until they were sickened by it. Looking for clues that didn't exist, searching for answers where there were none. Yet both were convinced of Kathryn's innocence.

'You know,' said Francesca, helping herself to a drink from the silver tray in the corner of the room, 'The most awful thing about Guy is that he was always self-destructive. Everything would be fine at the beginning, but there was something in him that wanted to spoil everything, as if he was trying to tear himself to pieces. I have a strong feeling that he brought about his own death, by something he did. The question is what, and how? I could never understand why you only separated and didn't get a divorce. Look how badly he treated you . . . Why didn't you tell him to go to hell?'

'Well, there were the children . . .' Diana's voice drifted off weakly. There was so much Francesca didn't know. So much she still kept secret, for the sake of Kathryn and Miles, and for her own sake too.

The most important thing now was to lodge an appeal to get the verdict overturned. Diana reached for her address book. There was a particular number she wanted to contact and she hoped she still had it.

When the telephone rang in his stateroom early the next morning, Marc picked it up lazily. A moment later he was sitting upright in his bunk, deeply startled.

The ship-to-shore operator had connected the *Sania II* on the radiotelephone and he found himself talking to Diana.

His steward, laying out his clothes for the day, listened with curiosity to Marc's terse comments.

'Sure, I understand what you're saying, but what's it got to do with me?' he was asking bluntly.

There was a pause, and Marc ran a hand through his tousled hair. 'Well, if it's all that urgent . . . but why can't you tell me what it's about?'

There was another long pause and then he heard Marc say, 'Okay. I'll come right away.'

A minute later Marc had bounded from his bunk and was starting to get dressed.

'Tell the captain I have to leave for London right away. I want a car to drive me to Malaga, and ask him to book me on the first flight out.'

'Very good, sir.'

When Marc came on deck, he found his guests were already having breakfast or sunning themselves. He looked at them with distaste. They were a bunch of hangers-on and he was suddenly bored with the lot of them.

'Sorry, boys and girls, but you'll have to leave today,' he said cheerfully, watching their faces fall

447

in consternation. 'I've got to fly to London. The party's over. Thanks for coming anyway.'

A minute later he was walking down the gangplank into a waiting car. Quite suddenly he didn't feel depressed or bored any more, but he did feel uneasy. Could Diana have somehow found out the dark secret of his life? Only if Carlotta had talked, and she'd have been unlikely to talk to Diana, whom she had banished from his life. And yet, why should Diana be trying to involve him in her daughter's affairs now? None of it made sense; he just hoped he wasn't walking into some goddam trap.

Kathryn was awakened at dawn on her second morning at Holloway Prison by the acrid smell of smoke and the sound of screaming in the corridor outside her cell.

'Fire!' someone yelled, their voice immediately drowned by raucous shrieks of abuse. 'Fucking pigs!'

'Up yours, yer cunt!'

'Fuckers! Fuckers!' The other prisoners set up a chant as two of the women warders struggled to extinguish the smouldering bedding in the adjoining cell.

Kathryn sat up in alarm, her heart pounding. She looked at Jenny and Tina, her two young cellmates whom she had joined the previous night.

'There's a fire!' she cried, springing out of her bunk, trying to wake them.

'So what?' mumbled Jenny who was twenty, and serving time for stabbing her boyfriend. She turned over in her bunk, asleep again instantly.

'The place is on fire!' By now Kathryn was frantic. They were going to be roasted alive in this stinking hell-hole.

'The mother-fuckers are always starting fires,' said Tina, sitting up sleepily. 'That's the third one this week.'

Kathryn sank down weakly onto her bunk again. She'd never get used to the violence here. Apparently only 'the Muppet house', as the psychiatric unit was referred to, was worse. Already she'd learned that Jenny had been attacked with a knife. Tina had tried to cut her wrists with a broken electric light bulb. A girl had hanged herself from a high window catch using a torn-off strip of her skirt. Another had gouged her eyes out with her fingers in an explosion of rage and frustration. The list of horrors grew, but this was Kathryn's first experience of fires being started.

'We're not allowed matches,' she said to Jenny, later in the day. 'How do these fires start?' In fact, if anyone wanted a cigarette a warder had to light it for them through a 'letter box' in the cell door.

Jenny shrugged. 'All sorts of things find their way in here,' she replied casually. 'We're not supposed to have scissors, but someone got hold of a pair and attacked her best mate with them last week.'

Kathryn knew her sentence wasn't just fifteen years of confinement, away from Carlos and her family. It was fifteen years of trying to survive the attacks of her fellow prisoners. From sullen resentment a flashpoint of fury and hysteria could spring up in seconds. Warders, though strong, tough women, were constantly being assaulted and injured, and all day long and sometimes until late into the night, cries and screams erupted with startling suddenness. The slightest thing could start it. Kathryn was locked in her cell with Jenny and Tina for hours on end because there weren't enough warders to supervise them all. She sat on her bunk trying to force her mind to ignore the obscenities and the violence. It was the degrading lack of control among the prisoners, as they screamed and smashed their heads against the wall, that so horrified her. They were like demented creatures, and she watched her cellmates warily, wondering when they might suddenly turn on her. And it was the smells that got to her too. The stink of ammonia, excrement and unwashed bodies, overlaid with wafts of strong disinfectant. The odour clung to her clothes and stifled her breathing.

That afternoon a hard-faced warder, dressed in her uniform of navy serge skirt and white blouse with navy epaulets, a bunch of keys hanging from her belt, told Kathryn she had a visitor.

Kathryn tucked her shirt into her jeans and ran her hands through her long flowing hair, thankful that at least prisoners were allowed to wear their own clothes. If by any chance it should be Carlos she wanted to look as good as she could.

She found herself being led down corridors, the yellow painted walls brightly lit by fluorescent strips, the linoleum on the floor scuffed and worn. This was not the first time she had noticed her surroundings, but even so she was more aware than ever of the baying and shouting of the other inmates, their eyes glaring fiercely at her through the 'letter boxes' in their cell doors, maddened that she had a visitor and they hadn't. She'd heard that a girl who had a visitor the previous week had been attacked with a broken cup on her return to her cell. She'd needed twenty-six stitches in her neck.

The visitors' room was long and bare and resembled a disused canteen. Tables and chairs, fixed to the floor, were arranged down one side. Kathryn glanced round quickly, hopeful yet fearful, desperate for some reprieve that would take her away from this place.

A well-dressed woman with thick chestnut hair and warm velvety eyes rose to greet her.

'Francesca!'

They hugged briefly under the watchful eye of the warden, then settled themselves on either side of a table.

'How are you doing, honey?' Francesca asked gently. Kathryn's face was bleached white and her large eyes held barely controlled terror.

'I can't tell you what it's like here,' Kathryn whispered. 'I thought it was bad before, when I was in custody, but this . . .' She glanced around the long room, nervous at being overheard.

'We're doing everything possible to get you out,' said Francesca swiftly. 'Your mother and Charlie, all of us, are mounting an appeal as soon as possible. Try and hang in there, darling. I'm sure something can be done.'

'I got a life sentence.' Kathryn said the words

451

flatly, despair and tension robbing her of expression. 'I know that with good behaviour, plus the time I served when I was on remand, it might be reduced, but what to? Five years? Ten years? *How can I stay here for ten years?*' It wasn't a question, it was a desperate plea for help.

The tragedy of the situation hit Francesca forcibly and she felt utterly helpless at that moment. No amount of money or power or influence could free her niece, and yet those were the things that had always dominated her life up to now.

Francesca clasped Kathryn's hand across the plastic table top and looked at her steadily.

'Your mother's coming to see you tomorrow; she's tied up with counsel all today, working on your appeal. Kathryn, we *will* get you out. Believe me. This is the most terrible miscarriage of justice, and we're still doing all we can to find the real killer.'

'Thank you.' Kathryn's voice was still flat, though her eyes seemed to brighten slightly. 'Francesca . . . I don't know how to ask you, but could you do something for me?'

'Anything. Just ask me.'

'Could you find out where Carlos is? Do you think he knows what's happened? It's months since I've heard from him, but of course, maybe now that this has happened . . .' Her voice sounded pitiful and Francesca felt a wrench of sorrow for her.

'I'll do what I can, darling,' she promised. 'I haven't heard anything from him, but then I didn't expect to. Has your mother relented about letting you see him again?'

'We haven't discussed it. I was going to plead

with her when – I thought I'd be going home, after the case . . .' Kathryn's voice broke and her hands twisted together on the plastic-topped table.

'We'll find a way to get you out of here,' said Francesca sturdily. 'We're doing everything we possibly can. Don't give up, Kathryn, whatever you do. We'll have you out of here, somehow, just as soon as we can. And meanwhile I'll talk to your mother about Carlos. I knew his father a long time ago, you know,' she confided suddenly.

Kathryn's eyes widened, and for a split second she looked almost happy. 'Did you?'

'Yes. He was a very nice man, Kathryn, and I'm sure Carlos is too.' Francesca decided to say no more for the moment. To tell Kathryn everything would only complicate the issue, and anyway she hadn't talked about Marc to anyone for twenty years.

'Time's up,' said a surly voice a few minutes later, and looking up she saw a warder eyeing them contemptuously.

The visit was over. Kathryn was being conducted back to her cell.

Francesca felt unutterably depressed as she left the old red brick Victorian building and made her way in her car through the surrounding slums of north London back to Eaton Terrace.

What happened if they didn't win an appeal?

A few reporters were still lurking outside Diana's house when Francesca got back, determined to glean every last bit of information out of the case before the scandal finally died. Everyone entering

453

or leaving was pounced upon, while a couple of tired-looking photographers flashed busily.

'Been to visit her in prison?' demanded one, without preamble, as Francesca stepped out of her car.

'Excuse me,' she said, trying to push past him and get to the front door.

'How is Kathryn bearing up? Is she okay?' asked another in a sympathetic voice.

Francesca spun on him angrily. She knew the type. They started off by speaking gently and compassionately, putting you off your guard so that they could then relentlessly extract everything from you.

'That is none of your business,' she snapped. 'Please go away.' A flash bulb went off half blinding her, and at that moment Bentley opened the front door and she tumbled into the house.

'Christ, what a bunch of creeps,' she expostulated.

'Her ladyship will be down in a minute,' he said primly, ignoring her remark. 'She has a visitor waiting in the drawing-room. Would you care to wait in there too, madam?'

'Thank you.'

Francesca strode across the hall and down the corridor to the drawing-room. Bentley had drawn the heavy curtains and the room was bathed in the soft light of several table lamps.

The figure of a man, familiar and yet strange, rose from a deep armchair and for a moment they stared at each other in stunned silence.

'Marc!' she gasped.

'Francesca . . . Francesca, what in the world are you doing here?' He sounded equally shocked.

'Why, I . . .' she croaked. He looked exactly the same, except that there were now flecks of grey in his mane of dark hair. He still looked rugged and muscular and in spite of his prosperous air he still had that attractive lived-in look.

'Do you two know each other?' said a voice in the doorway and Diana hurried into the room, fixing the clasp of one of her bracelets. She looked from one to the other, a puzzled expression on her face.

'We knew each other a long time ago,' murmured Francesca, wondering if Marc's presence had anything to do with Carlotta having been substituted for her by the terrorists during the hi-jack.

'Oh! I didn't know.' Diana looked mystified. 'How extraordinary. What can I get you both to drink?' she asked.

Francesca asked for Perrier water, Marc a whisky on the rocks. He was more convinced than ever now that he'd walked right into a trap. Why hadn't Diana mentioned Francesca when he'd arrived earlier? In fact she hadn't even told him why she'd summoned him. They'd talked for a few minutes, awkwardly, uneasily, and then she'd been called to the phone. Five minutes later Francesca had walked in.

'What's this all about, Diana?' he asked abruptly.

Francesca looked at Diana too, wondering the same thing.

Diana seemed to hesitate as if gathering strength, and then she spoke. 'You've presumably heard that my daughter has been convicted of murdering Guy,' she said slowly.

Marc nodded.

'I need your help, Marc. She is innocent. This is the most terrible miscarriage of justice and I need all the help I can get to prove her innocence. You may not be able to do anything, but I felt you had the right to know what was happening. There is also the question of her affair with your son, Carlos.'

Marc looked at her in blank astonishment, not knowing what the hell she was talking about. 'Wait a minute,' he interjected, 'what's Carlos got to do with this?'

Francesca leaned forward anxiously. 'Diana, I think you must let Kathryn talk to Carlos if she wants to. She mentioned him this afternoon and I promised to talk to you about him. Why are you forbidding them to see each other again?'

Diana hesitated, and Marc turned to look at her.

'Is your daughter Carlos' girlfriend?' he asked slowly. 'He did mention he had someone, but he never told me who.'

'Yes, and we've got to put an end to their relationship. Even though she's in prison he must not be allowed to contact her, nor she him.'

Marc's jaw dropped at her vehemence and for a moment he looked angry. 'Why the hell not?' he thundered.

'For God's sake, Diana, what is this all about?' demanded Francesca.

Diana levelled her eyes at Marc, took a deep breath, and then she spoke.

'Because Kathryn happens to be your daughter, Marc,' she said clearly.

'S-she's ...?' Marc's eyes widened and he looked dumbstruck.

'She's *what*?' gasped Francesca.

Diana turned to look at Francesca, who had paled. 'I never told you because I never thought it would come out, but Marc and I had an affair nearly nineteen years ago. If I'd known you knew him I might have told you in confidence, but the whole thing had to be hushed up.' She put her hand up to her forehead for a moment, then she turned to Marc.

'I couldn't tell you, Marc. I tried to get hold of you dozens of times but Carlotta ... well, you know, it was impossible. And you had said that if I ever tried to contact you again it could ruin you ... And so Kathryn was born. When Guy realised she couldn't possibly be his, because we hadn't slept together for over two years, he threatened to drag me through the divorce courts if I told anyone. The scandal in those days would have ruined me and my family. Guy said he was prepared to accept Kathryn as his daughter if I, in return, helped to preserve his public image as a normal family man.' There was pain in her voice and remembered unhappiness in her eyes as she spoke.

Marc was staring at her, believing what she said, yet struggling to come to terms with this astonishing information.

Francesca was looking dazed, her mind reeling with the thought: *Kathryn has been sleeping with her half-brother!* And then she looked at Diana and

457

a wave of anger and jealousy swept through her. She would have given anything, at one time, to have borne Marc's child, and all the time Diana had been nursing her little secret in order to protect herself and Guy. If the truth had been allowed to come out Kathryn would not be in the position she was today. There would have been no Carlos in her life for her to quarrel with Guy about. And then Guy might not have been murdered. And Kathryn would not be in prison now, accused of killing him.

'How *could* you?' she raged at Diana. 'How could you let this mess happen? Why didn't you at least tell Kathryn when she was old enough to understand? It's terrible – after all she's been through she's now got to face the fact she's been having an affair with her half-brother!'

'It was a chance in a million that she'd ever meet Marc's son,' Diana said coldly. 'We have your mother to thank for that.'

The two women glared aggressively at each other, then Francesca turned sharply to Marc.

'Let's face it, as far as women are concerned, Marc, you're bad news –'

Marc interrupted her roughly. 'Stop it, Francesca, before you say something you'll regret. May I help myself to another drink, Diana?' She nodded and he went to the drinks tray and poured himself a large whisky.

'I think I owe you both an explanation,' he said heavily, when he took his seat again.

'I think you do.' Francesca's tone was crisp.

Diana looked from one to the other, suddenly suspicious. 'Marc had no idea I was pregnant when we parted,' she said defensively. 'I didn't know it myself. All we've got to do now is stop Kathryn and Carlos seeing each other again.'

'There's no need,' said Marc.

'What do you mean, no need!' cried Francesca. 'It's incest!'

'There's no need, because Carlos isn't my son.'

Both women looked at Marc as if he'd gone crazy. Francesca was the first to recover.

'For God's sake, you left me because you'd got Carlotta pregnant!'

'Left you . . .?' echoed Diana.

Marc rose so that he faced them, his back to the fireplace. His face was grim, and in the depths of his eyes angry daggers of light flashed in the way that Francesca remembered so well.

'I'll have to tell you the whole story, from the beginning.' His voice rumbled deep in his chest and there was bitterness in his tone. 'If it gets out, if you both go off and tell everyone, then I shall be totally discredited in the eyes of my readers. But as I'm probably not going to be able to write any more books in the future, perhaps it doesn't matter now.'

As Diana listened, she was thinking: thank God Kathryn and Carlos are not related. At that moment it was all that mattered to her.

Francesca leaned forward expectantly. After all these years, years in which she'd wondered and worried over what had actually happened that night at Sarah's Christmas party, she was going to get the answer. Suddenly it was almost more important to her to find out the truth than it had been at the time.

'You remember my first book, *Unholy Spectre*, was a phenomenal success,' Marc began. 'It put me right at the top of the heap and I was hailed as a great new writer in the genre of Ernest Hemingway.'

'I remember,' said Francesca.

'The truth is, I didn't actually write it.' Marc paused. It was obviously painful for him to continue. 'You'll remember, Francesca, I was sharing rooms with a bunch of writers and artists in Greenwich Village at the time. One of them was a brilliant young man called Larry Fisher. He had an amazing talent. Just the sort of talent I didn't quite have. Nearly, but not quite. I helped him a bit with the book and I got someone to type it for him. I loved that book. It was exactly the sort of novel I wished I'd written. But Larry lived in a dream world, and he was so absorbed in writing his next book, he forgot to post the manuscript. When I found that it had been lying in a drawer for months, I mailed it myself.' Marc paused, and took a gulp of his drink. 'But first, I put my own name as the author. Maybe I didn't think anyone would accept it. Maybe I was just curious to see if anything would happen. When I got a letter to say the book had been accepted and the publishers were raving about it – they were offering me a hell of a lot of money – well, I went along with it. I was suddenly successful, famous, and they wanted my next book!'

'What did Larry Fisher have to say?' Francesca was watching him closely.

Marc drew in a deep almost throbbing breath and for a second his eyes closed. When he opened them, his expression was tortured.

'He committed suicide.'

'Oh my God,' murmured Diana, shocked.

'When he found out what had happened, it unhinged him. The day he killed himself is something that will haunt me forever,' said Marc, his voice catching. 'But the damage was done. I had no choice but to go on. You remember, Francesca, what hell I had trying to write that second book?'

She nodded, as realisation dawned on her. 'And no one ever found out what had happened?'

'Someone did. The girl Larry had been seeing. Carlotta.'

'Carlotta! Then you already knew her when – '

'No. The first time I actually met her was at your mother's apartment,' said Marc.

'But I don't understand,' said Francesca.

Marc began pacing up and down Diana's drawing-room restlessly. The room seemed to have shrunk since he'd begun talking and he was feeling oppressed by its fussy little tables and chairs and dainty *objets d'art*.

'She was already pregnant when we met.'

Diana's eyes clicked wide with relief. So it was true. Carlos really wasn't his child. He took another gulp of whisky and continued.

'As you know, Francesca, Carlotta was living with her aunt in a tacky downtown apartment. She'd been very strictly brought up and the shame of being an unmarried mother, with no money, would have been the end of her as far as her family were concerned. She knew Larry had written *Unholy Spectre*, in fact she'd even made a lot of good suggestions about the plot. Apparently he'd

461

talked about me, and before he killed himself he told her I'd stolen the book from him. After he died she started going with an artist who got her pregnant and then ditched her. That's when you and I came into the picture, Francesca. When she found out you knew me, the day you met at an art exhibition, she befriended you. Then it was only a short matter of time before you introduced us and she could put her little plan into action. She knew I was successful and would be rich one day, and she also knew she'd get me off guard if she sprang her ultimatum on me at some large social gathering. She'd reckoned on my not wanting to make a scene at your mother's party.'

'It was blackmail, wasn't it?' said Francesca.

'Yes. She said if I ran away with her that night, married her the next day in Las Vegas and let everyone think the baby was mine, she'd never tell anyone Larry was the real author of the book.'

'My God.' Francesca leaned back, remembering that dreadful night so long ago. The implications of what Marc had just said were immense. It meant he hadn't been having an affair with Carlotta while he'd been her lover! It meant he hadn't ditched her on an impulse. He'd been blackmailed over something that would have ruined his career and his credibility if it ever got out. No publisher would have touched him again. Everyone – reviewers, the press, his reading public – would have been revolted and shocked. She felt a flicker of understanding for the first time.

'But if only you'd told me,' she burst out. 'You've no idea what I went through, wondering what had happened. I rang all the hospitals . . . I was going crazy trying to find out why you walked out like that.'

'Francesca, I've always felt ashamed of the way I treated you.' Marc sat down again and his face was filled with regret. 'I was desperate to call you, but that bitch never let me out of her sight. We flew to her home in Spain the day after we got married, and if she even found me near a 'phone, she threatened to ring up the news agencies and tell them what I'd done. Besides,' he gave her a wistful smile, 'I didn't want you to know I'd never written *Unholy Spectre*. You always admired my work and that was an ego-trip for me. I'd rather you'd thought of me as a class one shit than someone who'd deceived the world into believing I'd written a good book when I hadn't.'

Francesca smiled back at him. She did understand. Writing meant more to Marc than anything else in the world, just as Kalinsky's meant everything to her. There was just one thing that still puzzled her, though.

'If you didn't write the first book, how come you've written a dozen successful ones since? Are you sure there wasn't more of your work in *Unholy Spectre* than you're giving yourself credit for?' she asked.

'What was the cleverest thing about that book?'

Francesca hesitated for a moment, recalling her admiration of it the first time she'd read it. 'The plot, I suppose,' she said slowly. 'There was such a fantastic twist at the end.'

'Exactly. And do you know whose idea that was?

Carlotta's. Of course at the time Larry told me it was his. Carlotta had the most fertile imagination. She also had a naturally twisted mind. Put the two together, and you've got a winner. I've written all the subsequent books myself, but the ideas were hers.'

'What will you do now?'

He shrugged. 'Give up writing altogether, or adapt other people's books into films. Who knows?'

Diana had sat very still while they'd been talking, staggered there'd been so much between them in the past, amazed at the truth behind his marriage to Carlotta. She looked at Marc and remembered her own affair with him and how heartbroken she'd been when he'd had to go back to Carlotta. But it seemed as if it had happened to another person, in another life. Even their love-making was hard to remember now.

But Kathryn was their daughter, and it was because of her that she'd asked him to come.

The three of them sat until late that night, discussing her case, going over the evidence again and again. Someone had killed Guy, and that some-one was still running around loose. Someone with a grudge, or a motive. Maybe someone in politics! Perhaps Guy had been killed because he knew something under the Official Secrets Act?

'Would it be possible for us to go down to Stanton Court?' Marc asked Diana at length. 'I'd like to see the place, see exactly where it happened.'

'Of course. I'll call Charlie in the morning. But what exactly are you looking for?'

Marc shrugged. 'Who knows? But a fresh eye might turn up something. I'll also put you in touch with a brilliant lawyer to conduct the appeal for you. It's the least I can do for my daughter,' he added with a wry smile.

That night none of them got much sleep. Francesca lay gazing into the darkness, thinking about Marc's confession, and she felt a curious sense of release. Marc hadn't abandoned her for another woman on a whim; he hadn't been playing around behind her back either. For the first time she felt she could forgive, and the last of her bitterness melted away. She also felt she could trust again. Really trust. Thoughts of Serge came racing into her mind and she wished he were here with her now. That had been her trouble, she'd never really trusted him not to go off and abandon her without explanation, the way Marc had done. She'd thought that as long as she remained unmarried she'd have a kind of shield behind which she could guard her vulnerability. Maybe, when this was all over . . . Her mind drifted and she fell into a light sleep.

Marc lay in his suite at the Dorchester thinking about Kathryn. He'd always loved Carlos, but to find he had a child of his own was a revelation. He'd always wanted children, but along with so much else, Carlotta had denied him that too. He wondered if Diana would tell Kathryn the truth now.

* * *

Diana spent the night as she had spent so many nights, going through every minute detail of that fatal Sunday in her mind. She tried to recall anything that might lead them to the real killer, but came to no conclusions.

In death, as in life, Guy had created around him a morass of evil and mischief. And, as always, others were having to pay the price.

Stanton Court was barely visible through a heavy curtain of rain as Diana accelerated her Jaguar up the long drive the following day. With her were Francesca and Marc; a strange trio, she thought, as the overhanging trees sent flurries of large droplets on to the windscreen and the wind shook the branches angrily.

Twenty years ago we could not have sat together in the confines of a car, she reflected. Twenty years ago Francesca and I would probably have been at each other's throats, each wanting this man who now sat quietly beside her, each consumed with jealousy of the other. It shows how the passing of time can erase passions, change attitudes, give a new dimension to circumstances, she thought. She glanced at Marc's profile as he looked intently ahead, and to her surprise she felt nothing for him but the warmth of friendship. She was sure it was the same for Francesca. In fact, last night she had sensed Francesca moving from a state of stiff wariness to a mood of understanding. Of course, Francesca had Serge, but she had no one. There'd been no one in her life for so long now, and she'd been so wrapped up in her children and her business that she'd hardly noticed the absence of love. Some deep instinct had told her it was better to have no one in one's life then the wrong person, and so it had been. Now she felt no desire for Marc even though he was a free man. She liked her life the way it was.

The rain continued to fall heavily for the rest of the day, but at about five o'clock the clouds suddenly lifted and bleak sunshine filtered through, brightening the landscape.

Diana had taken Francesca and Marc on a tour of the house earlier in the day. Now they walked round the estate, Marc asking Diana which path led to which exit gate, which gates were always kept open and which were locked. He interrogated her about each member of the indoor and outdoor staff in a desperate search to find a clue that would lead them to the killer.

By seven o'clock they had drawn a complete blank. On the face of it, as the police had insisted all along, no one but Kathryn could have committed the crime.

Dinner was a gloomy affair, with Charles and Sophie, seated at each end of the long table, struggling to keep the conversation going while Francesca, Diana and Marc seemed submerged in their own thoughts. Mary Sutton had intended to come over from the dower house, but at the last minute she had said she felt too tired, and so John had stayed with her to keep her company.

At last the long evening came to an end, and they all went up to bed dispiritedly. They were no nearer solving the problem.

Around midnight, Francesca was still awake and decided to go down to the library for a drink. Normally she didn't drink much, but sometimes a nightcap cured her insomnia, and she felt it was less harmful then sleeping pills.

Going quietly down the long curved staircase she made her way to the library and was just about to open the door when she heard a chilling cry. Pressing her ear to the door she suddenly sprang back, her flesh freezing. Uncanny wailing and howling was coming from the room, like the sound of a wounded animal – or a spirit damned. Who could be there?

Chapter Twenty-One

Francesca inched open the heavy door and peered into the library. Only one lamp was lit on the desk by the window and it cast a murky glow over the book-lined walls and heavy oak furnishings. At first the room seemed empty and the sounds had stopped, but suddenly they started again, eerie and filled with unutterable anguish. Stepping forward cautiously she saw the figure of a man lying face down on the leather sofa.

At that instant, as if he felt her presence, he stumbled to his feet and turned to face her.

Francesca stood still, numbed with shock. He was so changed she hardly recognised him. His once handsome face was ravaged, stained with red blotches, and his swollen eyes glittered feverishly. He had lost a lot of weight and by the way he stood swaying, he was obviously very drunk.

'John!' she exclaimed.

He looked at her as if he'd never seen her in his life before, then he staggered over to the desk and picked up several sheets of writing-paper. From where she stood, she could see they were covered with sprawling handwriting. Fumbling and shaking, he was trying to fold the papers in four.

'Are you all right, John? I'm sorry if I disturbed

you . . .' Floundering for words, embarrassed that he had started to sob again, she hurried to the drinks table at the far end of the room and poured herself a whisky.

The crash of a desk chair being flung sideways made her spin round, watchful and wary. She didn't know much about Diana's younger brother. Maybe he got violent when he was drunk. She had decided to slip out of the library and go back to her room, when John suddenly lurched towards her, tottering on legs that looked as if they might fold up beneath him any minute. She stepped quickly sideways, gauging the distance to the door, but he passed her and almost collapsed on to the drinks tray. He managed to seize hold of the whisky decanter and was slopping a measure into a glass when he spoke.

'Fucking bugger! Why did Guy have to be such a fucking bugger?' he sobbed. 'But I miss him so much all the same . . .'

For a moment she'd forgotten that John had been Guy's private secretary for many years, so of course he must miss him, but this orgy of grief puzzled her and made her feel uneasy.

'Come and sit down,' she said quietly.

'Fucking bugger!' he repeated, between his sobs. 'I loved him. From the beginning. He was my life.' He flung himself on the sofa again, while Francesca watched him with eyes aghast. 'I gave my life to him – I even gave up painting to work for him . . . he was everything to me.'

Francesca sat down suddenly, John's words hitting her with hammer blows. Guy and John!

470

She'd never realised! John's sorrow blazed naked now, his wretchedness reaching out to her with such overwhelming power she felt smothered. Trying to keep calm, she tried to absorb these new implications.

After a few minutes he seemed to grow calmer, but it was as if he was unaware of her presence. He was gazing with unseeing eyes into the ash filled grate of a dying log fire and his eyes looked blank.

'I've written it all down,' John suddenly muttered, his bloodshot eyes flickering towards the desk.

'You have?' said Francesca, thinking it must be the story of their affair.

'Everything. I had to. There's no other way.' He took another gulp of whisky.

'Did it help?'

'Help?' He looked at her as if he'd only just noticed her presence. 'It's not going to help me,' he said bitterly.

'I know nothing will bring him back. Sarah, my mother is deeply unhappy too. But life has to go on, John.'

He sprang to his feet, as if what she'd said had made him suddenly angry.

'You're his fucking sister! I've just realised ...' His face contorted for a moment into a paroxysm of pain and he could hardly get his next words out.

'He deserved to die!'

For a moment Francesca felt scared. He's really flipped now, she thought.

'He deserved to die?' she whispered.

'Yes. That's why I killed him.'

Pale and drawn, Francesca sat with the others in the drawing-room the next morning, waiting to make her statement to the police. She knew she'd never be able to go into that library again as long as she lived.

They had all heard her story of the previous dreadful night, and now she was going to have to tell it all over again to the police. Only Mary Sutton was absent. The local doctor had been called in to see her in the early hours of the morning when she'd heard what had happened, and now, heavily sedated, she was being watched over by a hurriedly hired nurse.

Diana, sitting on the sofa beside Sophie, had an expression on her face of profound shock. Charles, slumped in a deep armchair, picked absently at a loose thread in the chintz cover. Only Marc was able to remain detached, and with a glimmer of her old humour returning, Francesca wondered if he'd found a ready-made plot for his next book.

No one spoke. At last a servant ushered in Detective Inspector Alan Timpkins from the local police constabulary. He was accompanied by two policemen, one of them carrying a notepad and pencil. They questioned the other members of the family briefly. It was really Francesca they wanted to interview, so once again she was forced to relive the nightmare of degradation and remorse she had witnessed last night.

Clasping her hands tightly around her crossed knees, she started in a low voice.

What John had told her the previous night had

supplied the missing link they had been seeking for so many months.

On the particular weekend of the murder, John had been so angry when Guy had insisted on going to Stanton Court alone, saying he had private business to discuss with Diana, that he decided to drive down himself on Sunday to see if he could find out what was going on. He'd arrived at the dower house around lunch time, hoping to question his mother, but when he found her out he stayed in the house alone, brooding. He was sure Guy was up to something and, already rather drunk, his imagination took hold . . . John was sure Guy wanted to get rid of him; their relationship had gradually soured during the previous year and Guy went out every night without him. John was convinced Guy had come down to Stanton Court that weekend to try and persuade the family that it would be better if John gave up working in London and returned home and took up painting again.

The reason he had these suspicions, Francesca told the police, was because he'd found out, quite recently, that Guy had been conducting several other affairs. He'd even been paying young boys to come back to his flat in Westminster, having first sent John down to Wilmington Hall to carry out constituency business for him.

'It seems,' Francesca continued, 'that John was faithful to Guy all the years they were together, which is unusual in the gay scene. John found out Guy had had literally hundreds of lovers and when it occurred to him that Guy might want to get rid of him completely it was the last straw.'

Their faces expressionless, the police listened intently, making notes all the time.

'I asked him how he managed to get into this house – and out again – in order to kill Guy without anyone seeing him,' Francesca continued.

John had told her last night how simple it had been. He'd already planned what he was going to do – shoot Guy when he was out walking and say it was an accident. But when he arrived at the house, having walked through the orchard from the dower house, he was able to enter unobserved through the French windows in the library. Everyone was having luncheon in the dining-room and the servants were in the kitchen. His plan was to go to the gun room, collect a gun and some ammunition and then slip out again the same way. He had just loaded up a gun when he heard voices coming out of the dining-room, and he could hear Charles and Guy talking about going clay pigeon shooting. Alarmed, he replaced the loaded gun on its rack and slipped into a small cloakroom next door, locking himself in. He supposed it would only be for a few minutes, then when Guy and Charlie had gone out he'd collect the gun and follow them. The fact that they were going shooting would, he thought, make it look more like an accident than ever.

That was when things started to go wrong. Charles was called to the 'phone and then he left for the farm. The next thing John heard was Guy and Kathryn shouting at each other and he could hear every word they said.

Kathryn's words, 'You've never loved anyone but yourself, you don't know what love is ...'

struck John with their unerring accuracy. He recalled hearing the terrible things Guy had called her, and then he heard Kathryn sobbing as she fled across the hall and out of the front door. The next few seconds passed in such a frenzy that all John could remember was coming out of the cloakroom, hurling himself into the gun room, seizing a gun that lay on the table and firing it at Guy. His distraught brain told him Kathryn was right. Guy had never loved anyone but himself, and so he deserved to die for all the pain he'd caused.

A minute later John had slipped out through the dining-room windows, which could not be seen from where the others were drinking coffee on the terrace, and he'd sped back to the dower house by way of the orchard, getting soaked to the skin by the storm. Then he'd jumped into his car and headed back for London. Five minutes ahead of him, on the same road, Kathryn was also speeding back to the city.

'And you let Kathryn take the rap for killing Guy?' Francesca remembered asking John as he poured out his story, sobbing and gulping whisky as he did so.

'I thought she'd get off,' he mumbled weakly. 'But it's no good. Guy may have treated me badly, but I can't live without him. Life means nothing to me now. She can be set free, but I'll never be free for as long as I live.'

Francesca felt a wrenching pity for this man, weak and dissolute though he was. Another of Guy's victims, made to suffer for years by her brother's total selfishness.

'He's written a full confession,' Francesca reminded the Detective Inspector. 'He'd just finished it when I came into the library last night.'

'Can I have it, please?'

'I have it here.' Charles rose from where he'd been sitting huddled in the chintz chair wondering how he could have been so blind, and handed them the writing-paper, crested at the top with the Sutton arms, covered in John's large erratic handwriting. It was the most terrible moment of his life, and Sophie moved over to him, putting her arms around his shoulders.

The Inspector read it rapidly and nodded. 'Signed and dated,' he remarked. 'That's good.'

A heavy silence got a paralysing grip on everyone in the room, and then the Inspector rose and looked at Charles.

'Lord Sutton,' he asked grimly, 'where's the body?'

'It's still in the library,' Charles replied gruffly.

Francesca covered her face with her hands, trying to blot out the images that scarred her mind and would stay with her as long as she lived.

When John had finally finished telling her everything, he had handed her his signed confession, his face pale and set. 'Well, that's it,' he said with sudden calmness. Then he walked over to the French windows and pulled back the long velvet curtains. He gazed for a long time into the blackness of the night, lost in thought, and for a moment Francesca thought the storm had blown itself out. Then, without warning, John picked up a revolver from beneath a sheaf of papers on the desk, raised the muzzle to his open mouth and fired.

The shot rang out sharply, ricocheting round the book-lined walls, bouncing off the carved ceiling, echoing around the long room as Francesca stared, immobilised with horror. The force of the bullet seemed to raise John bodily into the air, lifting his hair until it stood upright on his head, and for a second he had looked surprised. Then he crashed to the floor, his brain and part of his skull spattered around him.

Sobbing with shock, Francesca dropped to her knees, hands clasped over her mouth as a wave of nausea left her bathed in sweat.

She would never be able to forgive Guy now.

When Francesca arrived back in New York two weeks later, she felt as if she had been away ten years. Serge was there to meet her at Kennedy Airport, a warm and comforting smile on his face, his arms tight and reassuring around her.

'God, I'm sure glad to get home,' she murmured as he held her close.

'I'm glad to have you back,' he said simply, kissing her. 'It sounds like you've been to hell and back.'

She gave him a wry smile and nodded. 'How's Mom?'

Serge raised his eyebrows and his expression changed to one of surprise. 'Incredible as it may seem,' he said, 'She's ... well she's sort of a changed woman.' He shrugged as if he couldn't understand it himself. 'I flew to Palm Beach last weekend to give poor old Henry a break, and frankly I'm not sure what's come over your mother.'

'In what way?' Francesca looked alarmed. 'Has she lost her mind or something, gone senile?'

'On the contrary, she seemed more lucid and sensible than usual. She wants you to go and see her as soon as you can. Henry is still with her, of course, but she's out of hospital and back in her house.'

'She heard about John, I suppose?'

'Yes.'

They climbed into the waiting limousine and Francesca sank back wearily on to the pale-grey suede while Serge supervised the loading of her luggage into the trunk. When he joined her inside the car she slid her hand into his, drawing comfort from its warmth.

'I have so much to tell you, Serge. So much has happened.' Her voice sounded distracted and he could see she felt very shaken by the events of the past two weeks.

He squeezed her hand. 'Just take your time, honey. You've all the time in the world, but now you need to rest.'

'At least Kathryn's been freed,' said Francesca. 'You've no idea what a relief that was. The poor girl had the most terrible time in prison, and when she was told she was being released she didn't believe them! She thought it was some trick. It took days before it sank in. It's going to take her a long time to get over the ordeal.'

'I can imagine. What about that business with

Carlos? Has Diana relented into letting her see him again?'

Francesca smiled and then told him the whole story.

'Diana has decided to tell Kathryn the truth about Marc being her real father. She feels she owes it to her. And, of course, as Kathryn and Carlos are not related there's no reason why they shouldn't go on seeing each other.'

'Who would have thought that Diana had been such a hot number,' said Serge, thoughtfully. 'To look at her you'd never think it.'

'That's typical English reserve,' replied Francesca. 'I'm sure Henry would have a ready platitude to describe it.'

' "Still waters run deep"?' he suggested, with a twinkle.

'Oh, darling, it's wonderful to be back,' Francesca clung to his arm, laughing.

Later, as they dined quietly in their apartment, she told him about John's inquest.

'They brought in a verdict of suicide while the balance of his mind was disturbed,' she said. 'In fact, I think John knew exactly what he was doing, especially at the end.'

'It was for the best though, wasn't it?'

'Undoubtedly. I don't think he could live with himself, knowing how Kathryn was suffering, and I don't think he could live without Guy.'

'It's a pity he didn't do it sooner then and spare everyone a hell of a lot of misery.'

They were silent for a moment, and then as if she wanted to blot out the memory of John she asked, 'So tell me more about Mom?'

Serge smiled mysteriously. 'Go and see her, find out for yourself,' he said, refusing to be drawn any further.

The next morning, having spent a couple of hours at her office, she caught a plane to Palm Beach.

Carlos flew in to England two days after Kathryn had been released from Holloway Prison. Marc met him at Heathrow and as they drove in to London he told Carlos the truth about his birth.

'Your father was a painter,' Marc explained. 'I never knew him, but I believe he was quite talented.'

Carlos was silent for a long time, trying to come to terms with a revelation that left him badly shaken. Then he turned to Marc, and there was gratefulness in his eyes.

'So you married Mom and brought me up as your own son,' he said quietly.

'Don't endow me with heroics, Carlos. There's a lot you don't know and the time has come to explain a few things to you. Once you were born, I grew to love you, but it wasn't like that at the beginning,' said Marc.

And so painfully and slowly, sparing himself nothing, Marc told Carlos the whole story.

'Are you telling me all this because Mom's dead now?'

'I would probably have told you sooner or later, but whilst Carlotta was alive it was a closely guarded secret, even from you I'm afraid. That was the way she wanted it.'

'If Mom provided you with the plots for all your books, how are you going to manage now?'

Marc shrugged. 'I'll work something out. Carlos, I had another reason for wanting you to know all this and it may come as a shock to you.'

'Well?' Carlos visibly braced his shoulders and his jaw tightened.

'It's not exactly bad news, son,' said Marc, slipping automatically into his usual tone of affection. After all, Carlos would always be like a son to him, nothing could change that.

'You're in love with Kathryn, aren't you?'

'Yes.' Carlos glanced at Marc with suspicion. 'Why? Has her mother suddenly relented towards me?'

'She thought she had good reason to keep you away from Kathryn. If only Diana and I hadn't been so fucking hamstrung, not daring to tell the truth, none of this would have happened! But we were both so busy protecting ourselves, and to a certain extent the people we were married to, that it nearly led to a real screw-up between you and Kathryn.'

'I don't understand. What's Kathryn got to do with any of this?'

And so for the second time that morning Marc had to reveal a truth that he had only known for a week himself.

'You mean . . .? Shit!' cried Carlos. 'So what does that make Kathryn to me? Step-sister?' He was pale now and sweating.

'It means you are not related at all,' said Marc firmly. 'Your mother was Carlotta and your father

481

was an artist. Diana is Kathryn's mother and I am her father. There's nothing to stop you two getting together.'

'Jesus wept!' Carlos shook his head, his mind spinning with the incredible situation. 'And so Diana thought . . .? Christ, no wonder she wanted to split us up. Does Kathryn know any of this?'

Marc smiled, remembering the previous evening when he and Diana had told Kathryn everything.

'Yes. She was quite shocked, of course, but when it dawned on her that Guy hadn't been her real father she seemed relieved. She'd never got on with him and when it became public knowledge, after John's suicide, that Guy and John had been having an affair for years and that it was John who killed him, she was horrified. Thankful she was cleared of the murder, of course, but still horrified. Telling her I was her real father sort of helped wipe the slate clean. She also understood why Diana had tried to stop her seeing you again,' Marc paused, glancing at Carlos.

'Poor kid. She's been through a hell of an ordeal. Does she still want to see me? I mean, it's been months since we've spoken,' said Carlos.

'I'm sure she does.' The car was entering Chelsea now. In a few minutes they'd be at Eaton Terrace. 'Do you still feel the same way about her?'

Carlos looked nervous. 'I'm not sure,' he said wretchedly. 'Hearing she's your daughter, and the fact that I will always look upon you as my Dad . . . well, it sort of feels strange.' Panic swept through his dark eyes. 'Oh, Jesus, Dad, can we drive around the block for a bit?'

'Sure.' Marc eased the steering wheel to the left and they cruised round Sloane Square and up Sloane Street. 'How about a drink?'

Carlos let out an audible sigh of relief. 'Great. I've got a bit of adjusting to do. What happens to you and Kathryn's mother, now you're both free? Are you going to marry her?'

'That is a big question,' said Marc drily, as he slid the Mercedes into a gap outside the Hyde Park Hotel. 'I've got a bit of adjusting to do myself.'

They entered the hotel and headed straight for the bar. Marc ordered a Campari soda for himself and a Pernod for Carlos.

'Diana's changed,' Marc reflected as they sipped their drinks. 'You'll like her, Carlos. She's a terrific lady, but she isn't the Diana I knew.'

Carlos observed, 'Nineteen years is a long time.'

'Too long, I fear. She's strong now and greatly changed. You never knew Guy, but to have survived being married to him is a feat in itself. He blackmailed her to stay with him and act as a cloak of respectability to hide what he was up to, and it's made her tough and independent. She's got a very successful business, you know, arranging parties and that sort of thing.'

'Kathryn told me.'

'We haven't talked about getting together and I think I'll leave it, for the time being. This whole thing has been such a trauma, and of course she's upset about her brother John . . . I reckon she just needs a good friend right now.'

'I wonder what Kathryn needs.' Carlos sounded unsure of himself, awkward and embarrassed at the thought of seeing her again under these changed circumstances.

Marc smiled understandingly. 'The same as her mother; kindness, friendship, a bit of tenderness. It'll be okay, son. Finish your drink and we'll go and see them now.'

'I'm kind of nervous,' said Carlos, finishing his Pernod and rising.

'We'll face them together, eh?' Marc slung his arm around Carlos' shoulders.

'Sure, Dad.'

Bentley opened the door and let them in when they arrived, and it was obvious to Marc that Diana, with her flair for organising social occasions, had stage-managed her first introduction to Carlos. She came swiftly into the hall, her hands outstretched, a warm smile of welcome on her face.

'Carlos, I'm really glad to meet you.'

'Hi, there.' He gave her a quick look and instantly liked her. 'It's good to meet you too.'

Diana looked questioningly at Marc, and he gave an almost imperceptible nod.

'You'll find Kathryn in the drawing-room, just along the corridor and on the right,' she said. 'She's longing to see you again.'

'Okay.' Carlos gave her a nervous smile.

'How did it go?' Diana asked Marc softly as Carlos loped off.

He looked at her tenderly. One of the things he'd always loved about her was her compassionate nature, the way she cared for others.

'I think he was a bit stunned, and nervous of

seeing Kathryn again, but he'll be all right.' His eyes twinkled. 'Are we leaving them alone for a bit?'

'I thought it best.' Diana's eyes were sparkling now and Marc began to see, through the mask of anxiety that had clouded her face for so long, the delicate beauty and the vibrance that had marked her features when he'd first known her. As he'd said to Carlos, he didn't plan to rush things. Nevertheless, the future looked brighter than it had done for many years. With a light step, he followed Diana into the cosiness of her study and closed the door behind him.

In the drawing-room, Kathryn's heart pounded as she heard Carlos coming down the corridor. This was the moment she'd dreamed of during those long nights in prison, when the air had been rent with screaming obscenities and her future had seemed like a solid blackness through which she could never escape.

'Carlos. . .' Her voice was a whisper.

For a second she thought she detected an uncertain look in his eyes, as if he doubted something. Then it cleared, and a moment later she was in his arms. He kissed her gently at first, and then with growing passion, holding her tightly.

'Oh, darling . . . My darling Kathryn – My little Kate,' he murmured, breathing in the sweet scent of her hair, pressing his cheek against the softness of her face. 'I was scared I'd never see you again.'

'I was afraid too. I thought I'd lost you forever. I can hardly believe you're really here now.' Kathryn pressed herself closer, wanting to reassure herself that this was really happening.

'I'm here all right, and we'll never be apart again,' he said softly.

Carlos led her to the sofa, his arms still around her, and their whispered kisses were the only thing that broke the silence of the room.

'I'm coming to live in America, you know,' Kathryn said at last, and her eyes were shining. 'Francesca says she can get me a job at Kalinsky's. It's what I really want to do, and it means I'll be near you.'

'Nearer than you think, sweetheart. I shall be in New York too. I've just signed a contract with the television studios there.'

She jumped up, pulling him to his feet. 'That's marvellous!' she cried. 'Oh Carlos, everything's going to be all right, isn't it? Does your father – I mean . . .' She broke off, blushing in confusion, and then she laughed. 'I mean, does Marc know?'

Carlos shook his head, laughing also. 'Not yet! Shall we go and tell him and your mother now?'

'Why not?' Grabbing his hand, she ran towards the drawing-room door. 'I wonder where they are?'

They went into the deserted hall, and through the closed study door they heard Marc's laugh, rich and deep.

Carlos and Kathryn looked questioningly at each other. 'Shall we leave them for a bit?' he asked, amused.

Kathryn looked disconcerted, and then she smiled. 'Perhaps we'd better. They've got a lot of catching up to do,' she said.

'And so have we, my love, so have we,' said Carlos, taking her in his arms again.

Francesca found Sarah sitting under the trees in the garden of her Palm Beach house. She was wearing a loose beach robe made of Indian cotton, her hair had been done and her face was exquisitely made-up. Beside her, Henry sat quietly sipping mint tea and reading *The Wall Street Journal*.

'Hi, Mom!' Francesca kissed Sarah on the cheek, marvelling at how well she looked. 'I don't believe you've been in hospital with a heart attack at all,' she joked. 'I think you've been having yourself a face-lift!'

Sarah laughed. 'Maybe next year! Lying in bed makes one terribly saggy.'

'Well, you look great to me. Hi, Uncle Henry! Good to see you.'

Francesca sat down on one of the sun loungers facing her mother, stretching her long legs out before her.

'Isn't Serge with you?' Sarah enquired.

'He couldn't get away. He's got a mass of work on. I'm only here for the weekend myself, Mom. Things are really piling up at the office.'

'Well, I'm glad you came, honey. I'm going back to New York myself next week. It's getting positively boring here, in spite of Henry's company.' Sarah smiled affectionately at Henry, and he leaned forward and patted her hand.

The conversation remained light and jokey as the servants served them luncheon under a bright yellow canopy. Guy was not mentioned at all, and neither was John's suicide. Sarah welcomed the news that Kathryn would be starting work at Kalinsky's next month, and it was as if the past three months hadn't happened. Perhaps this is what Serge meant, thought Francesca, when he'd said Sarah was a changed woman. She seemed to have brought down a shutter, blocking out everything that was unpleasant, and her remarks were both witty and relaxed.

Francesca watched her, a faint line of worry creasing her brow. Perhaps Sarah was becoming senile, returning to a childlike state of mind dominated by the trivia of a day-to-day existence.

It was after luncheon, when they were sipping their coffee by the pool, that Henry rose to his feet, stretched, and announced he was going indoors for a siesta.

'Aren't you going to have a rest too, Mom?' asked Francesca.

'Not yet. Maybe later, dear,' she said, exchanging a knowing look with Henry. He ambled off, taking his newspaper with him, and with gentle eyes Sarah watched him go.

'Can you pour me some more coffee, Francesca?' she said, holding out her cup.

'Are you sure you should? Isn't coffee a stimulant?'

'Just this once – I'll be good tomorrow.' She gave a roguish smile.

Francesca refilled her mother's cup and her own, then lay back on the sunbed and closed her eyes. She really wanted to talk to Henry, to find out what was going on and what the doctors had said, but it was obvious her mother wanted to talk to her alone. An awkward silence fell upon them now and Francesca searched her mind frantically for something to say. The only sound that broke the stillness of the air was the chink of china as Sarah put her coffee cup down on a nearby table. Then she spoke.

'I wanted to have a private talk with you, Francesca.'

Francesca opened her eyes and sat up. Sarah was looking at her directly, and that look swept away all doubts that her mother might be becoming senile. It was the old Sarah speaking and Francesca braced herself for another avalanche of hurtful words and bitter accusations.

'Yes, Mom?' she said guardedly.

'When I was lying in hospital, thinking I was going to die, I realised how unfair I'd been to you all these years, putting Guy first.' She was stroking the folds of her beachwrap and her hands shook.

Francesca looked at her, startled.

'It was wrong of me to idolise Guy so much,' Sarah continued, 'but he was my son and I loved him.' Her voice dropped almost to a whisper. 'But I always loved you too, honey, and I want you to know that I think you've done a wonderful job of running the company.'

Tears sprang to Francesca's eyes and her throat tightened in a painful paroxysm of emotion.

'Oh, Mom,' she whispered brokenly.

'You know how much the company has always meant to me, but I realise now that I was wrong in wanting Guy to take over. I'm afraid his heart was never in it and I should have accepted that fact years ago.' Sarah sighed deeply, and her lips trembled. 'I shouldn't have pushed you away in favour of him.'

For a moment Francesca felt like a little girl again, hanging on her mother's words, longing for a note of loving reassurance.

'Kalinsky's means as much to me as it does to you, Mom. All I ever wanted was to be part of it.'

'I remember.' For a moment Sarah smiled. 'From the age of six you were determined. Well, you did it, and you did it very well. I've made a new will and you are now my heir. That's what I want to say to you, Francesca, and I'm proud of you and I hope in the future we can be closer than we've been.'

Francesca felt bereft of words. Giving a little sob, she reached out and clasped her mother's hand.

'I'd like that very much, Mom. I always wanted you to approve of what I was doing. As a child I wanted to be just like you.'

'Not too much like me, I hope. I didn't really treat your father very well and I made a lot of mistakes as a mother. I put the company first and that was bad. Your father deserved better – because he was a fine man. What I'd really like to see now is your marrying Serge. Why don't you?'

Francesca stood up slowly, wiping away the tears. She was no longer that little girl, craving her mother's attention, trying to push her favoured brother out of the way, so that she could have a chance. She was a mature woman whose mother had given back to her a feeling of her own worth, a feeling of being loved.

'You're right, I should marry Serge and suddenly I'm no longer afraid to. In the past I've always felt a need to hold on to the business tightly; I suppose I was afraid that one day Guy would come home and snatch it all away from me. And I was afraid of being hurt. . .' She took a few steps and then stood by the edge of the swimming pool, looking down into its shimmering depths. When she looked back at Sarah, her face was radiant.

'Would the mother of the bride be fit enough to fix up a summer wedding for her daughter?' she asked.

'Francesca!' Sarah's face lit up, and she stretched out her hands. 'You couldn't have made me happier than by saying that. Oh, darling, I'll give you the loveliest wedding there's been for years, and I will be the proudest mother in New York.'

When Henry strolled back to the pool a little while later, he found Francesca and Sarah, sitting close together, talking. They both looked happier than they'd done in years. Seating himself opposite them he gave a bland and indulgent smile.

'Ah well,' he said philosophically, 'All's well that ends well.'

'Henry, you're *so* predictable!' said Sarah, as she and Francesca burst out laughing.

Marc fastened the last of his cases and then glanced around the hotel suite to make sure he had left nothing behind. Checking his passport and air-line tickets, he called the front desk and asked them to fetch his baggage. His plane left Heathrow for San Francisco in an hour and a half. It was time to go.

Downstairs in the Dorchester's foyer, he paid his bill, bought *The Herald Tribune* and *The Times* and a pack of Marlboro. Then on impulse he walked over to the telephone booths, jingling the small change in his pocket. He dialled the number he wanted and almost immediately the 'phone was answered.

'Hi, Diana,' he said softly. 'I'm leaving in a few minutes and I just wondered if you'd changed your mind?'

There was a long pause before she answered, and then he heard her voice, warm and gentle. 'I haven't changed my mind, darling. I explained it all to you last night. I'm a very different person from the young woman you used to know – you admitted that yourself. Don't take it personally, Marc, please. I really want my independence, and with Miles away at university and Kathryn going to the States, I want to build up my company into something big. You do understand, don't you?'

'Aren't you afraid you're going to be lonely?'

Diana gave a reassuring laugh. 'I got so used to being on my own, years ago, that I think I actually prefer it now. It isn't you, darling, it's that I don't want to get married at all. Now that Guy is gone, I feel so enormously free and it's a wonderful feeling. We can't turn the clock back, Marc, even if we'd like to. Time, and all that has happened, have changed both of us too much for that.'

'Okay, sweetheart.' Marc spoke reluctantly. 'But if you ever have second thoughts . . . well you know I'll always be there for you, and of course Kathryn. I'm looking forward to getting to know her better.'

'Thank you, Marc. It's wonderful to feel we'll be friends, if nothing else.'

'I've got to go now or I'll miss my plane. Take care of yourself, Diana.'

'I will,' she promised.

He replaced the receiver and strode out of the Dorchester to his waiting car. If he felt a twinge of sadness it was mingled with a tiny spark of relief. How sure was he, anyway, that he wanted to marry again and give up *his* new found freedom?

Serge awaited Francesca's return from Palm Beach with anticipation. He knew Sarah planned to talk to Francesca, for she had told him the weekend before – her guilt and her regrets, her fears for Francesca's future and her horror at Guy's past. She had laid her soul bare, and Serge had been shaken to see the normally controlled and dignified Sarah humble herself before him. It was as if all her illusions had been stripped away when she heard that John had killed himself over Guy, leaving the bare bones of a sordid reality. Sarah told Serge she feared Francesca would refuse to vindicate her of blame and would reject her apologies, but Serge knew better. Francesca was not a woman who harboured grudges and resentment. He was sure she would meet her mother half way and that they would at last be reconciled. He glanced at his watch as he waited at Kennedy Airport. Her plane had already landed. He patted his pocket nervously. He'd got his hopes raised and he hoped to hell he wasn't going to be disappointed again.

Francesca saw him the moment she emerged from the arrivals gate and her heart gave a little leap of delight.

'Serge!' she cried, running towards him. 'What a lovely surprise! I thought you'd be too busy to meet me.'

His kiss was warm and deeply loving. His arms held her strongly and reassuringly. 'I'm never too busy to meet you. How are you, darling?'

'Great!' Francesca's eyes sparkled as she stood, looking up at him.

At that moment she knew her mother was right. She should marry Serge. He had been such an integral part of her life for so long that she wondered why she'd ever been scared of marrying him in the first place. Perhaps seeing Marc again, and listening to his explanations, had washed away her lingering doubts. Perhaps the knowledge that she need no longer prove to Sarah that she was as tough a business woman as her mother, had wiped out her misgivings. Perhaps she had at last grown up. Whatever the reason her doubts had vanished. She just hoped it wasn't too late.

Serge guided her to the waiting car, chatting about inconsequential things, and it wasn't until they were seated that he turned to her with a quizzical smile. Her manner had told him that the weekend had gone as he'd hoped, and he squeezed her hand gently.

'You know how I always seem to be carrying bits

of jewellery around with me?' he began, conversationally. Francesca nodded, laughing. At times Serge was like a conjuror, pulling earrings, brooches, bracelets, some still unfinished and missing their stones, out of various pockets. It was as if he couldn't bear to be parted with a new design while he was still working on it.

'So you've got the Star of the East diamond tucked somewhere about your person!' she joked.

'If you reach into my pocket you'll find my latest design,' he replied. 'It's for you, if you want it.'

'For me?' Francesca always wore a lot of jewellery, but mostly as an advertisement for Kalinsky's and it went back into stock in a few days. Only a few gold chains and her jewelled watch belonged to her personally. Intrigued, she groped in the pocket he indicated and withdrew a small leather case bearing the familiar gold K on the lid. The lid snapped open at a touch. Lying on the blue velvet was a ring set with a large, square diamond, as deep as it was broad. It flashed and dazzled as she took it out of the case, and then she let out a little gasp. It was an illusion. It wasn't one stone, but eighteen diamonds, each cut precisely so that they fitted together like a perfect cube. Technically it was brilliant, for no clawed setting showed. It would put Kalinsky's once again ahead of all their rivals with a design that was innovative and totally original. But Francesca knew it was more than that. Serge had created it with love and care, and it symbolised the intricate joining together of many elements – brilliance, strength, fire and purity, cleaved from rough stones and fashioned into a likeness of their love.

'Will you keep it?' Serge asked, and there was a tremor in his voice.

'Yes, but on one condition,' she whispered.

'What's that?' His voice was gruff.

'That you give me a plain gold band to wear with it.'

More compulsive fiction from Headline:

RICHES

— A NOVEL —

UNA-MARY PARKER

RICHES

Tiffany – by day a successful costume designer working
from her luxurious Park Avenue apartment. By night,
the 'other woman' in the arms of film director
Hunt Kellerman.

RICHES

Morgan – her only ambition is marriage to an English
aristocrat. And in Henry, Marquess of Blairmore,
dubbed one of Britain's most eligible bachelors,
she finds just the man.

RICHES

Zac – their younger brother is the odd one out. Spending
his time in sleazy bars, he's on a downward spiral to
despair . . .

The three Kalvin children come from a background of
wealth and privilege, but each has to learn the hard way
that there's more to life than

RICHES

"A swingeingly accurate and sexy romp . . . " DAILY MAIL

"A truly delicious example of the genre . . . guaranteed
to make you gasp, giggle and stretch your eyes as you
gallop through the pages at one sitting." COMPANY

FICTION/GENERAL   0 7472 3013 7   £3.50

*And coming soon from Headline – SCANDALS
– Una-Mary Parker's stunning second novel.*

Headline books are available at your bookshop or newsagent, or can be ordered from the following address:

Headline Book Publishing PLC
Cash Sales Department
PO Box 11
Falmouth
Cornwall
TR10 9EN
England

UK customers please send cheque or postal order (no currency), allowing 60p for postage and packing for the first book, plus 25p for the second book and 15p for each additional book ordered up to a maximum charge of £1.90 in UK.

BFPO customers please allow 60p for postage and packing for the first book, plus 25p for the second book and 15p per copy for the next seven books, thereafter 9p per book.

Overseas and Eire customers please allow £1.25 for postage and packing for the first book, plus 75p for the second book and 28p for each subsequent book.